THE PEREGRINE CONJECTURE

SHANE STADLER

Copyright © 2023 by Shane Stadler

All rights reserved.

No part of this book may be reproduced in any form or by any electronic or mechanical means, including information storage and retrieval systems, without written permission from the author, except for the use of brief quotations in a book review.

Deception is the road to annihilation

CHAPTER 1

My entire life is deception, Anders Bennett thought as he slipped and nearly fell on the wet concrete beneath the awning. It was unlike him to be nervous.

He approached the door and waited, as the driver had instructed.

It was late February in Washington, DC, which often meant snow, but rain was even worse this time of year. He shivered as the damp air invaded his bones.

A long minute later, the door opened and a Secret Service agent stepped out and patted him down as he spoke.

"Welcome to the White House, Mr. Kellen," the husky man said, using Anders' alias. The agent then waved him into a warm foyer where he grabbed Anders' umbrella from his hand and slid it into a clay vase on the floor, near a coat rack. "This way, please."

After passing through a metal detector operated by another agent, Anders followed his broad-shouldered escort down a carpeted corridor. A minute later, they arrived at a door on the left.

"This is the Map Room," said the agent as he stepped aside and nodded for Anders to enter. "The president will be with you shortly."

Anders went in, and the door closed behind him.

He was alone.

It was a spacious area, maybe 30-by-30 feet, well-lit, with a chandelier in the center and a dozen small lamps on narrow, console-style tables along the perimeter. A couch and three padded, wooden chairs were clustered around a coffee table to his left. There was a similar arrangement in the corner to his right, next to a dormant fireplace. On the far wall, opposite the entrance, was a window, drapes closed.

As he tried to calm his mind and collect his thoughts, he strolled around the room on its red, patterned carpet and admired the paintings on the walls. The largest of them was of a tall sailing ship on gray, stormy seas. Others depicted national monuments and portraits of historical figures.

On one wall, above a narrow table that held an assortment of flowers, was a large mirror. He went to it and looked over his image. His disguise did well to cover his God-given light hair and pale skin, and the tone looked natural, even in the bright light. His fake, dark goatee, together with his disheveled, brown hair with a few gray strands – a wig – made him look ten years older than his 34 years. The key to creating a distorted look of age, however, was in the eyes, and he'd skillfully shaded in subtle, dark circles beneath them. Colored contacts were another disguise variable that he used regularly, but his natural, brown eyes fit well with his current look.

The art of disguise was a required talent in Anders' line of work. This one was good, but he should have thickened his eyebrows a little more. He wore extra-flat shoes that made him seem shorter than his natural height of five-foot-ten – normal shoes would add an inch – and he'd applied a makeup foundation to all exposed skin that was a few shades darker than his natural tone. He also wore thicker clothes than usual, with two layers on the top, to make him seem a little heavier than the 150 pounds that his thin frame currently supported. It also helped him to stay warm in the frigid weather.

The sound of a closing door came from behind him. Anders turned.

A tall man in his mid-60s stood before him in what appeared to be comfortable night clothes. He looked athletic for his age, and larger than Anders had anticipated – well over six feet tall, and thickly built. His otherwise stylish, gray-black hair was matted on one side as if it had been resting on a pillow. It was the president, Thomas Crownbrook.

The man walked over and stuck out his hand. "Anders Bennett, I presume," he said, almost under his breath.

"Yes, sir. Nice to meet you, Mr. President," Anders replied as he grasped the man's heavy mitt. He didn't feel comfortable with him mentioning – even whispering – his real name.

"I was expecting someone younger," Crownbrook noted as he gestured toward the cluster of furniture that Anders had noticed on the left when first entering the room.

"I'm in disguise," Anders whispered as he went to one of the wooden chairs and sat.

"How old *are* you?" the president asked as he sat on the couch, directly across the table from him.

"Thirty-four," Anders replied.

Crownbrook nodded, apparently in approval of Anders' disguise. "Still, I had it in my mind that you were just in your mid-20s – time really flies," he said. "You come with the highest of recommendations. You speak Russian and Chinese, correct?"

"My mother is Russian, so I speak fluently," Anders explained. "My dad, as you know, was in Hong Kong for four years with me and my mother when I was young. So I speak Chinese fairly well – but with an accent. I also speak Spanish."

"Henry was quite a man," Crownbrook said. "He's part of the reason why you're here now. I knew him personally, of course. It's been three years now, hasn't it?"

"Three years last November," Anders confirmed. Mention of his father's unexpected passing always set him into a state of sadness and disbelief. "He told me that you two had been on a few missions together. He gave me no details, of course."

Crownbrook nodded and smiled. "Yes, CIA officers must take some secrets to the grave with them," he said. "You're here because I trust you – and that's partially because of your father, of course. But you also come highly recommended by an extremely dependable, non-government entity."

"You mean the 'entity' for which I currently work."

"You've been with the company your entire professional life –12 years now, I understand," Crownbrook confirmed. "I know the founder of that organization well. His company provides quite an assortment of useful services. He says your skill set is perfect for your role."

"I'm a *courier*," Anders said. "I'm no CIA case officer."

"I know," Crownbrook said.

"I don't understand why you don't use the services already at your disposal," Anders said. "You have government resources under your command that are unmatched by any private firm – you already have excellent couriers."

Crownbrook nodded as if he'd anticipated the question. "Our agencies have changed over the past few decades, including my beloved CIA, to which I've dedicated most of my professional life," he explained. "They now think that *they* should be running things, rather than the president and the people. Same goes for the FBI and NSA."

"I see," Anders said. He'd developed a similar impression of those agencies – he interacted with them on a regular basis. "And you need to deliver something without government interference?"

"Yes," Crownbrook said. "As you probably know from the news, everything leaks these days. From the CIA to the FBI, information – including classified material – makes its way to the media, which then use selective parts to advance themselves, or their ideologies. But the problem is that our adversaries get that same sensitive information and use it to their advantage. I can't even trust my own aides, which is why had to invite you here to make the pickup."

Anders knew that even the US Senate Intelligence Committee leaked information constantly. "What's the job?" he asked.

"Should be routine for you, but it will be a recurring task," Crownbrook said as he reached into his pocket and pulled out a tiny red device and handed it to him. It was a data-storage drive shaped like a smooth, oval pill. "You'll deliver this to a contact in Alexandria. The information will go both ways – you'll be bringing a thumb-drive back to me as well. Future exchanges will occur in different locations, but mostly within US borders."

"Sounds easy enough," Anders said. He was grateful that the first exchange would be so close – he lived in Alexandria, Virginia.

"It is of utmost importance that you understand that you will *never* hand anything off to anyone but me on the return," Crownbrook said. "If someone tries to collect something from you on my behalf, then you're in grave danger."

"Understood," Anders said as he reached into his pocket, extracted a mobile phone, and handed it to the president. "This is a direct link to my boss, as requested. It's secure and encrypted – a satellite phone. We'll discuss possible data transmission using this device in the future."

"I think I'll stick with hand-to-hand delivery for now," Crownbrook said and slipped the phone into his pocket.

"Who's my contact?" Anders asked.

The president gave him the details and a code phrase for verification. He then stood and led Anders out of the room and into the hall. "Good luck," Crownbrook said, and then retracted into the room and closed the door.

The same Secret Service agent who had brought him in now guided Anders down the corridor toward the exit. When they reached the foyer, the man extracted Anders' umbrella from the vase, handed it to him, and directed him out, into the cold, rainy night.

"Have a nice evening, Mr. Kellen," the man said, again using Anders' alias, and then closed the door, leaving him beneath the awning where the wind blew drops of freezing rain into his face.

A gray SUV was waiting to take him to the DC Metro. From there, he'd ride the rails for a while before hiring a car and, finally, walking a meandering path back to his company's home base.

As he rode in the back seat of the SUV and looked out the window into the wet, frigid night, Anders' chest tensed with anxiety. There was something different about this job – and it wasn't only that the US president was the client. He knew nothing about the information that was on the thumb-drive in his pocket, which wasn't unusual, but something made him feel uneasy. What could be so sensitive that the president didn't trust his own intelligence services to handle it?

"Good morning, missileers," Colonel Maurice Spelling said as he greeted the more than 30 Missile Operations Officers in the briefing room at Minot Air Force Base. Minot, North Dakota was brutally cold in the winter, and he saw it on the reddened faces of the US Air Force officers seated in front of him. The weather back at his home center of operations, Malmstrom Air Force Base, in Montana, was currently no better.

"You should be happy that it's up to zero out there," Maurice said, knowing that the temperature was going to take a dive in the afternoon. "We're all reminded of where the phrase 'Why not Minot?' comes from."

Maurice was sure he heard a few expletives mixed in with the groans in their responses.

"I'm here to give you a briefing on some recent occurrences," he continued. The crowd was composed of the senior command structure of the three missile wings that curated the nuclear might of the United States – intercontinental ballistic missiles, or ICBMs. The three wings included the one which Maurice commanded, the 341st Missile Wing at Malmstrom, Montana; the 91st at Minot, North Dakota; and the 90th Missile Wing at F. E. Warren Air Force Base, in

Wyoming. Maurice was the most senior of the three wing commanders, so it was his job to take the lead in such situations. "You all know why you're here."

"Aliens," said a young officer in the front row, inducing some chuckling.

Maurice was expecting some friendly banter, but the situation was more serious than they appreciated. That was okay for now – only the three wing commanders were aware of the severity of the incursions.

"I don't care *who* they are, but they better stay away from our facilities before something serious happens," Maurice said. "In that regard, each site is undergoing security upgrades that include installations of surface-to-air missile rigs for immediate, local protection, and regular fighter flyovers for more blanketed support. Apache helicopters will also be on the ready."

"Sir, have any of the infiltrating crafts been identified?" a woman asked from the back.

"Not yet," Maurice replied. "But we suspect that they're Chinese or Russian drones. Until we figure out who they belong to, each site will also be fitted with special, ground-based sensing and imaging equipment to capture information that might help us identify these things. So far, satellite surveillance has been unsuccessful."

"Sir?" a man from the back called, raising his hand. "Have they figured out how the drones were able to mess with the computer control systems in the M-8 and A-11 silos?"

Those were two missile silos in North Dakota separated by over 50 miles, and Maurice vividly recalled that frightening night. The computers, and redundant power sources, at M-8 had shut down – something that wasn't supposed to be possible – and the A-11 silo had spontaneously started a live launch sequence, which had been stopped by an emergency shutdown procedure. "We have no idea at this point, but we're working on it," Maurice replied.

"But those failures *did* occur simultaneously with the appearance of the objects, correct?" the man asked. "I spoke with one of the officers who was on duty at A-11 when it occurred, and I'm stationed at M-8."

"Yes, they did happen concurrently," Maurice admitted. The brass above him was trying to play down that fact. "The point is that we're going to catch the intruders, and there will be a price to pay when we do."

"Can you tell us any of the running theories, sir?" the same man asked. "About who's behind it, that is."

He was expecting the question, and Maurice took a deep breath and recalled what he was supposed to say. "Okay, this isn't official – just talk," he said. "But the Chinese have come a long way with smart drones that have stealth technology. And the drones might be what are known as quiet-fan dirigibles."

"What do you mean, like silent, hot-air balloons?" a woman asked as the rest of the group hissed in derision.

Maurice was reminded of the Chinese "weather balloon incident" that had occurred early the previous year. One of their high-altitude balloons traversed the entire continental US, passing directly over his home base at Malmstrom, its missile fields, and the missile fields in North Dakota. After shooting it down and analyzing the debris, the US Department of Defense and CIA confirmed that there was advanced sensing instrumentation aboard capable of gathering information beyond the abilities of a spy satellite.

"They moved way too fast to be hot-air balloons," one man said.

"Not hot air, *helium*," Maurice clarified. "And the propulsion – the quiet-fan system – is a new technology that's more like a jet engine. It provides a formidable, quiet thrust."

"That still doesn't explain the malfunctions in the silos," the woman added.

"I'm just telling you the running theory," Maurice said. The fact was that there was no theory whatsoever. The only information they had was from eyewitnesses outside the silos – and it had been in the dead of night in all cases. Those on the inside could only corroborate the malfunctions.

Some discussion followed but then Maurice got them back on track, delivered their orders, and dismissed them.

It had been a tumultuous few weeks, and Maurice had hoped that the Air Force would've gotten its act together and identified who was responsible for the tampering by now. But it hadn't. During his 25 years in service, he'd experienced nothing as disturbing as the possibility of unintentionally initiating a nuclear attack.

LIGHT FLAKES of snow caught on Anders Bennett's eyelashes as he walked along the Potomac in Alexandria's Old Town district. The damp rain from the night before froze as a new weather system pushed into the area. Virginia, and the entire East Coast, was getting the front end of a winter storm that was to hit in full force by morning. It made for a cold, damp evening, and the streets and sidewalks were slick, despite the sand and salt that had been applied.

He was making his way to a popular pub called "The Swashbuckler," which bragged a large assortment of imported beers but was also known for its rare spirits – mostly whiskies. Thursday had been chosen for the rendezvous since the bar had drink specials on those nights: hopefully, the place would be crowded enough so that he and his contact would blend in and not draw any attention.

As he turned west, away from the river and down King Street, he spotted the sign for The Swashbuckler and glanced at his phone. It was 10:52 p.m. He was right on time.

Anders entered the crowded bar and casually searched for his contact. He was supposed to be a heavy-set, Chinese man wearing a black jacket and a Washington Nationals baseball cap. As he found an opening at the bar to place an order, he spotted him in a booth in a poorly lit corner in the back, near an antique jukebox that was currently silent. It was a good location. Even though Anders was in disguise – a light beard and mustache, a wig of curly blonde hair, and black, square-framed glasses with partially reflective lenses so that cameras would have difficulty picking up his eyes – it was always best to avoid light.

After getting a whisky, he casually made his way through the crowd and approached the man, who looked up at him with an expression of anticipation.

"The Nationals need some better pitching," Anders said.

The man smiled. "They'll have some new blood in the spring," he said with an almost imperceptible Chinese accent. It was the correct "all safe" response phrase.

Anders sat across from his contact and set his whisky tumbler near the man's beer glass.

"I'm Hwang," the man said. He looked to be mid-30s, chubby, and his cheeks shined as if they were covered with a thin film of sweat.

"I'm Thomas. Seems like we'll be meeting on a regular basis," he said, using an alias as he was sure "Hwang" was also doing. Anders pulled the red device the president had given him out of his pocket and set it near his tumbler so that only Hwang could see it.

Hwang reached for his beer and snagged the device along with his glass and took a drink. When he set the glass back on the table, a tiny blue object was sitting next to it. It was another storage device – the same shape as the red one – and Anders picked it up along with his whisky tumbler.

"You know why they're shaped like this, right?" Hwang asked under his breath, referring to the drive's smooth design.

"Easily swallowed," Anders replied.

"And later recovered," Hwang added, and chuckled. "It seems like our two countries are having some troubles."

Anders nodded. The US currently had an aircraft carrier strike group in the South China Sea, barely in international waters, and China had one near Guam. Tensions were escalating quickly. But the US also had other problems: Russian bombers were constantly violating US airspace in the Pacific Northwest, and it was getting worse. "You have direct contact with your president?" he asked.

Hwang nodded. "All communications go directly to him, and are from him," he explained. "No intermediaries, only me."

It made Anders again wonder what information could be so sensitive that the presidents of both countries didn't trust their own intelligence services with it. Diplomatic discussions shouldn't have had such paranoia associated with them, nor such secrecy. Perhaps they weren't conveying diplomacy.

They took another ten minutes to finish their drinks – so that they'd arouse no suspicion – and then Hwang headed for the restroom as Anders returned his glass to the bar and went for the exit.

Next stop, home base.

Harrison Palmer shook his head and sighed. He closed his laptop and pushed it away, stood from his desk, and walked over to the window. It was going on midnight, and the snow was coming down harder now and accumulating on the streets four stories below. It looked like he'd be spending the night on the couch in his office. Anders Bennett, his best courier, was expected to check in at any moment.

There was something strange about this operation, but Harrison couldn't figure out what it was. He'd learn more soon.

His eyes refocused on his reflection in the window. The close-up details were not flattering, although he probably looked a bit younger than his 51 years. His hair was still thick and his hairline was mostly intact, but the dark brown was starting to show some gray, as were his short sideburns. He was still in good physical shape. He'd been a swimmer in college and managed to keep a regular regimen of that, as well as a weightlifting routine at his private athletic club. The exercise, and reasonable diet, kept his weight below 215 pounds, which was about right for his six-foot-two frame. The physical activity also did well to manage his stress.

Harrison's company, DMS, Inc., had blossomed in the past decade as its selection of services had expanded to include all kinds of spook-related needs. It had started as a simple check-in system for retired spies who still felt the post-traumatic stress and paranoia of their dangerous, former lives. In fact, "DMS" stood for "Dead Man's Switch," which was a mechanism by which some action would occur if a client missed a regular check-in, which could be set up as a regularly scheduled email, phone call, or even an in-person visit. If the "switch" were triggered – the client didn't execute a check-in – and all attempts to make contact failed, an armed DMS team would be sent out to find them. There had been only a few incidents in the past decade in which customers had been in legitimate trouble, but DMS had come through every time.

Since its inception, DMS had expanded first to include money laundering – in the mostly legal sense – identity transformation, courier services, and, most recently, cyber services and surveillance. A few years prior, the momentum of the company had halted due to a pandemic – a nasty virus referred to as "RAT-32C," which had killed millions, and ravaged the world's economy. Since then, however, DMS had resumed its development and its employees now numbered just over 600.

Anders was his best and most trusted courier, and that's why he'd been selected for the job with the president. Although, the connection between Anders' late father and President Crownbrook had also been a factor. Inside DMS, only Harrison and Anders knew about the arrangement. No other personnel were aware of the client's identity.

Harrison's cell phone chimed. It was a text from entry security: Anders Bennett was on his way up to his office.

It was always a relief when his people returned safely from a mission. Harrison knew well the dangers of the life of a spook. He'd been one for about 20 years – with the CIA – and his own paranoia was what had driven him to create DMS, Inc. His wife had often speculated that it was his way of coping with his own situation –

giving him control of something while simultaneously building a wall around himself – a virtual castle, in his case. She put her foot down when he wanted to extend the castle walls around her, however. She refused to comply with a "Dead Woman's Switch" protocol. It still made him laugh when he visualized her expression when he'd asked her about it so many years ago. Still, he wished she'd agreed to it.

Two minutes later, a clean-shaven, slight man of five-foot-ten with thinning blond hair appeared at the door. It was Anders, no disguise. Harrison invited him in and closed the door.

"Everything go smoothly?" Harrison asked as he went around his desk and sat in his leather office chair. He offered Anders a seat on the opposite side.

"Yes," Anders replied as he sat. He pulled a small object out of his pocket and set it on the desk.

"Ah, a blue one," Harrison said as he picked up the thumb-drive and examined it. "You know why they're smooth, like a pill – "

"I do," Anders replied before Harrison could finish. "I'd prefer not to have to swallow one."

Harrison laughed. "The worst part comes afterwards."

"I'd think such a practice would cause problems – people getting cut open for whatever they swallowed," Anders said.

"It's more for dealing with overt entities – like the police," Harrison explained, "so that it won't be found during a body search. If a foreign intelligence service gets you, that's another story."

Harrison made a call to a DMS cyber specialist and asked her to come up to his office. The device was never to leave the immediate sight of Anders, and he was to report every touch of the device to the president.

"When's the drop off?" Harrison asked.

"Tomorrow, on the president's call," Anders replied. "Probably in the evening."

A light knock came at the door and Harrison looked over to see a stocky woman with thick, red hair tied in a bun on the top of her head. She had a laptop and a briefcase.

"Diana, come in," Harrison said as he stood and walked around the desk. "You can set up here, on my desk."

Anders vacated his chair and pulled it to one side, clearing space for the woman.

Diana placed the briefcase and laptop on the desk and flipped open the computer. She then unlocked the briefcase and opened it, exposing a dense console of electronics. She connected a cable from a port inside the briefcase to the laptop, and then scrolled out a power cord from the backside of the briefcase and plugged it into a wall socket.

"The first check is for explosives," she explained as she put on a pair of latex gloves. "Can I have the device?"

Harrison handed it to her. He knew that even a tiny object could pack enough high-energy-density explosives to kill someone. This was going to the president.

"Cute," she said as she examined it and then placed the drive in a tiny compartment in the briefcase. "First, we'll get rid of any germs with UV light."

She pressed a button on a small control panel in the briefcase and the tiny compartment glowed in a bright, purple-blue light for a few seconds. She then extracted the drive and put it into another compartment that had a lid with a rubber sealing gasket around the edge.

"This will do a residual gas analysis to detect signature traces of explosives," Diana explained. She pressed some buttons on the control panel and then went to the laptop and started some software. The briefcase hummed and then some peaks started to form on a graph on the computer screen. A minute later, she said, "All clear on that."

She then extracted the drive and put it into another compartment and started a new process on the computer. A whining sound and then a sequence of sharp clicks emanated from the briefcase. An image of the innards of the device appeared on the screen.

"The X-ray scan shows nothing unusual, either," she said.

Next, she removed the drive and pulled a strange tool out of a pocket on the lid of the briefcase. It had handles like a set of pliers but had oddly shaped jaws. "These caps are a pain, but you wouldn't want one coming off inside your gut," she said as she squeezed the handles and extracted the device's rounded lid, exposing its metal and plastic innards. "It's a standard USB-C connector."

Harrison looked to Anders. "These sometimes have tampering mechanisms," he explained. "Even though we're only checking for safety – not trying to read it – we have to be careful."

After irradiating the device in UV light again, this time with its lid removed, Diana plugged it into a port in the briefcase. "This is what's called a passive sensing port," she explained. "It means that we're not supplying power to the device – at least not enough for the device's electronics to sense it."

"We have to be extremely careful, as this could be a 'read once' device," Harrison commented to Anders.

"You mean like in those old spy TV shows, where tape recordings describing the missions to the agents spontaneously self-destructed?" Anders asked, grinning.

"Exactly, but the digital version," Diana said as she punched some keys on the computer. "In some cases, if a password prompt appears, it's too late. If you don't enter the password in a given amount of time, it will melt down."

"And sometimes you only get one shot at the password," Harrison added.

"This device has a tiny battery, according to the X-ray image," Diana said as she put the device in yet another cavity in the briefcase. "It means that it probably has a meltdown mechanism."

She tapped some keys on the computer and a set of electromagnetic-wave spectra appeared in the form of peaks on a graph. "It has no receiving or broadcasting capabilities from millimeter wavelengths to radio waves," she said as she put the cap back on the device and handed it to Harrison. "This is all I can do without risking triggering a software startup for login. In my assessment, it's physically safe. It's unknown, however, if it's software-safe – meaning it could have a computer virus on it. I'd recommend using it on a standalone computer that's not connected to any network."

Diana packed up her equipment. "Anything else?" she asked.

"Not now, thanks, Diana," Harrison replied. "But this will become routine for a while."

The woman left and Harrison handed the blue device to Anders.

"Tell the client what we've done here," Harrison said. "And tell him that we recommend going through this process every time."

Anders left with the device.

Harrison went back to his desk chair and pulled out a cigar, sniffed it, and cut off the end. He lit it and began puffing. Almost everything the company did was right on the edge of legality. The simple check-in service was completely legit, but the surveillance, money laundering, and transporting of sensitive materials were all skating on thin ice. Delivering back-channel communications for the president of the United States was a new level for DMS, and he was concerned about how things might develop if word ever got out about it. The compensation was good, but it wasn't worth losing the company, or worse.

After a few minutes of mulling over the situation, he put out the cigar, and then went to his personal bathroom and changed into shorts and a tee shirt – sleeping clothes he had on hand specifically for times like this. The roads were too dangerous to drive home.

As he brushed his teeth, he wondered how his wife had enjoyed her night out with colleagues, celebrating their recent acquisition of a grant to restore a historical building in Old Town Alexandria. Lauren was a historian working for a non-profit organization that specialized in preserving old structures in the Northeast, especially those with connections to the Revolutionary War. Harrison found some of it interesting, but much of her work was about structural details, like materials and hand-manufacturing of various things, which he didn't. The grant was a big deal, however, and he was sure they'd gotten some good food, and a fair amount of wine had been consumed. He wished he could have joined her in the celebration.

With the storm intensity building, he became concerned. Still in the bathroom, he sent her a text. She responded immediately, indicating that she had a good time and had gotten home safely.

He finished in the bathroom, retrieved a blanket and pillows from a closet, and set up his office couch as a bed. He turned off the lights, lay on his back, and took a deep breath and sighed. The snow was coming down harder now but the storm would be over by morning, and the roads would be cleared by the time he'd have to drive home the next night.

As he drifted off, Harrison wondered what was on that data drive.

ANDERS GOT the call from the president's aide at 11:00 a.m., and they set up a meeting for 9:30 p.m. that evening. As far as the aide knew, Anders, or "John Kellen," as he was going by for the White House operation, was the manager of a charity fundraiser for families displaced by a series of floods that had devastated the states of Missouri and Arkansas the previous summer. It was Anders' cover story for this mission.

Anders had played so many parts in the past year – with corresponding disguises – that he was starting to forget his true identity. It was getting to the point that he barely recognized his real face in the bathroom mirror.

He spoke four languages – two with minimal accents, English and Russian – and had a computer science degree from a good state school. Other than the languages, what had best prepared him for his job were his acting classes, and his participation in the theater programs in high school and college. It was in theater that he'd learned both to keep in character under duress, and the elements of disguise – clothes and facial modifications. He'd also learned to change his voice – not only accents but also tones and cadences.

DMS, Inc., had taught him spook skills such as surveillance and avoidance, self-defense, and how to use firearms. His main function, however, was to carry sensitive materials and make exchanges, which required many skills, including how to assess whether or not an exchange location was safe, or to determine if someone was observing him.

Harrison, the man who had first interviewed him at DMS, and then directly hired him, had been a CIA case officer for nearly 20 years before retiring and creating DMS, Inc. Harrison had told him that DMS had better couriers than most intelligence agencies. Even though Harrison had known President Crownbrook before DMS got the job, the president had likely chosen the company for its reputation within the intelligence community. Former spooks spoke well of the enterprise, and that helped, even though most of them were involved with DMS only for its "retirement" services. Anders had been selected for the current operation, however, because of the connection between the president and Anders' father.

Anders relaxed in his small, cozy apartment for the afternoon while the plowing services cleared and salted the roads. At about 6:00 p.m., he ate a light meal of chicken soup and then went to his bedroom to apply his disguise.

He stared at his naked face in the mirror. The fake goatee he was about to apply was darker than the natural blondish-brown color of his hair. He'd cut his hair short just a week ago and decided to use a wig on this job with the president so that he could make a quick change, if needed. He could peel off the wig and goatee in seconds. He often carried a razor with him so that he could modify his *real* facial hair in a few strokes, but he was already clean-shaven for this job.

One important rule of disguise in his work was that convincing concealment should always be paired with mechanisms for quick change. And the two looks should be as orthogonal as possible: taller to shorter, dark to light, thin to heavy, and fast to slow. And it was important to change the gate of one's walk. For instance, he'd concentrate on changing from his normal gate to a slight "pigeon-toed" or "duck" walk when changing his look on the fly.

One thing that he had going for him from the beginning was that his appearance was "average" in so many ways: about five-foot-ten, blondish hair, brown eyes, clear skin, average weight – if not a little light – indistinct natural voice, slightly better than average looks. He was generally unremarkable, which was a good thing.

At 8:35 p.m., he scheduled a "SuperLift" pickup, one of those services in which the drivers used their own cars as taxis, and ventured out into the frigid evening. Fifteen minutes later, he got out at a DC Metro entrance. Rather than taking the stairs down to the subway, he went to a side street and waited. Five minutes later, a dark SUV pulled up, and he got into the back seat and closed the door.

The next stop was the White House.

COLONEL MAURICE SPELLING squinted at the incident report in his hands and then dropped it on the stack of a dozen others on his desk. He rubbed his eyes and then kneaded his temples with the heels of his hands. It was going on 7:00 p.m. and it was time to start the frigid drive home, something he dreaded.

February could be brutal in Montana, and the current temperature was well below zero. The wind chill factor, however, is what made it intolerable. The oil-pan heater in his truck was plugged into an electric outlet in his assigned parking place, so at least it would start, but it would take at least 15 minutes before the interior warmed to a comfortable level, which was about how long it took him to get home. On nights like this, the cold seeped into his bones, making those he'd broken over a decade earlier throb with a dull ache, especially his right femur and hip, which he'd injured while ejecting from a plane. He was only 49, but he felt like an old man. Going from test pilot to desk jockey was psychological agony at first, but he'd evolved, and he now satisfied his adrenaline addiction in different ways. In this case, it was a mystery – a serious one.

For weeks, someone had been infiltrating and manipulating his missile launch sites – and those of the other two missile wings. The latest intrusion on his, the 341st Missile Wing at Malmstrom, had occurred just five days prior, and it had been a dangerous situation. One silo had even gone into a launch sequence – as had occurred a few days before at the 91st wing, at Minot. Both incidents required emergency, manual shutdowns, causing those operators great panic, some of whom were still recovering their wits. The upper brass was still rattled by the events.

The incidents seemed to occur simultaneously in lots of two or three, and only in the dead of night. Each of the three main missile wings had been affected. However, Maurice's wing had the highest frequency of incursions. During those events, there had been direct sightings of strange objects in the local airspace by security personnel on the surface, but they couldn't provide any detailed information. Everyone was referring to them as "drones," although that name might change if they ever got a clear sighting of them. Even vague descriptions of the sounds made by their propellers or jet engines would have been helpful.

Other than overseeing the readiness of the five alert stations, 50 control stations, and 150 missile silos in the 341st Missile Wing, it was Maurice's responsibility to make sure that the details about the incursions experienced by *any* of the wings did not get out to the public. Such a leak would reveal the apparent vulnerabilities of the entire US nuclear missile network. If details *did* get out, and a few rumors already had, he was to muddy the waters with stories that contaminated the facts. Such misinformation avenues included injecting tabloid-style rumors into public outlets which reported anything from power failures in the missile network to encounters with aliens. The latter had already emerged decades ago in the form of government conspiracy theories, and Maurice intended to take advantage of them.

There were at least two serious consequences that could emerge if the real story got out. First, the recent, inadvertent launch sequences would both panic the public and result in a review of the entire missile program. Such assessments could be hazardous: they often resulted in leaks of critical information that weakened the overall system. In fact, Maurice suspected that the current problems were caused by a major investigative probe carried out four years earlier. At the time, the Pentagon had deemed that an audit was best carried out by a private firm, which Maurice thought was always a colossal mistake when it came to top-secret systems and information. That particular firm had, among other sensitive things, access to the entire missile network's control software. It also had links to China, as discovered by the Defense Intelligence Agency just a year later, triggering a complete software reinstallation. Another consequence of the real story leaking was the inevitable disclosure of a weakness in the system. Even though it was clear that someone, probably Russia or China, already had knowledge of this vulnerability, it would be disastrous if it became public information.

The Defense Intelligence Agency had placed *him* as the point in the internal investigation into the incursions suffered by the three missile wings, and it was his job to identify all the witnesses to the events. The DIA would then interview them.

Maurice's money was on China being the intruder. First, it was well known that the Chinese had acquired a colossal amount of info about the US missile systems through espionage – including the infamous spy balloon incident where a Chinese balloon carrying surveillance equipment traversed the entire continental US, West Coast to East Coast. Maurice still didn't understand why it hadn't been shot down as soon as it had crossed into US airspace. Next, India had already accused China of similar, drone-like incursions at their own nuclear sites – even power plants, in their case. This had occurred just months before the recent wave of US incidents. He figured the Chinese might have tested their technology on their neighbors to the south before deploying it in the US.

Within weeks of the first US incident, both China and Russia had reported similar intrusions – each blaming the United States. Maurice thought it was too convenient, although he did acknowledge the possibility that the US had developed technologies that it first tested on its own missile systems, and then deployed them strategically around the world. He still doubted, however, that they'd put an ICBM station into a live launch sequence and risk such a story getting out.

His thoughts were redirected to his chiming phone. It was a text from his wife asking when he'd be getting home. He sent her a message saying that he'd be there in 20 minutes. He was exhausted and hungry but thought it unlikely that he'd be able to relax when he got home.

ANDERS FOLLOWED his Secret Service escort to the Map Room. When he arrived, the president was standing in the open doorway.

He followed Crownbrook inside, and then to the same cluster of furniture in which they'd sat during their first encounter. They took the same seats as last time. Two bottles of water sweated on the coffee table between them.

Anders thought the man looked deprived of sleep. He handed Crownbrook the blue storage device and explained everything that had occurred – specifically, who had handled the drive and why.

"DMS is quite careful and thorough," the president commented, apparently pleased. "This is a single-read device. If it gets plugged into a computer, a password prompt appears, and you have one minute to enter it. And the password must be entered correctly the first time – no deletes or redoes allowed."

"You mean a mistake can't even be corrected before you hit enter?" Anders asked.

"That's right," the president responded. "One incorrect keystroke and it melts its own innards."

"It must be extremely sensitive information," Anders noted. He was naturally curious but wouldn't ask questions.

"After the password is successfully entered," Crownbrook continued, "one has a preset amount of time – depending on the volume of info, I suppose – to examine the contents before it melts down. Any attempt to copy it also results in the immediate destruction of the drive."

The president then reached into his pocket and pulled out a green device, identical, other than its color, to the other two, and handed it to him.

"Your contact is in Miami this time," Crownbrook explained. "Russian."

Anders slipped the thumb-drive into his pocket.

Crownbrook then reached into a briefcase on the floor next to his chair, extracted a manila folder, and handed it to Anders. The label on its tab read "Heartland Flood Assistance."

"This is all the organizational documentation for the charity we set up for the floods," Crownbrook said. "From now on, you'll collect materials like this from me and bring it all with you every time we meet. Understood?"

"Yes," Anders replied as he thumbed through the materials. There were about 75 pages of documents including lists of financial donors and assistance distribution details.

"Make yourself familiar with the contents," Crownbrook added. "I have other people carrying out the real work, which is not extensive, but at least something is really happening."

Anders nodded. It would shore up his cover story.

Twenty minutes later, Anders was shivering on a street corner, near a trendy DC restaurant – his first stop on his way back to DMS.

He thought Miami was going to be a nice reprieve from the Northeast winter.

At 10:25 p.m., just five minutes after making the request on his phone, a Toyota SUV with a bright, green light in its windshield that read "SuperLift" picked him up and, after a ten-minute jaunt on the highway, dropped him off a couple blocks from DMS, Inc.

After a five-minute walk in the frigid wind, he passed through a rear entrance to the building that took him directly to a changing room, where he removed his disguise and changed his clothes. The rule was that no DMS personnel, other than top-floor personnel and drivers, on occasion, would ever see him in disguise.

Anders had a car, but he was never to take it to work. He was what DMS called a "non-person employee." His official job title was Senior Computer Programmer. His paychecks were in his real name, with legitimate accounts, but no one could connect him to any of his fictitious identities – all made to look authentic through DMS services. He had passports, driver's licenses, credit cards, and bank accounts in aliases, all of which would be expunged after a mission. The only things that could connect him to his clandestine activities were biometric data – fingerprints and DNA – and video, which disguises were supposed to at least mitigate. A problem was arising, however, with modern face-recognition software that could identify people through disguises by looking at ears and noses and cheekbones – things that weren't easily modified with conventional façades.

When interacting with normal DMS staff, Anders went by the name "Tom Johnson," which was his employee alias. Only the big boss, Harrison, knew his real identity. Human resources had his real name on an account somewhere so that he could get paid, but there were no photographs of him on file. His identity was treated like those of DMS's CIA retiree clients.

The changing room had its own elevator entrance, which Anders opened with a special electronic key and stepped inside. He inserted the same key next to a button on the panel that took him to the fourth floor, where he stepped out and into a foyer.

A woman behind a receptionist's counter looked up and said, "You can go right in, Mr. Johnson."

When Anders entered the expansive office, Harrison was on a couch against the far-left wall, smoking a cigar. "Come in, Anders, have a seat," he said as he nodded to a leather chair opposite a circular, stone-topped coffee table. "I hear you're going to Miami."

Anders closed the door behind him, sat in the chair, and pulled the green data storage device out of his pocket and set it on the table. "Yes, another exchange," he said. "This one with a Russian."

Harrison nodded. "The woman goes by the name Alina Petrova," he explained. "You'll collect instructions when you arrive in Miami – in a safety deposit box at a bank."

Harrison slid a round, silver key across the table and it skidded to a halt near the green thumb-drive. "The security box is in the name of one of your aliases, so it's all set to go," he added.

Anders grabbed the key and drive and put them into his pants pocket.

"I just want to reiterate that, other than the usual protocols for screening the devices you bring in, you will never interact with anyone else on this project," Harrison said. "Only me and the president. Is that absolutely clear?"

"It is," he replied. He found it odd that Harrison would echo a common security practice to a seasoned operative. "Is something wrong?"

Harrison rested his cigar in a thick, glass ashtray, and picked up a tumbler with just a swallow of whisky at the bottom. "I don't know," he replied, and then downed the last of his drink and winced. "I have a bigger picture of the landscape than you do. I can't divulge anything sensitive, but I assume you've been watching the news."

"I have," Anders replied. He was a news junkie. "I assume you're referring to the geopolitical posturing – China, Russia, the US, and also Israel and India."

Harrison shrugged. "Yes – there's a lot of the usual stuff happening," he said. "China is trying to dominate the South China Sea and is threatening areas east – like Guam. They have another carrier group headed in that direction. Russia has invaded Ukraine – and is threatening the rest of Europe – but has also been attacking our power grid through cyber-attacks."

"And invading our airspace with their bombers," Anders added, which he had recently seen on the news.

"What has *not* been reported in the news is that China or Russia, or both, have been probing sensitive military sites on the US mainland," Harrison said.

"What do you mean, like hacking?"

"That's always happening, yes," Harrison replied as he shook his head, "but it's more than that. They've been physically present, in the form of drones, and have interfered with the operations of those facilities."

"Interfered?" Anders said. "How so? Jamming radar or getting in the way of our planes?"

"Even more serious," Harrison replied. "They're meddling with the control systems of our missile silos."

That was an odd, and frightening, occurrence, Anders thought. "I thought those systems weren't on the network."

"They're not," Harrison replied. "They operate on a closed system. Whoever's doing this has to be physically present to interfere."

"Who's the more likely culprit?" Anders asked. "Russia, or China?"

"Unknown," Harrison replied. "And no one knows how it's being done. The problem is, Russia and China are both accusing us of doing the same to them."

"Well, that's nothing new," Anders said and chuckled. "Are we?"

Harrison laughed. "I think we would if we could, but I'm pretty sure we're not technically capable of such a thing. Those are highly secure sites, with severely monitored airspace. Even a drone the size of a sparrow couldn't get close to them. And it's the same for our sites."

"So how are they doing it?"

"No one knows, and that's what's scaring the defense department," Harrison replied. "My feeling is that this is what the communications you're handling are about."

"But why go through dark channels?" Anders argued. "Why not direct talks?"

Harrison shrugged and shook his head. "That I don't know, but clearly the president is worried about leaks of some kind," he explained. "Perhaps we have a vulnerability that can't be made public because the administration is worried it would cause panic."

Anders thought that was plausible, but still odd. "Is there anything else I should know before heading to Miami in the morning?"

"Yes," Harrison said. "Get back as soon as you're finished down there – no dawdling. I'm told this is extremely time-sensitive, and you'll have more to do when you get back."

Although he was looking forward to the warm weather, Anders wasn't planning on making a vacation out of it. "Understood," he said, and they wrapped up the meeting.

Anders would immediately head home to pack. It was going on midnight and his flight was leaving at 6:00 a.m.

CAPTAIN ANTHONY GRIMES cursed under his breath as he glanced at the clock in his quarters. It was 3:17 a.m., and someone was knocking on his door. Sleep cycles on an aircraft carrier could be erratic, even for the captain, but he'd been in deep sleep when the disruption came. He got down from his bunk and flipped on the light.

"This better be urgent," he muttered as he opened the door. He was surprised to see his executive officer, Chuck Sanders. His XO looked flustered. "What is it, Chuck?"

"We're being stalked, Captain," Sanders replied.

"Subs?" It was a constant worry for a carrier strike force, but the USS *Stennis* had ships that specialized in submarine defense.

"No, Captain," Sanders replied. "Aircraft."

"Chinese?" They were currently in the South China Sea, and they'd recently had encounters with Chinese fighters and surface vessels.

"Unknown," Sanders responded. "Radar can't identify them. They're quick, and they have a strange radar signature. We have two Hornets on the flight deck ready to launch on your order."

"How far away are they?" Grimes asked.

"They've come as close as 10 miles," Sanders replied.

Grimes flinched. "Get those Hornets in the air immediately," he said as he started to close the door. "I'll meet you in control."

"Aye aye," Sanders said and went on his way.

Grimes shut the door and slipped on his coveralls, hat, and shoes as his heart seemed to beat in his temples. He took a gulp of water from a bottle on his desk, and headed out. Five minutes later he was in the main control room where he found Chuck Sanders leaning over the shoulder of a radar operator.

"Our birds in the air?" Grimes asked his XO.

"Second one is launching now," Sanders replied and waved him over. "Take a look at this."

Grimes stepped up to the screen and spotted two faint, green spots on a polar grid that were flagged with red question marks. "What are they, OS?" he asked the Operations Specialist, a young man seated at the radar controls.

"Unknowns, sir," the man replied. "We're having a hard time tracking them – they disappear and then reappear somewhere else, miles away. And they're fast – supersonic – and change altitude quickly."

"Supersonic?" Grimes repeated. His throat tightened.

"Yessir," the operator confirmed.

"Are you sure these aren't just artifacts?" Grimes asked, now skeptical. All the *Stennis'* computer systems had undergone software upgrades when last in port.

"We're not the only ones seeing them, sir," the controller replied. "We've confirmed with the other ships in the group and – " The radar specialist cut his statement short and leaned toward the screen, eyes wide.

"What is it, OS?" Sanders asked.

The operator made some adjustments and seemed to look over the screen to confirm something to himself. "They're now less than a kilometer off our stern," the young man finally said.

Grime's blood seemed to freeze. "Are you sure?"

Before the OS could answer, the radar screen fluttered, and the other operators in the room started to chatter.

"We're being jammed," the operator said. It rendered the radar useless.

"That's an act of war," Grimes muttered and turned to Sanders. "XO, ready weapons operations, and get more birds ready."

"Aye aye, Captain," Sanders said as a communicator chimed on the wall near the entrance.

A sailor answered it and summoned Sanders who took the call, hung up, and rushed back to Captain Grimes.

"Something's going on with the reactor. The engineers are trying to shut it down," Sanders explained. "It's in danger of melting down."

"My God," Grimes said. "Shut it down and move to auxiliary diesel propulsion."

Another call came in and Grimes took it. It was a weapons officer named Smith.

"Sir, all missile systems are nonfunctional," Smith said in a panicked voice. "The computer controls are frozen."

Just as Grimes hung up with Smith, a communications officer called out from across the control center. "Our missile cruisers are experiencing the same problems, sir," he said.

"Where are our aircraft?" Grimes asked.

"Can't tell, sir," the radar operator responded. "The jamming."

"External radio comms are down as well," said the communications officer from the other side of the room.

For the next 15 minutes, internal comms streamed in from all over the ship reporting various system failures, including the diesel backup engines.

"Son-of-a-bitch," Grimes hissed. The entire carrier group was blind, defenseless, and dead in the water. "What the hell is happening?"

After another ten minutes of futile brainstorming, Grimes caught a glimmer of light on one of the screens.

"Radar is up again," the controller yelled.

"Where are the bogies?" Grimes asked.

"Nowhere in sight," the OS replied. "But our fighters are on-screen and heading back."

Other positive reports then started coming in and, one by one, all systems came back online, including the reactor.

Grimes turned to Sanders. "Send an encrypted emergency message to Naval Command describing what just happened," he said. "And I want a full report from the entire group by 0800."

Captain Grimes became lightheaded for a few seconds and then recovered. What had happened was an act of war. It was a horrifying demonstration: an entire aircraft carrier task force had been rendered defenseless to the point that it could've been destroyed using crude World War II technology. The entire US Navy was in trouble.

ANDERS ARRIVED at Miami International Airport at 9:30 a.m. and hired a SuperLift car. A half-hour later, he arrived at a chain coffee shop just a block away from a local branch of the International Canyon Bank, where he was to obtain instructions from a safety deposit box.

He ordered a coffee and sat at a small, outdoor table that faced northeast. The light-blue ocean was in the distance, and his near view was filled with a marina, its long aisles of slips filled with gently bobbing boats of various sizes and types. A catamaran, its sail painted in bright aquamarine and yellow, crawled through the calm water at a leisurely pace. It was something from a dream, he thought.

The morning sun warmed his face and a light breeze soughed through the fronds of two pudgy palms near the café's entrance. The air ruffled his hair, but he could hardly feel it through his wig – short, dark, and curly hair, with matching eyebrows. He was wearing sunglasses, but would change over to clear specs when he approached the bank. He was in khaki shorts with a white, short-sleeved, button-down shirt, matching the usual attire of the locals. Leather sandals finished the outfit. The weather was much nicer than in DC, with low 70s in the morning and a high of 81 expected for the afternoon.

He often enjoyed the lull time before missions, as long as it wasn't too lengthy. If there was too much dead time, he'd get fidgety and start thinking too deeply about unrelated things – like his personal life, which, although not tragic, was peppered with various disappointments. This included his "love life," which could be best summed up as *frustrating*. It was best to keep his mind busy.

He pulled out his phone, found the BBC News website, and perused its headlines. There were updates about China's scuffle with India along their common border, and with the US in the South China Sea. China was also in a territorial conflict with the Philippines over some islands that China had confiscated, and with Australia over economic issues.

Russia was another persistent troublemaker, the latest example being their bomber incursions into US airspace near Alaska and, much more severe, their invasion of Ukraine. NATO was finally starting to react, and there seemed to be a wider war brewing. The Russians now had ships heading toward the Hawaiian Islands, and the US was sending a carrier strike force to intercept them. The US countered further by deploying a carrier group to the Barents Sea, north of the Russian mainland.

Anders thought what was happening now didn't greatly exceed the usual level of geopolitical posturing in the world at any given time. However, as Harrison had informed him, the latest twist was that these countries were starting to accuse their historic adversaries of probing their inland nuclear sites and other military facilities. He figured new problems would constantly arise as spying technologies advanced.

He read a story about how artificial intelligence technologies could be employed to investigate common citizens through publicly available Internet sources and determine if they were cheating on their spouses or stealing money. It could also predict their future actions, such as traveling, buying a home, changing jobs, or committing a crime. It disturbed him due to the potential impact it would have on his profession: he was supposed to be effectively nonexistent, and certainly not predictable.

It was time to head to the bank.

As he strolled west, down Northeast 6th Street, he contemplated how his mission with the president fit in with global events. As all the state-run intelligence agencies were clawing for information about the geopolitical turmoil, Anders was a link in an underground communications channel connecting the three largest world players which was designed to circumvent those same agencies. Perhaps the leaders of those nations were trying to avoid leaks in order to prevent the situation from escalating to more than just poking and banter, but he was confused as to why it had to be so secretive. There must be more to it.

At 10:40 a.m., he entered the International Canyon Bank and requested access to a safety deposit box in the name of Theo Goddard. He provided the required ID and key, and followed a bank employee, a thin woman in her 50s with short, black hair and wire-rimmed glasses, into a safe with hundreds of rectangular doors, each about six inches tall and twelve inches wide, arrayed on the walls.

The woman pulled out a key and slid it into one of two slots in door number 842. Anders slipped his key into the second slot and they turned their keys simultaneously. The woman opened the door, pulled out a metal box, which was about two feet long, and carried it into one of two small side rooms.

Anders followed.

She set the box on a table and pointed to a white, round button on the wall next to the light switch. "Press the button when you're finished, and someone will come by to help you lock it up again."

Anders thanked her, and she closed the door as she exited.

He turned his attention to the box. He found two buttons, one on each side, near the front and top, and pressed them simultaneously, releasing the lid. He flipped it open, revealing its contents.

The first thing that caught his eye was the gun. It was a black Glock-19 with a single magazine. He checked the chamber, inserted the magazine, and slipped the weapon into the deep front pocket of his khaki shorts.

Next was a slip of paper that gave the name and address of a hotel with corresponding reservation information, some simple instructions, and two sets of phrases. One was for positive identification, with a corresponding "all clear" response. The other set – one phrase for him and the other for his contact – meant trouble and would abort the mission. He supposed the gun was for the latter scenario, but he wondered why complications were seemingly expected. Perhaps Harrison was just being extra careful. It seemed his boss was on edge about the whole arrangement with the president.

Anders closed the box and then pushed the white button on the wall to summon the bank employee. The exchange was to take place in 12 hours.

MAURICE LOGGED INTO THE SECURE, online meeting and found a dozen stern faces looking back at him. The only ones he recognized were those of his immediate boss, Major General Dario Moore, Sonya Goldman, an Air Force intelligence officer, and General Kennedy Frank Tillman, Chairman of the Joint Chiefs of Staff. Others were from the CIA, DIA, and NSA, and from other groups unfamiliar to him. Maurice was the second-lowest ranking attendee, just above the captain of the *USS Stennis*.

"I'd like to start this meeting by reminding you that the information discussed here is classified as top secret," General Tillman explained as he launched the meeting. "Any leaks will be investigated thoroughly, starting with all of you."

Maurice felt oddly threatened by the statement, but it made him even more intrigued about the information that was to come.

The general continued. "Each of you is here to report on strange, and potentially hostile, actions made by what are most likely advanced drones operated by either Russia or China, although China is the more likely culprit," Tillman explained. "Let's start with the most recent event – Captain Grimes, if you could get us started, please."

Grimes' camera feed filled Maurice's screen. The captain seemed to be inside a small compartment, and his signal flickered on occasion.

"Good evening," Grimes said. "I'm the captain of the *USS Stennis*, and we're currently deployed in the South China Sea, which is public knowledge. I will now describe our recent encounters with strange craft that we think might be advanced Chinese drones, based solely on our proximity to the China mainland, and our most recent encounters with Chinese planes and vessels."

The captain then displayed clips of radar traces from various sources within the carrier group.

"As you can see, these objects have tremendous maneuvering abilities," Grimes explained. "However, that's not the most serious aspect of our encounter. It seems these drones were able to hack into our control systems and could manipulate our nuclear reactor. They brought it close to meltdown."

Maurice found *that* to be extremely familiar, and now hoped to learn something that would help him with his own problems.

Grimes went into the specifics of the intrusion, which included descriptions of various systems shutdowns, soliciting gasps and questions from the audience.

"And then they just went away – the objects disappeared – and everything went back to normal," Grimes said at the end of his report. "No permanent damage."

After another half-hour of discussion, nothing conclusive, or even helpful, had been revealed other than a confirmation that the drones were quite advanced.

Maurice was next, and he described the eerily similar set of encounters experienced by the three missile wings, including the launch sequences that had to be manually aborted. Just as with the naval encounters, no one had gotten a direct visual of the aircraft.

Next was Valerie Stark from the DIA who described encounters at secret sites such as Area 51 and other, more obscure, facilities. In those cases, drones had apparently scanned advanced research project sites, including computers containing electronic files on the latest stealth bomber that was under development.

Representatives from the CIA and NSA followed, both reporting on what they suspected were massive data extractions by aerial objects from their unconcealed headquarters complexes, as well as their respective secret facilities around the country. The NSA rep added that drones had even hacked into the Internal Revenue Service and Social Security Administration databases, which brought up the question as to whether such a data breach should be reported to the public. The short and *final* answer to that question was, "No."

After a long discussion between the participants in which they tried to identify commonalities between the events, General Tillman added one more event to the list.

"Two days ago, one of our boomer subs was essentially hijacked in a manner comparable to that which you have all described, and especially similar to what the *USS Stennis* experienced," Tillman explained.

Maurice knew that the boomers carried nuclear missiles – they were the undetectable, mobile sisters of his missile fields.

"The captain of the sub in question could not participate tonight," Tillman continued. "His vessel is deployed in the South Pacific. It was a harrowing experience for his crew. First, their reactor went out of control and, like the *Stennis*, was on the verge of meltdown. Next, the sub went into a dive on its own, bringing it to just above its crush depth. After that, it surfaced on its own."

Maurice was shocked. This meant that the drones could go underwater, or there were underwater versions of the craft that could disable nuclear submarines. It was more than disturbing.

"Things were also happening with the nuke launch systems onboard," Tillman added. "They were malfunctioning during the entire event."

"What will we do if we verify who is responsible for these acts?" the woman from the DIA asked.

Tillman nodded, apparently expecting the question. "It's an act of war," he replied. "However, I'm not sure, exactly, how we'd retaliate. At first sight, it would seem that our aggressors have made a game-changing advance in technology. This, of course, would make us think twice about threatening a military conflict."

When the meeting finally ended, after nearly three hours, Maurice sat motionless in his desk chair. His ears were ringing as if a firecracker had exploded near his head. He reached into his coat pocket and extracted a pack of cigarettes and lit one, even though smoking was forbidden on the base.

The worst-case scenario was that someone was making a test run in preparation for a massive attack on the United States.

AFTER RETRIEVING his instructions from the bank, Anders checked into a five-star hotel in Miami Beach. This was unusual in his line of work – he usually stayed in fleabag hotels where he could pay in cash – but it was a part of his character in this mission. He was to meet his contact in the hotel's restaurant in the evening.

He spent a part of the afternoon on the beach, being careful not to get too much sun on his fair, Northeastern winter skin, and the rest of the time he strolled around the area and had iced coffee at an outdoor café. For dinner, he found a street vendor and bought a Cuban sandwich made with cheese, pulled pork, peppers, and onions. As he ate it, he thought he might come back to Miami someday just to have another one.

Around 9:00 p.m., he went back to his hotel room on the 11th floor and stepped out to the balcony, where he had a view of both the ocean and the pool area below. Cuban music came from multiple directions, and the moon was rising over the sea. It was beautiful scenes like this that sometimes saddened him. One source of this melancholic feeling was something he should have gotten over by now. It had been almost a decade since Tracey, his college girlfriend of six years, had rejected his marriage proposal. Just 18 months later she'd married a medical doctor. Within the next four years, she'd had two kids and a divorce. She was now on her second marriage.

He couldn't entirely blame her for passing on his proposal. Ever since they'd graduated from college, there had been a part of Anders' life that he'd had to conceal from her, to be revealed only after they got married. That was the protocol in his business. He suspected that Tracey had seen him as an underachiever. After hiring him out of college, DMS had created a low-profile, cover job for him as a computer programmer at an insurance firm – a job he'd never done, in a place he'd never seen. As a computer scientist, there were many better-paying jobs he could have pursued out of college, and Tracey had encouraged him to try for some of the well-known, big-tech companies. What she didn't know was that he, in fact, *had* applied for those kinds of jobs and turned down numerous offers, choosing instead to join DMS. And now she'd never know. Perhaps it all had worked out for the best, but there were times when the loneliness got to him.

Anders opened his disguise kit and got to work. An hour and a half later, his short, blonde-brown hair was replaced with longer, curly hair of a slightly darker shade. He then installed darker sideburns and a mustache, and wore round, wire-rimmed glasses that were partially reflective and slightly tinted. He donned loose, beige pants and a white, button-down shirt, which he wore untucked, with the sleeves rolled up to the forearms and the neck unbuttoned to expose some of the hair on his chest. His brown shoes were otherwise nondescript – shoes were difficult to change on the fly if the need arose, so they shouldn't otherwise attract attention – and he wore a large, gold watch that *did* attract modest attention. The watch he could discard easily – a cheap facsimile of an expensive brand.

He looked himself over in the mirror. If he took it any further he'd start to look like a 70s porn star. As it stood, however, he'd fit right in with the rest of the clientele.

At 10:15 p.m., he slipped the Glock into his front pocket, rode the elevator to the floor below the lobby, and went into an expansive bar-restaurant that had one end open to a large, outdoor pool. The place was filling with people and a band was setting up to play near the open area.

Anders went to the bar, ordered a whisky, and took it to a small booth for two in a corner as far from the band as possible. An inset light in the ceiling lit the table in a dim, golden hue, and a small candle burned in a pink glass holder against the wall. He had a good view of the area, including the bar and pool.

All he knew about his contact was that she was a woman who went by the name "Alina Petrova," and that she'd be carrying a red handbag with a gold keyring on one of the straps that had the words "I love Jamaica" on it. All she knew of him was that he'd be wearing a large, gold watch, round glasses, and a white shirt. She was to approach him, not the other way around. All he could do was sit and wait.

At around 10:45 p.m., the music began and the crowd grew. The band played Cuban music, and people started dancing and getting noisy.

His contact was expected to appear between 11:00 and 11:30 p.m. If no one showed by 11:35 p.m., he was to abort and evacuate – not even go back to the hotel room.

At 11:10 p.m., a young woman approached his table and smiled at him.

"Are you all by yourself?" the woman asked. She was probably in her late 20's, and blonde, tan, and attractive. She wore tight, white shorts and a bright green tank top. An intoxicating bouquet of coconut-scented suntan lotion emanated from her skin.

She had no handbag, and hadn't used the correct greeting.

"Just waiting for someone," he replied in a friendly tone. "She should be here any minute."

"Oh," the woman replied. "Well, enjoy the music."

"Thanks, you too," he replied, and the woman left. He saw her enter a restroom on the opposite side of the bar.

Strange women didn't usually approach him, and he found it amusing that his current look would attract anyone. It exposed how little he knew about what women found attractive in men – although he figured that tastes varied widely.

He ordered and received a second whisky from a cocktail server and, at 11:22 p.m., he spotted his contact. She was about five-foot-seven, thin, with short blonde hair, early 30s he guessed, and dressed to fit in with the crowd – tan shorts, a white tank top, and a red handbag over her shoulder with the identifying keyring. She was holding a beer in her left hand, and a cell phone in her right.

He could tell that she hadn't seen him yet, and he observed how she casually scanned the place for him. She was a professional.

With barely a glance in his direction, and with no hint of recognition, she made her way to his booth and then looked at him and smiled.

"Are you in Miami for the music?" she asked. She smiled, and her expression became friendly, as if she really knew him. She had a mild Russian accent.

He stood, smiled, and hugged her as if he knew her. Her perfume was pleasant, but it was a mistake to wear it. "Yes, but more for the weather and the food," he replied with the appropriate phrase. "How are you?" They both played it up, although quietly, like they were old friends, and then sat across from each other in the booth.

"I've enjoyed Miami," she said. "But I'll soon be heading back to the cold."

"Me too," he said. She'd be going back to Moscow, he presumed, and he to DC. A miserable time of the year for both places.

They were to make small talk for at least 15 minutes before making the exchange, and then wait another ten, at which point he'd head for the restroom, and she'd disappear.

"How long have you been in your career?" she asked.

"A little over ten years," he replied. "You?"

"Same," she said. "Like you, I'm in a private firm."

"It's odd how our respective clients have taken such a route," he said.

"Indeed," she said. "I try not to ask questions, but I must admit my surprise when I learned the details of this mission."

After an extended conversation about the city's attractions, she reached across the table and grabbed his hand. He was holding the item deep in his palm. She held it for a second and looked into his eyes as he felt her simultaneously extract it and replace it with another. "I hope we're doing the right thing."

"Me too," he said as she let go, and they both casually slipped their newly acquired data storage devices into their pockets.

"Now we just have to get out of here," she said.

"A friendly word of advice?" Anders said.

"Yes?"

"Nix the perfume," he said.

She flashed a look of anger and embarrassment at him.

"No – please, it's wonderful," he said. "Unfortunately, it can also be used to locate you."

"Locate me?"

"In case we're chased," he explained.

"I've never been chased."

"I have," he said.

"I'll take your recommendation into consideration," Alina said dryly.

As they chatted for another ten minutes, Anders regretted offering his unsolicited guidance, as he could tell that her demeanor had changed to something a little less friendly. She probably took it as an insult, but that was not his intention. It was probably another reason he didn't have a girlfriend.

"I need to use the restroom," he said and stood. "You want to get us a couple of drinks?"

"Sure," she said as she got to her feet. "Meet you back here."

Anders made his way to the bathroom and went into a stall. He pulled the horse-pill-shaped object out of his pants pocket and examined it. It was identical to the one he'd given Alina, but blue rather than green.

After he flushed the toilet, he went to the mirror and checked his disguise. Everything was intact. He was ready to go.

He went back into the bar, passed their vacant booth, and made his way out to the pool. It was crowded, and people nearest the band were dancing. Alina was nowhere to be seen. He then made his way back inside to an elevator and was in his room five minutes later.

Anders turned on a cable news station as he removed his disguise. The Russians were now accusing the US of infiltrating one of their submarine bases at Novorossiysk, in the Black Sea, where they'd been docking one of their newest subs, the *Kolpino*. This latest addition to their Black Sea Fleet was otherwise known as the "Black Hole," due to its supposed groundbreaking stealth capabilities. The

Russians were complaining that the US was using drones to access the sub's control systems. It was never mentioned whether those "drones" were of the airborne or underwater type.

After cleaning up and changing his clothes, Anders packed up his things and left the hotel without checking out. On the street in front of the hotel, he pulled out his phone and arranged for a SuperLift car to meet him at a nearby corner. On the way, he dumped his untraceable gun into a garbage can. He'd be back in Washington, DC by 3:30 a.m.

CHAPTER 2

A SuperLift car picked up Anders a few blocks from his apartment at 7:00 a.m. on a frigid, overcast, Monday morning.

DMS had a useful software app that arranged for hired cars from various companies, including SuperLift, SideKarr, and other networked services, and randomized pickup locations so that his path to work would be different every morning. This sometimes called for long walks and rides using cabs, buses, and rail. Occasionally, it would take him an hour to get to work, even though he could make the direct drive himself in 15 minutes. He carried only a backpack for these little adventures.

The app also paid for everything automatically under an alias that he referred to as his "morning commute persona," even though he used the same for his return home. When on a mission, the program would automatically use credentials that were consistent with his current alias. DMS had people working 24-7 on keeping track of its operatives and making sure no mistakes were made along the way, meaning that alias identities were consistent across the board – passports, flight reservations, car services and rentals, credit cards, and hotel rooms were all perfectly integrated. Even the slightest discrepancy could be fatal, but he trusted the DMS people.

It amazed him how oblivious common citizens were to many things that were happening right under their noses. There was a dark underworld that operated in parallel to that which existed in the light. People who seemed ordinary might be carrying out secret tasks, some of which had literal life-or-death consequences. Anders found himself entwined in this world of secret objectives, just like his father had been. People disappeared without a trace in this business, and he made sure to always keep this in mind. His dad had often reminded him that few people in his specific line of work within the intelligence community died of natural causes – and many didn't make it to 40 years of age.

Anders was not in the same cloak-and-dagger business as his father had been but, even though he worked for a private entity, he faced similar dangers.

The last leg of this particular chilly morning commute was a half-mile walk that took him past a local coffee shop called the Count Cristo Coffee House. It was an encouraged practice to deviate from a direct path in any segment of the trip – so that was his excuse. He climbed a set of concrete steps to the entrance and read a sign in the window that advertised the coffee and pastry of the day – Costa Rican medium roast and blueberry muffins.

He opened the door and was hit by a rush of warm air infused with the intense aroma of coffee and the softer scents of bakery goods. He stepped inside.

To his right was a coffee bar with a line of patrons placing orders. To his left was a room full of tables, three-quarters of which were occupied by what looked to be professionals on their way to work, about a dozen pensioners, and a few others who looked to be college students. Anders got the Costa Rican medium roast in a ceramic mug and took it to a small table near a window.

He sat, pulled his laptop out of his backpack, and opened it. It was a DMS computer, which meant it was secure. It operated in two modes: classified or benign. In the "benign" setting, no sensitive information could be accessed, and only some common software programs and an Internet browser were available. It was not connected to local Wi-Fi, but to an encrypted satellite link. He went to the main BBC News site.

He'd been paying close attention to the rising strains between the US, Russia, and China, and they confused him. Their respective leaders were communicating directly – privately – yet things seemed to be getting *worse* between them. They were all now openly accusing each other of the same things, and Anders had no idea which one of the three was responsible for the antagonistic behavior. He supposed it was possible that all three were provoking each other simultaneously, but it wasn't likely. What were the chances that they'd all developed the same technology at the same time? Even if one country had stolen it from another, there would at least be some delay before the thieving nation developed it and put it to use. In the end, he sensed he was in the middle of it somehow, but had no idea what was really happening. The BBC and other news sites provided nothing enlightening and only heightened his feeling that the situation was rapidly declining.

The day before, the morning after returning to DC from Miami, Anders had delivered the blue data storage device to President Crownbrook. Their conversation had been short, but Anders sensed anxiety in the president's demeanor. He supposed the man had a lot on his mind with the escalating global tensions.

Their meeting had also seemed rushed – he'd gotten the impression that Crownbrook was itching to see what was on the device – and Anders had been ushered out quickly. Before he'd left, however, the president had warned him that the frequency of the exchanges was going to escalate, but only after a lull of a week or two. Anders was to remain in the DC area at all times, and to be ready to act on a moment's notice.

He finished his coffee and returned the mug to the front counter on his way out. He'd been to this coffee house multiple times during the past few years, but made sure to visit it only once or twice a month. Although he thought he'd enjoy it being a part of his daily routine, he had to make sure it would not be a predictable stop for him.

It took him 20 minutes to meander his way to DMS on slippery sidewalks riddled with patches of thin ice. He'd stay at headquarters during normal business hours until he got the next call from the president. In the meantime, he'd try to be an astute observer of the news.

He took the special elevator, designed for identity-sensitive personnel, to his office, somewhere in the bowels of the five-story DMS building. The structure had three sublevels that originally served as an underground parking garage. They now functioned as a bomb-proof space for computer servers, control rooms, and isolated offices, like his, which was on the second sublevel.

Anders' workspace was square, only about 12 feet on a side, but was efficiently fitted with a tiny refrigerator, microwave, and sink on the wall to the right of the entrance when viewed from the inside. A small couch and a set of inset bookshelves were on the left. On the far side, opposite the entrance, was a desk with a gigantic computer monitor. Immediately to the left of the entrance was a door that led to a small bathroom with a shower that Anders compared to an airplane lavatory.

The floor was covered with short, beige carpeting and the walls and ceiling with glossy, pine paneling that made the space resemble the captain's quarters of an old sailing ship. A three-by-three array of dimmable, inset lights in the ceiling provided an adjustable level of illumination that ranged from a low, warm hue to a brightness that rivaled the lights at an athletic stadium. Overall, the place was compact but comfortable.

He sat on the couch and paged through the contents of the folder President Crownbrook had given him to study as a cover story. It occurred to him that he was actually building his knowledge so that he'd be able to answer questions about his relationship with the president that might one day be posed by the FBI or CIA. He also knew that he and DMS were probably on the fringe of legality in this case. He'd been involved in other things that could have been construed as, at the least, shady, but this was much more serious.

Another strange realization was that Anders, and the two other independent couriers with whom he'd interacted, essentially mirrored the leaders of the three feuding countries. The couriers knew what was happening, at least in the broad sense that information was being conveyed through backchannels, and so did their respective "firms." In the old days, before special, encrypted data devices with built-in, anti-tampering mechanisms, the couriers might be privy to some of the content of those messages, or at least be able to view the information in code. Codes could be broken.

Anders realized where his thoughts were heading and veered away. He wasn't going to tamper with the devices to try to figure out what they contained.

His daydreaming was interrupted by a knock on the door.

It was his boss.

"Good morning," Harrison said as he went to Anders' desk chair, turned it to face the couch, and sat. "I have some disturbing news."

Anders sat up and leaned forward on the couch.

"Someone tampered with the device you handed off to the Chinese courier in Alexandria," Harrison explained. "The Chinese president was delivered a nonfunctional device."

It was more than disturbing in Anders' view. Since he was one of the couriers who had handled it, he was an immediate suspect.

"Don't worry," Harrison said, seemingly sensing Anders' anxiety. "It didn't happen while in your possession."

"How do you know that?"

"It turns out that the tampering mechanism doesn't kill the entire device," Harrison explained. "There's separate memory allocated for monitoring software that logs various things, and it captured the time and date when the device's tampering mechanism was triggered."

Anders felt the swell of anxiety drain away. "When did it happen?"

"About 24 hours after you handed it off," Harrison replied. "The man was already in Hong Kong at the time."

"Did the Russian device make it through?" Anders asked.

"Ours did," Harrison answered. "However, as you might have guessed, the Russians and Chinese are also making exchanges. The Russian leader also received a burned device from the same Chinese Courier, and the Chinese president got a fried device from the Russians."

"What about the one I delivered from that courier to Crownbrook?"

"Intact," Harrison said. "It was the first delivery by that operative – maybe we got lucky."

"There's only one Chinese courier, right?" Anders asked. "Same as we're doing?"

"Yes, and it's clear that everything he handled after his delivery to us was compromised," Harrison said. "They're dealing with him now."

Anders knew what *that* meant. He wouldn't be seeing "Hwang" again, and neither would anyone else.

"Good thing you always operate in disguise," Harrison said. "Otherwise, you'd be compromised and out of the operation, as would DMS."

"What do we do now?" Anders asked.

"You need to make a delivery from the White House to a different Chinese agent," Harrison said. "You're scheduled to see the president tonight."

"And the exchange?"

"Tomorrow, here in DC," Harrison replied.

"That's quick."

"I've spoken directly with the president – he used the satellite phone we provided," Harrison said. "Everything is time-sensitive, and he seems flustered. We need to catch up – redeliver the message that was burned as soon as possible."

Harrison left and Anders remained on the couch, his mind spinning. All of it was odd, and now the US president was communicating with a private security firm with an encrypted satellite phone. Also, someone was trying to intercept the messages – so there was another, unknown party involved. Perhaps the intentions of the Chinese president had already been discovered by his own intelligence services.

Everything had just gotten much more dangerous.

MAURICE WATCHED CLASSIFIED footage of drones interfering with a US carrier group a few hundred miles off the coast of North Carolina, an incident which had occurred just 12 hours prior. He was with a dozen others at CIA Headquarters in Langley, Virginia, inside a viewing room that was set up like a mini movie theater. He'd been summoned to the impromptu meeting by the Deputy Director of the CIA.

The video was out of focus and grainy, but it was the only direct imaging of aircraft that they suspected were of the same type that had infiltrated numerous sensitive intelligence and military facilities around the mainland US. The video clips – which recorded normal light rather than thermal emissions – came from fighter jets. They were a bit shaky but showed off-white objects that looked nothing like conventional aircraft – pill-shaped, with no visible wings – and were extremely fast and maneuverable. They were, in fact, so agile that they were assumed to be unmanned since no human could survive the observed accelerations.

The thermal imaging footage was even more perplexing. Conventional aircraft have heat signatures from their propulsion systems – hot areas around the engines that drive their props, or hot plumes resulting from the expulsion of heated gas from their jets.

The objects in the video, however, had strange temperature profiles, as if there were cool shrouds around them that shielded the warmer innards of the craft. Their propulsion mechanisms therefore remained a mystery.

The screen went blank, the lights illuminated, and a CIA analyst who went only by "Janis" went to the front of the room and addressed the attendees.

"We cannot verify that these are the same type of craft that interfered with our inland assets," she explained. "However, this is the only direct footage we have of any of the objects. We also have some shadowy radar data, and a few visual sightings by military personnel on foot at some of the missile silos, but they provide no additional insight."

The meeting ended after another 30 minutes of unenlightening discussion and, as Maurice packed up his briefcase and put on his coat, the CIA Director entered and approached the woman who had led the meeting. She pointed at Maurice and the director waved him over.

As Maurice approached, the man took a step toward him and held out his hand. "Hello Colonel Spelling, I'm Clay Radcliffe, the Director of the CIA," he said.

"I know who you are," Maurice said as he smiled and shook the man's hand. Radcliffe was an easily recognized man: tall, thin, and his bald head shone like a polished, chrome trailer hitch.

"You command the 341st, and oversee the 90th and 91st, correct?"

"Yes sir," Maurice replied, although his so-called oversight of the other two wings was just a formality. He didn't interfere in their day-to-day operations.

"Good. I was wondering if we could have a word in private," Radcliffe said and then gestured to a door at the front of the theater, to the right of the screen. "We have a secure room back here."

As Maurice followed him toward the door, he noticed that the woman who had directed the meeting, Janis, did not follow them. It seemed he was about to have a one-on-one conversation with the CIA director.

ANDERS SPENT the afternoon analyzing open information sources, including news articles and blogs, about current geopolitical conflicts around the world. He found it odd that, in December, just over two months ago, the US president had met with his Chinese and Russian counterparts at a climate change summit in Norway. That meeting had taken place behind closed doors, and they'd been completely alone – not even security or translators had been present.

That rare meeting had been unscheduled – or at least not publicly disclosed on their itineraries – and the specific subject of their conversation had never been revealed, despite the media bombarding the US president with questions about it on his return to the States. President Crownbrook had told them that they'd discussed strategies to reduce carbon emissions, and "other things that had potential impact on the global environment."

Within a week of that meeting, two US carrier groups had been redeployed from their current missions. One went to the South China Sea, which wasn't unusual, although it was eventually positioned just barely outside Chinese waters. The other had been given delayed orders to deploy to the Barents Sea, north of the Russian mainland, which was a rare occurrence. That US strike force had now settled in just outside Russian waters. Both areas were now current locations of naval stalemates that could boil over at any time. There were also other naval skirmishes brewing between the three countries near Hawaii, Guam, and the Philippines.

Next, a new land-border dispute was emerging between China and Russia. In the end, there was a three-way standoff between the three most powerful countries in the world, all developing after that climate-change summit.

What had happened during that strange meeting in Norway? Had there been an argument? Had threats been made? Whatever had transpired, it seemed that all parties had gone away with negative intentions.

The question now was what underground information was currently being passed between the players, and why was it kept secret? Their geopolitical conflicts weren't secret but, he supposed, the *reason* for them was unknown, even though the US president claimed the posturing with China had to do with their unlawful occupation of disputed islands in the South Pacific, and the confrontation in the Barents Sea was in response to Russia's invasion of Ukraine and their threat to cut off the natural gas supply to the EU. That conflict also had an adverse effect on the world's food supply, with Ukraine being a major producer of grain.

Anders sensed that something *else* was occurring beneath all the geopolitical actions on the surface, and he was now in the middle of it.

MAURICE SAT across a table from Clay Radcliffe in a room designed to muffle sound, giving it the feel of a recording studio.

"Thanks for making the trek all the way to DC for this meeting," Radcliffe said. "Since your missile network is deeply entwined in this mystery, we would like to involve you in our investigation of this matter. We're developing plans to reveal who's behind this."

"What do you mean, like a trap?" Maurice asked. He'd been thinking about some possibilities along those lines.

"Something like that, yes," Radcliffe replied. "What we've been exploring will require extensive reconfiguring on your part – to some of your missile silos and control stations. Some of the actions we're considering are quite brazen."

"Such as?"

"In one scenario, we plan to initiate a mock launch sequence," Radcliffe replied.

A high-pitched ringing filled Maurice's ears for an instant. It came from an alarm sounding inside his own head. What the director suggested could start a war if not handled with care, and was a risky proposition. "What would that accomplish?"

Radcliffe shifted in his seat and leaned over the table, closer to Maurice. "Assuming that these drones are monitoring our internal activities – and we assume they are – they'll detect the launch activity very quickly."

"And then?"

"They'll report the actions to their country of origin," Radcliffe explained. "As you well know, we monitor our adversaries' nuclear sites very closely. The first to react to our mock launch is probably the country responsible for the drones."

"I see," Maurice said. It wasn't a great plan, but it could provide some circumstantial information. "A little risky, considering the consequences of taking it too far. Suppose the other country overreacts."

"That's something we've considered," Radcliffe said. "We'll just need to terminate the operation – shut down the launch – at the first sign of a reaction."

Maurice was already analyzing the complexity of such an operation. There'd have to be many people knowing what was happening. The potential trauma on his missileers, if left out of the loop, could cause problems in the future – for them, and for the entire program. He couldn't imagine being in their place and really believing they were on the brink of nuclear war. The other problem was that such an operation could easily be compromised if too many people knew about it.

"We figure this strategy would force the offending nation to back off," Radcliffe added. "Presumably, they don't want to go to war either, and this may send a clear message that we will no longer tolerate their incursions."

"It will require careful planning," Maurice said. "And, as you know, I cannot make modifications to the missile networks on my own."

Radcliffe nodded. "You'll be granted the authority to carry this out," he said. "Only the people in your direct chain of command will be aware of it. The order will come directly from the president."

In that case, Maurice would have no reservations about setting it up.

"Whether or not we'll actually go through with this has not yet been decided. But there's something else we're planning which is much more extensive, and more important in the long run," Radcliffe explained. "We're developing a mobile, auxiliary system to launch missiles from disabled sites. Is it true that, up to this point, the control systems in the silos and stations have only been disabled, and nothing has really been *damaged* by the drones?"

"Yes, as far as we know," Maurice replied. "Everything has always come back online afterwards, so it should still be operational after the meddling."

"Our assumption is that, in a real attack, the drones will disable a control station in the same manner and keep it in the inoperable, but undamaged, state," Radcliffe explained. "But now we'll have new, external launch vehicles – essentially mobile launch stations – to carry out the launches instead. They'll essentially bypass the entire control system of a disabled underground site, and carry out the launches."

"But won't these mobile stations circumvent the entire interlocked safety system that prevents rogue launches?" Maurice asked, startled by the concept.

"They'll still be safe," Radcliffe argued. "They'll continue to require the launch codes, and the two-key interlock system will remain. Just think how shocked the offending country will be when we initiate a launch from a silo that had supposedly been disabled by one of their drones."

Maurice thought it would send an effective message. "Is it just Malmstrom involved in these modifications?"

Radcliffe shook his head. "You'll get it started at Malmstrom, but the other missile fields will follow. For now, you're not to share this with anyone – this is top secret," he warned. "This means no one, not your superiors, not the director of the Missile Defense Agency, not the FBI, and no one other than myself in the CIA until I directly connect you with someone else. Essential CIA people and your colleagues at the other two missile wings will be brought up to speed later. Understood?"

Maurice nodded. He appreciated the importance of secrecy in the matter. He just hoped that they knew what they were doing.

ANDERS RETURNED to his apartment just after midnight and got into the shower. Just two hours prior, he'd met with the president and collected another data device to pass on to a Chinese contact the next evening. It would be a new courier, since the first one was either a mole for some unknown party, or a Chinese spy – an actual *member* of the Ministry of State Security (MSS) – which meant that the Chinese president was already compromised.

President Crownbrook seemed especially nervous while they'd met. They had spent an unusual amount of time talking about the mock charity work Anders was supposed to be performing, and the president had passed him a note with the relevant information about the next evening's rendezvous. Nothing was spoken aloud about the operation. Anders interpreted this as the president assuming they were being observed – bugged.

As the warm water soothed his nerves, he mulled over the situation. If the president's paranoia was based on anything real, then Anders should be just as paranoid. If they were suspicious of something, the CIA and FBI would keep tabs on anyone meeting alone with the president. They did anyway, along with the Secret Service, but this might now evolve into extended surveillance of visitors, including tracking.

Anders was well-versed in the practices of surveillance and avoidance, and had taken every precaution. Now, he just had to boost his avoidance efforts and maybe spend a few nights in his office at DMS. He'd also elevate his disguises, especially when leaving his apartment. A good thing about living in a large complex was that it was difficult for anyone watching from the outside to notice him coming and going since there were a few hundred other occupants in his building. There were also multiple exits.

In addition, DMS had installed a sophisticated security system in his apartment, and in the corridor leading up to it, which would detect anyone trying to break in or set up electronic surveillance. He could imagine that, if that had not been done, someone could install a camera near his apartment door and get a make on him in the disguise he was using for the day. From that point, he could be tailed by a team, and then he'd give away everything, including DMS, or whatever mission he was conducting at the time.

He'd been living in the apartment for almost two years. However, DMS would move him at some point, and also change his "home identity." According to the management of the apartment complex, his name was Richard Stiles, single, 38, with a stable, annual income of 92 thousand dollars. He paid his rent and utilities on time, didn't make any noise, and parked his gray Toyota Civic in his assigned parking spot.

Anders tolerated little risk. Outside of work, he mostly kept to himself. When he had the need for a retreat, he'd either immerse himself in a video game or, when he wanted something in the *real* world, he'd look up some secluded used bookstore or coffeehouse – sometimes over 100 miles away – and make an adventure of it. It wasn't that he hadn't had enough "adventures" in his life, but sometimes he needed to do something that wasn't dangerous.

There was another part of his life, however, where he was somewhat more exposed. For the past two years, he'd been involved with a woman who wasn't officially his "girlfriend," but was definitely more than a friend. Her name was Delilah, or "Del," Emery. She was a pediatrician and, after completing her residency six months ago, she'd relocated to Nashville, Tennessee, not far from her hometown. They'd met in a hospital in DC after Anders had undergone emergency surgery for appendicitis. She'd walked into his hospital room after he'd awakened from the operation, and then stopped and stared at him with a perplexed expression. She'd said, "You look a little old for seven."

He'd learned later that the hospital had made a typo entering his birthdate, and she'd been called in from home to look in on a young boy.

Anders had been attracted to her immediately – her smile, her long, blond hair, and her kind eyes. He'd figured out what must've happened, and replied with, "I think it might've been the cigars," which made her laugh. They hit it off right away.

Since she'd left DC, they'd made a few trips to each other's locations for a weekend here and there, but it was sporadic. Now, they would talk on the phone once every couple of weeks, but there was no mention of any visits. He was convinced she'd found someone locally – probably another doctor – and was sure their relationship would soon dissolve completely, if it hadn't already. It was probably for the best.

One major, and perhaps irrecoverable, problem with their fragile connection was that it was one-sided. He was hiding a major facet of his life from her – just like he'd done with his girlfriend in college. It was a catch-22: he couldn't tell her about his job *until* they were married, and he couldn't be completely open with her about his life *before* they were married. He wasn't desperate to get married anyway. And it wasn't fair that she was in the dark about his secret life. What if she didn't approve of what he did for a living – meaning that she didn't approve, ultimately, of who he *was*? It was a sacrifice he'd made for his career, and he sometimes wondered if it was worth it.

The timing worked out, however. If there was ever a time when he needed to be single, it was now. How could he explain multiple nights out per week – and coming home late? To her, he was a computer scientist – a programmer – and they typically weren't called in at odd hours. And what if she discovered his disguise kits? He concluded that things were as they should be, for now.

He got out of the shower, slipped on a pair of shorts and a tee shirt, went to the couch in his living room, and started up his latest video game. In the back of his mind, he was formulating the elements of his disguise for the rendezvous with the Chinese operative the next evening. This meet was going to occur at a popular wine bar near the University of Maryland campus.

Although he usually looked forward to some action, the situation seemed to be getting riskier than his usual missions. There was something simmering in the back of his mind: something was wrong about this operation.

"THIS GUY'S A SLIPPERY SONOFABITCH," Candace Wright muttered as she pushed away from her desk and leaned back. "We lose him every time."

"Definitely a professional," Timothy Barilaro said.

"We're fucking professionals, too, Timmy," Candace griped, using the form of his name that he despised. She was trying to get a rise out of her FBI partner, who was seven years her younger at 32.

"I know, Candy," he retorted.

She narrowed her eyes and grinned. He knew exactly how to counter her provocation. Other than her father and her husband, Tim was probably the only person who could get away with calling her "Candy." And, although she found Tim attractive – he was tall and rugged-looking for a man his age – she thought of him more as a younger brother. Her husband was about the same height at six-foot-four, which made them both nearly a foot taller than her. Oddly, Tim's fiancée happened to look a lot like her: short, dark blonde, and athletic, although Candace's hair was starting to show some gray.

She and Tim had a good rapport from the very beginning, and their first project together, three years prior, had resulted in her being promoted, and him being permanently placed in her "domestic counterespionage" group. This "group," which was tasked with exposing classified information leaks from upper-echelon government administrators, was comprised of only her and Tim. Unfortunately, according to the FBI's upper brass, their past successes didn't warrant any new personnel, nor an upgrade from their stuffy, shared office, with no windows. The workspace one got at FBI Headquarters was based entirely on politics, and she and Tim were at the bottom of that food chain.

Tim looked back to a large computer monitor that had multiple open windows with paused video images. "It's not easy to track someone on patched video footage when they change everything – appearance, mode of transportation, time of travel – and take crazy routes," he said. "It's as if he knows exactly where the dark areas are in this city. We can't track him in places where there are no cameras."

"We're the FBI," Candace argued. "We have the best surveillance equipment and have access to all public resources – including all the cameras in the broader DC area. And we even have drones. Dammit!"

"We don't have access to the drones. But we'll need a full surveillance team to follow this guy," Tim said. "Should we put in a request?"

She shook her head. "You know what's going on – this involves a sitting president," she said. "The more people who know what we're doing, the higher the chance of a leak. And, if it got out that we're investigating Crownbrook, well – "

"Scandal," he interjected. "And our careers might come to an abrupt end."

"Exactly," she said. "So let's concentrate on things that we suspect *connect* the president to this guy, rather than on the president directly."

"The Single-World Alliance," Tim said.

As a part of their "domestic counterespionage" work, Candace and Tim investigated subversive groups both inside and outside the government. The president's name had come up in connection with one called the Single-World Alliance, or SWA.

"We have no idea who this mystery White House visitor is. And do you really think Crownbrook's covert message channel has to do with the SWA?" Tim asked. "I mean, hypothetically, what could he be communicating to them?"

Candace shrugged. "No idea. But it doesn't matter. We can use it as an excuse to look into him and those with whom he has contact," she said. "He's a suspected SWA member and, if he's communicating with them at all, it's a problem."

"All we have are 'suspected' members of this organization – no one confirmed," he argued. "The group is pretty tight, if it really exists."

"If it exists?" she repeated in a derisive tone. "We have their *manifesto*. They have dangerous ideas."

"Just because we have a manifesto doesn't mean the group really exists," Tim rebutted. "I could write a manifesto for an organization that only exists on paper, and then spread rumors about certain people being members of it."

Candace shrugged. "The Deputy Director put us on this case for a reason," she said. "Our objective is to find out who is visiting the president and, allegedly, delivering messages that bypass normal channels – which is suspicious behavior. The only person we are unable to track and identify is *this* guy." She pointed to a screen with a still photo of a man holding a closed umbrella in the visitors' foyer of the White House.

"Yeah, the guy going through avoidance protocols as he goes back and forth from the White House is suspicious on its own," Tim said.

"And he's damn good at it," she added.

"Okay, no surveillance team at this point," he said. "Especially not one to start following him directly from the White House. So, what do we do?"

"We need more information – something to give us *cause* to look deeper," Candace said, and then looked to the screen. "All of this footage is useless. And we don't even have his name."

"He didn't sign in at the White House?"

"Not with his real name," she replied. "And we can't even ask about it or they'll know we're looking into Crownbrook. I got the alias he's using from a friend in the Secret Service."

"We could feed video frames into the new facial recognition system," Tim suggested.

"We'd need justification for that as well," she replied. "Plus, the anti-terrorism group has a monopoly on it. Could you imagine if word got out that we were cooperating with the anti-terrorism group to track someone who is meeting with the president – and is probably a US citizen – on US soil?"

"Yeah, okay," he said. "But if it really exists, the Single-World Alliance could easily be considered a terror organization."

"But it's not – not officially," she replied. Although, she knew it had been suggested in some internal reports that the SWA was involved with the RAT-32C virus, which was responsible for the worst pandemic in the last century. That would certainly qualify the group as terrorists, but it was all conjecture since no one could prove who was actually in the organization.

Tim shrugged. "So, what do we do?"

"We stick with investigating the SWA and hope we get a lead," she replied. "If we find a solid connection between the SWA and this guy, or to the president, our resources will widen."

"There are others investigating the SWA – maybe we should reach out to them," Tim suggested.

"Already did that, and got some info," Candace said. "At least two suspected SWA members are going to be in the same place – in public – tomorrow night. It might just be a coincidence but it's all we have right now."

"In public?" he asked. "Are we going to have someone there?"

"Yes," she said. "Us."

"Oh," he said with a look of surprise. "I haven't been in the field for a while."

"We're just going out for drinks," she said. "But bring your gun."

Tim gave her an alarmed look. "I'm more of an analyst," he said.

"I know. Me too," she said. "And we'll be there to analyze."

"Will anyone else be with us?"

"No idea," she replied. "My sources in Homeland Security just told me not to interfere if something goes down."

"Goes down?"

"I doubt anything's going to happen," she said. "They're going to try to ID the SWA suspects and see who they talk to. Maybe they'll get a few more names to put on the members list."

She winced at her own words. There was a fine edge between linking people together in order to reveal their collective intentions and tagging them as a threat, throwing them all into the same cage without definitive evidence. However, Candace felt that she could ride on that edge in this case. According to their manifesto, one objective of the Single-World Alliance was to exterminate a large fraction of the world's population.

Anders was in his DMS office by 8:00 a.m., sipping hot coffee and studying his usual news sites. The BBC presented numerous stories on the confrontations between the US, Russia, and China. The UK was now involved, as were Israel and India. India again accused China of invading their airspace with drones, and Israel and the UK did the same regarding Russia.

The clashes between the US and China in the South Pacific were escalating rapidly. China threatened Taiwan, Guam, and Hawaii, and the US responded with aggressive moves toward Chinese military vessels and disputed islands in the area. Up to this point, however, no action had taken place – not even warning shots – so Anders suspected that most of it was just posturing.

Next, he studied the location of that evening's exchange with the new Chinese op. It was a bar called "Grapes of Wrath," located just far enough away from the University of Maryland campus so that it wouldn't be overpopulated with students. The clientele would probably be professionals around his age, which made his choice of disguise straightforward. He'd go with brown, bushy sideburns, and a medium-length, curly wig that was one shade lighter. He'd otherwise be clean-shaven, and would wear glasses. He planned to pose as a software engineer, and DMS had already printed business cards that were consistent with his cover story.

The full DMS machine was in the game: if someone called the number on the cards, they'd get someone from Springwell Solutions, Inc., a software applications startup company. If DMS got a call on that number, it would set into motion a safety protocol in which Anders would get a text message or phone call. If he didn't answer with the correct phrase, or didn't answer at all, DMS ops would set out to find him.

Anders was confident in the operation, and his safety, but he still had more anxiety than usual. Perhaps it was the potential stakes of this job, and the concurrent overt interactions between the involved countries he'd been witnessing in the news.

Over the past decade, he'd read a lot about the espionage and tactics of the Cold War, where many in the intelligence services had been assassinated by their adversaries. He was always troubled by the idea that those who currently worked in the underworld, like him, might someday be cast into that same situation. The only problem now was that the available tools were far more sophisticated – from weapons to surveillance. Even his disguises would become obsolete in a few years when facial recognition and artificial intelligence technologies took hold.

In one sense, such advances might improve people's lives – perhaps they'd reduce certain types of crime and better secure people's identities. The opposite edge of that sword, however, was the elimination of anonymity and privacy. In fact, it would be a mechanism that would eventually render every aspect of one's life as public knowledge. Governments would have complete control over the people they supposedly served. It would end up being about power and a tool for control, and it would be abused. It had "Orwellian implications," as his father had often put it.

As technology advanced, democracies were becoming increasingly more vulnerable. Control of people was becoming digital, and each successive administration, especially in the US government, was becoming progressively more difficult to uproot once it was embedded. The governing administration controlled the FBI, CIA, NSA, IRS, EPA, and the Justice Department – the president appointed their leaders, or at least had great influence over who was installed. The ruling party could even change the rules of the Senate and House of Representatives to get what they wanted in a "legal" way. Although one might think that the CIA and FBI were the most powerful of the government entities in the executive branch's toolbox, the Internal Revenue Service wielded power that was often underestimated. The IRS could exact devastating effects on political adversaries by controlling their money. Finally, if high-tech social media companies, the news media, and individual government agencies, had a common political objective, they could effectively eliminate the democratic process. Anders figured that this could be accomplished through the coordinated effort of about 100 well-placed people.

Regarding his own profession, Anders was trying to stay informed about developing technologies in surveillance and espionage, hoping to learn how to utilize them, and to defeat them. He knew of weaknesses in some of the methods, and how to exploit them, but those holes were quickly closing. The extrapolation of the current trajectories of the technologies, however, was frightening.

Elements of the wider, new-world technologies were not yet perfected, and still disjointed. But he imagined that, as those individual pieces improved, they'd eventually coalesce with each other. For instance, facial recognition might develop to the extent that a person couldn't go into any public place without being recognized. At that point, you wouldn't have to carry a cell phone to be tracked. That technology could then be integrated into artificial intelligence algorithms to map every place you'd been and, based on your patterns, which you may not even know existed, predict where you would go next. This idea had already been implemented through the monitoring of credit card transactions – credit companies had programs to detect activity that was outside your "normal behavior" in order to diagnose credit card fraud.

Anders' job depended on him being unidentifiable and untraceable. The methods available to him for maintaining that state of existence were starting to evaporate. Eventually, and he hoped he wouldn't be alive to experience it, technology would be perfected that could extract DNA from the air – that which a person exhales. He imagined a day when he'd walk into a place and a computerized sensor system would identify him, unequivocally, using the DNA he expelled with his breath. Between that, facial recognition, cell phones, credit cards, and, finally, smart, continuous satellite imagery, every place he went and everything he did could be cataloged. On top of that, artificial intelligence could predict his future actions. It would be an intolerable situation. His profession was doomed.

A knock at the door broke him from his spiraling thoughts.

Harrison walked in and took a seat on the couch. "Some updates for you," he said. "Apparently, the CIA and FBI have gotten wind of something going on with the president."

Anders shook his head in disbelief. "Already? What do they know?"

"They don't *know* anything," Harrison replied. "They just have strong suspicions."

"Was it the captured Chinese courier – he spilled the beans to the MSS and the CIA got wind of it?"

"Possibly," Harrison answered. "But it's more likely that he'd been working for Chinese Intelligence from the beginning. And I don't think that *you* have been compromised."

Anders was pretty confident of that as well. "What do we do now?"

"First off, you won't be meeting with the president anymore," Harrison explained.

"How will we make the exchanges?" Anders asked.

"Another person has to get into the loop – someone close to the president," Harrison replied.

"But doesn't that defeat the purpose of the single-contact exchange?" Anders asked. "Won't that person know what the messages are, and where they're going?"

"They won't even know that they're carrying them," Harrison replied.

"How does *that* work?" Anders asked, skeptical, although he was familiar with the function of a *mule*.

"We're still figuring that out," Harrison said. "For now, you'll be picking up the president's outgoing messages outside the White House."

Anders wasn't clear whether that posed more or less risk for him. But he wondered about the integrity of the messages themselves. Extra steps meant a greater chance for interception or tampering. If the information was important enough to be sent through covert channels – even around the CIA – then he wondered what risk was acceptable.

"Are you ready for tonight?" Harrison asked, redirecting the conversation.

"Yes," Anders replied. "I'm just studying the local area and checking evacuation routes should something go wrong."

The emergency protocols were a bit different for this mission compared to those of a "normal" operation. In this case, if he were pursued before making the exchange, he was to destroy or lose the outgoing data device – the red one coming from the president to be delivered to the Chinese leader. If he were chased *after* the exchange, he was to swallow the device he'd acquired from his contact, and then conduct the unpleasant process of extracting it later, if he got away.

The plan now was for Anders to leave the DMS building on the shift change at 5:00 p.m., along with about 200 other employees. He would be in disguise, and there was no way anyone staking out the building could follow everyone simultaneously. At that point, he'd have over five hours to burn before the rendezvous, and he'd spend it at a large coffeehouse in College Park, Maryland, which was also a used bookstore. He was looking forward to it. He'd rely on SuperLift or SideKarr services for transportation. There'd be DMS operatives close by the entire time.

Harrison wished him luck, and left.

For the rest of the afternoon, Anders read up on pertinent current events and then donned his disguise. In the end, he'd easily pass for the shaggy software engineer he set out to emulate. He chose a black, knee-length, wool coat with a high collar. Beneath it, however, he wore a thin, blue jacket over a sweater. If he had to, he could lose the sideburns, wig, glasses, and long coat, and change his appearance in a matter of seconds.

At 5:05 p.m., he arranged for a SuperLift car on his DMS-managed phone application, and left the building with the dayshift people. He felt unusually electrified for this mission. He didn't know whether this confluence of excitement and anxiety derived from the mysterious importance of the information he was exchanging, or if it was the high degree of risk associated with it, like walking a high-wire.

MAURICE WAS BACK IN MONTANA, behind his desk in his office at Malmstrom Air Force Base. He'd been catching up on paperwork ever since getting back from DC at 4:00 p.m. that afternoon. It was now 9:00 p.m.

He got up, went to a closet, and started donning extra layers of clothes to make the drive home when he heard the ringing coming from his desk: it was the "red phone" – the one used for emergencies.

It wasn't unusual to get a call from one of the 150 silo sites managed by the 341st Missile Wing – things went wrong on a regular basis – but Maurice's anxiety was growing at a steady pace. He'd been waking up in the middle of the night with his mind spinning out of control, and was now suffering the symptoms of sleep deprivation. The apprehension was becoming intolerable.

He went to his desk and answered the phone. It was the senior operator at Silo E-09, just northwest of Hilger, Montana. They'd detected an unidentified aerial vehicle and concurrently suffered a complete power shutdown, including the backup power systems. No launch sequence had been initiated, but this one was still more serious than most of the others. This system not only had backup generators but also had recently been upgraded with a new, long-life battery backup system that could keep it functional for up to 12 hours if both the external power and standby generators malfunctioned. In this case, *all* power systems went offline – including the new battery backups, rendering the silo nonfunctional.

Maurice hung up the phone and realized he was starting to sweat. He peeled off the layers of clothes he'd just put on, sat behind his computer, and sent an email to his Air Force superiors. He'd have to wait for a response before heading home, and that could take hours.

He inserted a coffee pod into a single-cup coffee maker, placed a cup beneath the nozzle, and pushed the button to start the brew. He paced back and forth as the device gurgled and hissed, emitting its comforting aroma about the room.

He'd get the full report from the silo operator in the morning, but he was certain the event was like the others, although more serious because of the failure of the upgraded battery system. The time to implement the trap suggested by the CIA was now – immediately – but he knew there was a lot to be done to prepare the ruse.

The event reminded him that he needed to finish the misinformation report to be released to his outside media sources. They'd disseminate it to the public through their positions at internet news and magazine sites. Nothing like conspiracy theories mixed in with a little truth to muddy the waters. It was a part of his unofficial job that he both enjoyed and despised. In the end, he had to remind himself that the deception was for security purposes. Besides, a few entertaining stories never hurt anyone.

When his coffee was ready, he took it to the large, north-facing window of his office. Since his building was on the north side of the base, he had a good view of the northern skies without much light pollution. It was a clear night, and he could see the northern lights, although just faintly. They were fluttering bundles of vertical waves, colored with pinks and greens this time, overlaid on a field of stars.

Suddenly, a luminous streak flashed across the sky – a shooting star – redirecting his attention to his problem. Who in the hell was screwing with his missile silos?

HARRISON SPUN a pen around his fingers and fidgeted with paper clips in a tray next to his computer. Anders' operation was about to commence. It might be another overnighter at DMS for both of them.

With the new exchange arrangement, which Harrison wasn't sure was a prudent or premature reaction, he'd become privy to information that would put him, and DMS, into an uncomfortable position. The president would funnel encrypted messages to Harrison using the satellite phone Anders had provided him. DMS would then apply various decoding-encryption processes before loading it onto a data storage device, which would then be delivered to the foreign couriers by Anders.

Harrison worried now that he'd soon know too much – or at least have access to too much information. Of course, he could argue that, although DMS *could have* accessed the messages at some intermediate step between receiving and re-encrypting them, they *hadn't* – that was the deal they'd made with the "client," who just happened to be the president of the United States. He wondered how that would fly during a trial.

He put down the pen, went to the table next to the couch, and poured a finger of scotch into a tumbler. He sat on the couch and mulled over the situation as he sipped.

After some thought, he realized that his anxiety wasn't driven by knowing too much, or too little. It came from being somewhere in between. It was clear that whatever was going on between President Crownbrook and the Russian and Chinese leaders was bigger than the usual geopolitical saber-rattling that occurred on a continuous basis between the three nations. What was most confusing was that those leaders seemed to be cooperating, even though their countries' overt actions propagated and accelerated the conflict.

Harrison then realized that the underground messaging between the three leaders might not be a channel of collaboration but, instead, a conduit of provocation. Were they quarreling amongst themselves and using the resources of their respective countries to threaten each other? The only thing Harrison knew was that he had to make a choice between trusting the president, or not. He'd chosen the former at the beginning of the operation, and would stick with that choice until overwhelming evidence showed that he should reverse course.

At some point, however, he had the feeling that he'd learn more about the messages – that he'd be forced into the information loop. Other than experience and intuition, he didn't know why he believed that was the case.

Harrison took a sip of whisky just as his cell phone vibrated. It was a text message from one of his DMS operators: Anders was entering the Grapes of Wrath.

ANDERS ENTERED the pub and casually scanned faces as he approached the bar. He spotted a bearded, Asian man sitting on a stool next to a round, wooden table on the far side of the main room. The place was at about three-quarters capacity – around 50 people, he figured. The bar on his left was crowded with an eclectic assortment of patrons ordering drinks that, according to a chalk-written menu on the wall, included wines and some expensive cognacs.

He squeezed his way through the people clustered around the bar and ordered one of the wine specials, a merlot. After getting his order, he casually made his way to his contact, who wore the prescribed brown and white pullover sweater and a black, knit hat.

"Have you tried the house merlot?" Anders asked. That's when he noticed the three empty glasses on the table, and a fourth in the man's hand, half empty.

"I prefer cabernets," the man replied in a thick, Chinese accent. It was the correct response, indicating that the situation was safe. If it weren't, he was to say that he preferred ruby ports. Anders sat across from him but was not happy that his contact appeared to be getting drunk.

The pudgy, Asian man's thick beard was about an inch long, and he wore small, square glasses with black rims and a gold chain around his neck that wasn't gaudy, but had just enough flash to be a memorable feature. Anders knew it was a disguise, and approved.

"My name's Barney, and I can drink a bottle of wine without feeling anything," the man said, seemingly sensing the need to explain the empty glasses on the table.

Anders noticed that his utterance was not slurred at all, and was impressed how such a thing might add to the man's identity deception. Surely, a spy would not get drunk during a mission.

"You can call me Frank," Anders said. "Apparently, your predecessor made some mistakes."

Barney nodded. "Different contractor," he said. "And I don't think he made any *mistakes*. He was probably working for Chinese intelligence from the very beginning."

In a casual move with his left hand, Barney set something near the three empty wine glasses, and then used the same hand to lift his fourth, which was still half full. Anders then made a similar move, exchanged his red device for the blue one Barney had just dropped, and slipped it into his pocket. Barney picked up the red device when he set down his glass, now down to about a fourth of its capacity.

It was a smooth exchange but, even though Anders understood why they went to the trouble of executing such a simple transfer in a public place, he always thought there should've been a better way. The reason for the status quo boiled down to control and paranoia, both of which were important for survival. The planning was crucial. First, the location in which an exchange was to be made should be indoors, and not have extravagant security technology – especially cameras. DMS had scouted out the location, and both Anders and "Barney" were seated at a table that was out of view of the few poorly placed cameras in the establishment. When meeting outdoors, even at night, anyone could be watching or filming from almost anywhere in the vicinity – a car, a building, or from the trees in a park a hundred yards away. The disguises went further to mitigate any problems that might arise if investigators did happen to find good video footage; it was impossible in this age to avoid all cameras.

Requiring the rendezvous to occur in a public place had to do with mistrust. For instance, in the case that a hostile actor – perhaps the other party in the exchange – intended to steal the package, a public arrangement made this risky. One reason was that there would be multiple witnesses to the deed. A more menacing reason, however, was that either party could have friendly ops nearby, even in the crowd. Anders knew that DMS had backup in close proximity to the bar, but not inside the building. He was sure Barney had friends close by as well.

"Did you hear the rumors about what happened with the captured device?" Barney asked.

"No," Anders replied, but he hoped that the anti-tampering mechanism had done its job.

"They were able to get part of the message in what's called a flash extraction," Barney explained. "And they deciphered it. The gossip in Chinese intelligence is that our respective leaders are discussing nuclear war – or at least the rules for it."

"The *rules* for it?" Anders didn't like the sound of that. "As if – "

"Yes, as if they're actually making plans to conduct a nuclear war," Barney cut him off. "It makes me wonder if it wouldn't be best if our corresponding intelligence services *were* in the loop."

"But they only got a part of the message, right?" Anders asked.

Barney nodded. "They say only about ten percent."

"So whatever information they obtained could've been taken out of context," Anders argued.

"Of course," Barney said as he slipped on his jacket and downed the last of his wine. "Just something to think about."

The Chinese courier then disappeared into the crowd on his way to the exit. Anders remained and sipped his wine while he waited for the prescribed 15 minutes.

Why would the leaders of quarreling countries be negotiating the rules of nuclear war rather than discussing how to avert it? And why would this be happening through dark channels?

Anders wondered if he should even bring it up with Harrison. With only ten percent of the message being retrieved – if *that* rumor were even true – drawing any conclusions from it would be nothing short of irresponsible.

He ordered a SuperLift ride, made his way out of the wine bar, and walked to another pub two blocks away called Old Style Spirits, which its patrons called the "OSS," after the old-time, spy agency that had been replaced by the CIA after World War II. His car arrived after only a few minutes of him standing in the cold wind on the street corner, and he got into a large SUV with a female driver in her 50s who was singing along with a Taylor Swift song playing on the radio. As they made their way toward a restaurant in Alexandria, where Anders would jump into another hired car, he clenched his hand around the device in his pocket. He fought the need to know what was on it.

He generally mistrusted his courier contacts and was continually concerned about a possible setup, or the risk that they might scam him. For all Anders knew, Barney had just given him a worthless piece of plastic and had gotten away with authentic information. That would be determined soon after arriving at DMS, although only the president could verify whether or not the data the storage device carried were genuine.

After a car exchange near the restaurant with a different service, and then a final transfer to a DMS car and subsequent ride back to the home facility, Anders found himself in Harrison's office with the computer tech. The device seemed legit and was deemed ready to deliver to the president.

The tech packed up her equipment and left, and then it was just Anders and Harrison.

"How are we going to get this to Crownbrook?" Anders asked.

"You'll hand it off to an intermediary," Harrison replied.

Anders shook his head. "I don't get it. How is that any different from me going directly to the White House?" he asked. Someone still had to finish the delivery. "I thought the fewer hands to touch it, the better."

Harrison smiled and poured whisky into a tumbler and handed it to Anders before pouring the same for himself. "You'll be handing it off to the president's niece," he explained.

"His *niece*?" Anders asked, confused, and now also concerned about the security of the situation. "Does she know what's going on?"

Harrison shook his head. "No," he replied. "She's an antiques dealer, and Crownbrook collects old model trains, among other things. When he finds something he likes, he often sends her out to authenticate the item, and then acquire it and bring it to him."

"I see – the device will be hidden inside a train car," Anders said. "Sounds risky."

Harrison shrugged. "The president thinks it's pretty reliable, at least in the short term," he said. "His niece isn't a model train expert, so she won't be able to tell whether anything we give her has been altered. She'll just meet with you to check the general condition of the piece, inspect the paperwork, and then execute the purchase. She and her uncle get along well, and she visits him often at the White House."

"So Crownbrook is effectively using his niece as a mule," Anders said, and then realized how horrible it sounded. He didn't have her running illegal drugs across the border. "I mean – "

"No, you're right," Harrison interjected. "But it seems that the situation is that vital."

"That reminds me," Anders said. "You'll see it in my report tomorrow, but maybe you should know now."

Harrison nodded for him to continue.

"My contact said that Chinese intelligence was able to extract a small fraction of the data from the device they intercepted, and deciphered some of the text," Anders explained. He'd decided to tell Harrison everything, even if it was unreliable intelligence. "That information has somehow leaked, and it apparently has to do with rules for conducting *nuclear war*."

Harrison's expression flashed to alarm, and then quickly to calm.

"That's probably misinformation," Harrison said. "It could be a way of checking if you're a leak. If this nugget of information spreads, it means you're the source. Small talk from other couriers should always be taken with a grain of salt."

"So you don't think there's a chance it could be legit?"

Harrison shook his head. "I think that if they were only negotiating new rules about nukes, then this whole operation – meaning the covert communications – would not have been necessary."

"I suppose not," Anders agreed. "But the implication was that they were actually *planning* a war, and are now negotiating the rules before starting it."

Harrison remained still and quiet for a few seconds as he seemed to mull over what Anders had suggested. "Assuming that were the case, what would be the endgame? What would any of them have to gain?"

Anders shrugged. "That, I don't know," he admitted. "I'm just taking my contact's words at face value, which I know is unreliable, and considering the extraordinary situation that this is – meaning the unusual, underground communications. I'm not saying they're trying to start a war, but there must be something of great significance going on to warrant this."

"I agree," Harrison said. "But let's not jump to any farfetched conclusions without solid evidence. Even if the recovered message fragment was genuine, it's just a snippet, and could easily be taken out of context."

Anders figured the same, but it wasn't enough to ease his mind.

They chatted about other things while they finished their whisky, and then Anders took the elevator down to his office where he removed the remaining components of his disguise. He'd taken it off in stages between rides in order to alter his appearance, making it more difficult for anyone to track him. Only the sideburns were left now, and the glue that held them on required a solvent if they were to be removed without pain.

It was going on 2:00 a.m., and he decided to spend the night in his office. He took a shower in his tiny bathroom, donned shorts and a tee shirt, got a blanket and pillow out of a cabinet, and went to the couch.

As he lay on his back, the Chinese courier's mention of nuclear war spun in his mind. Something of great significance was happening, and the anxiety building in him seemed to indicate that, whatever it was, it had existential consequences.

CHAPTER 3

Anders was impressed that the DMS people had been able to acquire a rare model train collectible in such a short time, along with the appropriate paperwork that indicated its authenticity. Harrison was adamant that whatever they passed on to the president be genuine in case anyone decided to scrutinize it. They settled on "HO gauge" train cars, which meant that they were at $1/87^{th}$ scale of the real thing. Most cars in this class were between five and seven inches long and two to three inches tall, making them a good size to hide a horse-pill-sized data storage device.

Anders did some background research just to be conversational if something came up during the "deal." He understood the sizes to some degree, and some of the terminology. DMS had acquired a Märklin, HO-gauge, three-rail locomotive, and its "tender," which was another car that hauled its fuel and supplies. This particular set was supposedly once owned by Frank Sinatra, a famous model train enthusiast, and paperwork was included to support that. Anders would deliver the locomotive, and the tender would be used for an exchange at a later time.

It was a sunny, frigid morning, but Anders was looking forward to the midafternoon rendezvous with the president's niece, Sara Bradbury. They were to meet at a coffeehouse inside a large, used bookstore – one of Anders' favorite kinds of places. He was comfortable with the plan, but he made an extra effort to be prepared for all contingencies. One could be taken by surprise when too relaxed.

The coffeehouse was in rural Maryland, and Anders headed northwest out of Alexandria, Virginia at noon.

MAURICE SAT across the table from his CIA visitor in Malmstrom's main cafeteria. When CIA Director Radcliffe had told him that someone would be out to the base to meet with him, he didn't think it would be so soon. It was Thursday, and Maurice had just been at CIA headquarters that Tuesday.

Christine Johnson – probably not her real name – was thin, late 30s, and dressed in dark blue slacks and a matching jacket. Her brown hair was pulled back in a tight ponytail that seemed to stretch her entire face backward, and her brown eyes looked stressed. Maurice thought she looked like he felt – nervous, on edge, anxious.

They were sitting at a small table in a corner of the large cafeteria, with a lot of background noise. She didn't seem to be enjoying her food.

"So, our renovations are to start right after next month's inspection," Maurice said, summing up what they'd discussed in his office that morning.

Christine glanced around, apparently searching for anyone who might be within earshot, and then nodded. "It will give you a few weeks to devise a plan and assemble a crew to construct the auxiliary systems and override electronics," she explained. "How long do you think it will take to get 15 silos ready?"

The original number had been 12, now it was 15, and he knew the final number could be 25, or more, if his experience with government operations served him well. "If I'm able to assemble the crew I have in mind for this job, it should take 7 to 10 days each," Maurice said. "That's 15 weeks at least. But my guess is that it will take 20, or more, factoring in delays with getting equipment, and other problems."

"That's fine," she said as she took a bite of a ham and cheese sandwich and set it back on her plate. She took a sip of iced tea and seemed to force a swallow. "We want this ready in mid to late summer."

"Regarding the mock launch – the traps we're setting – are you sure that warheads need to be on those missiles?" Maurice asked, wanting to go deeper into the discussion they'd had that morning. "I think that might be risky since we'll be bypassing the interlock systems. If something happens – an accidental launch – it might be difficult, if not impossible, to abort it."

"Director Radcliffe wants to be sure the event looks authentic," Christine explained. "Also, it's possible that the drones can detect the presence of fissile material. If none is there, they'll know it's a bluff. And so will the technicians who replace the live warheads with dummies."

Since the drones had commandeered computer-interfaced controls over 50 feet below the surface, it wouldn't surprise Maurice if they could detect a live nuclear warhead as well.

"Besides, we want those missiles to be deployable in case of a real attack," Christine added. "And there will be missile upgrades to those silos, but I don't know the timetable on those."

"Oh?" Maurice asked. "What kinds of upgrades?"

"The missiles themselves, but I can't say anything more about that now," she said. "If you're on schedule, we may select a few more silos to upgrade in addition to the original 15."

That's what Maurice figured, but he now wanted to know more about the missile upgrades. "Will there be additional changes needed to accommodate the new missiles?" he asked.

"Minimal – the new ones are being designed for the existing silos," she replied.

He wondered why he hadn't heard anything about this from his superiors, and found it odd that the CIA would be involved at all. He understood, at least to some degree, why they'd be involved in setting the trap to identify who was responsible for the drone incursions, but the CIA normally had nothing to do with actual missile defense operations. In fact, all his drone reports went from his superiors in the Air Force to the DIA and Department of Defense. The CIA had started getting copies of them just recently.

"You should give us the name of the control systems mechanic who will lead the crew," Christine said. "This person will have to come to CIA headquarters to be vetted, and will need to know some of what's happening. After this person is cleared, you can select the rest of the crew. They'll all need to be vetted as well, but those will just be standard background checks."

"I know exactly who should lead the group," Maurice said. The man in question was near retirement, and Maurice had an idea of who that senior mechanic would select for the rest of his crew.

They finished lunch, and then got into Maurice's truck and headed for Great Falls International Airport, which was just 15 minutes west. Christine's next stop was Colorado Springs for a meeting at the North American Aerospace Defense Command, or NORAD, whose airspace and monitoring systems had also been invaded recently by the mysterious drones.

After dropping off his CIA visitor, Maurice headed back to the base. He found it ironic that communications had been reduced to face-to-face meetings. The CIA and NSA had deemed everything electronic to be insecure for the time being. People involved in this project were never to mention anything regarding the operation over the phone, through email, or in electronic documents. And nothing sensitive was ever to be written down.

The whole thing made his nerves charge up like the paddles of a defibrillator. He was in a strange position: even though his direct superior was aware of the operation, there were people above him in the Air Force command structure who had no idea what he was doing. Why should he obey the commands of the CIA, or even the president himself, over those above him in his own organization?

Maurice realized he was already formulating his testimony for his court-martial. He'd say something like, "The president supersedes everyone, and his order came through the CIA to me. I followed the president's orders."

He didn't think that would fly.

ANDERS TRIED to relax during the sunny drive northwest and arrived early at a coffeehouse-bookstore called The Page. It had a medieval theme, and even had a full-sized model of a knight in shining armor in a big window holding a cup of coffee in one hand, and a book in the other. Anders was hooked on the place before he even entered it.

The outside air was crisp and cold, and the warm, java-infused breeze that hit his face as he opened the door was a welcoming sensation. He was looking for a blonde woman, near his own age, with a green coat. He was wearing a red ski hat with a white tassel – she'd be looking for it.

To his right was a coffee bar and a cluster of a dozen small, round tables with wooden chairs, and a red sofa on the far wall. The couch, and about half the tables, were occupied with patrons. To his left, and directly ahead, well past the coffee bar, were tables stacked with books. Along the walls were tall, wooden shelves stacked with the same. He could smell the old tomes under the aroma of coffee.

He went to the coffee bar, ordered a medium roast, and took the piping-hot, glass mug to one of the empty tables next to the front window, not far from the knight. It gave him a good view of the entrance.

He was carrying a leather knapsack that held the model train engine and the accompanying paperwork. DMS personnel never ceased to amaze him: the train was genuine and a true collectors' item, with definitive evidence that it had once belonged to Frank

Sinatra – "Ol' Blue Eyes" – himself. More importantly, this particular piece had an enclosed void that could be accessed without damaging it. Two, nearly undetectable, screws on the front end fastened a metal plate to the frame. The data drive was secured in the compartment behind the plate and embedded in clay to keep it from rattling around.

At ten minutes before 2:00 p.m., a blue Toyota Civic parked across the street. A fit, blonde woman with large, black sunglasses and a green coat emerged. She trotted across the street, entered The Page, spotted Anders almost immediately, and approached him.

"Are you Don Keller?" she asked.

"I am," Anders replied as he smiled and took off his hat. He had all the paperwork for the alias, which he'd use more than once since this was expected to be an ongoing relationship. "And you're Sara, I presume?"

She nodded, smiled, and stuck out her hand.

Anders shook it and said, "Good to meet you."

"Likewise," she said and glanced at his coffee mug. "I'm going to grab a coffee, too. Would you like anything else?"

"No thanks," he replied, and she headed for the counter.

Deception sometimes made Anders feel guilty. This was one of those times, even though Sara would not be harmed by anything they were doing. He supposed it bothered him to be taking advantage of someone who was innocent of whatever wrongdoing was actually happening. Well, he wasn't sure of any "wrongdoing" just yet, although he felt it was all at least "shady."

Sara came back with a mug of coffee, sat across from him, and smiled. Her skin was perfect, and her bright, green eyes seemed almost too large for her face. Her blonde hair was tied in a ponytail that was rooted near the top of her head so that it mushroomed out like a plume.

"So, Don, how did you get into the model train business?" she asked.

"I'm not really *in* the business," he admitted. "It was my grandfather who was the expert. When he passed, he left me and my dad all his trains." It was a cover story that explained his lack of model train knowledge.

"And you're selling them?"

He nodded. "My parents are selling the estate – they can't afford the property taxes anymore – and neither I nor my parents have room for all of my grandpa's collectibles."

"I see," Sara said. "Maybe my client will be interested in more of your collection. Let's see the item you brought."

Anders reached into his backpack, extracted a cardboard box, and set it on the table. He removed the lid, slid out a rectangular Styrofoam container, and removed the top half to reveal the engine, which was securely embedded in the lower half.

Sara seemed to be mesmerized by it as she lowered her head to get closer and view it from different angles.

"What a beautiful, intricate contraption," she said, her eyes widening in approval. "So much detail. Can you pull it out of its holder?"

Anders put on some thin, cloth gloves and described some of the details he'd memorized as he carefully extracted the engine. He tilted it at various angles as she directed and then slipped it back into its Styrofoam container, replaced the lid, and slid it back into the cardboard box.

"Can I see the documentation?" Sara asked.

He reached into his knapsack and pulled out an envelope, removed its contents, and spread them out on the table. Included in the documentation were the bill of sale with Frank Sinatra's signature, the instruction manual, and a random assortment of other things, including a photo of Frank himself in front of a large model train set with the engine clearly visible.

"This is *amazing*," she commented. "I had no idea Frank was into model trains."

"As are a lot of other people who you might not expect," he said.

"It can be an addicting hobby. I'm on the twelve-step program, and about free of it now."

Sara laughed.

"Actually, I thought they were neat when I was a kid," Anders said. "But they were just toys to me."

"Well, I'm convinced that what you have is authentic, and I've been authorized to make the purchase," she said. "You said $3,500, right?"

"That was with the tender," he replied.

"The *tender*?"

"The old locomotives had an accompanying car that carried fuel – coal, wood, or oil," Anders explained. "But the tender is currently being refurbished. It should be done in a week or two. The price for the engine without the tender is $2,750. You can tell your buyer that they can have first chance at the tender."

"Okay, I will," Sara said. "Can I have your FlashPay number?"

She was asking for his account number for a popular fund transfer service, and Anders gave it to her. DMS had set up the account for his alias.

They chatted as they waited for the payment to show up in "Don Keller's" account.

"Do you live around here?" Sara asked.

"No," Anders replied. "I live near DC. But my grandfather's house is in this area – and that's where the trains are."

Anders didn't know why he revealed that he lived near DC other than that he knew she lived in the area, and he was attracted to her. But he knew he couldn't see her outside this fictitious persona he was developing. It made him think about his sunsetting relationship with Del, and realize that any future relationships he had would likely follow that same path.

"Oh, I live near DC as well," she said. "Where do you live, exactly?"

"Alexandria."

"I live in Gaithersburg, but I'm in DC often," she said. "Maybe we could get coffee sometime. You have my number."

A pit formed in Anders' stomach. He knew he'd never be able to do that.

"That would be nice," he said as his phone buzzed. A text message informed him that the funds had been deposited into his account.

"Looks like our deal is complete," he said, and then signed a transfer document and put it in the envelope. He then slid the box and envelope to the center of the table. "I hope your client enjoys the new piece."

Sara stood, shook his hand, and picked up the items.

"Pleasure doing business with you, Don," she said.

"Likewise," he replied.

"Oh, and I'm sure my client will want that other item – the 'tender' – as well," she said.

"Great," Anders said. "Then we'll be in touch."

Through the window, he watched as she exited the store, put the train in the back seat of her car, and drove away.

He then sent a message to DMS confirming that the exchange had been made.

Anders went up to the coffee bar, got a refill, and went to the back of the store to peruse the used books. Sometimes he didn't know what to think about his life. His career was exciting, but it didn't come without sacrifices. He was his job. And it was difficult to be anything more.

He just hoped that whatever he was currently doing was for the better good. The problem was that there was something in the back of his mind suggesting that it was just the opposite of that.

It was going on 7:00 p.m., and Candace sat at her desk and wrote up the report on their surveillance operation from Tuesday night. She'd wanted to get it out of the way on Wednesday, but her in-laws were visiting, and she had to pick them up from the airport that morning since her husband was out of town. She'd had to take a vacation day to accommodate them, which wouldn't have been needed if they weren't such high-maintenance people. They weren't leaving until Sunday afternoon, so her weekend was going to be filled with shopping, museums, galleries, and restaurants – none of which interested her.

The report on Tuesday night's surveillance was short, since nothing happened other than that she and Tim had spotted two suspected Single-World Alliance members in the same place. Both had been women, and they'd never even come close enough to speak to each other in the crowded bar.

There were over 400 people on the SWA "active" list Candace had found in the FBI archives. Two of those 400, the two women, had been on the guest list of about 150 people for a fundraiser for a US Senate candidate from Virginia, who would now be investigated for SWA ties herself.

Candace thought it was a dead end. She concluded that the two SWA women were in the same room only by chance. What were the odds that, when cross-referencing two lists, one of 400 and the other of 150, that two people would appear on both? Add in the details that they lived in the same area, were both in the economic upper class – the minimum donation to get into the event was ten thousand dollars – and the candidate's politics were apparently complimentary to the SWA's objectives, and the chances were high enough for Candace to dismiss the meeting altogether. She concluded it was only a coincidence that both women were there.

She now wanted to focus on some new information the FBI's counterintelligence group had passed along to her regarding a possible rendezvous between a domestic courier and a foreign operative who were somehow linked to the alleged dark communications channel used by the president. The tip had supposedly come from

Russian intelligence, so she was skeptical but would look into it since she had no other leads.

Tim strode into the office and set his briefcase on the floor. "I was halfway home. What's up?"

Candace stood, grabbed a file from her desk, and handed it to him. "Read this," she said. "We need to get authorization for a team right away."

"What is it?"

"A tip," she replied. "From counterintelligence – they got it from the SVR." The SVR was the agency that replaced the Russian KGB in the early 1990s, but their methods of operation were similar. The new organization was as untrustworthy as its predecessor.

Tim flipped through the file. "They're looking for a private courier – a woman – but they only give a basic description," he said. "There are at least 50 thousand women in DC alone who fit this description."

"Read on," she said. "They have a lead on an upcoming meeting where she's supposed to pass information to someone."

"And this might be connected to Crownbrook?"

She shrugged. "We're following up on a lead involving a Russian – we're not investigating the president," she argued. "But who knows, maybe he'll come into it somehow."

"Sneaky," Tim said. "I like it. So, what do you want *me* to do?"

"Devise a plan to surveil the meeting," she said. "And then write an authorization request to do it, and also to form a team."

"That's a big operation for a tip that has nothing more than the vague description of a woman," Tim argued. "There's not even mention of what kind of information she might be passing."

"I know," Candace said. "They won't authorize the team, but they'll probably give us the go-ahead to stake out the place."

"I see," Tim said. "You're asking for more than you really want."

"You're learning," she said. "Now, get to it. We'll want that request to be in by noon tomorrow."

Candace felt like she was flailing, but she couldn't stand idle in the hope that better information would just fall into her lap. If she could link the president to dark-channel communications, he might be impeached, or at least be investigated with ample public exposure. It wouldn't do much to change *his* future – it was his second term – but it might quash his vice president's chances of being the next presidential candidate.

Candace figured she was a part of the so-called "deep state" that this administration had been complaining about ever since Crownbrook had taken office. She was happy to do her part.

IT WAS GOING on 10:00 p.m. when Anders stepped into the hot shower in his apartment. He let his mind wander and, after just a few minutes, something that had been causing him anxiety earlier in the day came back to him.

The method DMS devised for getting the data drives to the president could only be used a couple of times. *What would they do after that?* Crownbrook could only buy so many trains before someone got suspicious. More concerning was that Anders was unaware of any plans for getting information *out* of the White House. It reminded him that, for the two operations DMS was lining up for the next weekend, he'd only be *receiving* items.

After the shower, he got dressed, made a cup of Ramen noodle soup, and sat on the living room couch with the used books he'd purchased at The Page that afternoon. They reminded him of Sara Bradbury, and how he looked forward to seeing her again. It also reminded him that he'd missed a call from Del the day before. It was going on three weeks since they'd last spoken. Their relationship had clearly been reduced to barely more than friends.

The musty smell of the books brought him comfort. It reminded him of the cozy library in which he'd studied during most of his evening hours in college. Two of his three acquisitions for the day were early editions of works by one of his favorite writers, Fyodor

Dostoyevsky, and the other was a history of the KGB by an author he hadn't heard of, published in 1974, in Russian. He'd always been interested in the early development of intelligence services, and he'd been looking for a book on the Chinese agencies but had no luck so far. Learning about their histories helped him to understand their current methods and idiosyncrasies. He didn't know if this actually helped him in any way, especially since intelligence methods and technologies were constantly evolving, but reading about them did seem to calm his nerves.

He finished his Ramen noodles and, just as he was about to pour a glass of wine, his cell phone buzzed. It was Harrison.

"I need you to come in," Harrison said without saying hello.

"Right now?" Anders asked and glanced at a clock on the wall opposite the couch. It was going on 11:00 p.m.

"Immediately."

Anders agreed, and ended the call. His ears rang as he remained still in the silence. The adrenaline that now coursed through his body suppressed his longing for the warm couch. It wasn't often that he'd been called into work at odd hours, but each time it happened it had been justified. Something big was happening.

He got dressed, scheduled a SuperLift ride to pick him up at a nearby convenience store, and headed out, into the cold.

Harrison poured a finger of scotch into a tumbler, downed it in one swallow, and refilled it. It was a waste of expensive whisky but he needed it. In fact, he was needing it more and more lately and figured he should cut back. Tea might be a good alternative for a while.

It was going on midnight. Anders would be arriving soon.

Harrison had just learned that the president was being investigated by the FBI, and he was now worried that DMS might be compromised. He knew that was unlikely, considering he had his best courier on the job and they'd only carried out a few minor operations so far. However, he had to address their client's concerns immediately.

More alarming, however, was that a Chinese operative had been picked up by the FBI not long after Anders had made the exchange with the courier at the Grapes of Wrath. It was unknown, however, if the man the FBI had brought in was "Barney," Anders' contact, but the timing was alarming. Things were becoming complicated far more quickly than Harrison had anticipated, and it created a cloud of anxiety in his mind.

Anders arrived at 12:07 a.m., and they sat across the coffee table from each other at the far end of the office.

Harrison explained what had happened.

"What's the plan?" Anders asked. "Are we going to continue?"

Harrison had been struggling with that question since learning about the potential complications a few hours prior.

"It was the president who informed me of the situation," Harrison explained. "He's not sure if it was our contact who was brought in, but he could've withheld that info and let us go on, oblivious to the situation. Also, he *is* our client, and we knew what we were getting into from the beginning. That said, it doesn't mean that *you* have to continue with the operation, and I wouldn't hold it against you if you opted out. It's probably going to get dicey."

Anders stared at him in silence for an awkward few seconds before he spoke. "Do you trust Crownbrook?"

Now it was Harrison who took some extra time to mull it over. Finally, he said, "I have no reason *not* to trust him," he said. "He has a storied background in intelligence, and I just can't see him being a traitor. And I don't think he's crazy. Not yet anyway."

"How did the FBI catch wind of the backchannel communications?"

"My sources came across the president's name in their investigation of a dark-state society – an organization that believes in a single, global government," Harrison explained. "The FBI apparently intercepted a communication – this was before we got involved – that was supposedly from Crownbrook. It made them suspicious about dark-channel comms."

"You don't think he's one of those one-world government advocates, and now he's conspiring with China and Russia to make it happen?" Anders asked.

That possibility, along with numerous others, had already crossed Harrison's mind. "I think neither the Russian nor the Chinese president would tolerate a one-world government unless *they* were going to be the one-world leader."

"Right now, three people already rule the world – *effectively* anyway," Anders said. "If they conspired in some way, they could crush the rest of the planet in a short time."

"To what end?" Harrison asked. "The three largest countries would divvy up the spoils amongst themselves? And then what?"

Harrison opened a cigar box and offered one to Anders, who politely declined, and then took one for himself, nipped off the end, and lit it.

"There's something else going on here," Harrison continued, as he puffed. "And I have some theories as to what it is."

"Yes?"

"This is entirely conjecture," Harrison started, "but, during my time at CIA, I learned a lot about foreign intelligence agencies."

Harrison set his cigar in the oversized, glass ashtray on the coffee table, sat back, and rested his foot on his knee. "Most people think that the leaders of these giant countries have all the power. But that's not really true," he explained. "It's the intelligence agencies and policing entities that have the real control."

"But they're just employees of the government – the president can fire them," Anders argued. "Even the CIA director is appointed by the president."

"In principle, that's true," Harrison agreed. "But the president, and other elected and appointed officials, do not have all the information. It's the people who are the *lifers* – those who come up through the ranks of the CIA over a span of 20 to 50 years – who have access to *all* the information."

"Can't the president just ask for anything – and get any information he wants?"

Harrison shook his head. "Not exactly," he replied. "There are things that the CIA deems as 'need-to-know only,' or 'above top-secret,' that the president will never get to see except under very special circumstances. There are at least two reasons for this. First, most presidents don't have an intelligence background, and can't be trusted not to *accidentally* spill information. The slightest misspoken detail could crush an operation, or destroy an otherwise unknown intelligence or military advantage."

Anders nodded. "And the other reason?"

Harrison picked up his cigar and relit it. He puffed on it as he spoke. "The president doesn't know what he doesn't know. He has no idea what questions to even ask."

"Are you talking about big things – like major black operations, or just shady details of missions, like what we're doing?" Anders asked.

Harrison cringed. He supposed what they were doing for the president could be construed as "shady."

"I mean there are major blocks of information to which only long-time CIA personnel have access," Harrison explained. "It's compartmentalized so well that new people come into the fold of a specific 'compartment' only when the old guard dies."

"I don't understand," Anders said. "How old are we talking here when you say 'old guard?'"

"How old was your father when he passed away?"

Anders stared at him with a blank expression for a few seconds before responding. "He was 77," he finally replied. "But he retired at age 65."

Harrison smiled to try to soften the blow. "It might have *seemed* like he retired," he said. "But he was still active in the CIA – in his compartmentalized area – and was directly involved in recruiting his replacement. He was active until the day he passed."

"How do you know this?" Anders asked.

Harrison took a drag of the cigar and sighed as he expelled the smoke. He was conflicted about telling Anders – or anyone – anything about his CIA past, but this was for a good reason. "Because I was supposed to be his replacement."

"What?" Anders asked, his eyes bulging. "Replacement for what?"

"His role in an internal CIA group – a secret organization within the CIA itself."

"What organization?"

"I never found out. I didn't take the offer, and I retired soon thereafter."

Anders seemed to mull it over for a few seconds. "You knew my dad well?"

"Not too well, no," Harrison replied. "I declined the offer pretty quickly and we didn't interact much after that."

"Why did you reject it?" Anders asked. "You didn't learn anything about it at all?"

Harrison shook his head. "I didn't like the idea of committing to something about which I was not completely informed, and which I'd never be allowed to quit," he replied.

"Can't quit?" Anders asked. He looked rattled. "And you don't know *anything* about this group my dad was in?"

"Only minor details, but I'm not allowed to discuss them," Harrison replied. "Don't worry though – your dad was a good man, and I'm sure whatever he was doing was in the best interest of the country."

That was only an assumption on his part, but it seemed to have a calming effect on Anders.

"The point of the matter," Harrison continued, "is that there are self-contained compartments within the CIA from which no information is shared – not with the outside, the elected politicians, or even within the CIA leadership."

"Seems like we've gotten off track," Anders said. "What does this have to do with our operation with the president?"

Harrison sat back and crossed his arms. "As you already know, your father and Crownbrook worked together on missions," he said. "And your dad was a senior member of this so-called informational compartment – the group I described. The important part, something you don't yet know, is that the *president* was in that same group."

Anders seemed to go into a daze.

"You have questions," Harrison said.

"A million of them, but one comes to mind immediately," Anders said. "You said you can never really leave that group. But what about Crownbrook? He's no longer in the CIA, is he?"

Harrison shook his head and grinned. "That's the point," he said. "Crownbrook, in fact, *is* still in the CIA. He can never really leave that secret group. He knows too much."

"I see," Anders said. "So you think that his covert actions now – the ones we're helping him carry out – have something to do with this secret organization."

"It's possible."

"Does the group have a name?"

"Long ago, when I was invited, I got a typed message that read 'We want you to join the CG.'"

"The CG," Anders repeated. "What does 'CG' stand for?"

Harrison shook his head and smiled. "No idea," he replied. "But the president knows. Whether or not his CG connection is part of what is driving his current actions, I don't know."

"Since the FBI found a connection to him in their investigation, could the CG involve the people who are pushing for a one-world government?"

"It's possible."

"But you think we should continue to help him."

"I do," Harrison said. "He has a view of the bigger picture, and I have no reason not to trust him, like I said."

Anders nodded. "Okay," he said. "Is this why you called me in?"

"This, and I want you to spend the night in your office," Harrison explained. "And maybe the next *few* nights. The FBI is usually slow but, on rare occasions, can act quickly. I'm probably being paranoid, but I think you'll be safer here for the next couple of days."

"You think they'd raid my apartment?"

Harrison shook his head. "Probably not," he said. "But I'd hate to look back on the situation and regret not taking action after a foreign courier involved in our operation had been taken in by the FBI – if it really was our guy, that is."

"I understand," Anders said.

Harrison saw Anders out and then went back to the couch and relit his cigar, which was getting short now. Ever since declining the offer to join that "special group," he'd always wondered what information the CG was preserving, and what its purpose was.

Sometimes agencies like the CIA had global objectives that conflicted with the immediate interests of the nation they served. Harrison just hoped he wasn't helping the president to accomplish one of those objectives.

MAURICE BELCHED and then winced as an acidic concoction erupted from his stomach and seared his throat. He took a sip of coffee, but it had the predictable effect of making it worse, so he chased it with a gulp of bottled water. It was going on 2:00 p.m., and he was waiting in his office for a man who was, in his opinion, the most experienced and talented of all maintenance personnel in any of the missile wings.

His anxiety had been building over the week. Things were moving more quickly than he'd anticipated, and the complexity of his part in the project, and of the broader operation, kept his mind spinning. His head ached and his eyes burned from lack of sleep.

At the top of the hour, a knock came at his door, and a clean-shaven man with high-and-tight, black hair entered and said, "Good afternoon, sir."

He was about five-foot-eleven and unusually skinny. His stature, along with his ability to contort himself to work in tight places, had earned him the nickname "Gecko." It was Captain Eduardo Pacquiao. The man's face seemed somewhat weathered for being in his mid-40s, but his dark eyes looked clear and energetic.

Maurice offered him coffee, which he accepted, and they sat near a window in facing upholstered chairs, between which was a small, round table.

"How did the briefing go at the CIA?" Maurice asked.

Eduardo smiled and shifted his eyes to meet Maurice's. "It was an experience," he replied. "I'd never been to Langley, and I never thought I'd meet a CIA director. But the novelty wore off quickly when we got to discussing business."

"What did you think of the plans?" Maurice asked. He'd been informed that Director Radcliffe had made a strong case for the mission and, apparently, Eduardo had been convinced.

Eduardo's face flashed with an expression of panic for an instant but then became calm and serious. "I still have to keep careful track of who I can talk to about this."

"It's easy: you can talk to me and the CIA director. Tight lips, otherwise," Maurice said. "Relax, Eduardo, I'm in this with you. I report only to the CIA director and a couple of others. None of my direct superiors are in the loop – at least not entirely – which makes this quite unusual. But it must be done this way."

"I understand the two phases of the operation," Eduardo said. "The part in which we develop an auxiliary, mobile launch system is a straightforward concept, and we should be able to construct it without too much trouble. The second part is a little worrisome, however."

"How so?"

"I understand that the idea is to set a trap to see which country reacts first to our missiles going into a launch sequence," Eduardo said. "But do we have to do it with live warheads?"

"You know well how many people would have to be involved in replacing them with duds," Maurice said.

Eduardo closed his eyes and nodded.

"This way, we only need to alter the electronic systems, and no one will suspect anything else is happening," Maurice continued. "Besides, those warheads can only be armed with the launch codes – and those would have to come from the president himself."

Eduardo seemed to relax. "So, the same system we develop for the mobile instrumentation will be used to initiate the faux launches for the trap?" he asked.

"That's right," Maurice replied. "When they detect us initiating a launch from a silo that one of their own drones had supposedly just deactivated, it should send them scrambling. And we'll be monitoring their reactions – we'll see who acts first, and how."

"There's a lot to do before we get to that stage," Eduardo said. "We have to complete the silo upgrades and construct the launch vehicles, and then train the new, mobile launch crews. In the meantime, the drones will still be creating havoc."

"Right," Maurice replied. "So we need to get started as quickly as possible."

"But what about the crews in the launch stations who don't know what's going on?" Eduardo asked. "I mean, when the mobile launch systems take over their stations."

"They'll be panicking," Maurice replied. "Which is unfortunate."

"What if we design the mobile systems to deactivate the monitoring systems inside the permanent stations?"

"No good," Maurice said. "In the case of a real launch, we'll want the crews to see what's happening. Maybe we'll need them to do something in a pinch."

"I understand."

"How will you proceed with the modifications?" Maurice asked.

"They should be straightforward," Eduardo explained. "First, we'll install a series of remotely activated switches that bypass the override systems and interlocks in the launch stations. Next, full control will go over to a mirror computer system and communications electronics, located in the specialized launch control vehicles."

"What will be the range of these vehicles – how close will they have to be to the control stations?"

"Within a mile," Eduardo answered.

"How long will it take to complete the project?" Maurice asked.

"If we have everything we need on hand – including all the new electronics – it will take a solid week per silo," Eduardo said. "There are 15 silos on the list. I'd say 20 weeks would be a safe estimate, accounting for unforeseen complications."

"That's reasonable," Maurice said, not telling him that the number of silos to be modified would likely increase – the most recent number he'd heard was 25. "You'll have to choose your team soon since they'll need to be vetted by the CIA. Do you think you'll be able to keep them in the dark on this?"

Eduardo nodded. "The *official* plans – the ones my crew will hear – are to install a portable, emergency launch system," he explained. "It's something that will be easy to justify considering that drones have somehow been able to mess with the underground electronics and computer systems. There will be no mention of a faux launch plan to unmask the intruders."

Maurice was satisfied, and his own anxiety was now diminishing. What they were doing wasn't so outrageous, considering that the modifications could pass as a legitimate response to the recent intrusions.

"You need to provide me with two things," Maurice said. "First, a list of your team members within the next 48 hours. They'll need to undergo extensive background checks before we can get started. They won't go to Langley for that, and they're not to know that this job is in any way special – other than it's high priority because of our recent intrusions."

"And the second thing?" Eduardo asked.

"An equipment list," Maurice replied. "Everything you'll need, from electronics to computers to vehicles. I'll be your direct contact for these things and will put them through as high-priority acquisitions. Any questions?"

"No, sir," Eduardo said as he got to his feet.

Maurice stood. "Good. Keep me informed," he said. "Dismissed."

Eduardo left, and Maurice went back to his desk and opened a spreadsheet listing all launch-site personnel. He now had to find teams to *operate* the new, portable launch control systems.

His anxiety was building again. Those teams would also have to be carefully screened by the CIA. Everything took time.

But there was another potential problem that loomed in the future. Given the command, *would those mobile teams actually launch their missiles?* Being underground and executing a launch sequence under normal procedures was difficult enough. However, launching from a truck while circumventing normal protocols might be another story.

CHAPTER 4

At 8:30 a.m. on Monday, Anders sat in front of the giant computer monitor in his office at DMS. He sifted through the news from multiple sources which reported on the geopolitical turmoil building between the US, China, and Russia.

He'd spent four nights away from his apartment, on Harrison's order, due to the rumored capture of the Chinese courier. It turned out that the FBI had instead captured a Chinese intelligence officer – MSS – who had probably been *tailing* "Barney." That wasn't all good news – clearly, the MSS was aware of the Chinese president's underground comm channel – but at least it seemed that the FBI didn't yet know about Barney. With that new information, Harrison thought Anders was in the clear, so he'd go back to his flat this evening. It was evident, however, that the broader situation was becoming more treacherous.

It had been a week since he'd made the model train delivery to the president's niece, Sara Bradbury. Harrison had informed him that she'd passed it along to Crownbrook the next day without issue.

Crownbrook had almost no privacy, as would be expected as president, and he certainly couldn't meet with anyone without others knowing about it. It hadn't been a problem in the beginning, but now that the FBI had suspicions, significant resources might be allocated to track everyone who met with him. It meant that even Crownbrook's niece would be scrutinized. There'd be at least one more train purchase – the tender car for the engine she'd already delivered – but that would likely be the end of that mode of transfer.

Harrison had informed Anders that they were working on another method of getting info *out* of the White House, but Anders would still be making the external exchanges in the usual manner. The president had a DMS phone, and that was one possible instrument for sending data electronically. It was something DMS comms specialists were exploring.

Anders scribbled some notes in a notebook he'd been keeping on public media sources, including the BBC, *The New York Times*, and *The Jerusalem Post*, as well as intelligence reports that DMS obtained through various contacts.

All three nations were claiming drone intrusions at their nuclear sites. US intelligence agencies denied any involvement, as they always would, but they also pointed out that India and Pakistan were blaming China for similar events at their facilities. China and Russia blamed the US, and the US openly expressed suspicion toward them in return – with the main focus on China.

In terms of the "blame game" that was occurring, the situation was far from extraordinary. However, the capabilities of the drones were described by all parties as astonishing. They were apparently advanced far beyond conventional technologies, and Anders suspected that whatever nation actually owned them was intentionally making the other two nervous.

Anders was still pondering what Harrison had told him about his father. It made him want to visit his mom and ask her what she knew. She still lived in the house in which Anders had been raised, near Savannah, Georgia. What was most intriguing was that, according to Harrison, his dad had still been active in the CIA right up until he passed away. Anders figured his mother would know something about it.

He suspected that there would be a lull in activity until Harrison and the president opened a new channel of information transfer. Maybe this was a good time to take a few days off and make a trip south.

HARRISON STARED out his office window and contemplated the situation. It was a frigid but sunny morning, and he observed people as they bustled about on the icy sidewalks below.

DMS had developed the original method for getting information into and out of the White House after being contacted months ago by the president through a liaison. It was supposed to have been a simple courier job, although some processing of the actual data storage devices had to be carried out before incoming deliveries got into the hands of the president.

An important aspect of the arrangement was that Harrison, and DMS, would have *no* knowledge of the information carried on the devices. That worked for both sides. First, the president required the highest security – the information was "hot," as Crownbrook had put it – and it had to be as secure as possible. Second, DMS would have plausible deniability – effectively acting as nothing more than a secure mail carrier.

They were now going to have to make adjustments that eroded both sides of that arrangement. DMS was going to be more integrated into the operation. The messages would now come directly from the president via the encrypted satellite phone provided to him by DMS through Anders during his first visit. After being received on the DMS side, the data would be decrypted, encrypted again using a different method, and loaded onto a thumb-drive. The decryption-encryption was supposed to be a one-step, hidden process so that a readable message would never be seen. However, the problem for everyone involved was that, if he really wanted to, Harrison could get his computer specialists to insert an intermediate step so that the original message could be read before undergoing the re-encryption. It made the information vulnerable, and it made DMS potentially culpable in the case of an investigation.

It came down to trust – on both sides. Did the president trust Harrison enough to handle the so-called "hot" information? Did Harrison trust Crownbrook enough to deliver his underground messages, despite rumors that the three battling countries were discussing nuclear war? On top of that, what about the president's suspected involvement in a controversial global-government organization?

The "model train method" had worked for one delivery, and Anders would make one more exchange in the same fashion. Afterwards, they'd have to devise something new. Getting information out of the White House would be easier than getting it in since the latter would still require the physical delivery of the devices. Although, the president could provide DMS with the passcodes for the incoming devices, in which case the messages could take the reverse route to the president via the satellite phone. That, however, would require an extra step on the part of the president: he'd have to implement two successive decryptions to read the messages, one for the satellite data transfer, and one for the original decryption implemented by the source in Russia or China.

Harrison's thoughts turned to his plans for the evening. It was his eighteenth wedding anniversary, and he and his wife, Lauren, had reservations at a posh restaurant in Alexandria. She loved seafood, and that was the restaurant's specialty. He preferred a good steak but this was an easy concession for him.

He had to be home before 7:00 p.m., so he had time to accomplish a few things before then.

He pulled out his phone and called Anders up to his office. Anders had a mission planned for the evening.

CANDACE WAS with Tim in their shared FBI office when the email from their supervisor arrived.

"Figures," she hissed. "They're not giving us backup."

"But we're getting the go-ahead on the stakeout?" Tim asked.

"Yes," she replied. At least they got that. "I wasn't expecting help, but it's still annoying. We're going to have trouble following anyone if we make a positive ID."

"We only have one tip, right? The woman?"

"Yes, and little to go on other than her general appearance, and that she has a Russian accent," she replied.

"We'll just have to play it by ear then," he said.

"Very funny," she said. His puns sometimes made her want to scream, especially when she was stressed. "There'll be a lot of people there, so hearing her might be challenging."

"What time will they meet?" Tim asked.

"Between 10 and 11 p.m., according to the intel," she said. "We'll be there by nine."

"Do we get to drink?"

She nodded. "We'll need to fit in," she said. "You'll have to dress a little better. Go home and put on a jacket – something nice, but loose, like you're there looking to pick up a date."

"And you?" he asked. "How are you going to dress?"

"Cocktail dress," she said. "I'll pick you up at your place at 8:30 – we'll take my car."

"I get to ride in the Beemer."

Tim packed up his briefcase and headed for the door.

"Oh," Candace said. "Come armed."

He stopped and looked at her. "I planned on it," he said, and then left.

Candace had worked some strange cases in her career, but this one was unique. They were delving into things that were connected to the dark, geopolitical underworld. She was happy to contribute to tarnishing the current president – even though it was unlikely that he'd be removed from office no matter what they discovered – but she didn't have any experience in the spook world, which was where the investigation seemed to be heading.

ANDERS ASSEMBLED his disguise for the rendezvous, which was to occur at 10:30 p.m. in a hotel bar in DC. He was going with dark hair and goatee with square, black-rimmed glasses and a black turtleneck. He thought he looked like an eccentric artist, or maybe an English professor.

He was meeting the Russian courier this time – Alina – the woman he'd met in Miami. He hoped she wasn't still miffed about his advice to nix the perfume.

He slipped on a long, black wool coat, exited his apartment, and scheduled a SuperLift car to meet him at the corner of State Street and Townsend Boulevard – three blocks east of his apartment building. Twenty minutes later, he was dropped off at a French restaurant in a trendy DC suburb, ordered another ride from "D-Car," one of SuperLift's competitors, and got dropped off at a microbrewery just two blocks from the Orion – one of the most expensive hotels in the DC area.

Anders meandered through the busy business district, keeping an eye on any potential stalkers, and finally passed through a set of massive, rotating doors into the warm lobby of the Orion. It looked like a palace, with white marble floors that matched six massive pillars reaching four stories to a domed ceiling that looked like it was painted by Leonardo da Vinci. Hanging from a thick chain attached to the center of the dome was a colossal chandelier that was designed to resemble "Orion's Belt," one of the most recognizable constellations in the night sky.

Anders passed through the lobby and went directly to a wall with six, side-by-side elevator doors. He pushed a button and the one on the far left opened. He stepped inside and held an access card provided to him by DMS next to the control panel. The console beeped, and the buttons to all the floors illuminated, indicating that he had access to everything. His card was a master key to all levels, including the roof. It didn't, however, get him into the rooms.

He pressed the button for the second floor, on which was a popular bar and lounge that was frequented by everyone from movie stars to politicians, and was busy every night of the week.

The elevator halted, and the first things he noticed when the doors opened were crowd noise and cigar smoke. It was one of a few places of its sort in the DC area that ignored the no-smoking mandates and wasn't held accountable. He knew that was because the politicians wanted it like that, and the rules never seemed to apply to them.

The room took up an entire half of the second floor, and was dimly lit. A man played a smooth jazz tune on a piano in the far-left corner, and an expansive bar lined the wall opposite the elevator foyer. To the right was a small stage, but it was dark.

Near the bar was a cluster of tall, circular tables with stools, and about a dozen booths lined the walls on the right and left. The rest of the floor was carpeted and clustered with couches, upholstered chairs, and coffee tables.

The place was busy, which was good, but there were plenty of open seats.

As he made his way to the bar, meandering around groups of chatting clientele, he spotted Alina in a dark booth on the right-side wall. She wore a black cocktail dress and stiletto heels. Her hair was short and reddish-brown, rather than the blonde she'd had the first time they'd met.

He found an opening at the bar and ordered a single malt scotch, neat. When it arrived, he took a sip and glanced into a mirror behind the bar and scanned the scene behind him. Nothing suspicious stood out to him.

He fit in well with the crowd, except that he might have been on the young side, as was Alina. He estimated the average age to be about fifty, and mixed evenly with men dressed in jackets, and women in classy dresses, except for a few younger women robed in more revealing attire who seemed to be paired with much older men.

Anders casually weaved his way around the room and then approached Alina's booth. She was texting on her phone and suddenly looked up, startled.

"How long have you been waiting?" Anders asked, smiling.

"Not too long," she replied with a barely discernible Russian accent.

If she responded by looking at her watch and reporting a specific number of minutes, like "45 minutes," then something was wrong, and the exchange was to be aborted.

He sat across from her and set his drink on the table next to a glass of white wine.

She reached her left hand across the table and he took it with his right. He felt the device in her palm – he'd only be picking up during this meet.

"Things are getting a little crazy, don't you think?" she asked. "Especially with the capture of our Chinese friend by the MSS."

"That courier was probably an MSS mole," Anders said, assuming she was referring to the first guy. The Chinese intelligence service had people everywhere. "A new operative took his place – one vetted by all three security firms involved in this venture."

"Sometimes I think I should have stayed in the employ of the Russian government," she said.

"You still are," Anders said. "Your company works directly for President Kurmaev."

She shrugged, pulled away her hand, and spoke after taking a sip of wine. "I sometimes wonder who is really in control – the president, or the security services."

"I wonder the same," he said, as he slipped the thumb-drive into his pants pocket. "I suppose the answer is obvious since we're acting on behalf of our respective leaders to circumvent those agencies."

Alina nodded. "I suppose so," she said. "You've heard the rumors about the intercepted message?"

"I have," he affirmed. He felt odd about gossiping with agents from the other side, but it wasn't like either of them belonged to a formal intelligence service. "But even if that info is accurate, it's just a fragment with no context."

"Still, it reveals something," she argued. "The mere mention of nuclear war in a secret communication is alarming."

He couldn't argue with her on that point. "It comes down to who you trust."

"Do you trust your president?"

"I trust him more than the embedded bureaucrats in our intelligence agencies, or the FBI," he replied. "How about you?"

"I trust Kurmaev over the security services, but not by much," she replied. "I would feel better if I knew more about the information we were carrying."

Anders felt the same.

"Do you know anything beyond these rumors?" Alina asked.

"Yes," he replied. "Your SVR or FSB supposedly tipped off the FBI about our new Chinese counterpart, and it was rumored that they picked him up. It turns out that the FBI nabbed a Chinese agent – MSS – instead, who was probably tailing him."

Alina looked horrified for an instant and then recovered. "If true, it means my government – the SVR – is aware of the communications," she said. "President Kurmaev might be at risk."

"The FBI has also been tipped off about the information leaving the White House," he replied. "But they have nothing definitive. It does, however, make things more difficult for us. What about you – you know anything else?"

She nodded. "We have Chinese contacts who have reported recent movements in China."

"Movements?"

"Nuclear warheads – mostly land-based systems," she explained.

"You mean intercontinental missiles?"

"Yes, ICBMs, and also some jostling of personnel."

"Missile operators?"

She nodded.

"And these are more than just rumors?"

"Yes – the info has been corroborated through independent, reliable sources," she said. "But it could just be a coincidence – they're constantly making adjustments."

Alina suddenly reached over the table and grabbed both of his hands. She smiled and said, "There's a man at the bar that I recognize – and he just looked over here."

"Recognize? How?" Anders asked and smiled back without moving his eyes from hers. He maintained his composure but his heart rate ticked up a notch.

"He was at a political fundraiser I attended last week," she said. "Maybe a coincidence, but he might be following me. Time to evaporate."

Anders let go of her hands, slid out of the booth, and leaned over and kissed her on the lips.

"I'm going to the restroom," he said. "You mind ordering me another whisky?"

She smiled, grabbed her purse, and slid out of the booth. "Sure, what did you have?"

"The Balvenie Portwood, 21-year," he replied. He kissed her again and headed to the bathroom. As he walked, it occurred to him that Alina had taken his advice: he detected no perfume.

He made his way to the bathroom at a modest pace, and entered. It was large and smelled clean. Six urinals lined the wall to his right, and there were four sinks at a counter to the left. The only other person there was an obese man with short, gray hair, washing his hands at the nearest sink. On the far end were six stalls on the right with metal walls that went all the way to the floor.

Anders went to a urinal and pretended to relieve himself as the man at the sink dried his hands and left. Anders then went to the far end of the restroom, closed the door on the third stall, and then stepped into a stall two doors further down and locked the door.

He took off his jacket and hung it on a hook. He then peeled off his fake goatee – a painful process – removed his wig, and replaced his dark-rimmed, square glasses with circular, gold-rimmed ones. He took off the turtleneck to reveal a thin, maroon, long-sleeved shirt, and turned his jacket inside out – it went from black to light gray. Finally, he donned the jacket, put all of the unused items in a plastic bag, and double-checked that the thumb-drive was in his pants pocket.

He exited the stall and closed the door. He dumped the bag in a garbage can, went to the large mirror above the sinks, and checked himself over. The transformation was complete.

Just as he was about to leave, the bathroom door opened and a man entered. Anders pretended to ignore him – didn't even glance in his direction – and began washing his hands. He watched in the mirror as the man first looked in the direction of the stalls, and then proceeded to the bank of urinals. It was the man Alina had identified in the bar.

As Anders dried his hands, he got a look at the man from behind – tall with short, dark hair, wide shoulders, and shoes with thick soles that looked less like dress shoes than tactical boots. If he'd seen Anders enter the restroom, he now probably thought he was in the closed stall.

Anders exited the bathroom and went back into the main bar area. He concentrated on walking slightly "pigeon-toed," and from heel to toe, in order to change his gait. Someone else might be watching for him. Alina was nowhere in sight.

He casually weaved his way through clusters of patrons to the elevators, and entered one that had just arrived. As its doors started to close, he spotted the large man exiting the bathroom, and got a good look at his face. He seemed to be looking for someone.

While the elevator descended, he pulled out his phone and ordered a SuperLift ride to meet him two blocks from the hotel.

Anders knew there was a smaller exit on the west side of the hotel – he'd entered through the main lobby on the south side – and got off the elevator and headed to that west door. A minute later, he was in the cold air, heading north toward a bar called "The Senate," which was known for being a seedy pickup joint frequented by the Washington elite.

Just as he approached the place, his SuperLift ride arrived. It was a blue, Honda minivan, and it was to take him to another hotel near a subway stop. He'd then take the subway to a place where a DMS team would pick him up.

As he rode, the adrenaline that had been flowing through his body waned, and he relaxed. He wondered if Alina had gotten out safely.

He didn't think she was just being paranoid. In fact, being a little paranoid was okay as long as one controlled it and didn't allow themselves to panic. That he and Alina had followed protocol was a good thing. He had the device, and no one had chased him.

It struck Anders as odd that Alina would attend a local political event – where she'd seen the man who'd followed him into the bathroom. Did she have other contacts?

Fifteen minutes later, he was on a subway car with a group of teenagers, and got off at the first stop. He walked a few blocks down empty streets into a residential district. Just as he approached a cross street, a black SUV pulled up and one of its doors opened. He got into the back seat, next to a burly man dressed in jeans and a sweater, and closed the door. The vehicle sped along.

"Welcome back, Mr. Johnson," the man said.

Anders welcomed the use of his DMS employee alias. "Good to be back," he replied.

"Harrison is waiting for you," the driver said.

It was going to be a late night.

HARRISON HAD dinner with his wife and was back in his DMS office by midnight. Having a direct line with a client wasn't his usual method of operation, but this was the president of the United States. It meant that Harrison was on call at *all* times – even on his wedding anniversary. He was grateful that the call had come just after dessert.

Anders would be in soon: Harrison had just gotten word that the exchange went as planned. He'd also learned from his FBI moles that Anders had successfully avoided a pair of agents in the FBI's counterespionage group who were looking for him, or his contact, at the Orion. He hadn't yet learned the status of the Russian courier.

That morning, another DMS operative had met with Crownbrook and installed sophisticated encryption software with file upload capabilities on his DMS satellite phone. The president then made a practice data transfer to DMS to test the encryption-decryption-encryption process, the final product of which was then loaded onto a thumb-drive identical to those used to deliver the messages to the foreign couriers. This drive would now be delivered to the president to decrypt on his own computer. If he's able to extract the message, and it is identical to the one he'd sent, then the new process is ready for use. If not, DMS people will have to debug it, or scrap the idea altogether.

The problem was that the first "test" message that Crownbrook sent contained vital information – a warning: the FBI had gotten a tip that something was going down at the Orion Hotel regarding "secret messages" sent from the White House. The tip had supposedly come from Russian operatives who had gleaned information from the CIA's own electronic surveillance in Moscow. It was disturbing that Russian counterintelligence was able to tap into CIA resources abroad. It was also alarming that the CIA had information about the meeting in the first place.

Harrison grabbed a whisky tumbler from a cabinet and then put it back. He didn't want to dull his nerves right now, plus he needed to reduce his overall alcohol consumption. What he needed was coffee, so he called the nighttime receptionist and ordered a carafe – strong. Anders was going to need some, too.

There were so many disturbing questions to contemplate. First, how did information leak about the communications? It seemed that the adage, that three people could keep a secret if two of them were dead, held true. Which of the three players in this situation had the leak? Perhaps there were multiple leaks. It was apparent that there were at least some glitches on the Chinese side, since one of their devices had already been intercepted, but that was a problem within the private, Hong Kong-based firm – there had been a Chinese mole in exactly the right position. The Chinese president had since changed security firms.

There was a light knock at the door, and the overnight attendant delivered a tray of coffee and mugs, and some other items, including cookies.

"Thanks, Eldridge," Harrison said. "You can put it on the coffee table."

Another knock came from the open door. It was Anders.

"You're just in time," Harrison said to Anders as the attendant left and closed the door. "Have a seat."

Harrison sat on the couch on one side of the coffee table, and Anders took a chair directly across from him.

"Our situation is evolving quickly," Harrison said as he filled his mug with the black brew.

"I'm pretty sure someone was tailing us tonight – my Russian contact spotted a man," Anders explained. "Thinking back on it, it might have been a hairier situation than I thought it was at the time."

"There were, in fact, *two* FBI agents there," Harrison nodded. "It was good you took proper precautions."

Anders looked like he was going to be sick. "How did they know?"

"There could be leaks anywhere," Harrison replied. He didn't want to worry Anders with the details.

"Did Alina get away?" he asked.

"She got out of the hotel with no one in close pursuit," Harrison replied. "After that, we stopped watching her. She should be okay – she wasn't carrying anything after the exchange anyway. You were."

Anders nodded, reached into his pocket, pulled out a blue data storage device, and placed it on Harrison's side of the table.

Harrison pulled out his phone and sent a text to the computer specialist. She was on standby for this delivery.

"We have the next train car – the tender. We'll load it here, tonight," Harrison explained. "The president will inform his niece of the new purchase, and you can set up a meeting in the next few days for the delivery. You should use the same place you did for the first exchange. I know that's unusual, but changing locations might make his niece suspicious."

Anders nodded. "It's also unusual for one party to be completely oblivious to what they're doing," he said.

"It works in her favor – plausible deniability," Harrison argued. "However, things are more dangerous than when we started. She'll be out of the picture after this one."

"Alina had some new information," Anders said. "Just rumors, but concerning nonetheless."

"Go ahead."

"The Chinese are reconfiguring their ICBM sites, moving mobile launch vehicles, and shifting personnel," Anders explained. "It's consistent with the rumor that the leaders are discussing nuclear war."

"Where did she get this information?"

"Multiple, independent sources."

A knock came at the door.

"Come in, Diana," Harrison said.

She came in carrying a laptop and a briefcase. Her red hair was wrapped in a bun on the top of her head. She looked tired.

"Set up on my desk," Harrison said as he stood, snatched the blue device from the table, and walked it over to her.

They watched as Diana put the thumb-drive through the usual checks, which took about five minutes.

"Do you want me to load the test device as well?" she asked.

"Please," Harrison replied, walked around his desk, and pulled a purple device out of the top drawer, along with an ordinary, black thumb-drive. "The text is in a file on the black one. The filename is Test-1. Encrypt that file and load it onto the purple drive."

The purple device was to be loaded with the message the president had sent to DMS using his encrypted satellite phone. Harrison was to send that message back to Crownbrook along with the device Anders had just collected. If the test was a success, they would use the satellite phone method from this point forward to get information out of the White House. They were still working on a new method for getting information back to the president.

"They're all ready," Diana said as she packed up her equipment and placed three drives on the desktop: one each of blue, purple, and black.

Harrison put the black one, which was just an ordinary thumb-drive, back into his desk drawer. The blue and purple ones remained.

"The purple one is the test message," Diana reconfirmed.

"Very good," Harrison said. "We'll talk more tomorrow about setting up our client to receive encrypted messages on his phone."

Diana collected her briefcase and laptop, and left.

Harrison went to a cabinet behind the desk, retrieved the train car, and set it near the data storage devices.

"This is the tender," he explained as he retrieved a thin, Phillips-head screwdriver from a drawer. He turned the car on its side, removed four screws from its underbelly, and pulled off a square, metal panel, revealing a void. He turned it so that Anders could see. "I already put some putty inside to hold the devices securely."

Anders leaned in closer. "Looks like there's just enough room for them," he said as Harrison pressed the first, and then the second device into the black putty.

"A perfect amount of space," Harrison said and then reached into his desk drawer and pulled out an open package of putty and packed more around the devices to ensure they had no room to jostle. He then replaced the cover, tightened the screws, wiped the car's underside with a tissue and glass cleaner to remove any putty residue, and set the car on the desk. "This is in your hands now. Set up the exchange for Sunday."

As Anders picked up the car and examined it, Harrison retrieved its plastic storage box from the floor and placed it on the desk. "The paperwork is in there as well," Harrison said.

After wrapping the tender in a plastic bag, Anders placed it in its form-fitted foam insert inside the box, closed the top, and slid two metal clips to secure the lid. "Will the president's niece initiate contact?" he asked.

Harrison nodded. "You should turn on the phone you used for your first meeting with her," he said. "Now, we have some other things to discuss."

They went back to the coffee table and retook their seats. Anders placed the box containing the train car on the empty chair to his left.

"The situation is heating up more quickly than I anticipated," Harrison said.

Anders shifted in his seat. "I was getting that impression tonight," he said.

"As you now know, the FBI is getting nosy," Harrison explained. "And now the CIA might be involved – or factions within it."

"Are we going to suspend the operation?"

"No," Harrison replied. "But we're going to take some precautionary actions."

"How so?"

"After your delivery on Sunday, you're going to take a week off and get out of town – far away," Harrison explained. "Think of it as a paid vacation, although I'd recommend you keep up with the news."

"The operation comes to a halt in the meantime?"

Harrison shook his head. "We'll be running some decoy missions," he said. "Other DMS couriers will visit the president and make some exchanges – nothing to do with our current operation."

"What's the purpose?"

"Anyone surveilling them will be taken on a wild goose chase," Harrison replied. "What's more, if our people get questioned, or the materials going in and out of the White House get confiscated, they'll all be found to be benign. In short, the FBI might deem it all waste of time, and conclude that there was nothing to the rumors in the first place."

"Sounds good," Anders said. "I'll head out of town after the exchange – I won't even stop back at my apartment."

"Good plan," Harrison said. "Where will you go?"

"Probably Savannah, to visit my mom," Anders replied. "It's been a couple of months since I've seen her. And I think the Georgia weather will be a nice break."

Harrison took a drink of coffee and leaned back on the couch. "I also wanted to let you know that we're in a different situation now," he said. "Our plausible deniability is gone."

"How so?"

"If we wanted to, we could read the president's messages," Harrison said. "He's given us the encryption software – meaning that we'll have his original text files from this point forward."

"But we won't read them."

"Of course not," Harrison said. "But who would believe that we didn't?"

Anders seemed to get the point. "We're in pretty deep then," he said.

"We'll be okay," Harrison said, half-believing his own words. "We'll take whatever precautions we can. The devices themselves destroy the data after the messages are read, so there won't be a trail."

"What about the transmissions?" Anders asked. "Could they be intercepted?"

"Yes, but they're encrypted," Harrison explained. "We should be safe, at least regarding the content of the messages. We can only be linked directly to the transport of the devices."

They chatted for a few minutes about geopolitical events before Anders left for his office and Harrison went to the closet for his coat.

As Harrison donned his knit hat and leather gloves and headed toward the elevator, an unnerving thought entered his mind. There might be a time when he'd have to read the president's messages.

CANDACE ENDED the call and slapped her cell phone on the desk.

"Dammit!" she cursed.

"Still no resources, then?" Tim said. "I told you."

"I know, I know," she said. "But we're on to something here. The man you followed into the bathroom just evaporated." They'd waited for an hour for him to come out but he never did, and the woman had gone to the bar and then seemed to disappear into thin air.

"I swear there was no other exit in that restroom. This is cloak-and-dagger shit," Tim said. "Something was definitely going on, but there's no way to prove it's connected to our investigation."

"What did you dig up on the Single-World Alliance member list?" she asked. She'd given him the task of finding old documents.

Tim pulled a thick folder out of his briefcase and flopped it on her desk. "These are the files I found in the archives," he said. "Some old ones, dating back to the 60s."

"It all started long before that – in the late 40s or early 50s," she said.

"The earliest FBI file I found is from 1961, but it has old member lists – I assume it must include some of the founders," Tim explained. "Most are dead now, of course, but I found at least three who are still alive. One is located in Hawaii."

"We're not going to Hawaii, Tim," Candace said without hesitation. "Where are the other two?"

"Santa Barbara and Seattle," he replied.

"Shit," she muttered. "I don't want to go all the way across the country."

"I can go interview them on my own," he said, seemingly eager to take a trip.

"We have to go together – you know the rules," she said. "The question is whether we really have a reason to talk to them."

Tim shrugged. "Hard to know unless we talk to them," he said. "Catch-22. What can we learn from them?"

Candace shrugged. "We could get more details about the SWA's objectives, more names, some historical facts," she replied. "We have our in-house research, and some files from the CIA, but these people would be *direct* sources."

"Right from the horse's mouth," Tim said. "We might catch some nuances that were missed in those earlier investigations."

"That, and we'll try to trace forward in time," Candace said.

"What do you mean?"

"Usually, we try to work backward," she explained. She typed an email as she spoke. "We get recent, active sources and find out who preceded them, etc. This time we ask for names of younger members, and hopefully progress forward."

"I'm sold," Tim said. "Now you just have to convince Neumann."

Candace clicked the send button. "I just emailed him," she said. Now they just had to wait for authorization from Jack Neumann, who was their immediate boss, and Associate Deputy Director of the FBI.

CHAPTER 5

Anders thought it was nice to wake up in his apartment after spending the previous five nights in his office. The sleepovers at DMS had started as a precaution after his hurried exit from the Orion Hotel, where he'd made the exchange with the Russian courier, Alina.

He'd spent the extended time at DMS looking into "deep-state subgroups" within the global intelligence community that included operatives from almost all major nations. Some of these secret organizations were benign – and not very secret – while others had goals that spanned everything from population reduction to world domination. Others wanted open access to all information otherwise hidden by the government – including military secrets. He figured anyone who believed in *that* would be the worst type of person to work in intelligence.

It was now Sunday, and at noon Anders started assembling his disguise for the meeting with Sara Bradbury. It wasn't too complicated, just a reddish-blonde goatee and blonde wig with thick, curly hair, but it was important to keep track of every detail to repeat the look she'd seen the first time. One never knew what specific feature someone else noticed in their appearance. He'd have to become "Don Keller," amateur model train trader, for another afternoon.

By 1:00 p.m., he'd picked up a rental car and was on his way to The Page. It was a cool, clear day, with just a few fluffy, white clouds inching across the sky. It was the first week of April, but it still didn't feel like spring to him.

He arrived 15 minutes before the scheduled meeting at 2:30 p.m. Sara was already there, sitting at the same table they'd shared during their previous meet. She was in the chair he'd occupied that first time. The place was busy and loud.

He approached her and set his leather knapsack on the floor next to the chair across from her. "Good to see you again, Sara," he said.

She smiled and said, "Likewise, Don, how are you?"

"Just enjoying the beautiful day," he replied as he detected stress in her green eyes. There was a cup of steaming coffee on the table. "I'm going to grab a coffee before we get started. You want anything?"

She declined, and he went to the coffee bar.

The tension he sensed in her now transferred to him, and he needed to scope out the place to check if there were any suspicious characters around. The bookstore was bustling with people, so it would be difficult to identify anyone unless they were completely incompetent, but he'd look anyway.

He ordered coffee and casually took in the scene. No one seemed out of place.

He went back to the table with a hot mug, and sat.

"I take it that your client was pleased with the engine," he said.

"Very happy," she said, smiling. "And now he wants the accessory – the tender."

Anders reached down, opened his backpack, extracted the plastic case, and set it on the table. He slid the two metal clips on the top and opened the lid, revealing the tender, wrapped in plastic. He lifted it from its foam insert, removed it from the bag, and placed it on the table.

"It's not as impressive as the engine, but they make a collectible pair – worth much more as a set than individually," Anders explained as he reached into his backpack and extracted the paperwork. "This has the maintenance records – one of the wheels was loose. My grandfather's restorer repaired it."

Sara looked over the paperwork and nodded. "Looks like we have a deal," she said as she took her phone out of her purse. "Same account?"

"Yes," he replied. "We agreed on $750, right?"

She nodded, tapped a few times on the phone's screen, and said, "It's on the way."

This was the time that made Anders uneasy. Sitting around with the package and waiting for the money to clear was allowing time for someone to close in. It reminded him that Sara had no idea what was really happening.

"Now, new business," Sara said, and then reached into a blue gift bag on the floor sporting The Page logo – the coffee-drinking, book-reading knight. She pulled out a cardboard box and set it on the table.

"What's this?" he asked.

She opened the box and pulled out a plastic-wrapped locomotive. She unwrapped it and set it on the table in front of him.

"It's beautiful," he said, wondering what else he could say since he knew nothing about trains. It was black, and it looked like an old steam engine.

"My client wanted you to have a look at this, and hoped you might know someone who could appraise it," she explained.

Anders felt a prickly sweat start to itch the back of his neck. "This belongs to the same client?"

She nodded. "He said he's had this one since he was 12 years old – a gift from his uncle," she explained. "He wants to know what it's worth. Do you know someone who can evaluate it?"

Anders wanted to say no, but he knew he couldn't. What was Crownbrook doing?

"Sure," he said. "I know just the person."

"Good," she said and smiled. "Then it looks like we'll meet at least one more time."

Anders wasn't sure that was true. "That's great," he said, as she packed the engine back into the box, closed it, and slid it to his side of the table.

She then pulled a form and pen out of her purse and slid them over to him.

"Please fill this out," she said. "And I'll need your ID."

Anders had one – always did for his aliases, no matter how minor the meeting. He filled out the form, which asked for his name, address, and phone number. It also had details of the locomotive in the box, including a serial number. He signed the form with his alias information, and slid the pen and paper back to her.

"This could take a few weeks," Anders said. "It really depends on how busy my grandfather's colleague is."

"I understand," she said, and then stood, put on her jacket, put the box with the tender car under her arm, and picked up the blue gift bag along with her purse and coffee mug. "We'll be in touch."

As she returned her mug to the counter and walked out, Anders took her seat so that he could see her exit the building. He watched as she got into her car and drove away.

He glanced at the box on the table and sighed.

The original plan was that he'd start driving south, toward Savannah, immediately after the exchange, but now he had to go back to DMS.

Why wouldn't the president give DMS some kind of warning that he was sending a package? Anders' nerves tingled, and he decided to take extra precautions on his unplanned trip back to DMS.

IT WAS SUNDAY, but Maurice regularly came into the office on weekends to make the schedule for the coming week. This time he'd also arranged a mid-afternoon meeting with Captain Eduardo Pacquiao. Last week, they'd met and discussed Eduardo's assignment of assembling a team to develop the mobile launch systems. That task had been completed, but the crew members were still being vetted by the CIA.

Planned for this week were mandatory, standard training sessions for current missileers, including updated protocols for security and reporting. With all the strange events occurring around the missile launch sites and control stations, a more organized method of documentation was being implemented. There were also new options to consider: each site was being equipped with new defense measures, including updated sensing instruments, and surface-to-air missile launchers. And, of course, there were other "renovations" happening that he couldn't divulge to anyone. That's what the meeting with Eduardo was to be about.

A knock came at the door at 3:00 p.m. sharp, and Maurice called in Eduardo. At 46 years old, the master missile mechanic had already put in his 20 years and was beyond retirement age, but his level of expertise was so rare that the Air Force made it worth his while to stay. His income would be even larger this year with the added supplement from the CIA for his part in the operation.

Maurice directed Eduardo to a set of upholstered chairs next to the floor-to-ceiling, north-facing window. On the small table between them was a carafe of coffee and two mugs.

"The crew members you've selected are currently undergoing background checks," Maurice said as he filled Eduardo's cup, and then his own. "The CIA updated you on Friday regarding the details of the work. Any questions?"

"A million," Eduardo replied. "But they told me I can't ask any of them."

Maurice laughed. "You can ask, but you might not get answers," he said. "Do you think you've convinced everyone on your list to join?"

"Pretty sure, yes," Eduardo replied. "They're all younger than me, but still near retirement. I don't know how pleased they'll be with the hours, even with the extra money."

"I've thought about that," Maurice said. "They'll be working full-on for however long it takes – four to five months – and it will be rough. However, they'll be granted standby duty for six months after the job is complete."

"That's practically a six-month, paid vacation," Eduardo said, apparently impressed.

"Yes," Maurice said. "They'll still have to be on base from time to time for training updates and general inspections. And, of course, anything construed as an emergency. But maybe they can use it to make up for lost time with their families."

"I think they'll be amenable to the idea," Eduardo said.

"I've already ordered some of the equipment you listed, but I'm going to need a full list of the big-ticket items by the end of the week," Maurice said.

"It's going to be expensive," Eduardo said. "To get started, we're going to need eight M36 military trucks with climate-controlled interiors, and two or three HG-P801s – those will be needed for bad weather. Later, we'll have to order more to accommodate the rest of the silos."

"You're right – that's going to be a big bill to pay," Maurice said, knowing that a single HG-P801 was over two million dollars. It was an eight-wheeled, all-wheel-drive truck with a specialized, climate-controlled, rear compartment designed to house sensitive electronics. These were also going to be modified to carry super-quiet, electric generators and powerful transmission antennae.

"With the specialized electronics, the trucks, and the personnel costs, I expect the total cost to be over 50 million dollars," Eduardo said.

"Probably more," Maurice said. "But that's nothing compared to the cost of just one of our B-1 bombers. We have the money for this – it's been marked as a level-one priority project."

Eduardo shrugged. "I think having a completely mobile auxiliary launch option is well worth it," he said. "One of these drones could shut down a normal silo, but our mobile units could drive in and launch the missile anyway. Even if all the redundant systems at a silo or control station were disabled, we'd still be able to launch. It will only take the flip of a switch to give control to a truck, which can be done by hand if the remote switch fails."

"That's what I wanted to hear," Maurice said. "I need you and your crew on site I-1 by Friday of this week. I'll need decisions from each of your crewmembers by Wednesday, and the names of the replacements for anyone who declines."

"Okay, but there's something else," Eduardo said.

"Yes?"

"If funding isn't a problem, I'd like to add two more to the crew," Eduardo said.

"Why's that?"

"If time is important, extra hands are good," Eduardo explained. "More importantly, however, we can have two engineers prepping the next site on the list as work on the current one is finishing up."

"Okay," Maurice said. It increased the crew from eight to ten, but it didn't matter as long as they were vetted. "I'll need the two new names by noon tomorrow."

"The drones must really be an imminent threat if we're pressing forward this quickly," Eduardo said. "As we both know, neither the Air Force nor the Department of Defense acts with great pace in these kinds of things."

Maurice chuckled. "That's an understatement," he said. "As it turns out, the brass is pretty panicked by the drone incursions. And I have to warn you, once again, that this is as top-secret as it gets. My feeling is that the CIA, as well as defense intelligence, is going to be watching you and your crew very closely. I'm sure they're monitoring me as well. So, tight lips, right?"

"Yes, sir," Eduardo said. "My crew will know very little about the big picture – even I know very little – but they *will* know what they're doing. I mean, they'll understand the functionality of the upgrades and the mobile apparatus they're constructing. They're all experts in this field."

"I know," Maurice said. "But they need to keep quiet about it. They'll be briefed, and well-informed about the rules on this project."

"Understood," Eduardo said and stood. "I better go find two more crew members."

Eduardo left, leaving Maurice standing at the window with a mug of coffee in his hand. He hoped Eduardo and his engineering team could keep their mouths shut. If word got out, the trap would be ineffective, even though the mobile upgrades would still be an immense improvement to the system.

He went to his desk, picked up the phone, and called Christine, the CIA contact who had made a visit to Malmstrom two weeks ago.

Maurice notified her that the operation was moving forward and on schedule.

AFTER DROPPING off the locomotive he'd gotten from Sara Bradbury at DMS on Sunday afternoon, Anders had headed south on Interstate 95 toward Savannah, Georgia. Having to go back to DMS had delayed his departure by a few hours and, rather than driving late into the night, he'd decided to make a stopover in Raleigh, North Carolina, where he'd visited a bookstore, and then gotten a hotel room and ordered a pizza.

Now it was 10:30 a.m. on a bright Monday morning and he was on the road, just an hour away from the house where he'd grown up. More accurately, it was the house in which they'd lived while in the United States. The rest of the time they were living abroad, which was how he'd learned multiple languages and experienced other cultures through complete immersion. He'd had no idea that his father had been working for the CIA at the time. Anders had always thought he'd been a businessman who'd dealt in computer technologies. To the present day, he'd never really known what his father had done in the CIA – at least no specifics. He had known, however, that he'd worked with the current US president on some missions.

As he got closer to his childhood home, it felt as if he were going backward in time. He recognized the houses as he got closer; most everything was the same, except the trees were much larger, or missing altogether. He passed the house of his former high school girlfriend and, through muscle memory, almost pulled into her parents' driveway. His mom had mentioned during his previous visit – Christmastime – that they still lived there.

He opened the car window and, as the sweet southern air brushed over his face, he caught the scents of dry pine needles, magnolias, and early-blooming flowers – most of which he knew were just the blossoms of weeds poking up through the fields. The smells brought everything into context – early spring in southern Georgia was very different from that in DC.

Five minutes later, he pulled his rental car into his mother's driveway and cut the engine. His mom stepped out the front door and onto the porch of the three-story house, which looked unlike any other in his hometown of Genesee Lake, located 45 miles northeast of Savannah. She was wearing dirty jeans, boots, and a green tee shirt with the yellow words "Go Hornets!" on the front, above "GLHS" – Genesee Lake High School. Stitched in cursive on the right shoulder was the name "Gigi," which was her nickname, derived somehow from Griselda.

He got out of the car and rushed over a cobblestone walkway and up a series of brick steps to his mom.

"Andy, my dear," she said as they hugged. "I'm so glad you're here!"

As they separated, he looked at her muddy boots and pants. "What are you doing?"

"Potting plants in the backyard and working in the garden," she said and grinned. "You bring your work clothes?"

"I'm sure I have something up in my room," he said, and laughed.

His parents had done nothing with his bedroom since he'd gone to college.

"Let's have tea – I have some excellent lemon cookies from Mrs. Cranston," she said. Jenny Cranston was 70 years old – the same age as Gigi – and they'd been friends for as long as Anders could remember. He knew both of the Cranston kids, a daughter a year ahead of him and a son a year behind. The family lived a half-mile down the road.

"Sounds good," he said as he headed down the steps back to his car. "Let me take my things up to my room, and I'll meet you in the kitchen."

Anders grabbed the duffel bag and backpack out of his car, followed his mom into the house, and then climbed a wide, wooden staircase to the second level. From there, he could go forward, to a room with a large bay window that faced north with a view over the backyard, or left or right. He could also go up. To the right was a stairway that went up to his room. To the left were stairs that led to his father's study. His room and the study shared a wall on the third floor, but there was no door between them. Late at night when he was a kid, he'd hear his dad on the opposite side of the wall – sometimes talking on the phone, and other times playing music on the radio or on his old, vinyl turntable – mostly smooth jazz.

Anders took the staircase to the right and went up to his bedroom. In an instant, it was as if he'd been transported back to his childhood. The nostalgia often brought a tear to his eye, but it had happened so many times since he'd moved to the Northeast after college that the feeling was now short-lived. His current life was exciting, and going back in time wouldn't change much regarding where he was now.

His bedroom looked the same as it had when he was 12 years old, from the Star Wars posters on the walls to the twin-sized, loft bed above his wooden desk. The large throw rugs that covered the wooden floor were worn, but he thought they might last another 20 years.

The high, slanted ceiling followed the pitch of the roof, with horizontal beams that spanned the width. It was like living in a hayloft. Both rooms on the third floor were rectangular, each spanning half the level, with large windows at each end, one at the front of the house and one at the back, facing south and north, respectively. Anders' room had a cozy reading nook at the north window, overlooking the backyard and garden. At the far north end of their three-acre lot was a barbed-wire fence, and then a farmer's field that was sometimes filled with sunflowers. Further north, beyond the field, was a forest and a small lake in which he and the neighbor kids used to swim in the summers. From his window, he could see the lake through an opening in the trees.

Anders changed into some old jeans and a tee shirt he found in his dresser drawer. He'd wear his dad's old boots when he went outside to work.

He scampered down the stairs two at a time – his childhood habits were still hardwired into him – and met his mom at the kitchen table just as the teakettle whistled.

"English breakfast okay?" she asked.

"Perfect," he replied. Her two favorite teas were English breakfast and a strong, black Typhoo tea that Anders often enjoyed at night.

They sat across from each other at the table, each in their usual spots. The large window to Anders' right looked out to the backyard and garden. To his left was an empty chair. It had been three years since his dad's passing, but the void represented by that chair was heavy, and permanent.

"So what's the occasion?" his mom asked. "You were just here over Christmas."

"That was just a three-day visit," he replied. "I had some vacation time that I had to use or I'd lose it. It was between here and the Bahamas."

"Sure," she said and laughed. "How long will you stay?"

"This week and through the weekend, if that's okay," he replied.

"Of course," she said. "There are a million things to do around the house."

"You seem determined to put me to work," he said.

She smiled.

"Actually, it will be nice to do something physical for a while," he said, and took a sip of tea and a bite of a lemon cookie.

"Your work giving you some stress?"

He sighed and nodded. He wished he could tell her about it, but he was sure she knew that, just like his father, he couldn't divulge much. She knew *exactly* what his job entailed, but never any project details. "It's always a bit stressful, but I'm involved in a pretty big one this time. It's complicated, but I'll be okay."

"You sound just like Henry," she said, referring to his father. "I understand. As a translator, there were things I had to keep confidential as well – some of them were quite disturbing. It's stressful not being able to talk about them."

Gigi was fluent in Russian, and had rotated through just about every US embassy in Europe. That was how she'd met his dad.

They finished their tea and cookies, and went out to the garden. It was sunny, mid-70s, and no wind. Anders was looking forward to spending time with his mom, and unwinding.

In the evening, after she went to bed, he'd visit his father's study.

"I'm Special Agent Candace Wright, FBI," Candace said, "and this is Special Agent Timothy Barilaro. Are you Wilfred Carrigan?"

According to his file, the man before them was 91 years old and lived with his wife, Annalise, who was 87. He looked old, but not frail, and stared at them through the screen door with suspicious eyes.

"That's me," Wilfred said. "What do you want?"

"We'd like to talk to you about the Single-World Alliance," Candace replied. "Can we ask you a few questions?"

The man closed the heavy, inner door, and Candace glanced at Tim, who smiled and shook his head, seemingly conveying that he thought they were going to have a difficult time talking to the man after fighting to get the trip authorized by their deputy director, and a hectic trip from DC to Seattle, riddled with flight delays and cancellations. It was even worse with the sporadic downpours that were predictable in that they knew they'd occur, but just not specifically when. Candace's jeans were already damp, making her legs itch.

The muffled voices of the man and, presumably, his wife went back and forth for about 30 seconds behind the door before the inner door opened again – and then the screen door.

"My wife says yes," Wilfred said with a tone of disappointment. "So, come on in."

Candace followed Tim into a front room with a wood floor covered by a large, burgundy throw rug. A couch, and two upholstered chairs on its flanks, faced a large, flat-screen television mounted on one wall. On the opposite wall was a large window that faced the front yard and was covered by wooden blinds that were mostly closed, letting in just a fraction of the available daylight. Spider plants hung from hooks mounted to the ceiling in every available corner, and potted plants occupied almost every horizontal surface. Candace thought there wasn't enough light for the vegetation to survive.

"This is my wife, Millie," Wilfred said.

The thin woman was dressed in jeans and a red fleece, and her gray hair was pulled back in a ponytail. She looked much spryer than her husband, although the bald man seemed to move well for his age.

"So, what do want to know about the SWA?" Wilfred asked as he repositioned the two chairs so that they faced the couch.

Wilfred and Millie sat on the couch and Candace and Tim took the chairs.

"You were a member, back in the day," Candace started. "Can you tell us how it got started?"

Wilfred shook his head. "You were just here last year – well, other FBI people were here," he spat and glanced at his wife, who shook her head and sighed. "What more can I possibly tell you?"

"There were other FBI agents here a year ago?" Candace asked, surprised. The latest information they had on the SWA dated back almost a decade. If the FBI had more recent info, it should have been in the archives. "What did they ask you?"

"They wanted to know if I was still involved," Wilfred replied. "I'll tell you, like I told them, I've been out of it since I left the CIA in 1982."

Candace glanced at Tim, whose eyes widened. Neither of them had been aware that Wilfred Carrigan had been in the CIA. The files indicated that he'd been an engineer working for a private defense contractor.

"What did you do for the CIA?" Candace asked.

The man's eyes narrowed. "It's classified."

"That's okay," she said. "But can you tell us where you were located?"

"You already have that information," Wilfred said. "I was in Albuquerque and Las Vegas for most of my professional career."

"You were an engineer?" Candace asked.

"Yes, an electrical engineer – Purdue University," Wilfred said.

"What did you specialize in?" Tim asked.

Candace knew that Tim had a degree in mechanical engineering.

"Advanced circuit design," Wilfred replied. "But you're not here to learn about my education. You want to know about the SWA."

Candace nodded. "Can you give us the names of those you encountered in this group?"

Wilfred shrugged. "Sure, I suppose I can now. They're all dead."

"Do you know Peter Mackenberg?" Candace asked. "He's still alive, and about your age."

Wilfred's eyes widened for a split second, seemingly trying to place the name, but then replied, "That name's not familiar to me. But there were SWA members all over the world, so I couldn't know everyone."

"Well, Mr. Mackenberg was in the US and worked at Los Alamos National Lab during that time. He currently resides in Southern California."

Wilfred shrugged and shook his head. "Sorry, don't know him."

Candace pulled a piece of paper out of her pocket, unfolded it, and handed it to Wilfred. "Do you recognize anyone on this list?" It contained the names of about 100 suspected members.

Wilfred looked it over for almost a minute. "Sure, but again, they're all dead."

She handed him a pen. "Can you tell us who they were – what they did for a living and where they were located?"

Wilfred took the pen. "Okay, I recognize some of them," he said and began to go through the list.

Candace turned to Millie. "How long have you two been married?"

"Sixty years," Millie replied.

Candace now wondered what *she* knew – perhaps more than Wilfred realized. And maybe she'd be willing to divulge more.

"Were you also a member of the Single-World Alliance?" Tim asked.

Millie shook her head. "I didn't even know that Wilfred was involved with the SWA until those FBI agents showed up last year. At the time, it was still scary having people in our house, even though the pandemic had been winding down for over a year. We didn't let them in without wearing masks, even though Wilfred and I had been vaccinated."

Candace figured that nixed any hope of getting descriptions of the agents.

"What did you do for a living?" Tim asked Millie.

"I was a journalist, and then the kids came along – three of them, two years apart," she explained. "They took most of my time until they left home."

After about ten minutes, Wilfred handed the paper and pen back to Candace. He had identified 17 people, and noted what some of them had done for a living and where they had resided at the time. They were all technical people – scientists or engineers, some of whom were also in the CIA or in defense intelligence.

"This will be helpful, thanks," Candace said as she folded the paper, put it in her pocket, and pulled out another list and handed it to Wilfred. "The first list contained the earliest members that we know about – perhaps the founders of the organization. This second list is longer – 400 names – and contains more recent, and possibly *current*, members. Can you look this over and see if there's anyone you recognize on it?"

Wilfred sighed, took the list and pen, leaned back on the couch, and started reading.

Candace turned back to Millie. "Do you know what the SWA is all about?"

Millie's face took on a look of alarm for an instant but then relaxed. "Well, I only know what Wilfred has told me," she explained. "In a nutshell, they believe in a one-world economy and government, and a reduced population."

"Any idea as to how they planned to go about doing all of that?" Tim asked.

Wilfred sat up. "In the beginning, when I was involved, they intended to do it through government policies – politics and elections," he said. "The people that came into it after me were more radical."

"How so?" Candace asked.

Wilfred shifted in his seat. "They wanted to take people down – politically and otherwise," he said. "And they started suggesting methods to reduce the population by means other than attrition."

"Other than attrition?" Tim asked.

Wilfred glared at them. "You know exactly what I'm talking

about – the other FBI agents knew what I meant," he argued, and then seemed to realize something. "Can I see your badges, please?"

Candace glanced at Tim, and they both produced their credentials, holding them at arm's length.

Wilfred glanced at them and sat back again. "You must have the SWA manifesto in your files," he argued. "They want to overthrow the government from the inside, and exterminate the majority of the planet. It's not what I signed up for, so I got out."

"Did you recognize anyone on that list?" Candace asked, nodding to the paper in Wilfred's hands.

"Yeah, here, I put checkmarks next to a few," he replied as he handed her the list and pen. "I only recognize the names – I don't know anything else about them, other than that they must have been in New Mexico or Las Vegas when I was there."

"Are there any other names that should have been on this list – either list – that aren't?" Candace asked.

Wilfred looked at her and bit his lip. "Two, but you're not going to believe one of them," he said. "The first is Henry Bennett – he was CIA. I have no idea if he's still alive – he got in about the time I checked out."

Candace didn't recognize the name.

"And the other?" Tim asked.

"Thomas Crownbrook," Wilfred replied.

"You mean – "

"Yes," Wilfred said. "I mean the current president of the United States."

ANDERS SPENT the warm afternoon helping his mom repot plants and set up the garden. Afterwards, he fixed little things around the house including the doorknob on the door to the first-floor bathroom, a loose railing on the banister leading from the first to second floors, and went online and ordered a new thermostat to replace the one that was malfunctioning in his parents' bedroom on the second floor. The work settled his mind, and he made a long list of things to repair the next day.

After dinner, they watched a movie, and then his mom went to bed at 9:30 p.m., a half hour later than usual. Anders watched TV for another hour before heading up to the second-floor landing, where he stood and contemplated whether to take the left or right stairway – to his dad's study, or up to his bedroom.

He went left and climbed the steep, wooden stairs that terminated on a square landing in front of a tall, oak door. The heavy door creaked as he opened it, and he stepped in and closed it behind him before flipping on the lights.

The layout of the study was a mirror image of his bedroom. Track lights mounted to the overhead beams bathed the built-in bookshelves on the perimeter and a large, beige area rug in a warm light that was easy on the eyes. The smell of his father's pipe smoke still permeated the space, and Anders tempered the emotions that welled in him by focusing on the cozy environment. He understood why his dad had spent so much time in this place.

A massive, rolltop desk was against the east wall – the one between this room and his bedroom. It was one of his dad's favorite possessions, and it was magnificent. At about nine feet in length and four feet wide, it was much larger than a typical rolltop desk; there was enough space so that two people could work comfortably side-by-side, and it was tall enough to house a large computer monitor under the rolltop, which was currently closed.

The woodworking and carving were stunning. Supporting the work surface on the ends and center were beautifully crafted columns of wooden drawers. Mounted atop the housing that contained the rolltop mechanism, was a bank of cubby shelves – five columns of three, each about a foot and a half square, making the height of the desk reach almost eight feet. Each cubby had something in it, from stacks of papers to books to coffee mugs. One housed an electric teakettle and accessories.

His dad had gotten the desk as a gift from a wealthy friend in Russia when Anders was just seven years old. He recalled that they'd had to hire an antique furniture specialist to disassemble it in the garage and reconstruct it in the study. At the time, it was worth over ten thousand dollars. Anders figured it now might be worth many times that value considering the complexity of the piece – it was riddled with internal mechanisms and gadgetry – and the rare hardwoods of which it was constructed.

The bottom drawer of three on each of the three lower columns was a file drawer, and that's where he'd start looking. Before diving into that, however, he wanted to peruse the extensive collection of books on the shelves on the west wall, opposite the desk.

His dad was an avid fan of science fiction and had a vast collection that included the works of all the big names in the genre, as well as a fair number of novels from more obscure writers. His father had been particularly fond of anything that had to do with extraterrestrials – from stories about first contact to full-scale alien invasions. He had numerous autographed copies as well, which he kept on a dedicated shelf.

His dad had loved learning about longstanding alien conspiracy theories, from the Roswell Incident to "The Big Flap," when UFOs supposedly buzzed the White House on July 19th, 1952. In fact, Henry had been a donor and member of the Mutual UFO Network, or MUFON, as well as the SETI Institute, which stood for "Search for Extraterrestrial Intelligence Institute." Anders' mom would always tease him, and had once made aluminum-foil hats for them all to wear during dinner, which they did, and had a good laugh – including his dad.

After about 30 minutes of perusing, and taking note of which books he was going to read, he went to the desk. He pulled on the left file drawer but it didn't budge. He checked the others but everything was locked, including the rolltop.

He searched around for a key, but then realized that he couldn't even find a keyhole.

He wasn't going to force anything open – he didn't want to damage the masterpiece – so he grabbed one of the sci-fi novels from the shelves and headed to his room. He'd ask his mom about the desk in the morning.

CANDACE FLIPPED through her notes as the plane came in for landing at Los Angeles International Airport – LAX. They'd booked the first morning flight out of Seattle, and Tim was sleeping with his head against the window.

The day before, Wilfred Carrigan had provided them with some useful information, the most important of which was verification that President Crownbrook had been a member of the SWA. It remained hearsay that he was *currently* a full-fledged member, but they were getting closer to putting the president and his administration out of commission, or at least causing them trouble. For Candace, it would be fulfilling a dream, and something that would be a highlight of her career. Of course, she knew her current line of action could also land her without a job altogether.

The second person on their list of remaining – *living* – SWA founders was Peter Mackenberg, and it was to his residence that they were heading. He'd been easy to find using FBI resources. His location was further verified through social media, where it was clear he'd been posting too much personal information. Candace thought it was unusual for an 88-year-old man to be that active on the Internet, even though he'd been at the top of technology as an aerospace engineer right up until he'd retired from Lawrence Livermore National Lab at age 83.

The plane touched down at 6:45 a.m., and 40 minutes later they were in a rental car heading for Santa Barbara with Tim at the wheel. After getting a bite for breakfast, they'd stop at the FBI field office in Los Angeles to access some archived files on an SWA investigation carried out in the 80s. They'd knock on Mr. Mackenberg's front door around 6:00 p.m.

AFTER EATING a giant omelet with cheese, peppers, and bacon for breakfast with his mom, Anders went to the local hardware store and bought some things for the house, including a new light switch, a handle for the garage door, weather stripping, caulk, and a spigot for an outdoor faucet.

By noon, he'd made all the repairs and upgrades he'd planned for the morning, and then made a new list for the afternoon, which included air filters for the air-handling system, two bags of quick-setting concrete to reset a wobbly fencepost, and a new screen for the door in the back of the house.

His mom made homemade vegetable soup for lunch, and she and Anders sat at the table and chatted while they ate. Afterwards, she made a pot of coffee and brought out a lemon pound cake.

"Do you have the key to Dad's desk?" Anders asked as he took a bite of the dense cake.

"You want to get into his desk?" she asked, eyes wide. "Why?"

Anders knew he'd have to explain himself, and was as prepared as he could be for broaching the topic.

"Our latest client is a bigwig who worked with Dad in the CIA, and they worked on a project together," he explained. "I wanted to see if there's any evidence of that in Dad's desk."

"Is it something of current relevance, or just your curiosity?" she asked.

"Both," Anders replied. "I didn't follow Dad's career too closely, but our paths are crossing now."

"I see," she said as she looked at him and seemed to mull it over.

"Also," Anders added, "I need a floor plan of the house. Do you know where that might be, if not in his desk?"

She stood, went to a tall, narrow broom closet on the opposite side of the kitchen, and brought back a three-foot-long, cardboard tube. "This is it," she said. "The garage addition isn't on this blueprint."

She then went to a drawer under a countertop dedicated to the toaster, and opened it. It was a junk drawer, and had always been filled with miscellaneous things that ranged from screws to paperclips to rubber bands. But there were also loose keys, screwdrivers, and old reading glasses in it.

After a minute of rummaging through the mess, she said, "Ah, here they are."

She came back to the table with a silver, cylindrical key and a wooden object that was shaped like a Star of David.

"This is the key," she said and slid it in front of Anders. She then placed the star-shaped block on the table. "And this goes with it."

He picked up the wooden object and examined it. It was a six-pointed star but it was slightly irregular – not perfectly symmetrical – and it was heavier than it looked. It was about an inch and a half wide, point-to-point – and three-quarters of an inch thick. It reminded him of the geometric blocks used in the game for toddlers where they had to press them into matching holes. "What's this for?"

She shrugged and smiled. "Your dad said you'd have to figure it out."

"What do you mean?"

"He knew you'd need to get into the desk one day," she admitted. "It seems that day has come."

Anders had gotten along well with his dad, so much so that his father had wanted him to follow in his footsteps in the CIA. Anders had almost done it but, after contemplating the idea during his last year of college, decided against it. His dad had been a *real* spook, and had seen a lot of action. Anders had neither the desire nor the skills for such adventures – especially on the international platform where they played for keeps. His job at DMS, however, was the perfect compromise, allowing him some work in the field and to use his unique language skills, but keeping him away from most of the potentially lethal aspects of the profession. Also, his acting talents were of great utility at DMS, although he was sure they also would've been put to good use in the CIA.

"I don't understand why I'd ever *need* to get into his desk – or how he'd known that I'd need to," Anders said.

"Well, it seems that you *do* need to," she said. "So, you must know why that is."

The truth was that Anders didn't know what he was looking for in the desk, but it seemed to him that there might be something that connected his dad to the president, or to what the president was currently doing. He was searching for some kind of justification for Crownbrook's actions, and his secret communications with America's primary adversaries.

He placed the key and the wooden star at the center of the kitchen table. "I'll take a look at it tonight," he said as he pulled a folded piece of paper out of his jeans pocket. "Now, I need to get to the hardware store to pick up some brackets for the gutter and a new downspout for the side of the garage."

She smiled. "It will be nice to get that fixed," she said. "Whenever it rains hard, the overflow splashes down on the flower planter on that side of the house and washes out my tulip bulbs."

Anders stood, put the list back in his pocket, and kissed his mom on the cheek. "Thanks for lunch," he said, and then headed for the front door.

A storm of thoughts swirled in the back of his mind as he scampered down the porch stairs and into the driveway. *What was he going to find in the desk?*

MAURICE WAS in his office at noon when he received Eduardo's final construction crew roster. Everyone had been vetted and trained in top-secret information handling, which was just an eight-hour crash course on how to keep one's mouth shut. A few of them seemed uncomfortable when they were informed that they'd all be undergoing weekly polygraph tests. They wouldn't be privy to any critical information, but even the accidental leak of a tiny detail could compromise the trap they were setting. Only Eduardo had the bigger picture, but his view was only wide enough to give him an understanding of the operational goal: to create a mobile system to facilitate missile launches from outside the control stations.

Maurice ordered some of the required equipment, including the "conventional" trucks, and it all would be delivered in three days. He'd never experienced such a quick turnaround on any requisition, much less one with such a large price tag. The multimillion-dollar, eight-wheelers would take longer since they had to be modified.

A small hangar on the Malmstrom base had been cleared out and dedicated to the project, and the equipment and supplies would be stored there. Fully equipped machine and electronics shops had also been constructed in the hangar so that the team didn't have to involve anyone from the outside. The building would be guarded like any of the others on the base – nothing extra that would draw attention.

After lunch, he arranged for general maintenance work to be carried out on different, unrelated silos by three of his regular crews so that the work of Eduardo's group wouldn't stand out. He'd have to make sure that the silos that Eduardo's people modified were never inspected by any of the other crews, since they'd notice the modifications and probably file a report.

A thought suddenly struck him. If the alterations *were* discovered, all trails led to him. The CIA was notoriously effective at distancing itself from such things, especially regarding operations executed inside the US. They were also good at tying up loose ends – or removing them completely.

A wave of panic surged through him and he shuddered. It passed. Too many people knew about the operation now, and the CIA would have to "clean up" a giant mess if anything happened to any of his people.

Maurice walked over to the window. It was only 7:00 p.m., but it was already getting dark outside as gray-black storm clouds rolled in from the northwest. He caught his reflection in the glass and was confused for a few seconds. He'd aged. His short hair was still dark and only slightly receding, but it was his face that shocked him. Dark circles had formed under his eyes and his expression looked like it was frozen by stress, like a wincing frown that also wrinkled his forehead.

He went back to his desk, checked the status of a few orders, and put on his jacket. He was going to get home before the storm hit. He'd try to spend a relaxing evening with his wife – maybe have a little wine and light a fire in the fireplace. For some reason, it occurred to him that he'd better enjoy life while he could.

ANDERS SPENT the afternoon fixing the gutter and downspout, and repairing the automatic garage door opener, which only needed to be reprogrammed to utilize new remote controls. His mom seemed more excited about the garage door than his saving her tulips from gutter overspills.

They had vegetarian lasagna for supper, and ate popcorn with butter as they watched a movie until bedtime – her bedtime – which was getting later each day he was there.

After she retired to her bedroom, Anders made a cup of coffee in a single-cup brewer he'd given his parents for Christmas years prior, and took the coffee, key, and wooden star up to his father's study.

He set the coffee mug on a bookshelf and turned on a massive AM radio from the 1950s that was built into a wooden console. Its dial had orange backlighting and its innards hummed and whined until he tweaked the dial just a little to tune in his dad's favorite news station. Vents on the antique radio's cabinet emitted yellow light from the warming vacuum tubes inside. Like his dad, Anders concentrated best with a little background noise.

He stood in front of the desk and looked it over. With its rolltop closed, and its dimensions, it could have served as a coffin. He didn't know why such a dreadful thought had come to him, but he figured that he'd never get over losing his dad. It had been over three years now, but it seemed that the realization of the permanence of death came in stages. His father's passing was peaceful, but unexpected, and it seemed that his mom had accepted it more quickly than he had. He supposed that she was around his father's things all the time, whereas Anders was exposed to the tangible reminders, like the house and the desk and his father's empty chair in the kitchen, only a few times a year.

Anders took a sip of coffee, set the mug on the shelf next to the star and key, and went to the desk. It took him a few minutes to find a keyhole: it was on the upper, right-side frame of the rolltop. It was a circular hole, and the key was cylindrical.

He retrieved the key from the shelf, went back to the desk, and tried to insert it. It seemed to be the correct size, but it would only go about a quarter of an inch into the hole. He turned the key through every possible orientation, but it wouldn't go any deeper.

He set the key back on the shelf, returned to the desk, and searched for 15 minutes for another keyhole. No luck.

His thoughts then went to the wooden star, and what its purpose might be. He retrieved it from the bookshelf and examined it closely. As he'd noticed when he had handled it the first time, it seemed heavier than it should have been if it were made entirely of wood. He then spotted an almost imperceptible circle at the center of one of the faces, about a half-inch in diameter. Although the linear wood grains of the circle matched up with those on the rest of the star's face, a thin circular outline was still just visible. It seemed to be a plug. It meant that something might be embedded inside, and that gave him an idea.

Next to a shortwave radio set on an adjacent shelf was a metal box in which his dad had stored miscellaneous nuts and screws, change, small tools, and old watches. He brought the star up to it.

When it got close to the box, it suddenly snapped to it, making a clanging sound, and remained stuck to it.

"I knew it," Anders said aloud and grinned. "I know what this is for."

The magnet embedded in the wooden star was strong, and he had to pull with some force to remove it from the side of the box. He took it to the desk and searched the entire outer surface except for the backside, which was against the wall. After ten minutes he'd found nothing, and then turned his attention to the underside of the desk. Three columns of drawers supported the desktop – one on each end and one in the center – leaving two spaces for chairs. There was only one chair, which was currently beneath the right side, so he got on his hands and knees, crawled beneath the left, turned on his phone's flashlight, and examined the wooden surfaces of the desk's underbelly.

He found it in just a few minutes: a barely discernable, star-shaped outline on a side panel. Just like the circular plug in the wooden star in his hand, the wood grains in the star under the desk were aligned with those around it, and the colors matched perfectly.

Anders placed the wooden star on the outline of the same under the desk. The shape of the star was slightly irregular, so the wooden "key" had to be oriented properly to match the outline. As soon as he turned it into proper alignment, it clicked into place and sunk a little over a quarter of an inch into the desk's side panel so that about the same amount stuck out.

Anders stood, retrieved the cylindrical key from the shelf, went to the right side of the desk, and inserted it into the keyhole. This time it went all the way in – a full inch – and two metallic clicks came from somewhere inside the desk's interior. He turned the key a half turn clockwise, and the sound of a twanging spring came from the underside somewhere.

He went to the front of the desk and pulled gently upward on the two handles at the bottom edge of the rolltop. It slid up smoothly and latched in the fully open position.

His heart thumping hard, Anders stepped back and looked at it. The interior was riddled with shelves, slots, doors, and drawers built into an overhead hutch that bridged the full length of the desk. Dividing the desktop at its center was a support pillar, about eight inches wide, with small shelves, some of which had framed pictures of the family on them, and old ones of his mom and dad when they were young – just kids in their mid-20s. The exotic woodwork and finish reminded him of the captain's quarters of an old sailboat but was much more intricate. It seemed that the desk was designed to accommodate two people.

The items on the desktop looked as if they hadn't been touched since his dad had passed. A large, desk-pad calendar was on the March page of three years ago, with notes in his handwriting up to the day he died. Anders had been in Hong Kong, on a DMS courier mission on that day. It had been Harrison who had called to inform him of the devastating news. He'd never forget the support he'd gotten from DMS to get him home, and keep him company, during that horrible time.

Every exposed shelf, slot, cabinet, and drawer was occupied with something. He found notebooks, fancy pens, an antique Swiss Army knife, and a handful of data storage devices, some of which were quite old, based on their storage capacities.

He knew that the desk had numerous secret compartments. The friend from whom his father had acquired the desk had referred to it as "the spy's bureau."

Next, he checked the file drawers in the desk's support columns and found that they'd unlocked with the rolltop. He pulled out the one on the far left: it was nearly three feet long and packed tightly with file folders. It was the same for the one on the right side. The drawer in the middle column also contained files but was only about half as long as those on the ends. He'd nose through all the files during the next few days, although he didn't know for what, exactly, he was searching.

Suddenly, he was overcome with a wave of guilt. It wasn't just his intrusive actions – breaking into his father's beloved desk which felt like he was rummaging through his entire life, both personal and professional. It was that the desk held secrets, perhaps some that his dad didn't want to be disturbed, or revealed. But Anders now felt regret for not following in his father's footsteps: maybe he could have found a place in the CIA. Maybe he and his dad would've worked together at some point. Maybe his father had wanted to pass along his knowledge to someone – to *teach* him something.

Anders shook it off – there was nothing he could change about his past decisions. As for searching through the desk, he figured it was warranted in this case. He had to make sure that he, Anders, wasn't a part of something that might lead to an existential disaster – like a nuclear war. It wasn't that he'd necessarily be able to *do* anything to stop it, but he wanted to make sure he wasn't enabling it.

He glanced at his phone: it was 11:25 p.m., and he was beat from the early morning wakeup and the full day of home repairs. Stress and emotion also contributed to his fatigue – it was difficult to come home and see his mom living in the empty house all alone. He'd do his best to bring some positivity to her life while he was there, but that took a lot of energy.

He closed the rolltop, removed the star-shaped wooden block from its receptacle under the desk, and extracted the key. He turned off the radio, padded to the door and, just as he was about to turn off the main light switch, he turned and looked at the desk. A thought occurred to him: his father must have had a reason to lock it up every night.

He flipped off the lights, stepped out, and closed the door. Anders was going to do whatever he could to discover what his father was keeping there for him to find.

CHAPTER 6

Candace pressed her face against the cool window as the jet accelerated down the runway. Still groggy from the lack of sleep the night before, she struggled to keep her eyes open against the morning light.

Tim was in the aisle seat to her left, and they were lucky to not have a passenger between them on the nearly full, red-eye flight to DC. Tim looked as exhausted as she felt.

"I still can't believe it," Tim said.

She looked at him and then closed her eyes again as she spoke. "This case just got a whole lot more interesting," she said.

"A whole lot scarier, you mean," he said. "This is crazy."

There were no words that could describe how Candace was feeling, but fear was a major part of it. Peter Mackenberg and his wife were dead when she and Tim had arrived at the old couple's house in Santa Barbara at 6:10 p.m. the night before, and they'd been dead for approximately eight hours. Both had been shot in the head twice, and nothing had been stolen from their place. It was a hit.

Then, at 3:00 a.m. back in Seattle, Wilfred and Millie Carrigan had been found dead in their car which was hidden behind a dumpster in the parking lot of a local dog park. Candace had gotten the call just an hour ago. They'd been killed in the same fashion, except three of Wilfred's fingers had been broken. He'd been tortured.

"You think whoever did this is after us as well?" Tim asked.

Candace's eyes were closed, but she could tell by his voice that he was feeling the same fear that was invading her own mind. "Maybe," she said. "But it wouldn't be common."

Her response made her wonder why that was true. Killing potential sources or witnesses would draw as much attention to a case as would offing the investigators, but she supposed that eliminating all *witnesses* was a more permanent fix. To be thorough, however, one might kill everyone – witnesses and investigators. She'd be sleeping with her gun for a while.

"The big question is, who knew that we were going to visit the Carrigans?" Candace said. "That we were going visit the Mackenbergs might have come from the Carrigans when they were interrogated by whoever killed them. But how did the assassins know they had to get to the Carrigans in the first place?"

"You think there was a leak?" Tim asked, eyes wide. "From inside the FBI?"

She was leaning that way. "We gave names and details when we got authorization for this trip," she said. "There were at least six people who had to sign off on it, and probably a whole bunch of other eyes got a glimpse of the paperwork."

"What do we do next?" he asked. "Do we investigate these murders, or keep on our original path?"

"The local FBI field offices will handle those killings," she replied. "We'll stay the course with our own investigation – we're clearly on to something. Wilfred Carrigan verified other names on our lists. I suggest we look more closely into those people. But we will *not* leak the identities of anyone else we interview – not even to the FBI."

"Most of the people Carrigan identified are already dead," Tim said. "Wilfred had been out of the SWA loop for a long time."

"We'll look into them anyway," she said. "We'll need to check into spouses as well – see if any of them are still kicking."

"Not a bad idea," he said. "When people get old – really old – they sometimes spill information they're not supposed to."

It was something that Candace knew was true for a number of reasons. First, people sometimes wanted to relieve the burden of secrets they'd been holding from their loved ones. She was already feeling that burden herself – by keeping things about her job from her husband. Second, sometimes a person wanted to explain why they'd behaved a certain way for some span of their lives – why they'd been distant, or angry, or acted in suspicious ways. The last reason, however, was the one that was most damning and revealing. It was the guilt associated with the knowledge that something very wrong was occurring – or had occurred – and that they'd either been a part of it, or were concealing vital information that affected others.

Candace pulled the list of names out of her briefcase and looked it over. There were about a dozen checks made by Wilfred Carrigan next to the names of suspected SWA members. It was time to track them down or find the families of those who were deceased.

AFTER BREAKFAST, Anders made a trip to the hardware store and picked up four new electrical outlets. The ones they were to replace were over 30 years old, and his mother complained that one of the safety circuits in the kitchen often tripped when using the toaster and other appliances. In one instance, it had powered off when her slow cooker was supposed to be on for six hours, and she'd come home to an uncooked pot roast. He decided to replace the one in the kitchen, as well as those in all the bathrooms.

Gigi made grilled cheese sandwiches for lunch, and they chatted over tea and cookies afterwards. He explained how he'd unlocked the desk with the star magnet and key, and asked her what other tricks it had.

"It has numerous secret compartments," she said. "I know a few of them."

"What's in them?" Anders asked.

She shrugged. "Data drives, keys, things like that," she said.

"Were you involved in Dad's work?"

She blushed. The question seemed to take her off guard.

"Well, honey, I really wasn't supposed to say," she explained. "But I suppose it's okay now."

Anders had always suspected that she'd been working with his dad on some level, but her answer, and reaction, still surprised him.

"I'd think it would be, as long as you don't reveal any classified info," he said.

She nodded. "A lot of it is," she admitted. "You see, I was also a CIA employee."

"What?" he asked, astonished. It was a bombshell. He'd known she'd been a contract interpreter, but not an official CIA employee. "Really?"

She nodded and smiled. "At the end of his career, your father was a publicly known CIA official, and they wanted him to move into a leadership role," she explained. "Instead, he remained active as a 'retired analyst,' until he passed. So, he never really retired, and I only retired after he was gone."

"Why didn't you tell me?"

"I promised your father I'd keep it secret as long as possible," she said. "He worried about my safety, and he said he could think more clearly if he knew we were doing everything possible to keep me, and you, safe."

"Did you work together, or did you have your own projects?"

"Both," she replied. "I was an interpreter, but I was also a ciphers specialist. As you know, my college degree is in mathematics."

"Yes," he said. "But I thought you were working part-time as an actuary."

She smiled. "That was a cover, and I *did* take some of the actuary exams so I could get part-time work. It brought in a little money –

enough to pay for your college. But I also wrote computer algorithms to encrypt messages, right up until your father passed."

"For Dad's work?"

She nodded. "When your dad went into semi-retirement, I worked exclusively on his communications," she explained. "Before that, I did other work for the CIA, particularly in their campaigns in Eastern Europe."

Anders had been oblivious to it all. "What do you know about Dad working with President Crownbrook?" he asked.

"They had a couple of missions together," she answered. "After that, they were in a black operation that your father only revealed to me at the very end – just the week before he passed. He wasn't feeling well, and I think he knew something was wrong with him. He said he didn't want to keep any secrets from me, although he still didn't reveal any classified details about that operation."

It saddened Anders that his dad must have known his health was failing. He'd had some heart troubles in the past and was going in for regular checkups. Anders suspected that his doctors had told him that his time was coming to an end.

"Do the initials 'CG' mean anything to you?" Anders asked. It was all that Harrison knew about the group that Anders' dad had invited him to join.

She seemed to mull it over for a few seconds before shaking her head. "I can't think of anyone I know with those initials."

"No, it's not a person. I think 'CG' stands for the name of a secret organization within the CIA – maybe an informational compartment," he explained, recalling how Harrison had described it. "I think it's a top-secret group that's somehow connected to the operation in which I'm currently involved."

"Oh?" she asked as her eyes widened. "I thought you were separate from the government."

"I am – well, I'm supposed to be," he explained. "We were contracted by someone in the government."

"You mean *by* the government, or privately, by someone *in* the government?" she asked. Her tone seemed to reflect concern regarding the latter option.

"The second one," he said. "It's a high-level person who doesn't trust information going through formal channels."

"Hmm," she said and narrowed her eyes. "That must be some severely sensitive information."

"I have no idea what I'm transporting," he said.

"I understand your dilemma," she said and took a bite of a cookie and a sip of tea. "You could be passing information that might be part of some dark motive."

"Exactly," he said. "And I'm not even sure if it's legal – is our client committing a crime of some kind by circumventing proper channels? And then, how could my company be implicated – and how could *I* be implicated?"

She seemed to process what he said. "It depends on what they know – DMS – and what you know," she said. "The premise of your entire service is that you don't nose into anything."

"Right," Anders said. "And I don't know anything for certain. Only rumors. Bad ones."

"So, you think your father was involved somehow?" she asked.

"Not in what DMS is doing, of course," he said. "But my project might have to do with information managed by this special group of which Dad was probably a member. He invited Harrison to join, long ago."

"And you think there might be something in his study that reveals what this 'CG' is?"

He shrugged. "Maybe."

"If there is, are you sure you want to go looking for it?" she asked. "Aren't you eliminating plausible deniability?"

Anders had already contemplated the idea. "I'm not sure *what* I should do," he admitted. "I don't have enough information to make a decision."

"And acquiring that information – even enough to make a choice – means more risk," she said.

Anders was not surprised that she picked up on his predicament so quickly. "That's why I want to see if Dad knew anything about this CG group," he said. "Maybe I can learn something that won't put the mission, or me, in jeopardy."

Gigi took a sip of tea and set down her cup. "Well, then I suggest you explore his study, and the desk, thoroughly," she said. "Once you've exhausted your efforts, I'll show you a few hidden compartments that your father showed me. I don't know everything about it, but I can at least reveal a few things for you."

"Thanks, Mom," he said. "Now, I should replace those light bulbs above your shower."

"Yes, it will be nice to see in there again," she said and laughed. "I was too afraid to climb a ladder and do it myself. It's a pretty high ceiling."

Anders grabbed a cookie and stood. "After that, I'll remove those old paint cans from the garage and take them to the disposal center," he said. "Some of those are over 20 years old."

As he made his way to the garage to get a ladder, his phone vibrated in the front pocket of his jeans.

It was a text from Harrison. It read, "Alert: Sara Bradbury was picked up by the FBI this morning. We found a data device in the train car she gave you. You have a mission when you get back. We'll talk Monday."

Anders' eye twitched as he slipped the phone back into his pocket. If they were willing to bring in the president's niece, it meant they might have something solid.

His phone buzzed again, and he pulled it out. It was another message from Harrison. "The FBI reported two double murders on the West Coast that might be connected to our mission."

White sparkles appeared in Anders' vision for an instant and he suddenly felt queasy. *Two double murders.* That was *four* people – a *cleanup* process of some kind. If true, he was getting involved in a cloak-and-dagger operation – something for which he had neither the stomach nor the training.

He put the phone away and contemplated the new information. He might already be in too deep to pull out of the operation. He then concluded that he should sacrifice plausible deniability and learn whatever he could. Things were getting too dangerous to be in the dark for the sake of a client.

Anders would spend the rest of the day working on the house. After his mom went to bed, he'd head up to his dad's study and search for answers.

HARRISON ATE lunch at his desk as he read through emails from DMS operatives. Eight of his 22 couriers were on missions, all of which were benign – mostly the transfer of intellectual property belonging to industrial clients. Sometimes he wondered if he should have limited DMS to such things, but he knew that he wanted to provide more sophisticated services that made a global impact. Although he didn't know any real details, he sensed DMS was in the midst of just such an operation with the president.

Outside DMS, the only communications Harrison had regarding that operation were with the president himself. However, he'd gotten word from one of his CIA sources that Crownbrook was partnering with someone in the agency – most likely with the current director, whom Crownbrook had appointed. If so, that meant CIA Director Radcliffe didn't trust *his own* agency to handle the communications.

Next, the FBI was nosing around, and the president's niece had just been brought in by its counterespionage division. Saying that it was a startling development was an understatement.

What the hell is going on? he wondered.

He'd changed the mode of information transfer between DMS and the president just in time – otherwise, Anders might also be in FBI custody. It would have been a precarious situation, for him and DMS, even though no one knew anything about the actual content of the messages. But that wouldn't stop the US government from tearing apart DMS with search warrants.

If that should occur, he'd have to implement the "escape pod" operation for all DMS clients – which essentially meant destroying all records and rerouting their assets to predetermined accounts or safety deposit boxes. It was the company's self-destruct mechanism. The employees had their own escape protocols as well, which would make it difficult for anyone to track them down.

DMS had a close relationship with the CIA, and with its former personnel. The FBI, however, was another story. Whereas the CIA was okay with secrets being kept from them if they weren't of any use, the FBI was not. The FBI was about the law, and would probe and intrude without regard for whatever, or whoever, might be exposed. One branch of DMS worked much like the federal witness protection program, and leaking that type of identity information would ruin, or end, lives. And, whereas the federal protection program was designed to keep witnesses safe from mostly domestic criminals, DMS protected its clients from international threats. Such customers were often placed in other countries.

The courier division of DMS was Harrison's current concern. The services DMS provided were intended to ensure the secure delivery of extremely sensitive or valuable items, or information. Regarding the deliverables, there were limits: for instance, DMS wouldn't deliver contraband like drugs or weapons, or engage in anything akin to human trafficking. Acceptable cargo might be expensive prototypes of new technologies developed by private companies, such as advanced computer processors or samples of newly invented materials. On other occasions, they'd transported ancient artifacts or heirloom jewelry. Examples of information DMS had transferred were industrial blueprints of future tech devices, and computer code or data that was too sensitive to send electronically. They once even transported the electronic files of a highly anticipated feature film for a major studio. In all cases, Harrison had never feared culpability in a crime, such as industrial espionage or theft.

This time was different: he worried how things were going to develop now that Crownbrook's niece was being questioned. According to the president, the messages in the trains had been successfully delivered and read – so it seemed that nothing had been intercepted.

As a precaution, Harrison put a surveillance team on Anders' apartment, and set a trap. An operative made up to look like Anders stayed in his apartment for three days, and a DMS team was positioned nearby to monitor whether anyone was watching. The final consensus was that Anders was in the clear.

Even though it seemed that DMS was safe for the moment, Harrison was now considering learning more about the information he was relaying to and from the president. Once he breached that barrier, however, he knew he'd be at least partially responsible for whatever happened as a result of DMS's services. His plausible deniability would be gone, and he'd have his conscience to contend with – both for breaking his company's promise to its client and for his part in his client's endeavors.

Harrison's phone vibrated on his desk. It was a text message from a DMS operative informing him that Sara Bradbury had been released from custody fifteen minutes ago. It was a shorter stay than normal, which Harrison figured must have been a courtesy extended to the president – her being his niece.

He knew that Sara Bradbury knew nothing other than the number for Anders' burner phone, and his physical description. He'd been in disguise for their exchanges, and therefore she couldn't answer any of the important questions. But he wanted to know what questions she'd been asked. This could reveal two things. First, he might learn what the FBI really knew about the flow of information out of the White House. Second, he could get an indication of what the secret correspondence was about – what was in the messages themselves. Were they really discussing nuclear war?

Harrison was to attend a meeting for the next hour with a potential client in the banking industry. After that, he'd brainstorm how to approach Sara Bradbury without scaring her, or exposing DMS.

Anders watched a sci-fi movie and ate popcorn with his mom until she went to bed at 9:45 p.m. He then went up to the study.

He inserted the wooden, star-shaped magnet into its receptacle, unlocked the desk with the cylindrical key, and elevated the rolltop.

He pushed his dad's old leather chair up to the left side of the desk and sat in it. It was soft and comfortable, but its moving parts needed to be oiled as they squeaked whenever he shifted his weight.

Inside the desk's roll-top space was an expansive work surface and, deeper inside, an intricate configuration of wooden drawers, shelves, slots, doors, and latches. As his mother had explained, these things were supposedly riddled with hidden buttons and actuators that revealed even more concealed compartments. She knew of seven such secret spaces and had mentioned that there were many more. But those would all have to wait until another day. Anders first wanted to rummage through the things that were immediately accessible since it would take some time to go through it all. He'd start with the file drawer on the lower, left side of the desk.

He rolled it out about two feet. The entire drawer was about three feet long and packed solid with manila file folders of different colors with tabs labeled mostly with acronyms that he didn't recognize. Some, however, were labeled with things like "Hong Kong," "Paris Consulate," and "Company Receipts."

He pulled out one labeled "Security," placed it on the desktop, and opened it. A quick scan of the 30 or 40 pages of documents indicated they were about general cyber security and the safety of classified documents. Some of the papers were dated just months before his father had passed.

The file also contained papers that outlined procedures for storing sensitive materials on computers and storage devices, and transferring them securely. Anders hadn't found any computers in the study, which was strange. But then he figured his mom might have brought any laptops she'd found downstairs, to her own office.

The third-floor study was exclusively for his father's work, although he now suspected that his mom had spent a lot of time there as well. There was even another desk chair in the corner next to the entrance, so maybe they worked together on occasion. The first-floor office was dedicated to home management – tax records, house upgrade documentation, bills, and user manuals for every device and appliance in the house. Anders had searched through those files numerous times since arriving – including once to find the manual for the washing machine in order to locate a plugged filter, and again to find the instructions on how to reset the garage door opener and program its remote controls. He'd also pulled records on the contractor who did the annual furnace maintenance and set up an appointment, which was arranged for the next day.

That reminded him that it was already Wednesday night, and he'd be leaving on Sunday. The days were flying by, and he had a lot to do – both in the study and around the house.

For the next hour, he pulled all the files in the drawer, one by one, and paged through them. Although none seemed to contain top-secret information, some did seem sensitive. For instance, there were itineraries for trips, meeting schedules, and some travel receipts. What surprised him was that his father had been traveling frequently up until the week he died. His final trip had been to Moscow and, just before that, Hong Kong. The reimbursements were through a company called Space Systems, Inc., but Anders knew that must have been a CIA front company.

What was he doing in Hong Kong and Russia? he wondered. Those trips had taken place near the end of President Crownbrook's first term.

Next, he moved to the file drawer on the far right side of the desk. This one was also packed with file folders, some of which were more like sturdy, file-folder-sized envelopes, bound closed with strings. As he pulled one out and placed it on the desk, he felt a lump inside. The envelope's label read "TF-2020b Report." It meant nothing to Anders.

He unwound the string that held the top flap closed, tilted the envelope upright, and peered inside. There were about 50 pages of loose papers and one stapled document of about 30 pages. There was also a data storage device – a black thumb-drive – at the bottom.

He tipped the envelope and the contents slid out gently onto the desk. The first document he examined was a table of names, locations, functions, and statuses. The names were just first names and numbers, such as "Harry-0987," and "Angel-1223." The locations were not in code – they were all cities in Russia and Eastern Bloc countries. The functions were in code, like "TD" or "SF9," and some people seemed to have multiple functions – up to four in some cases. The statuses were also in code, but one code in particular had an ominous look: "XX" with a date next to it. To Anders, it suggested that those people had died, but maybe it just meant that they'd exited the mission.

He examined the other loose pages and found nothing that looked important, so he moved to the stapled document, which had a cover page with the title, "Operation Titan Feather (Unclassified)." Beneath it were the dates, "17 February 2012 – 30 June 2020." He opened it and read the opening summary, which described the CIA's longstanding mission to inhibit nuclear weapons development in Iran. This specific mission had to do with monitoring Russia's involvement, which was extensive, and interfering in the Iran-Russia partnership. It turned out that Russia had also helped North Korea go nuclear, and it was now providing North Korean technology to Iran. Russia was a troublemaker.

It always baffled Anders why Russia and the West couldn't have found some common ground after teaming up during World War II. He knew the history – many things contributed to the disharmony – but it was disappointing to him. He wondered what the world would have been like without the constant conflict between nations, classes, races, and politics. Would we be more advanced in some way? Or, was the constant, urgent competition generated by those things the mechanism that had *stimulated* development?

He gathered the papers, refiled them, and pulled another envelope. This one was for a project titled "Operation Blue Marlin (Unclassified)," dated 1 July 2015 – 30 June 2019. He pulled out the contents, which again included some loose papers, a stapled document, and a thumb-drive. The abstract described the acquisition of a Chinese spy satellite that had plunged into the South China Sea in early 2015. It had been covertly collected by Navy Seals and delivered to a government contractor called Interstellar Dynamics, based in the DC area, where it had been successfully reverse-engineered.

Anders slipped the folder back into the drawer and pulled another. This one was called "Operation Open Palm (Unclassified)," dated 1 July 2010 – 30 June 2017. He opened the file and pulled out a stapled document, on the front cover of which was his father's handwriting. It read "Third draft." He paged through the summary and found his dad's handwritten editing notes, and then realized that his father must have been the one writing these reports.

It seemed that, during his so-called retirement, Henry Bennett had been reducing classified information into unclassified documents. To write them, however, he must have had access to the classified versions. Anders then suspected that the accompanying thumb-drives contained this secret information, and that they must be ultra-secure, maybe even equipped with self-destruct mechanisms.

He pulled another file and read the abstract. This one was also unfinished and there was no data-storage device in the folder. Instead, there was a note that read, "Electronic files in secure location."

Anders returned the file to the drawer and pulled another. This one read "Custodial Group (Unclassified)." He stared at the title for a few seconds before it hit him: the initials were CG – those of the group to which Harrison had been invited to join as his father's replacement, and to which President Crownbrook supposedly currently belonged.

He pulled out the contents – no thumb-drive – and went directly to the stapled document. This one was only 12 pages and the words "Rough draft" were written on the cover. The dates on the cover page read "15 September 1947 – ." There was no end date, so Anders concluded that the group was still active, at least at the time of writing.

His hands shook as he read. He learned that the Custodial Group managed an off-the-books research operation in Nevada, associated with the famed Area 51. It seemed to be a technology development project, but there were no details. It was common knowledge that the CIA was designing advanced spy planes and carrying out other technological research at that facility and others around the country.

Anders paged through the report. It was so tersely worded that even his father had written notes in the margins saying things like "This says nothing," and "This will be flagged for more details." At the very end of the report, he'd written, "This entire document is unreadable and will irritate the reviewers. We have to at least give some specific technological information, even if it's obsolete, if we expect to be funded at the requested level."

The other papers in the folder were financial documents that had truncated numbers that Anders suspected meant they were in units of millions of US dollars. For instance, the annual personnel costs were 92.5, and the equipment costs were 1225.5. A new lab facility with a massive, underground hangar constructed in fiscal year 2013 reportedly cost 225. If he was right, it was an enormous budget.

At the bottom of the envelope, he found a note that read, "Electronic docs in safe, device# CG1947-1779."

"A safe?" Anders whispered to himself.

He stood and looked around the room. Just about every bit of usable space was occupied by bookshelves or furniture, and even the walls were mostly covered with paintings, maps, and pictures. A small safe could be hidden anywhere – behind a painting, or even in the floor.

Instead of searching for the safe, Anders stayed up until 3:00 a.m. reading every scrap of paper in the Custodial Group file. By the end, he still had no idea what the CG was about, and concluded that any revealing information would be on the thumb-drive stored in the safe, wherever it was. But even if he found the safe and managed to get into it, the device would surely be protected, and he'd risk it self-destructing and losing it forever if he tried to access its contents, even if he got help from DMS experts.

But suppose he made it through all of that and got the info: *should* he read it? He knew well that it was a crime to access top-secret information without authorization. And, even if it wasn't top-secret, he was really researching what the president was doing, and that violated the conditions of service between DMS and the client. It was also Anders' reputation that was at stake: how could anyone trust a courier who nosed into their client's business?

He decided he'd worry about the ethics of the matter when that time came. Meanwhile, he'd ask his mother about the safe, and do his best to get a hold of that thumb-drive.

ANDERS PADDED down the stairs at 6:15 a.m. and was greeted with the aromas of strong coffee and his favorite breakfast.

His timing was perfect: he arrived just as his mother slapped the last two steaming, blueberry pancakes onto a stack to make six.

"Good morning, dear," Gigi said. "How did you sleep?"

"Okay," he replied, as he took his usual seat at the table. "I was up past 3:00 a.m."

She set the plate of pancakes on the table and then went back to the counter and retrieved a carafe of coffee and a porcelain pourer filled with hot maple syrup. "That's just three hours of sleep," she said. "You must feel awful."

"I'm okay – I'm used to weird hours."

"What did you find?" she asked as she flopped two pancakes on his plate and filled his coffee mug. She followed by serving herself.

"How did Dad's CIA duties change after he took on the work-from-home phase?" asked Anders.

She hesitated for a second before responding. "He went to writing declassified reports for the CIA to present to Congress – to the intelligence committees," she explained. "He struggled with them – he said it was like writing stories with no names, no facts, and then trying to ask for billions of dollars to continue the projects. He said he felt like he was always lying by omission."

"Did he ever mention something called the 'Custodial Group' to you?" he asked as he poured hot syrup over his hotcakes.

"Yes, he belonged to that organization," she said, her tone suddenly more serious. Her eyes widened with realization. "My God – that's the 'CG' you mentioned, isn't it?"

"I think so, yes," he replied.

"Why didn't I make that connection when you asked about it?" she said, seemingly annoyed. "Anyway, I think that group scared him a bit and, because of that, it also frightened me. But he never divulged anything specific about it."

"It's classified as 'ATS,' *above top-secret*," he said. "I think it's somehow connected to the project I'm working on now."

"Okay, now it's scaring me again," she said. "What do you know about this *Custodial Group*?"

"Nothing other than it's been mentioned in connection with some serious rumors that have been going around," he explained. "There's something dark going on at the highest levels of our government and I'm not sure I should be a part of it."

"It seems you already are."

"Maybe," he said. "But I don't know if I should be trying to help or hinder what's happening."

"Did you find the files you were looking for?" she asked.

"Yes and no," he replied.

"What do you mean?"

"I have an unfinished report on the 'CG' – the Custodial Group – but it reveals nothing. It reads like, 'Some people are doing things in a secret location, and there are scientists involved. Please continue the funding.'"

She smiled. "That sounds about right."

"Dad even wrote notes saying that it was all rubbish," he said. "But there are *other* files."

"Oh?" Gigi said as she took a big bite of a pancake and a blueberry fell from her fork and splattered on the tablecloth. "Where?"

"Most of the files have data storage devices included with them that I think contain the corresponding classified files," he said. "The CG file, however, does not, but there's a note that says its thumbdrive is in the *safe*. We have a safe?"

She grinned as she moved the blueberry to her plate with her fork and tried to clean the stain it left on the tablecloth with a napkin and water. "Your father said you'd eventually get to this point."

"What do you mean?"

"Henry thought you'd eventually explore his work – starting with the study," she explained. "He figured your current job would lead to it somehow, and to the CIA. He also knew you'd eventually need to get into the safe."

"I'm not sure exactly how," he said, "but the CIA *does* seem to be entangled in my current project."

She nodded. "And it very well could be – or *parts* of it anyway," she said. "Your father told me that there are independent elements within the CIA which are separate from, and immune to, the administration's, or congress's, so-called oversight. And sometimes these internal factions are working against each other – and often don't even realize it. The Custodial Group might be one of these."

"So, there *is* a safe?" he asked.

"There is."

"You have the combination?"

She shook her head. "All I can tell you is that the safe's in the desk."

"Really – in a hidden compartment?"

She nodded. "Yes, and the combination is hidden in yet another compartment. I can show you the ones I know about, but you'll have to hunt for the others. Your father figured it might take you a few hours to locate the ones you need."

Anders' fingers tingled – he wanted to get to it right away. However, he had other things to get done around the house first.

"Do you ever go and poke around in there – try to find new secret compartments?" he asked.

She shook her head. "I haven't gone up there very much since your dad passed," she said. "It's been difficult with him gone."

"I understand."

"Besides, other than the classified details, your father didn't keep any secrets from me – except those about the Custodial Group, of course," she said. "Otherwise, I doubt I'd be surprised by anything you find."

"Can we go up there and take a look after lunch?" he asked.

"Sure," she said. "I'll do some gardening this morning and then we can head up after we eat."

"Sounds good," he said.

Gigi slapped the last two pancakes onto his plate. "More repairs today?"

"I'm going to the hardware store for some supplies to fix the faucet in the utility room, and I'll get a new vent for the clothes dryer."

"That'll be nice," she said. "It'll keep the squirrels out of the house. They got in twice already this year, just after the weather turned warm. I had to chase the crazy little monsters out the front door with a broom."

Anders laughed.

He'd get some satisfaction from doing house maintenance the rest of the morning, but his mind would be on the desk, and the contents of its safe.

It was midmorning on a cool, sunny Thursday, and Maurice had a lot to do if he was to get home in time. Both of his kids were coming home from college for a long weekend, and he wanted to be there for the special dinner his wife was planning for the evening. However, he was going to have to wait for Christine, the woman from the CIA, to get him the results of the background checks on the additional personnel that Eduardo had recommended. After that, he'd have to rush to process those extra crew members so that they could start work on Friday, and that could take hours.

Eduardo's entire team, including the new members, was to start working on Launch Control Station I-1, about 25 miles southwest of Malmstrom Air Force Base. Once the "extras" learned how to prepare the sites for upgrades, they'd move to Launch Facility I-2, another five miles to the south, and get to work. This was Eduardo's strategy to make the modification work more efficient, and Maurice agreed it was a good plan.

It was 11:45 a.m. when he got Christine's call, and he was given the green light on the additional crewmembers. During that call, however, he was informed that there would be other things coming that might require added tweaks to the sites. She wouldn't divulge exactly what those modifications were over the phone, but mentioned that it was a good opportunity to implement "additional upgrades." By the tone of her voice, it sounded like the enhancements would be significant, but wouldn't require much work on his part – or on the part of Eduardo's crew. The implication was that the upgrades would be in the weapons themselves – the missiles – which would mean complete replacements. It was something she'd hinted at during her visit to Malmstrom weeks earlier, and he'd heard the same from the CIA Director soon thereafter.

When he hung up with Christine, he called Eduardo and informed him that everyone on the list was cleared and they should start work the next morning.

Maurice ate lunch in his office as he sent emails to the Malmstrom staff who were responsible for processing new personnel, and arranging housing. He'd walk the paperwork through every office to expedite the process, which would be completed by Friday afternoon – so the crew would have proper, on-base accommodations that evening.

He was pleased to have the group in action in the third week of April, one week ahead of schedule.

Anders followed his mom up the steps to his father's study. When they entered, she stood still for a moment and seemed to take in the scene.

After a few seconds, while Anders thought she might break into tears, she smiled, and said, "I need to come in here and tidy up after you leave." She then went to the north window and opened the blinds. The daylight somehow changed the milieu of the room, giving him a brighter, more hopeful feeling.

"It's not too bad," he said. He could tell that she was straining to keep a happy face. "Just a little dusty."

She went to the desk. "Just like you needed to find the star-shaped button to release the lock so that you could open the desk with the key, you'll have to locate some cleverly concealed mechanisms that reveal other hidden compartments."

"And the safe is in one of those?" he said. "It must be pretty small."

"It's cubic, about 12 inches on a side," she explained. "I know where it's located, but I only vaguely recall the location of the actuator that releases the wooden panel that conceals it."

"The safe must be near the floor," Anders said. "I'm sure it's heavy. If it were too high, it would make the desk unstable. Also, it would require supports that might fatigue over time."

"Very good," she said. "It's in the lower, middle column – behind the drawers."

Anders suddenly recalled that the file drawer in that center column was shorter than those on the ends of the desk. The safe was behind it.

He placed the wooden star in its place, used the key, and elevated the rolltop.

Gigi rolled the chair up to the left side of the desk and sat in it. She then reached into the hutch and opened a tiny, square door to reveal a compartment that was big enough to hold a coffee mug. It was empty.

"This is it, I think," she said as she reached inside and slid her fingers around the interior.

Anders couldn't quite see, but it seemed that she pushed on something on the compartment's ceiling.

"Got it," she said and closed the door. She then stood, moved to the right side of the desk, where a second chair would fit, and felt along the underside of the desktop, near the central bank of drawers.

"Here, look," she said as she moved away from the desk and crouched down.

Anders leaned in and went to one knee to get a good view. There was a small, square hole, about an inch on a side, on the wall of the central column, close to the rear of the desk.

"Inside that compartment is a metal knob," she explained. "Go under there and pull it out about an inch."

Anders got on his knees and crawled under the desk. It was dark, so he pulled out his cell phone and activated its flashlight. It looked as if the square panel that had concealed the compartment had depressed inward and slid to the side. Inside was a silver knob, and he grabbed it between his thumb and forefinger, and pulled.

He had to tug with some force, as if he were working against a spring. At about an inch of displacement, a click and then a twang that sounded like a plucked piano wire came from somewhere inside the desk. He let go of the knob and it settled back into its original position.

He crawled out from under the desk. "Okay, now what?" he asked.

"Now, go under the other side and look around," she instructed.

With his phone still in flashlight mode, he crawled beneath the left side of the desk. He found it near the base of the central column. A square, wooden panel, about a foot on a side, had shifted into the interior and slid to the right, revealing the door to a gray safe with a black dial marked in white numbers from zero to 99.

"Found it!" Anders said as he reverse-crawled out and stood. "Now, where's the combination?"

She smiled.

"Another hidden compartment?" he asked.

She shrugged. "Yes."

"Any idea where it is?"

She shook her head and pointed to the complex of nooks, doors, handles, shelves, and knobs on the desk. "Somewhere in there," she said, as she moved closer to it. "I can narrow it down a little. I know it's a one-step process, unlike the safe's hidden panel, which required two. And I know your father used to fiddle around in this area when he needed it, although I never saw him actually extract something and look at it." She waved her hands around a cluster of doors and knobs on the far-left side.

Anders looked it over. "That might take a while," he said.

"You'll find it, eventually," Gigi said. "Teatime?"

Anders' blood was still doped with adrenaline from discovering the safe, but he could tell that his mom wanted to leave the room. He couldn't even imagine how it must have felt for her to lose her best friend of nearly 50 years, and then have to live in the house where everything from a favorite coffee mug to a painting to a piece of furniture reminded her of him. And he had the impression that the two of them had spent more time together in this room than he'd first imagined. He could almost *see* them working side by side at the enormous desk with soft music playing in the background and the aroma of Earl Grey tea in the air.

His mom was strong, but he was determined to visit her more frequently. He thought it would be good for her. It would be good for him as well.

He followed her down the stairs for tea and cookies.

It was 6:00 p.m. when Harrison got the report from his team about the president's niece, Sara Bradbury. He'd been waiting as patiently as he could in his office as DMS operatives made their way back to headquarters and reported what they'd discovered.

To his disappointment, they'd been unable to approach Bradbury directly but *had* been able to identify the two FBI agents who had interviewed her. DMS had sources inside the FBI, so Harrison would see if he could get more information from them as well. At the moment, he still didn't know what Bradbury had divulged – although he was fairly confident that she didn't know anything that would cause DMS trouble.

Anders was due back Sunday night, and Harrison would have a DMS team on the lookout for any stalkers after his return. He was certain that Anders was in the clear for the time being, but he wondered what was going through his head. From their discussions before he left, he knew Anders was just as suspicious as he was about what was going on with the president. He also wondered what Anders might learn from his mother. Harrison knew that she had been a CIA analyst – something of which he figured Anders was unaware. He had the feeling, however, that with her husband gone, Mrs. Bennett might reveal her past to her son, especially if he started asking questions about his father's involvement in the CG, whatever it was.

He was starting to regret giving Anders that information – especially since Harrison didn't know anything about the objectives of the mysterious group. But maybe Anders would learn something and share it with him. Harrison had always wondered what path his career would have taken had he accepted Henry Bennett's offer. He had the impression that the CG was more like a secret society than a mere club of CIA ops.

He grabbed a cola from a small refrigerator and then took his phone to the couch. There was some new information that was bothering him. His CIA sources informed him that an associate director of the CIA had been questioned by the FBI about the two double homicides in Southern California, and that the victims were connected to a secret group called the Single-World Alliance, or the SWA. Harrison looked into it and learned that the SWA was akin to the CG in some ways – meaning that it was a "deep state" subgroup that had its own agenda, independent of whatever administration occupied the White House. There seemed to be some differences, however. Whereas the CG was presumably composed exclusively of CIA people, the SWA was supposedly an eclectic group of domestic and foreign intelligence operators, politicians, and wealthy civilians – many of whom were affiliated with large defense contractors. More concerning to DMS, however, was that the CIA administrator, who was suspected of being an SWA member, was also being questioned about alleged, secret communications between the White House and foreign operatives.

Was Crownbrook using other communications channels for his secret communications? If so, it confused things, since DMS operatives could get reports about investigations into the president's dealings and not know whether or not they involved the company. This latest CIA report fit precisely into this category: it might not involve DMS at all. However, any investigation that involved the president at this point increased the risk to DMS.

He took a gulp of soda and leaned back on the couch. He usually loved mysteries. This one, however, had some potentially serious consequences. DMS was certainly at risk, but it was more than that. A queasy feeling had been welling in his gut for weeks. There was something significant going on, and it seemed to him that it was more serious than the usual political shenanigans that every administration was compelled to generate. There was a real feeling of danger, even impending doom, in this one, and it frightened him.

Harrison finished his soda, grabbed his jacket from the closet, and headed for the door. It was date night with his wife, and he was meeting her at his favorite restaurant – Argentinian food. He was in the mood for a steak. He just hoped he could calm his mind enough to enjoy it.

AFTER TEA IN THE AFTERNOON, Anders finished a few projects around the house, which included fixing a jammed drawer in the kitchen, and then had spaghetti and meatballs with his mother for dinner. After cleaning up the dishes, they watched two episodes of a popular TV series based on the thriller novels by Tom Clancy.

It was 10:00 p.m. when his mother went to bed and Anders headed to his father's study. He sat in the chair and used his fingertips to probe every surface and crevice in the general area his mom had identified that afternoon in search of the hidden compartment that contained the combination to the safe.

Within an hour, he'd revealed three such compartments. One was opened by twisting a knob whose function at first seemed to be only as a grip to open a tiny door. He discovered another by depressing a hidden button on the interior wall of a cubby shelf. Finally, a tiny door popped open on the left side of the desktop when he pushed on the edge of one of the six, letter-sized shelves in that same area. The revealed compartments were of varying shapes, but were small – just large enough to hold a coffee mug or a small book. Two of the three were empty. The third contained a silver wristwatch with a metal band, which looked rather plain but seemed to be valuable. It had the words "Vacheron Constantin" in small, black letters on its white face, and there were two dials, presumably for two different time zones. He put it back into its compartment.

He spent the next two hours pulling, pushing, and twisting every knob, drawer handle, and shelf, and poking on every exposed surface to see if he could find more hidden compartments. He discovered three more but they were all empty. Frustrated, he leaned back in the chair and sighed. Could it be that his dad had removed the combination from one of the voids he'd already discovered?

His attention was redirected to the only thing he'd found – the watch. He grabbed his phone and searched for "Vacheron Constantin." The results that came up startled him for a second. It was a brand that was even more prestigious than Rolex. He couldn't determine the model of this particular watch, but similar-looking ones on the website were listed for nearly fifty thousand dollars.

He retrieved the watch from its compartment and examined it more closely. He flipped it over and looked at its backside. There was an inscription:

May our eyes one day be opened ...
13-23-72

Anders stared at the words for a while. What did the inscription mean? And who had given the watch to his father? Was it the same person who had given him the desk? Then it struck him that the numbers couldn't be a date – none of them could correspond to a month.

Trembling with excitement, he pulled the chair away from the desk and turned on his phone's flashlight. He crawled beneath the desk and found the safe – the wooden panel was still open, as he'd left it that afternoon. He turned the dial to the right three or four rotations and stopped on the first number, rotated to the left, past the second number, and then landed on it the second time around. Finally, going to the right, he stopped on the third number. He took a deep breath and then tried to turn the handle. It didn't budge.

His heart sank.

"What?" he muttered.

He rotated the dial to the right a few turns and repeated the procedure. Again, the handle didn't budge. He then tried dialing it in with all the rotations reversed. No luck.

He looked closer at the safe and found a company name in white lettering on the bottom left: Sorensen Safes, Inc.

He backed out from under the desk, sat on the floor, and leaned his back against the left-side column of drawers. He turned off his phone's flashlight, opened a web browser, and typed, "How to open a Sorensen safe."

A long list of links scrolled down his screen with images of Sorensen-brand safes. Some were links to written instructions, and others went to videos. He clicked on a video that had an image of a safe that resembled the model in the desk. He soon learned that the combination wasn't entered in the same way as one might open a standard padlock. There were more turns between numbers, and it didn't even stop on the final number – there was a final one-eighth turn in the direction opposite to that in which the last number was approached.

Anders went back under the desk and carefully followed the prescription. When he reversed direction for that final one-eighth turn, he felt tension in the dial, just as the person in the video had described.

When he attempted to turn the handle, it moved with some resistance and clicked.

His heart picked up pace. He pulled the door open – it was heavier and thicker than he'd anticipated.

The first thing he saw inside was the black handle of a gun. It reminded him that, although this was some kind of an adventure for him, there were serious implications associated with everything he was doing.

He grabbed the gun, a Glock-19, and peeked into the chamber – it was empty. He placed it on the floor next to him.

Next, he spotted a rectangular, wooden box, about four by eight inches, and two inches thick. He reached in, extracted it, and set it next to the gun. Next was a bound stack of money, over a half-inch thick. He pulled it out and fanned through it. It astonished him that they were all hundred-dollar bills – meaning that it totaled in the tens of thousands of dollars. Deeper inside were six flat, one-ounce bars of pure gold, each sealed in clear plastic. These Anders had seen before. He recalled his dad had gotten interested in investing, and was convinced that everyone who had the resources should have at least some gold in their possession.

Finally, there was a letter-sized, brown envelope, which he removed and held in the light of his phone. His ears started ringing when he realized what was written on it, in his father's handwriting: *For Anders*.

He crawled partway out, sat on the floor, and leaned his back against the inner wall under the desk so that he could see the envelope in the overhead lighting of the room. He opened it and read:

WELL DONE, young man. You found your way inside – using the watch (which is now yours). I was hoping that, one day, you'd follow in my footsteps. However, I realized, and perhaps it was you who taught me this, that everyone takes a different path to happiness.

If you are still young, then you have searched for the contents of this safe for a reason. I, of course, cannot know exactly why, but you should proceed with great caution. If you are old, then I suggest you destroy the contents of the wooden box and live out your life in peace.

If your mother is still with you, please tell her that I love her.
I love you both with all of my existence.
-Dad

P.S. If you have not yet explored the "CG," you should. There are tightly-held secrets in your world.

. . .

A tear trickled down Anders' cheek as he read it again. He then folded the letter and slipped it back into its envelope. He missed his father, and he regretted not following in his footsteps. Nonetheless, he found himself looking inside the safe while he was still young. He *was* there for a reason, and he *was* going to explore the Custodial Group.

He put the money, gun, and letter back into the safe, picked up the wooden box from the floor, and crawled out from under the desk. He placed the box on the desk and examined it.

Its finished wood was dense, like hickory. It had golden-brass hinges and a heavy, matching latch that had a loop through which one could place a lock, but there wasn't one. He thought it resembled something that might hold an expensive piece of jewelry.

He unbuckled the latch, which made a sharp snapping sound, and opened the lid.

Inside was a five-by-twelve array of data storage drives, each held securely in a form-fitted, felt-lined depression. Of the 60 slots, only four were vacant. For an instant, Anders worried that the one he needed would be missing, but he disregarded his panic – his father had even mentioned "CG" in his note.

He extracted one of the devices: it looked like an ordinary, black thumb-drive, with a string of letters and numbers printed on its backside in white characters. He was curious about the contents of all the drives, but he wasn't going to plug any of them into his laptop. He'd get help from DMS experts to check for self-destruct mechanisms on the one he intended to take, and also to decrypt the information, if needed.

He pulled the CG file out of a drawer, opened it, and found the document that had the label for the drive: CG1947-1779. He then pulled thumb-drives out of the box, one by one, looking for the one with that ID. He started with the drive in the upper left and proceeded systematically down the row, and then back along the one below it. Somewhere in the middle, he found the one he sought. He placed it on the desk, closed the box, and went under the desk and returned the box to the safe. He grabbed the letter and then closed the safe, rotated the dial a few turns, and tugged on the door to make sure it was secure.

A panicked thought struck him: he had to make sure to never put the watch in the safe. He then figured that he better write the combination down or, better, store it electronically in a way that only he would know what it was.

He grabbed the watch again and examined it. It was simple but elegant. But it was definitely too expensive to be wearing on his own wrist. Maybe, one day, he'd have an occasion to wear it. He took out his phone and snapped pictures of the front and back: he now had an image of the combination.

He slipped the watch back into its hiding place and closed the door.

Anders then went around to the right side of the desk. Low, near the back, was a hole with a curved crank sticking out of it. Just as his mother had instructed that afternoon, he turned it clockwise. It required a fair amount of torque to rotate, and it made a sound like that of winding an enormous clock as he did so. After three and a half rotations, a loud click sounded from somewhere inside the desk. The spring that powered the multitude of concealed mechanisms in the desk's innards was reset.

He pulled the crank out of the hole and placed it on a nearby bookshelf.

He then peeked under the desk and saw that the panel that had originally concealed the safe was now closed. All the other hidden compartments had also reset.

With the thumb-drive in his front pants pocket and the letter in his hand, he headed to his bedroom. It was already 2:00 a.m. and breakfast would be ready by 6:30 a.m. He was going to have trouble falling asleep.

CHAPTER 7

The aromas of nutmeg, maple syrup, and coffee entranced Anders as he made his way down the stairs.

"Good morning," he said as he entered the kitchen and walked over to his mom, who was pouring hot coffee into a carafe. He kissed her on the cheek and grabbed two white, porcelain mugs out of a cupboard. "Breakfast smells great."

"Did you find what you needed last night?" Gigi asked.

He explained everything as they settled at the table and started eating French toast. He told her about the watch, and how to open the safe, and then described its contents. He handed her the note.

She read it and smiled.

"I was there when he wrote this," she said. "But I didn't know he added the part about telling me that he loved me." Her eyes became glassy.

"Are you okay?"

"I miss him," Gigi said. "But the things that remind me of him no longer make me sad. They make me happy. They make me appreciate him."

Anders understood, but they still made *him* sad. He supposed he hadn't been in the house every day for three years, as she had. Her grief must have progressed more than his.

"There's a stack of money in the safe," Anders said. "I didn't count it, but it was thousands."

"It's 20 thousand," she said.

"What's it for?"

"Emergency funds," she replied. "For you – not me, dear."

"What?" he said. "I don't need any money. That should stay here for you, just in case."

"And your father wanted you to have his watch," she said. "As you know, the safe's combination is inscribed on it."

"You knew."

"I was going to tell you this morning if you didn't figure it out," she said. "The watch came with the desk."

"The man who gave it to him must have been a good friend."

"You should take it when you go," she said.

"I can't believe I'm leaving the day after tomorrow," he said. The week had flown by but it also seemed like he'd been away from DMS for much longer than he had. So much was going on there – a week was like an eternity. "About the watch, I'll keep it here for the time being. I think I'll need to get it insured before I take it anywhere."

"You're taking the data drive?" she asked.

He nodded. "I'll let DMS take a crack at getting into it," he explained. "I need to know what this is all about."

"I understand," she said. "I'd help you myself, but I had nothing to do with encrypting those files. I only helped your father with direct communications – emailing files and the like."

"It's okay."

"You should be extremely careful about with whom you talk about this," Gigi said, her expression conveying anxiety. "Your father was beyond paranoid about keeping the Custodial Group secret."

"You don't know *anything*?" Anders asked.

Gigi smiled and shook her head. "Your father used to say that there was only one secret that he would keep from me – and that was it," she said. "He told me that it was something dangerous – that people would kill to get more information about it, or to safeguard it. He also said it was something that would alter my view of reality, and that it might actually change the world one day."

"Why did he arrange for *me* to get it?" Anders asked.

"Well, you don't exactly have it yet, do you?"

"No, but – "

"He figured you might need it one day," she said.

"The president is a member of the Custodial Group," Anders said. "And my boss, Harrison, was invited to join – by Dad – but he declined."

She raised an eyebrow. "Perhaps Harrison was smart to stay out of it," she said. "It was something that was constantly on your father's mind. Maybe your boss saved himself a lifelong obsession."

Anders sensed some resentment. "Are you disappointed that Dad didn't tell you about it?"

She glanced at him and her face flushed for an instant. "No, of course not," she rebutted. "I'm sure he had his reasons."

"If I find out what it is, I'll tell you," he said. "You must be able to keep secrets, too."

"I was just an interpreter and analyst – ciphers and things," she said.

"Yes, that was a great cover," he said and gave her a look suggesting that he knew there was more.

She smiled. "Okay," she said. "I *do* have a few secrets of my own – nothing that pertains to your situation though. If I did, I'd spill the beans."

She grabbed a second piece of French toast for herself, and then put two more on Anders plate. "What's on the agenda for today?"

"I need to replace a windowpane in the back of the garage," he said. "And the roof to your garden shed has a few missing shingles. I'll head to the hardware store after breakfast."

"They should know you by name over there by now," she said.

"They do," he said, and then sighed. "I miss working on the house with Dad. But now I find it to be calming."

"I understand," she said and smiled. "I'll be gardening in the morning, and then cooking your favorite for dinner later this afternoon."

"Homemade pizza?" Anders asked, knowing the answer. It was so thick that it was more like a pie, and he'd never been able to eat more than two slices.

They finished breakfast and Anders helped clean the kitchen before heading to the store. As he drove, he realized the coming weekend was the last span of relaxation time that he'd have for a while.

He was excited to learn what the thumb-drive had to tell him about the Custodial Group. But he had foreboding premonitions of where it might lead. He had no specific ideas – not even justified suspicions of what it was about – but his thoughts were somehow shrouded in darkness. Something unusual was afoot, and he sensed that it would have global repercussions.

It was 6:15 a.m. on Friday morning when Captain Eduardo Pacquiao briefed his team on the long-term task that lay ahead. Including him, there were ten in the crew, each of them one of the best in their respective specialties.

The job was originally planned to take 15 weeks but he knew they might expand the number of silos to 25. The bottleneck was in the delivery of some of the supplies, especially the communications gadgetry they needed.

Everyone on the team was required to reside on the base, under the watchful eye of CIA and Air Force security, when they weren't working in the field. Although they'd been informed of this requirement, some of the crew were already talking about holidays and family events, such as the Fourth of July, as if they were going to be able to make them. Unfortunately, they'd signed contracts in which they'd agreed to some things that were out of the ordinary. One such clause indicated that, even if they quit the team, they'd be confined to the base until the entire project was completed.

Eduardo doubted anyone would quit, but he might have to deal with some bellyaching when certain holidays or family birthdays came around, or when the weather got warm. But they were professionals, and he knew they'd work hard and produce a quality product.

His larger concern was with the questions that might arise while they were in the midst of the project. Everyone was smart enough to know that they were doing something unusual, and the severe secrecy requirement only brought about more suspicion. He'd worry about that later. In the meantime, he'd concentrate on getting the job done.

Eduardo went to his second in command, Second Lieutenant Sammy Paulson, a lanky, 40-year-old woman from northern Montana. "How are we doing, Paulson?" he asked.

"All packed, Captain," she replied. "We'll need to take a couple of hours tonight to get everything set up for tomorrow."

Today they were just going to disassemble parts of Launch Control Station I-1 in order to expose the areas on which they'd have to work the next day. It was convenient that Malmstrom was centrally located with respect to the distribution of the sites that they were upgrading, and I-1 was only 25 miles southwest of the base. If they needed something from their hangar at Malmstrom, they could get it within an hour.

The main problem with which they'd have to contend was the weather. April in Montana could be unpredictable, but his crew was used to it.

"Okay, let's move out," Eduardo yelled.

They all packed into three rugged, all-terrain military trucks, and Eduardo jumped into the cab of the one Sammy was driving.

"Lead the way, Sammy," Eduardo said.

"Yes, sir," she said and started the truck.

The sun was just starting to light the sky as they exited the enormous hangar and turned toward the base's southern exit. It was going to be a cool, clear day. It was also going to be a strange day for Eduardo. They were embarking on something that he didn't completely understand. Deep inside, he was uneasy, as if he sensed that what they were doing was leading somewhere dark.

To add to his anxiety, the CIA had given him an "extra" task about which even his commanding officer, Colonel Spelling, was unaware. They'd explained it to him when he'd gone to CIA headquarters in DC to be vetted and briefed. It was a job that Eduardo could easily handle, but it would put him in an awkward position if it were discovered. But it wasn't as if Colonel Spelling would inspect their work and, if he did, it was unlikely that he'd notice the subtle differences from the original plans: Spelling was no electronics expert.

Eduardo pushed his anxiety aside. He was only following orders, and he had to assume that those above him – those with the bigger picture – knew what they were doing. He just hoped they'd considered all the possible problems that could arise from having the ability to short-circuit the safety interlocks on an intercontinental ballistic missile launch system.

It was 10:00 a.m. when Maurice got the call on his office phone. It was Eduardo, who reported that the full contingent of specialists had entered the first missile silo on the docket, and started work. Before ending the call, Eduardo listed a few additional things that the crew would need once the installment of the auxiliary electronics had started.

To Maurice, it was an enormous relief that the project was starting on time – even a little early. However, new things were popping up, the most serious of which was that another missile site had been invaded by a drone during the night. This one, in North Dakota, was a part of the Minuteman III network controlled by Minot Air Force Base. It was the tenth incursion in the last three weeks, and every one of those reports made Maurice's mind go to the darkest of places.

The world had been relatively peaceful since World War II. There had been other wars, of course, but nothing that had been a threat to human existence. And why was that? Maurice figured it had to do with a balance of power, which meant some level of parity in technology, including nuclear weapons. At least it could be argued that no evil dictator had acquired a devastating weapon that no one else had. What would have happened to the world had Adolf Hitler acquired the atomic bomb before the Allies? The idea was not unique, of course, considering the innumerable alternate-history novels that had been written on this premise. And there were other versions of the idea: what if Russia had been the only country to develop nuclear weapons? Maurice knew that, had that been the case, the world would now be a very different place, and probably one he wouldn't like. Thus, nuclear weapons were the great equalizer between the most powerful nations, which had kept them from going to war with one another – even a conventional war. They only fought through proxies.

But it now seemed that things were starting to change. During the Cold War, the two adversaries were racing for advancements that would give them an edge. That edge had gone back and forth many times, but not enough to give one country the confidence to attempt to take down the other – the projected costs on both sides had always made it untenable.

Since the Cold War, countries other than Russia and the US had anted up to the nuclear pot. This put them, in some sense, on equal footing with the big two. Starting in the 1990s, China emerged both economically and militarily, and the two superpowers then expanded into the "big three." Now, the UK, Israel, Pakistan, India, North Korea, Iran, and others were in the nuclear weapons club, and the world was on the brink of war again, even though most people hadn't yet realized it.

It was as if a dozen monsters were all trying to get through the same door at the same time, and none were passing through because they were all jammed tightly in the frame, struggling, but making no headway. But there would come a day when one of them would squeeze through, and that one might be the overall winner. It would be the country that developed something that could defeat the superweapons of the others – either by rendering them useless, or by developing something far better. That nation, if it had such intentions, and had the right leader, might take over the entire world. And Maurice didn't think he could live in such a world.

Although no one could prove it definitively, the running theory was that the drones that had infiltrated the US launch sites belonged to China. Maurice, however, now leaned toward the Russians being responsible, based entirely on proximity. He thought it might not be difficult getting them from Russia into Alaska. From there, it would be much easier to smuggle the drones into the US through Canada.

On second thought, if they were small, it might not be difficult to get them into the US through any of its borders, or even through its ports. In fact, they could be brought in piece-by-piece, and then assembled near the location from which they were to be deployed. It wasn't the fact that they'd been brought into the US undetected that was the problem. All kinds of contraband, from guns to drugs to humans, were being smuggled over the borders every day. Instead, it was the very existence of the technology that was the real threat. Anything that could take control of a secure facility like a US nuclear missile launch station could also sneak up to the White House one night and destroy it, throwing the country into chaos – especially if no one could prove who was responsible.

Who was going to be that first monster to get through the door?

The problem with the latest string of drone incursions was that he was going to have to attend yet another briefing. As it turned out, the most recently violated site had just undergone security upgrades that included state-of-the-art tracking and targeting systems equipped with surface-to-air missiles. It was discovered that the drones could not be tracked, and the targeting systems couldn't lock onto them. In one case, eyewitnesses had claimed that the object they'd encountered moved slowly, and seemed to hover silently a few hundred yards from the control center, just 150 feet off the ground. These direct, visual observations were suspect since the incident had occurred at night, but the witnesses said it seemed larger than a typical drone – about the size of a twin-engine Cessna – although they couldn't describe its shape.

During this incursion, the entire missile site had blacked out – even the emergency circuits had been disabled. The craft then fled at great speed and low altitude and disappeared over the horizon. Twenty minutes after the incident, the control station came back online, and there was no damage except for some blown fuses on the emergency backup power system.

Those responsible for the infiltrations were becoming progressively more brazen. But that most recent event, and any new ones to come, would only strengthen his commitment to the mobile launch project. It was becoming clear that such an option was needed.

Maurice packed his bag and locked his computer before putting on his jacket and heading for the door. It was time to go to Minot, North Dakota for the briefing. One nice thing about working on an Air Force base was that air transportation was always ready to go, especially when traveling from one base to another. Technically, Malmstrom did not operate as an active air base, which one might think was odd. However, aircraft could still land for maintenance and upgrades, and personnel could hop on planes as they came and went. This time, he'd jump a ride in a KC-135 Stratotanker to Minot Air Force Base. The aircraft had just undergone maintenance service at Malmstrom and was due for a test flight.

Maurice twitched as a thought came to him. For some reason, this meeting had to be held in person rather than online. They must have acquired some new information. He'd find out in a couple of hours.

Harrison stared at the mobile phone vibrating on his desk. It was the line dedicated to the president – a satellite phone with heavy-duty encryption.

He picked it up and took the call.

"This is Bob," Harrison said.

"This is Frank," a man said. Even though the phone was secure, they never used real names.

Harrison recognized the voice, and the name the man used to identify himself indicated that everything was currently okay and he wasn't under duress, although that would be quite disturbing considering that he was the president. The codename he'd use if he were in trouble was either "Jim," or his real name.

"How can I help you?" Harrison asked.

"I have an outgoing message for both outside parties," Crownbrook said. "Coming to you now."

A message popped up on the phone informing him of an incoming file and asking permission to download it. Harrison accepted the file and the download was confirmed a few seconds later.

"Anything else?" Harrison asked.

"Incoming deliveries are expected soon. Be careful. People are getting suspicious," Crownbrook said. "Even family members are being harassed, as you know. That situation has come to an end – no big revelations."

Harrison knew that the president was talking about his niece, Sara Bradbury, being brought in by the FBI.

"Good to hear. We've confirmed that with our own sources as well," Harrison said, referring to the info he'd gotten from a recent chat between DMS personnel and an FBI agent who had been present during the interview.

"We're pushing things a little harder now," Crownbrook said. "Your activity will increase during the coming weeks."

"Understood," Harrison said, and then the president ended the call.

Harrison was glad that Crownbrook was familiar with secure communications equipment. It reminded him again that the president had been in the CIA – and was likely still active since he was a CG member. Harrison tried to recall whether there had been any other presidents who'd been in the CIA. He didn't mean those appointed to a position, as was the case with H. W. Bush. Rather, he meant someone who had come up through the ranks as a case officer, reports officer, or even an analyst. He couldn't think of any.

Then it hit him: not only was Crownbrook former CIA, but the Russian president, Anatoly Kurmaev, was former KGB and SVR, and the Chinese leader, Huang Jinping, had been an operative in his country's Ministry of State Security, or MSS. They were *all* former spooks. What did that mean?

Harrison knew that the CIA was a vast entity that held more secrets than any one person could be allowed to know – and that included the president. He could only assume that it was the same for the spy agencies of the other two superpowers involved in the underground communications threesome. But, again, the thing that was odd about the current situation was that *all three* leaders had full-blown careers in their respective intelligence agencies before ascending to power.

Harrison marked it as a unique occurrence, but probably just a coincidence. The concern, however, was that intelligence services were essentially conducting a war at all times – spying never ended, nor did the perceived need for every country to get an edge on the others. Perhaps the three leaders were just continuing the battles they were fighting when they were intelligence ops.

He took the data card out of the satellite phone and then picked up his desk phone and summoned the computer specialist. Two copies would be made of the outgoing data – one for China and one for Russia. The data would be decrypted, encrypted using a different method, and then written to a data storage device without anyone seeing any of it. It was a procedure that delivered the privacy and security that DMS promised.

Harrison had been contemplating, however, whether or not that promise should be kept, considering the rumors of what was happening, even though they were unsubstantiated. He supposed the stories connected to the partially decoded message intercepted by Chinese intelligence were also hearsay, but there were numerous other things – like the murders on the West Coast that were somehow connected to everything that was happening. There was a point at which circumstantial evidence warranted a closer look at things, and he felt the situation was approaching that point.

It reminded him that Anders would be back from his hiatus the day after next, and that he had something of importance which required the computer expertise of DMS – something to do with their current operation.

The idea that Crownbrook would now be "pushing things a little harder" incited a sense of urgency that Harrison had to resist. He had to delay his impulse to read the president's messages at least until more solid information was revealed. His company's reputation was at stake. If he did finally break DMS's confidentiality agreement, he would be compelled to act on whatever he discovered.

THE RULE WAS that his crew and equipment should be back in Hangar 14 before dark, and Eduardo nearly failed that order on the very first day. The reason for the curfew was twofold. First, no ordinary maintenance crew would work after dusk, and doing so would draw unwanted attention. Second, the drones came out at night, and all precautions were to be taken to make sure they didn't get a whiff of what Eduardo's people were doing.

Progress on Silo I-1 was going as planned except for a few minor glitches. The technical drawings did not exactly match the electrical wiring at the site, and some of the structural features deviated from the construction blueprints. It was his guess that every site would vary to some degree from their respective technical drawings. It was something that often happened when a construction crew had to improvise for some reason and didn't report the alteration since they figured it either didn't matter, or that it would never be noticed.

Eduardo went to the mess hall with the crew and then headed to Colonel Spelling's office by 7:30 p.m. for a briefing. When he arrived, Maurice's door was closed, but he could hear his muffled voice inside.

Eduardo knocked; someone seemed to mumble something behind the door and then went quiet.

"Come in," the voice finally said, and Eduardo entered and closed the door behind him.

Maurice was sitting behind his desk, on the far left end of the room. "How did it go today?" he asked.

"Other than the inaccurate blueprints, it went well," Eduardo replied. He wasn't going to mention that they'd barely made it in before dark.

"The extra equipment and supplies that you requested have been ordered," Maurice said. "It should all be here by Tuesday."

Eduardo was surprised at the quick turnaround. "We didn't anticipate having to cut through carbide plates to get access to some of the parts," he explained. "It wasn't in the plans."

"It's okay, we'll solve problems as they arise," Maurice said. "Did you get any questions from your crew about the project?"

Maurice shook his head. "No, I think they all know why we're doing it," he said. "It was clear to them that someone has found a weakness and we're constructing the patch."

"And that's all accurate," Maurice said. "Except we're not going through normal channels for these modifications."

Eduardo nodded. "And that's the only thing causing suspicion with my people," he said. "They were wondering why they had to go through extra background checks for a job that otherwise seems routine."

Maurice nodded. "I figured that might be the case, but the CIA insisted," he explained. "I think they suspect that someone from a maintenance crew was responsible for leaking vital information about the control stations in the past – giving our adversaries the intelligence they then used to cause the problems we're experiencing now. The CIA wanted to make sure that those involved in this crucial upgrade were squeaky clean."

"One of my crew asked whether the upgrades actually introduce a new vulnerability into the system," Eduardo said. "We're effectively creating a back door that can be exploited."

"That's true," Maurice admitted. "And that's why only a small fraction of the sites will have this extra functionality. It's also why this project is deemed top secret."

Eduardo was convinced that the operation was justified, though he still had reservations. But his opinions on the matter weren't relevant – such decisions were above his paygrade, and also beyond his responsibility. If something bad happened and someone got unauthorized access, that was on the brass, not on him or his crew. His job was to make sure the upgrades were installed properly and that they functioned as designed.

"Anything else?" Maurice asked.

"We're going to have to train crews to *operate* these new systems," Eduardo said. "We can't do that and work on the modifications at the same time."

Maurice nodded. "Working on it," he said. "The plan is for you to train the first mobile crew, and then that group will train the rest. You'll train that first crew after you've renovated a few launch sites."

Maurice dismissed him and Eduardo left the office building.

On his way back to the hangar, Eduardo stopped, sat on a bench outside an administrative building, and placed a call on his mobile to "Christine," the CIA contact who managed the project. He informed her of their progress, with a few details beyond what he'd reported to Maurice. He also gave her specifics regarding the additional communications equipment he needed for his "extra task," and she assured him that they'd be discretely packaged with the things he'd just ordered through Maurice. He was in an awkward position, having two bosses: his formal one, Maurice, and his secret one – CIA Christine.

After making a final check on his crew, Eduardo would make a stop at the base's general store to pick up some snacks and then head to his quarters. There was a soccer match he intended to watch at 8:00 p.m., and he'd call his wife at halftime. He missed her and the kids already. It was going to be a tough few months.

ANDERS THOUGHT DRIVING on a Sunday was always a good time since traffic was light. The weather forecast indicated clear skies all the way up to DC. He left Genesee Lake around 7:30 a.m. after a hearty breakfast of scrambled eggs and bacon. His mom packed him a bag of brownies for the ride.

He was sad to leave. They'd enjoyed a relaxing week together that was therapeutic for both of them. He'd also gotten some satisfaction out of making repairs around the house.

The visit had also been revealing: he'd learned some extraordinary things about both his parents. First, his mom had been a CIA analyst while he was growing up, not just a contracted translator. Next, his father had never really retired from the CIA. To the very end, he'd been declassifying documents for top-secret projects, and it seemed he'd been an active participant in at least some of those operations. Finally, his mom had confirmed that his dad had been a member of the mysterious Custodial Group, or CG, something about which Anders hoped to learn more in the coming days. That, of course, hinged on whether DMS would be able to extract the data on the thumb-drive he'd retrieved from the safe.

The hours of driving on the nearly vacant highway gave him the opportunity to think without distraction. It was clear that his dad had *expected* him to find the information about the Custodial Group, and had therefore not been concerned about Anders learning of his involvement in the secretive organization. On the other hand, it could be that he'd wanted Anders to *expose* the group, or at least to reveal the sectioned-off information that the organization was concealing, which was still an unknown. Anders had the impression that the CG was something like a clandestine society whose function was to maintain a specific secret and, possibly, had a central objective. Unfortunately, the watered-down file he'd read about it revealed nothing.

After ten hours of driving, and only a few brownies left in the bag, Anders pulled the rental car into the parking lot of a large home improvement store a mile outside downtown Alexandria. A DMS operative would eventually pick it up and return it to the car rental company. He then arranged a SuperLift ride, which dropped him off a few blocks from his apartment.

It was the end of April, and the Northeast was suffering a cold snap that involved harsh winds and temperatures. As he walked face-first into the cutting wind, he longed to be back in Georgia.

It was going on 6:00 p.m. when he got back to his apartment. He unpacked his duffle bag, ordered a pizza for dinner, and turned on the TV. For some reason, the remote wasn't where he usually left it and, when he turned on the television, it was on a reality channel that he never watched, which was odd. He then remembered that DMS had inserted a "stand-in" while he was out of town in order to test the security of his apartment, and to determine if he was being surveilled. It must have been deemed all clear.

He flipped through the cable news channels, which were focused on the story of a late winter storm that had hit the Upper Midwest, dropping more than two feet of snow, and forcing some businesses and schools to close for a couple of days. That front would make its way to him in the next few days, thereby extending the bad weather they were currently having. Between the weather-related "breaking news" segments were reports about the escalation of words and geopolitical posturing between the "big three" nations. They continued to blame each other for exactly the same things.

Anders thought it unlikely that all three would use the same method to probe and harass the others. He figured *one* country was behind all of it and, from that government's perspective, the other two blaming each other did well to confuse the situation.

He flipped the station to a sitcom just as the buzzer next to his apartment door sounded, indicating that his pizza had arrived. He hurried down to the lobby, picked it up, and was back on his couch a few minutes later, devouring a slice as he watched his program and tried to unwind.

Even though he had intended to ignore it for a while, his thoughts went to the flash-drive in his backpack. He had reservations about giving DMS access to its secrets before he knew what was on it. He wasn't sure that his father would have wanted it exposed in that way – maybe he'd intended for only Anders to see it, or at least to see it *first*.

Then why would he pack it away in such a secure storage device? he wondered. He was beginning to think that maybe it wasn't so secure – after all, it was already locked in a safe. What if it was just a normal thumb-drive and the documents it contained weren't even encrypted?

Anders decided that he'd ask the DMS computer techs to determine only if and how the device was protected, and not to do anything else with it. If it wasn't protected in any way, he'd look over the materials in private. If it *did* have anti-tampering mechanisms, then he'd have no choice but to let DMS specialists find a way around them.

With the usual uncanny timing, his phone vibrated, indicating he'd received a text message from Harrison. He was asking Anders if he'd made it home and informing him that he wanted to meet first thing in the morning. Then Harrison's second text came, which read, "Our client needs to accelerate activity."

Anders responded immediately, saying that he was home and that he'd stop by Harrison's office as soon as he got into work in the morning.

So much was happening, and Anders was in the middle of it all, like a fly entangled in a spider's web.

CANDACE WAS EATING a breakfast bagel at her office desk at 7:30 a.m. when she learned the news. It was an email from her supervisor.

Another man that the recently deceased Wilfred Carrigan had identified on the list of potential Single-World Alliance members was found murdered in his home. This one was another professional hit – two bullets in the 90-year-old's head. The former Area 51 engineer, a widower, had resided in Hawaii since he'd retired at age 84. They found him in a hammock on his back porch.

She felt sick to her stomach. Now *five* people were dead. Without a doubt, the hits had been triggered by their investigation. She could tell that Tim, who was sitting in a trance at his desk on the other side of the office, was feeling the guilt as well.

"You realize that we submitted his name with the Carrigans' and Mackenbergs' when we requested authorization for our West Coast trip," Tim said. "I remember because I was hoping for a trip to Honolulu."

"We provide no names from now on – to anyone," she said. If there was a leak in the FBI, then there was no one they could trust.

"I heard that they interviewed the president's niece," Tim said.

"Who did?"

"*We* did – the FBI."

"That's a big deal – calling in a president's family member," Candace said. "Why did they bring her in?"

"Rumors of backchannel communications," he replied.

"So, someone else is working on the same thing we are," she concluded.

Tim shrugged. "Maybe," he said. "But she was cleared."

"Who else are they looking into?"

Tim shrugged. "I've heard nothing else."

"We better get moving then – we don't want to get scooped on this."

She looked over the list of names that Wilfred had checked as confirmed SWA members. Most were dead, but some still had living spouses. For those who didn't, Candace was considering contacting their children.

The assassinations only strengthened her resolve. The added fact that the FBI had questioned Crownbrook's niece made her feel more urgency and anxiety about the investigation. It meant she and Tim were sticking their noses into something big.

ANDERS TOOK extra precautions while making his way to DMS headquarters in the frigid morning air. He made one stop at a drugstore and purchased some over-the-counter meds for migraines. He felt one coming on, and he was out of his medication and didn't want to get caught without it. The pills only helped if he took them right away – when the first symptoms appeared – otherwise he'd be out of commission for at least 12 hours. He was seeing hints of white speckles of light in his peripheral vision, which was the telltale indicator that one was developing.

He then made a second stop at a coffeehouse – one that he'd visited a month prior. The coffee selection at the Count Cristo Coffee House was impressive, and he wanted one of their apple fritters, which were so large that he'd had to skip lunch the last time he'd had one for breakfast.

He got his doughnut and coffee, and then found a table with a window that had a view of Swann Street, on which the coffeehouse's main entrance was located. He knew there was an emergency exit near the restrooms that led to a side street. He pulled his laptop out of his backpack, set it on the table, and flipped it open.

After downing two migraine pills, he opened a web browser – connected to the Internet via a secure satellite link – and perused his usual news websites.

The top story on every major news outlet addressed some facet of the accelerating conflict between Russia, China, and the US. The UK and Israel were starting to side with the US, and Iran and Syria were backing Russia. China only had North Korea, and India was not taking sides for the moment. The newest development was that the NATO countries were starting to organize and were mobilizing assets in case a member was attacked. This had already been happening in response to the Russian invasion of Ukraine, but NATO preparations were accelerating.

The next level of news reports had to do with the various types of weapons technologies each country possessed. On the top of the list were hypersonic missiles. Over the past 16 months, each of the big three countries had declared that they'd conducted successful tests of their hypersonics, claiming they could travel up to ten times the speed of sound, which was always deemed an exaggeration by the opposing sides. One advantage of such a technology came from the lower trajectories the missiles took in getting to their targets. This, along with the greater speed, not only decreased their time of flight relative to conventional missiles, but also made it difficult for radar to pick them up. In the end, hypersonic missiles could carry multiple nuclear warheads, and get them to their targets with the least warning time and the highest success rate.

Anders wondered why that even mattered. What was the difference between 30 minutes and 15 minutes of reaction time? Everyone was going to be dead in the end. He supposed that a nation attacked by surprise might get fewer missiles launched in response – but how many fewer? Would the return volley be weakened enough to save the aggressor from being completely destroyed? It was Anders' understanding that all-out nuclear war would be globally devastating no matter who was involved, or who supposedly won. It would mean nuclear fallout everywhere. At the least, society as we knew it would be destroyed.

Anders arranged for a SuperLift ride as he finished his fritter and coffee. By the time he'd packed up his laptop, taken his dishes up to a return counter, and stepped out of the building, his car pulled up to the curb. Ten minutes later, it dropped him off a few blocks from DMS, and he found his way to the "sensitive employee" entrance.

He entered the building and got into the elevator. Just as he was about to press the button to go to his office, his phone buzzed. It was a text from Harrison.

Anders pressed the button to take him directly to Harrison's office and, a minute later, he was knocking on his door.

"Come in," Harrison said.

The door was already cracked open, and Anders stepped inside.

"How was your trip?" Harrison asked from behind his desk as he waved him to the chair across from him.

"Refreshing," Anders replied as he sat and set his backpack on the floor next to him. "And enlightening."

"How so?"

Anders unzipped a pocket in his backpack and extracted the memory drive he'd gotten from his father's safe. He placed it on the desk.

Harrison picked up and examined the black thumb-drive. "What's on it?"

"I'm not sure," Anders said. "But it has to do with the CG – the *Custodial Group*."

Harrison's expression flashed from surprise to fear to excitement in quick succession. "CG stands for Custodial Group?" he asked. "And your father had this?"

Anders nodded.

"You haven't seen the contents?"

Anders shook his head. "It might have anti-tampering mechanisms," he explained. "I thought we should check it out first – get our computer people to take a look."

"Good idea," Harrison said as he sent a text message to Diana, the computer tech. He then looked back to Anders. "So then, you've confirmed that your father was a member of the Custodial Group?"

"I think so, yes," Anders replied. He wasn't sure how much he wanted to divulge about his mother and what *she* knew. "He was trying to write a declassified report on the Custodial Group before he died."

"Did you read the report?"

"I did," Anders replied. "It was short, and it said almost nothing. I didn't learn enough to speculate even vaguely about what the CG is. I did learn, however, that it was highly funded. Billions of dollars went to that group – dark money – and there were scientists and engineers involved, and lots of facilities and equipment based at a site near Area 51. The report was supposed to be a declassified description of the project to be presented to the intelligence committees – but it was useless. My father even wrote a comment on it saying that his report was rubbish."

"It give any hint as to what's on this?" Harrison asked as he twisted the thumb-drive around and examined it closely, apparently trying to read its white lettering.

"I suspect it contains the classified information that my dad was trying to boil down in the report," Anders replied, as he was trying to formulate the words to tell Harrison that he wanted to look at the documents before anyone else. "But the files are probably encrypted."

Harrison nodded. "That could be trouble," he said, just as someone knocked on the door.

"Come in, Diana," Harrison said as he stood and handed the data drive back to Anders. "You can set up on the desk."

The woman had changed her hair since the last time Anders had seen her: it was now short and black, rather than in a red bun, and she had square bangs.

Diana placed her briefcase and laptop on the desk and opened it. "What are we doing today?" she asked.

"Checking for anti-tampering mechanisms," Anders replied.

"Okay," she said and held out her hand.

Anders hesitated for an instant, but then gave her the drive. He knew there was a chance that it could be destroyed, but there was no other way.

Diana connected a cable from her laptop to a port on the exterior of the briefcase, and then plugged the data device into a slot in the briefcase's interior gadgetry. She hummed some unrecognizable tune as she tapped away at the computer.

After another minute, she looked up and said, "There's no physical self-destruct mechanism," she explained. "However, it has a shell protection program called Encryptocon that requires a password to get access to its files. In addition, the files themselves could be individually encrypted."

"So, there's no risk of destroying the data by trying to open them?" Anders asked.

"Unlikely," Diana replied. "However, you might have some trouble even getting to them. Encryptocon was developed by the NSA. It requires large passwords, and might be layered."

"Layered?" Anders asked.

"It means that there might be a second password," she explained. "It could also mean that the password is a *file*, rather than a string of characters. It might even be an image file."

Anders' worry now shifted from the risk of destroying the files to the possibility that he'd never be able to access them.

"This is an older version – Encryptocon 4.6," Diana added. "The most current version is 6.3. It means the version on your device is about five years old, or more."

"Have there been any successes in breaking into files encrypted with the older versions?" Anders asked.

Diana shook her head as she disconnected her laptop, extracted the thumb-drive from the slot, and closed the briefcase. "Not that I'm aware of," she replied. "All I know is that the newer versions keep getting more sophisticated." She handed Harrison the data drive.

Harrison handed the device to Anders, who then slipped it into his backpack.

"I'm afraid you might be dead in the water without the password," Diana said and looked to Harrison. "Anything else?"

"No. Thanks, Diana," Harrison replied. "You can go."

Diana packed up her things and left.

Anders felt a pit form in his stomach. He knew that his dad wanted him to see whatever was on that device, but it was looking like it might be a difficult task. He must have arranged a way for Anders to get to those files.

"You have any idea where you might acquire the password?" Harrison asked in a tone that hinted that his hope was waning along with Anders'.

"Not offhand."

"On to other business," Harrison said. "You have two exchanges scheduled this week in New York City. One is tomorrow night, and the other is still being arranged."

"You were able to receive a message coming out of the White House using the satellite phone?"

Harrison nodded. "Crownbrook seems to be comfortable with the technology," he explained. "He's been out of the spook business for a long time now, but must have been keeping up with the tech."

"He's certainly had the opportunity," Anders said. "He was on the Senate Intelligence Committee before running for president."

"Your first exchange will be with the Chinese courier – same one as last time," Harrison said.

"Is he still clean? Not too long ago, the FBI picked up his MSS tail," Anders said. "It means Chinese intelligence is onto him."

"His firm assures us that he hasn't been compromised."

Anders was doubtful. "I hope he's sober this time."

Harrison shook his head and grinned.

"When do I leave?" Anders asked.

"Tonight," Harrison replied, and then went to his desk and pulled out two pill-shaped, data storage devices, one red, and the other green, and handed them to Anders. "Red for China, green for Russia."

Anders slipped them into a pocket in his backpack. "Anything else?"

"Yes," Harrison replied. "It seems that the president's niece is in the clear."

Anders felt immediate relief – it had been in the back of his mind. "Did you get the data from the thumb-drive planted in the model train she gave me?" he asked, referring to the one he'd dropped off at DMS before heading to Georgia.

"Yes, and that outgoing message is on both of the drives in your possession, along with additional data Crownbrook recently transmitted," Harrison explained. "From this point forward, all outgoing electronic data from Crownbrook will be handled by satellite phone."

The meeting ended and Anders headed for the elevator. He'd spend the rest of the morning in his office organizing the details for his trip to New York, and then go to his apartment to pack and assemble his disguises for the mission. DMS had a safe house in Manhattan, so there was nothing to arrange regarding accommodations for the stay.

As the elevator descended into the bowels of the DMS building, there was something else on his mind: his father's encrypted drive. Anders needed to call his mother.

Maurice's flight departed for Washington, DC from Malmstrom Air Force Base at 5:00 a.m. He'd gotten the travel orders at 10:00 p.m. the night before, and a CIA jet was waiting on a runway at Malmstrom before daybreak.

A car was waiting for him when they touched down at Reagan International Airport, which took him to CIA Headquarters in Langley, Virginia. He was then taken through the main building to a secluded garage where he and his escorts got into the back seat of a large SUV with tinted windows. The driver and front-seat passenger were burly Secret Service types, wearing suits, earpieces, and sunglasses.

They drove off the CIA campus and got onto the highway. Maurice kept silent as he took in the sights. After a 25-minute drive, they entered what looked to be a complex of large office buildings. The names on their signs sounded like those of government contractors such as "Quantum Solutions," "Kerion Dynamics," and "Anderson Avionics." They turned into the drive of a place called "Space Systems."

Their SUV pulled up to a gate staffed with two armed guards, and stopped. The sentries looked like military types, but in plain, black uniforms. One of them peered inside the car and examined the ID of the driver and front-seat passenger. The driver then passed the man some paperwork, which he looked over, glanced at Maurice, and then handed back.

As the gate opened, the guard said, "Inside, another officer will direct you to a parking spot. Park, get out of the car, and follow his instructions."

The SUV moved out of the sunlight and into the dark bowels of the building. Another guard appeared on foot alongside them and directed them to a parking spot about 100 feet inside. They all got out, followed the man to an elevator, and rode it down five levels. The lift came to a halt, the door opened, and Maurice followed the others out and to the right, down a dimly lit hallway. The air smelled like wet cement, reminding Maurice of the basement in his childhood home. Closed doors, spaced about 20 feet apart, lined the corridor on both sides. Each had a sign near the door handle indicating whether the room was occupied, similar to that which appeared on lavatory doors in airplanes. About half of the rooms were in use.

After taking a few turns, and another walk down a long hallway, the guard in the black uniform stopped next to a door on the left and opened it. Maurice's escorts nodded for him to enter.

Maurice stepped inside, and was not expecting what he saw.

It was a miniature theater, with a large screen and stage, and stadium seating for about 100. There were roughly 25 people in the room, one of whom Maurice recognized as Thomas Crownbrook, the president of the United States. Another was the CIA director, Clay Radcliffe, whom he'd met a few weeks ago. The others looked to be military upper brass from the various branches, including that of the recently formed Space Force.

Radcliffe came to him. "Thanks for coming, Maurice," he said and held out his hand.

Maurice shook it.

Radcliffe then escorted him to a seat on the right-side aisle, about four rows from the front.

"Relax for a few minutes," Radcliffe said. "We'll get started as soon as our last participant arrives."

Maurice sat and leaned back in the chair. The president was chatting with someone else he recognized: the Chief of Staff of the Air Force, who was in uniform. Maurice, too, was in uniform, but in his less-formal, service attire.

After just a few minutes, the final guest arrived – a woman in civilian clothing – and the lights dimmed. CIA Director Radcliffe stepped onto the stage as the screen illuminated and showed white print on a black background:

PROJECT 1709874

THE PEREGRINE CONJECTURE

CLASSIFIED: TOP SECRET
NO PHOTOGRAPHS
NO AUDIO RECORDING
NO VIDEO

"THANK YOU ALL FOR COMING," Radcliffe said. "You've been summoned here so that we can present a new weapons system that has been slated for immediate deployment."

Radcliffe then nodded to someone at the back of the room and a movie started. It began with something that was at the center of Maurice's expertise: intercontinental ballistic missiles, ICBMs. The video ended 30 minutes later.

Maurice's gut churned with excitement, and trepidation.

ANDERS HAD ALWAYS FOUND New York City an exciting place to visit. He'd arrived late the previous evening and had spent the night in the DMS safe house, which was a large, well-furnished flat on the 48th floor of a swanky Manhattan apartment building. He was on the streets by 7:30 a.m. and was pleased that the weather was mild, as it should be in early May. However, a cold front would be entering the area by noon.

He found a large coffee shop a few blocks away from the flat and ordered a bagel and a cappuccino. He went to a tiny table in the back, set up his laptop, and scanned his usual news sources. He knew it was just an illusion, but it seemed like every story he encountered was connected to his work somehow. The bulk of the news was about the US-Russia-China conflicts, and the other countries that were now getting drawn into the fray. Russia was now amassing forces on its western border. That, along with increased activity at its nuclear missile sites, was making the European countries nervous, as well as the rest of the world. To turn up the heat even further, China had just disclosed the results of their test of a new missile that could supposedly defeat the radar detection systems of the US and Russia – their own hypersonic ICBM. This time there was video – but it was still nothing new, and wasn't conclusive. All three countries were doing the same, each downplaying the others' evidence of successful tests.

Anders had planned to call his mother the night before, but he'd gotten caught up with traveling. He'd arrived at the safe house after 10:00 p.m., and he knew she'd been long asleep by then, despite her staying up later while he'd been visiting. Although she used to stay up late with his father, she was now a morning person.

He'd left his father's thumb-drive locked in his desk at DMS, so getting in touch with his mom about that was no rush. He'd left it there so that he wouldn't be distracted during his mission, and also so that it would be safe in case he got into some kind of trouble. That device wasn't the type he could swallow.

After breakfast in the coffee shop, he found a used bookstore a few blocks away and spent the rest of the morning there. He promised himself he'd only buy one book since he'd be carrying it home with him. After an hour of perusing, he chose a science fiction novel from a modern, obscure author. He hoped it would keep him entertained during the afternoon.

It was just after 12:15 p.m. when he left the bookstore, and the weather had already turned overcast and chilly. He picked up a sandwich and soup from a deli and went back to the safe house, where he'd spend the rest of the afternoon. After eating his lunch, and a couple hours of reading his new novel, he looked over the online maps of the rendezvous location. For fleeing purposes, knowing the layout of the streets was important, but New York was relatively easy to navigate, and the foot traffic was dense enough to conceal someone on the run. He was more interested in the ground-level views offered by the map application, which helped him locate the exits of the building in which they were meeting.

This evening, the location was a bar on the ground floor of a fancy hotel.

After eating a light supper, Anders went back to his book, which was about government conspiracies, and the possibility of nuclear war. He was hooked. It was enough to keep his attention as he passed the time leading up to his mission.

At 7:00 p.m. he'd start assembling his disguise for the 11:00 p.m. meet.

THE FRIGHTENING PART to Maurice was that, although he'd known that the US would eventually develop such advanced weapons systems, he knew that their adversaries were not far behind. He quickly reformulated his thinking to acknowledge the possibility that America's enemies weren't behind at all, and could, in fact, be well ahead of them.

The disruptive technology that he'd just witnessed in the video was a hypersonic, intercontinental missile. Both Russia and China had been boasting similar developments for years, but US military intelligence agencies who monitored the tests of those systems were doubtful. It was clear to Maurice, however, that the US had succeeded, and the new system was ready for deployment.

The eclectic audience had questions, most of which were general inquiries regarding the importance of the technology, and commissioning timetables. The obvious difference between hypersonic missiles and conventional ICBMs was the greater speed of the former, which ranged between five to eight times the speed of sound. However, another important difference was in their trajectories. Whereas normal ICBMs followed high-arching paths that took them completely out of the Earth's atmosphere, hypersonic missiles took flatter routes that just skimmed the edge of space which, along with their greater speeds, reduced travel times from launch to target by a factor of two or three.

The lower trajectories of the hypersonics also helped them to avoid the line-of-sight of ground-based radar systems until very late in their paths, giving the target country little time to react locally, even though satellites could still detect and track them globally from the moment they were launched. Someone brought up the fact that nuclear missiles fired by submarine could do the same thing, but a naval intelligence officer pointed out that the hypersonic missiles could carry larger payloads. The hypersonics carried large, thermonuclear warheads that could take out entire cities. In addition, many missiles could be fired simultaneously, making an all-out attack extremely difficult, or impossible, to defend. They could even carry multiple warheads.

The new missiles weren't just "fully developed," they were ready to go. They'd been designed to be perfectly compatible with the current launch sites – with only minor modifications – and were to be deployed immediately. It made the hair on Maurice's neck bristle: he knew why he was there. He'd gotten hints about the missile upgrades from both CIA Director Radcliffe and his CIA liaison, Christine, while at Malmstrom.

When the question and answer session was over, the CIA director called him over. The president was standing next to him.

"I'm not sure if you've met President Crownbrook," Radcliffe said and then turned to the president. "This is Colonel Maurice Spelling."

Crownbrook stuck out his hand and Maurice shook it.

"Nice to meet you, sir," Maurice said as his mind tried to process the surreal events he'd experienced during the past few weeks.

"The pleasure is mine," Crownbrook said. "Director Radcliffe and I would like to speak with you in private after everyone else clears out."

"Certainly," Maurice replied.

It took another 15 minutes before the other attendees vacated, and then Radcliffe led Maurice, the president, and four secret service agents to an elevator. A few minutes later, they were on the 17th floor of the building, in an enormous corner office with floor-to-ceiling windows on the south and west walls. The view to the south was over a pine forest that Maurice thought was unusual in this area: it seemed to him that almost every square foot of property around DC had been developed.

With the secret service agents absent and the door closed, Radcliffe led Crownbrook and Maurice to the office's southwest corner where they sat in upholstered chairs arranged symmetrically around a square, wooden coffee table. The president sat directly opposite the table from Maurice, and Radcliffe was to Maurice's left.

"We had to discuss this in private since the rest of our visitors are unaware of your project," Radcliffe explained.

Crownbrook cleared his throat. "As you have probably guessed, the missiles in the launch sites you are upgrading will be replaced by hypersonics," he explained. "They've been designed for an immediate swap, with minimal alterations. They're ready to go."

"All of them?" Maurice asked.

Radcliffe nodded. "Yes, 25 are ready to ship to Malmstrom," he said. "You'll have to brief the crew doing the upgrades."

"You understand why we're doing this, right?" Crownbrook asked.

Maurice nodded. "After what's been happening with the drones — their ability to disable our launch control stations — we need to have auxiliary launch capabilities," he said. "I suppose the reduced flight time of the hypersonic missiles accounts for any delays in launching due to interference by the drones."

"Exactly right," Radcliffe said. "And not only will all the modified launch systems have hypersonics, so will about a quarter of the unmodified silos — eventually."

"This is top-secret information," Crownbrook said. "It shouldn't be shared with the missileers at this time."

"But won't my construction crew know — and also the operators and maintenance people at the modified launch sites?" Maurice asked. "The current missiles will have to be removed, and the new ones look very different."

Radcliffe nodded. "Yes, they'll know that the missiles are being swapped," he said. "They'll be informed that it's an upgrade to our conventional ICBMs. The story is that the new versions have improved engines and navigation instrumentation – but there will be no indication that they are hypersonics."

Maurice wasn't convinced. The problem was that the talented people he had on his crew might suspect that the missiles were special in a more significant way.

"We're going to have to change the upgrade plans to account for the new missiles," Maurice said. "Even though the alterations are minimal, they will take time. Plus, there will be extra time involved in removing the old missiles and replacing them with the new ones."

"Since the hypersonics are ready, you should have the old ones removed ASAP," Radcliffe said. "I know that will mean those sites will be offline for some time, but we'll activate others in the North Dakota fields to cover for them."

"We're supposed to have the first site set up for mobile launch by the end of next week," Maurice explained. "That will have to be delayed now."

"Understood," Radcliffe said. "We're sending two engineers to Malmstrom tomorrow to instruct your crew on how to make the additional alterations. It should add about a day's work to each site modification."

"Okay," Maurice said. That wouldn't be too bad, he thought.

"Now, let's talk about the drones," Radcliffe said.

"You have new information?" Maurice asked.

Radcliffe glanced at Crownbrook before responding. "Maybe," he said.

Maurice looked back and forth between the CIA director and the president. They both appeared hesitant. "What's going on?"

Crownbrook nodded to Radcliffe, who cleared his throat before he spoke. "We have evidence that there are more of these craft than we originally thought," he explained.

"How many are we talking about?" Maurice asked. "And how are you seeing them? I thought we couldn't track them."

"It's not definitive," Radcliffe explained, "but we have a few satellite images that caught faint heat signatures."

"Are they jet-propelled?" Maurice asked. He knew that the most likely source of heat would come from the hot gas expelled from jet engines.

Radcliffe shook his head. "It doesn't seem that we're catching the heat signatures from their propulsion systems. But rather from the heat generated by the friction between the drones and the air through which they are moving."

"They'd have to be moving pretty fast for that," Maurice argued. "How fast are they going?"

Radcliffe stood, went to his desk on the opposite side of the room, and returned with three photographs. "These are satellite surveillance images of the Montana-based missile facilities – your wing," he said as he handed one of them to Maurice. "This was extracted from satellite video footage, but the streaks that you see were only detected in a few frames."

Maurice looked over the photo. It was mostly black, with thin, colored traces overlayed on a background of the major roads and towns, and white dots that indicated the missile silos. The image spanned a thousand square miles of area. He counted over 40 red streaks, each following a path originating from either a control station or silo, and extending across the entire frame. "What am I seeing here?" he asked.

"We don't know," President Crownbrook replied.

"These tracks occur over just a few frames?" Maurice asked. "It means that they were traveling at unimaginable speeds. Could they be artifacts?"

"We calculated speeds of over 50 times the speed of sound, and accelerations over 200 times the acceleration due to gravity – Mach 50 and 200g. As you know, no human could withstand that acceleration. Therefore, they're clearly unmanned, as we suspected anyway,"

Radcliffe explained as he handed him another image. "This one was recorded by another satellite at the same time as the first."

Maurice looked over the second photo. It looked the same, but it was taken from a different angle.

"Clearly, it wasn't an artifact," Crownbrook said.

"Our spy satellites are coordinated, so we can process the two photos to get a three-dimensional perspective," Radcliffe explained as he handed Maurice a third printout.

In the third one, which took a longer view, it was clear that the streaks were nearly parallel to one another, and extended to a great altitude.

"How high do they reach?" Maurice asked.

"The lines disappear at about 100 kilometers up," Radcliffe replied. "Altitudes over three hundred thousand feet."

"But that's beyond the atmosphere," Maurice said. He'd been a test pilot and had flown some of the most advanced aircraft ever created, and none of them could breach space. "Surely, you don't think these represent real aircraft."

Radcliffe shrugged. "We have no idea what they are," he said. "And they are clearly trans-medium craft."

By "trans-medium," Maurice knew that Radcliffe meant that the so-called drones could travel from the atmosphere into empty space. And, based on the reports of the US submarine that had been commandeered by a drone, they could probably go underwater as well. Capable of traveling through water, space, and air: he doubted anyone had a craft that could do that. "Could these streaks be tracks from lasers?" Maurice asked.

"That has been suggested – that someone has shone lasers on our missile installations from a low-Earth orbit, causing the air in the beam to heat up," Radcliffe said. "But the streaks move far too slowly to be from light. And they also curve slightly – something a laser beam wouldn't do under these conditions. There'd also be some scattered light, and we'd be able to determine if it was from a laser."

"Also, the timing of these photos is crucial," Radcliffe said.

Maurice knew what he was going to say.

"They were taken at precisely the time at which the multiple incursions happened," Radcliffe explained. "It was as if someone were simultaneously meddling with 43 of the silos, but all the craft stopped simultaneously and fled."

"When did this happen?" Maurice asked.

"April 14th, just a few weeks ago," Crownbrook replied. "And there were nearly 200 others spotted at various times that night."

Maurice knew that was the night when multiple incursions had taken place in the Malmstrom missile fields. "But there were only three incursion events detected that night."

Radcliffe shrugged. "Maybe the other craft were doing things that you couldn't detect. Or maybe they were just observing," he countered.

Maurice nodded and conceded the argument. "Any new clues as to who's behind this?" he asked.

"We think it's more likely China than Russia, but we don't have any hard evidence of that," Radcliffe replied. "Can we count on you to get this done – the upgrades?"

"My best people are working on it," Maurice said. "It will be about one silo upgraded per week. The only foreseeable bottleneck is getting the equipment on time."

"Leave that to me," Crownbrook said. "Those special, eight-wheel-drive vehicles are on the way, and we added four more to the order. Later, we might also expand the number of silos to be converted, but we'll stay with the current plan for now, which is 25."

"If we extend the duration of the project, we might have to form another crew, or at least add a few members," Maurice said. "They'll be away from their families for over five months."

"If they stay on, we'll make it well worth their while," Crownbrook said. "In fact, with the added alterations for the hypersonics, you can tell your crew that their compensation for this job has been increased by twenty-five percent, and that there will be more work ahead if we decide to expand. You'll be getting extra for this effort as well. This is important."

Maurice was getting the idea. However, even though much new information – disturbing information – had just been disclosed, he still felt in his gut that there was something else lurking beneath the surface.

CHAPTER 8

Anders donned a brown wig, round, wire-rimmed glasses, jeans, a dress shirt, and a brown sportscoat that could be converted to black by turning it inside out. His short, fake beard was slightly darker than his hair but matched his enhanced eyebrows.

The meeting place was a popular whisky bar on the ground floor of The Emerald, a five-star hotel in lower Manhattan, which was frequented by an eclectic clientele. It was particularly popular with the art community.

He left the safe house at 10:15 p.m. and took a SuperLift ride to a coffeehouse just two blocks from the bar. He got a coffee and sat at a table near a window with a view of the north side of the hotel – the side with a direct street entrance to the bar.

It always settled his mind to find a calm place to observe the rendezvous point before engaging in an operation, if possible. He'd often learn something that would help him. It could be something as important as discovering a different exit to a building, or as simple as noticing that he'd be greeted by an employee upon entering an establishment. This time, he noticed two large men in winter jackets monitoring the front door of the bar and asking for IDs. Anders was ready.

At 10:45 p.m., he left the coffeehouse and headed toward the hotel. The temperature had dropped significantly – below freezing now – and the wind gusted repeatedly, making his sport jacket flap, and giving him a violating shot of cold air around his midsection. Two minutes later, he was standing in front of the bouncers who were more appropriately dressed for the falling temperature with heavy jackets and knit hats. One wore a red hat with a white, fuzzy ball on the top: it would've been just as disarming had it been worn by a bear.

The men looked rough but were pleasant as they requested his ID and looked it over. "We had some trouble in here a few nights ago, so they upped security," the one in the red hat explained as he returned the ID and then held out a coupon. "That'll get you a middle-shelf scotch."

Anders accepted the coupon. "Thanks," he said and then entered the bar. Under normal circumstances, the security personnel at the door would not have been a concern. In the current situation, however, the added security made him anxious, as if he could be trapped inside the establishment if something went wrong. Knowing that there was another entrance to the bar from inside the hotel eased his mind, but he knew that there might be bouncers monitoring that inner door as well. He also knew there was an emergency exit on the east side of the building, but opening that would likely set off an alarm.

He passed through a small foyer and into the bar. The ceiling was high, maybe 12 feet, crisscrossed with black, steel girders on which were track lights that illuminated the concrete floor, which was artistically stained in swirling, brown-red patterns. On the right was a long bar with a varied assortment of patrons that Anders figured represented a cross-section of the local art community. Many of the men were dressed in sportscoats and jeans, like Anders, and some of the women wore skirts or dresses – slightly above business casual. By his assessment, the ages ranged from 20s to 60s.

On the far wall were booths, most of them occupied, and to the left was an open floor with tall round tables and stools. On the far left wall was a stage, but it was dark. Paintings and drawings filled all available wall space, most illuminated from above with wire-caged lights mounted to pipes, as if the fixtures were connected to water spigots. It was then that he realized that the place brimmed with steampunk décor.

He could barely hear the light jazz playing in the background over the voices of about 100 people, some of whom were talking about the art.

Anders went to the bar and handed the bartender the coupon. "What can I get with this?" he asked.

The bartender, a tall bald man, late 30s, dressed in a white shirt with a black bowtie, pointed to a shelf on which were about a dozen bottles of various spirits, mostly whiskies, but a few cognacs as well.

"What do you recommend?" Anders asked.

The man set a glass on the bar in front of Anders and pulled two bottles from the shelf and placed them next to the glass.

"These have been the most popular," he said while pointing to the one on his right. "But I'd recommend this one – it's a donated bottle that's otherwise pretty expensive."

Anders looked at the label, which read, "Laphroaig, Quarter Cask." It was a single-malt scotch.

"Okay – I'll try that," Anders said. He didn't know anything about whisky but was now interested in trying this label. "Neat, please."

The bartender poured two fingers into the glass. Anders put a five-dollar bill on the bar for a tip, grabbed the whisky, and then turned and casually scanned the room for his contact. He spotted "Barney," his Chinese counterpart, sitting in one of the booths – the most dimly-lit one – at the far end of the room. He had a goatee this time, rather than the beard. Anders spotted two empty whisky glasses, and a third with some left in it, on the table. At least he knew he had the right guy.

Anders went over to the first piece of art on the wall nearest the entrance and studied it. It was a stunning charcoal sketch of a bird in a steep, vertical dive. Its wings swept backward and their tips blurred into linear trails like those seen emanating from the wingtips of jet aircraft. What was odd was that the background wasn't the usual sky, with clouds. Instead, it was stars – it was nighttime. The title was "Wings of Death."

Anders shuddered. The drawing invoked fear and anxiety and, above all, impending doom. He moved on to the next one, which wasn't much more inviting than the first. It was another charcoal sketch of a tall man – so thin and lanky that he didn't seem human – facing away and standing on a hill. Again, it was nighttime, and he was looking to the star-studded sky. He seemed to be watching a shooting star that was plummeting vertically downward, toward the horizon. The man's silhouette – his posture and sprawled arms – seemed to convey horror and fear. The title of this one, by the same artist, was "Revelation of Death."

After recovering from the emotions that the two drawings invoked, Anders sighed and chuckled quietly – nervously. He wondered what demons the artist had been fighting while creating those pieces. He acknowledged that they were good art – they clearly brought about emotion. They made him uncomfortable.

He stepped to the right to view the next piece. It was a painting of the overhead view of a small island, studded with a dozen red-brick structures, green lawns, and patches of pine forests that made him think of a quaint, college campus. He thought it looked like an isolated place – there were no people – and it was surrounded by a vast, blue ocean. On the far left side of the island, at the end of a peninsula, was a lighthouse. He glanced at the title below it, which read, "Jenna's Dream." It invoked feelings of comfort and excitement – opposite to those incited by the previous two works – and Anders hoped it might appear in his own dreams.

He passed from piece to piece while he moved around the room toward the location of his contact, sipping whisky as he went along. After 10 minutes, he finally approached the man in the booth, who glanced up at him and asked, "Does the art inspire you?"

It was the correct phrase for "all clear."

"It does, but I'm mostly here for the whisky," Anders replied with the planned "all clear" response, and then took a seat across from the man.

"Good to see you again, Frank," the man said.

"You too, Barney," Anders replied.

Even though there were only two empty glasses, and another nearly empty, on the table in front of "Barney," it was difficult to assess how much the man had actually consumed. Each of those glasses could have started with anywhere between one and three fingers of whisky in it. Anders still had one finger left in his glass when a server approached the table.

The woman collected the empty glasses and asked if they wanted anything. Anders declined, but Barney ordered a cognac called Hennessy Pure White, and the server left.

"I'm a connoisseur of fine whiskies and cognacs," Barney explained.

Anders was not surprised.

"I've been building up the nerve to purchase an expensive bottle one day – Hennessey Ellipse or a Remy Martin of some kind – but not yet," Barney said. "Perhaps after I retire."

"I like whisky – but I've only had cognac a few times," Anders said. "I think they're both an acquired taste."

Barney smiled. "Keep trying, they'll grow on you," he said, swallowing the last of the whisky in his glass just as the server came back and replaced it with a snifter of a reddish-brown spirit that seemed to fluoresce in the low light. She then placed a glass of water on the table, and left.

Barney took a drink of the water. "I need to cleanse my palate before switching to cognac," he explained and then shifted in his seat and cleared his throat. "I understand that your client has had some troubles recently."

Anders nodded, figuring that news was getting out to the greater intelligence community that the FBI was suspicious of the covert messaging. He didn't mention the rumor that Barney had been brought in by the FBI but the man they'd caught and interrogated had instead been an MSS agent who had been tailing him. "There were some complications, but they were taken care of," he said.

Barney nodded. "As you know, my client has had his own problems," he said, clearly referring to the data drive intercepted by Chinese intelligence. "And my understanding is that the third party in our partnership is now having some issues as well."

"Oh?" Anders said, his heart picking up pace. Alina Petrova's face appeared in his mind.

"The SVR intercepted a drive – one from us," Barney explained.

"I thought the Russian president had a stranglehold on the SVR leadership, and all his security agencies."

Barney shrugged. "So did I," he said. "But I also thought *my own* leader was in complete control – and then I learn that the MSS has taken an interest in our dealings. I'm now convinced that *none* of our leaders are in control. I've always thought that it was the intelligence agencies that had the real power."

That's what Anders thought as well. In the US, the FBI and CIA had more power than any of the elected leaders, even the president, since they could always conjure up something to take them out. Combine those agencies with a corrupt Department of Justice, and control was absolute.

"In our little circle – or *triangle* – we all work for private firms," Barney said. "And I'm happy to work counter to our intelligence services – or at least to circumvent them. They have too much influence, and I will take the side of my president in this conflict."

Anders understood his point, but he hoped he wasn't working *against* his own CIA – both of his parents had invested their lives in the agency, and he was sure that most CIA people weren't anti-

American, or looking to control the country from their concealed positions.

"I trust my president as well," Anders said. "Do you know whether Russian intelligence was able to break into the device – did they extract any information?"

"Only rumors – something about distributing and readying hypersonic nukes," Barney explained. "There was also mention of some new secret project."

"What kind of project?"

Barney shrugged. "No idea," he replied. "But it seems that it's being developed through unofficial channels – just like our current communication lines."

Anders wasn't going to bring up anything he'd recently learned – about the Custodial Group, or anything else. "Which of our countries is running this new project?"

Barney shook his head. "My feeling is that all three are equally involved," he said. "I suppose two could be doing something behind the third party's back, which happens continually in this business, but this situation is different from anything I've experienced before."

Barney picked up his drink, took a sip, and breathed in and out through his nose a few times. "This is a wonderful cognac," he said and then set the snifter back on the table. Next to its base was a blue data drive.

Anders picked up Barney's glass and the drive, swirled the cognac in the light, sniffed it, and set it down again, along with a red thumb-drive.

Barney cupped his hands around the glass, leaned over it, and inhaled. "I'd like to get a bottle of this to bring back to Hong Kong, but I'd never get it through the airport with all the restrictions."

When he retracted his hands, the red device was gone.

"From what we know so far, it sounds like there might be a conflict in our future," Anders said.

Barney nodded. "Could be," he agreed. "But this is an odd prelude to war, if that's what it is."

"Where's the restroom?" Anders asked. It was the exit phrase.

"To the left of the bar," Barney replied and nodded in that direction.

"Good luck," Anders whispered as he stood.

"You too," Barney responded.

Anders made his way toward the bar and then veered left, into the bathroom. There were two stalls on the far right, one with the door closed, but he couldn't tell if someone was inside since the walls went all the way to the floor. He checked his disguise as he walked past the mirror on his left, over a set of side-by-side sinks, and then went to one of two urinals on the wall to the right and pretended to relieve himself. After a minute, he went to one of the sinks and ran some water, and then got a paper towel from a dispenser, crumpled it up, and threw it into a trash can.

Someone flushed the toilet in the closed stall and Anders headed for an exit opposite the door he'd entered. He got past the stalls just as the occupied one opened, and then exited the bathroom into the main lobby of the hotel. There were no bouncers at the restroom doors. The bathroom entrance seemed to defeat the security of the whisky bar, although the hotel had guards at all of its external doors.

Anders emerged into the main lobby, near a foyer with six elevator doors, all on the same wall. The lobby was as extravagant as that in the Orion Hotel, back in DC. At the center of its high, central atrium was an enormous fountain with a 25-foot-tall statue of a green dragon at the center. The dragon's head was tilted back and water streamed vertically out of its mouth and rained over its body, running off into the emerald pool in which it stood. It was both beautiful and menacing.

He forgot about the dragon the instant he spotted the man sitting on a couch near a window to the right of the main entrance. It was the same man he'd seen in the Orion's bar, the one who'd followed him into the bathroom when he'd met with Alina – the man she'd seen at a fundraiser days before that rendezvous.

Anders only glanced at the man, and then reached into his

sportscoat and pulled out his cell phone, pretending he'd gotten a call. As he feigned a conversation, he activated the camera on his phone and rotated slowly as he talked so that he'd get the man on video. DMS might be able to identify him later.

Anders turned away from the man for just a second and, when he turned back again, the man was walking toward him.

He had to make a split-second decision whether to stay put, or flee. By the looks of the guy, fighting would not be a viable option. He was at least six-foot-three, and over 200 pounds. His brown hair was cut short, not quite military style. There was an intensity in his expression that implied urgency and desperation, both of which indicated danger.

As the man approached, Anders laughed into his phone, turned away from him, and continued the fake conversation as he walked toward the seating area near the hotel's front entrance. To his relief, the man continued past him and went into the restroom.

Just as the restroom door swung closed behind the man, Anders walked at a casual clip toward the exit, the phone still up to his ear. He had to maintain his current state for a while longer: it was a common tactic in this type of situation for the stalker to suddenly reappear to see what had changed, or if there were any "runners."

Anders kept a clear view to his rear in the reflection from the glass doors at the hotel entrance. On cue, the man reemerged from the lavatory and looked around the lobby, not focusing on any one of the 30 or more people milling about in the seating area, or the dozen others in line at the front desk, waiting to check into their rooms. The man just seemed to assess the environment.

Anders passed the dragon fountain and veered right, into the seating area. He sat in an upholstered chair about 50 feet from the exit, facing at an angle so that he could maintain sight of the man in his peripheral vision.

As the man wandered closer to him, Anders continued his faux conversation, making it sound like he was meeting a woman at another place. He said things like, "Who else is going to be there?"

and "Where is this place?" and, finally, he looked at his watch and said, "Okay, see you soon. Love you, too."

Anders ended his fake call, and then ordered a ride on the SuperLift app to pick him up at the hotel entrance and take him to a coffee shop near City Park.

The man passed in front of him, sat in a chair just a few feet away, and took out his phone and seemed to type a text message. A few seconds later, the man's phone vibrated, and he sent another message.

The map feature on the SuperLift phone app showed that Anders' car would be arriving at the hotel entrance in less than a minute. He waited another few seconds, and then, just as he was about to stand and head for the exit, the man looked at him and then back to his phone, as if he were comparing Anders' face to an image on the screen. Anders monitored the guy in his peripheral vision as his potential stalker glanced back and forth a few more times. He was confident that his disguise would hold up.

Anders finally stood and headed for the tall, glass entrance doors. His car had arrived, and he could see the green-illuminated "SuperLift" sign through the windshield of the midsized, Honda SUV.

The man then started for the door as well, giving Anders the urge to make a run for it, but then the potential pursuer stopped and looked behind him. Anders glanced in that same direction and got a glimpse of his contact, Barney, heading for the elevators – he'd exited the whisky bar through the bathroom.

As the burly stalker walked at a hurried clip toward the elevators, Anders took the opportunity to increase his pace and went through the glass doors into the drafty, outdoor air. Just as he closed the SuperLift car's door and it started pulling away from the curb, he spotted the man looking in his direction.

Anders smiled. Barney had gotten away. The pursuer was like a dog trying to catch two squirrels, frantically chasing them both, but each going up a different tree, out of reach. The problem was that, if the dog were persistent enough, it would eventually catch one of those squirrels.

The more serious problem was that the man had reappeared at another one of Anders' rendezvous locations – this one *in a different state*. It meant there was a leak somewhere. The other concern was that he had another exchange set up for the following night, this one with the Russian courier, Alina.

Harrison was on the couch in his office at 1:15 a.m. when he ended the call with Anders. The operation had been successful, but the tension was rising. There was either a leak, or one of the intelligence services, or the FBI, was onto them somehow. He was now considering delaying the exchange planned for the next evening.

After contemplating the situation for a few minutes he decided to let the next meeting take place as planned but, going forward, he'd direct the couriers to employ dynamic exchange methods. They were currently employing the so-called "static" rendezvous method, which meant that the operatives met at a predetermined public place and conducted a covert transfer of information – in this case, using data storage devices.

In contrast, dynamic exchanges could be carried out in a number of ways. One method was to give the operatives secure burner phones and let them communicate directly with each other as they navigated the exchange. In a dense, urban setting, like New York City, they might walk the busy streets of Manhattan, meet on a street corner, or in a line at a deli, make a quick exchange, and then scatter. In another effective technique, one party could get a SuperLift car, pick up their contact, and drive around. After making the exchange, one operative would get out and the other would drive away. In that way, although it was impossible to eliminate *all* risk, they'd at least not be trapped in a building. It also precluded a leaker from pinpointing a meeting location. Implementing this tactic, however, would take some time, as there would have to be at least one more "static" meeting with each foreign contact to discuss the new procedures. It meant that Anders was still on for the next evening.

Harrison had confidence in Anders' ability to make the right decisions under pressure – as he had just done. His best courier had even gotten a video of the man who had appeared at the previous exchange with the Russian courier. Harrison would put DMS resources to work on identifying who it was. However, since the man had now appeared at this latest rendezvous point, this time with the Chinese courier, he'd probably been stalking *Anders*, not the Russian contact, during that first encounter.

There were only three people on the US side who were aware of the meeting locations: the president, Harrison, and Anders. It meant that any leaks either came from the White House or from DMS. Harrison couldn't see how it could have originated from DMS. He only shared information with Anders, and both of their offices were swept daily for bugs. He concluded that any leaks on the US side had somehow come from the president. It was possible, however, even though Anders was apparently the one being tailed, that Russia or China was responsible for the breaches. After all, Chinese intelligence had already intercepted a device, and there was a rumor that the Russian FSB or SVR had recently done the same.

The other bit of disturbing news coming from this latest encounter was, again, the mention of nuclear war – now with hypersonic missiles. The individual bits of information they'd gotten about nukes up to this point had been construed as mere rumors. However, the consistency of the full collection of those rumors was starting to cause him concern.

More and more, Harrison wanted to know what information was passing through DMS.

"Well, *that* tip was a bust," Candace said as she took a bite of a bagel and glanced out the window of the breakfast café on the corner of two bustling Manhattan streets. She was referring to their fruitless surveillance of the night before. "Other than the whisky, it was a wasted trip to New York. We're burning through our travel budget."

"It was supposedly high-grade info from FBI counterintelligence," Tim argued. "We must've missed something."

"We're fish out of water on this," Candace said. "They could've made the exchange right under our noses. We need to let counterintelligence handle it next time."

"I thought *we* were counterintelligence," Tim said.

"A surveillance team," she said. "You know what I mean. We're desk-jockey investigators."

"They're spread too thin already," he said. "They don't have time for us."

Candace still couldn't believe that they'd had specific information about the meeting and were unable to spot the exchange, or even to mark anyone as suspicious. It was actually the opposite of that: *everyone* looked suspicious, which was the same thing. Either way, they'd gotten nothing out of the venture.

"The hotel was enormous," Tim said. "And why would they meet in a fancy bar, and not in a hotel room, or in Central Park?"

Candace shrugged. "It's complicated," she explained. "You have to realize that spooks aren't on the same side. If they're making an exchange, it's often more like a drug deal than a friendly encounter."

"I see – each side is afraid they'll be ripped off."

"Or worse," she added. "Spooks sometimes kill each other, too."

"The traffic in the lobby was heavy – almost like an airport," he said. "I can't see how I was supposed to identify anyone acting in a suspicious manner. A few of them were drunk and loud, but that's all I saw."

"It was the same in the bar," Candace said.

"So, what now?"

"Since we're here, we should follow up on the other tip they gave us," she said. "But it will be another sit-and-watch kind of operation."

"And after that?"

"Back to what we're good at," she replied. "Back to the lists."

"The spouses of the deceased?"

"And their children," Candace said. There were five names on the list she wanted to explore first. They were all dead, but she and Tim would interview their immediate family members. It was their only remaining course of action unless they got another tip. After that, their investigation would dry up.

Anders was up by 7:00 a.m. He stayed in the safe house all morning, reading, perusing news websites, and drinking coffee.

The two-bedroom flat was comfortable, with high ceilings and wooden floors covered with soft area rugs. The view on one side was of the skyscrapers across the street, which had always given him the impression of a lack of privacy, even though the windows on his building had a highly reflective coating that made it impossible to see inside during the day. At night, he could close the curtains if he wanted privacy, but the view was well worth the exposure.

The kitchen was equipped with modern appliances and was separated from the living room by a black, granite countertop. The living room was furnished with a couch and a matching set of two upholstered chairs arranged around a sturdy, wooden coffee table. On the wall across from the couch was a large, flat-screen television.

At 10:00 a.m. he had a bagel with cream cheese and found the BBC News channel on the TV. There were more stories about the geopolitical posturing by the big three, along with some jostling of alliances with some of the smaller countries. It was just more of the same, except for one story that described the relocation of Russian nuclear missile launchers, as well as the reconfiguration of some of their underground launch silos near Irkutsk, near the Mongolian border. In addition, China was supposedly arming a new missile field near Hami, in its eastern Xinjiang Province, with hypersonic missiles, although some of the analysts doubted they really had the high-tech weapons.

Although such information was not out of the ordinary, it did correlate well with the rumors he'd been hearing from both of his courier counterparts.

It seemed to him that, if he were ever truly convinced that those tales were true, it would be too late to do anything about them. And he didn't know what kind of proof it would take to convince him to act – perhaps only an admission by the president himself would be sufficient.

It made him think again about the data device from his father's safe. He might find some answers there.

He pulled out his mobile and called his mom. It was going on 11:00 a.m., and he knew she might be having company for tea, or preparing lunch for her gardening group.

"Anders?" she answered after just two rings.

They chatted for a few minutes, and he explained that he was on a mission and couldn't tell her where he was. He then explained what he'd learned about the thumb-drive.

"There were no booby-traps?" she asked.

"No, but the files are encrypted," he replied.

"I'm not surprised," she said. "But if your father wanted you to look at them, he would have given you the means to access them."

"Are you familiar with a program called Encryptocon?"

After an awkward silence, she said, "I might be."

"Do you have passwords that might get me into the drive?"

"Possibly," she replied. "But it might take more than that if he's done what I think he has."

"And what's that?"

"Have you tried to get into it?"

"Not yet."

"Okay, when you do, let me know what it asks for," she said.

"The passcode could be anything from a string of characters to a file of some kind."

"Will do," Anders said. "When I'm back in DC, I'll try it and let you know. Maybe we can figure something out."

Before ending the call, she'd given him an update on the latest happenings in Genesee Lake, which included a small levee on a pond breaking and flooding a neighbor's property, and a listing of the events scheduled for the annual Spring Festival, which was just over three weeks away. It was something that Anders had loved as a boy. The Spring Festival was a carnival, with rides, games, shows, great food, and a craft sale and farmers' market. It always happened on the last weekend of May, when the weather was getting warm but still comfortable. She wanted him to visit during the festival, and he promised he'd try.

He spent the rest of the afternoon reading the sci-fi novel he'd picked up from the bookstore the day before. He had just over 100 pages left when he had to quit and start preparing for the meeting. He'd already scoped out the location: it was a fancy restaurant that required reservations, which were made for 8:50 p.m.

The meeting location was organized by the Russian side, and Anders felt it was too rigid. Once he and Alina were sitting at the same table, and with reservations no less, there was no arguing that they didn't know each other. It was no random encounter when a man and woman had dinner together.

He assembled his disguise, which would be very different from the one he'd used the last time they'd met. This time, his hair was almost black, and curly and short. He had matching eyebrows and a short, thick beard. His black-framed eyeglasses were square and small. After he donned the jeans, white button-down shirt, and jacket, he examined himself in the full-length mirror on the bathroom door. It was about as far from his natural look as he could imagine without wearing a latex mask – something that looked unnatural under close inspection. He'd worn them a few times, but only for travel on public trains or buses, some of which had extensive camera systems – especially in the EU.

At 8:25 p.m. he ordered a SuperLift car. Before he headed for the door, he stopped at the kitchen counter, opened a drawer, and pulled out a Glock 19. He checked the chamber – there was a round in it, and he removed it. He then extracted the magazine, inserted the loose round, and replaced the magazine, striking it with the heel of his hand.

He slipped the gun into an internal pocket in his jacket – one designed for just that purpose – and did a final check of his wallet. His ID was in order: his name was now Terrance Fillmore, software developer. Everything was there – including business cards with phone numbers connected to specialized personnel at DMS.

Five minutes later, he was in a car, heading for a restaurant called "Gilligan's Isle."

MAURICE LANDED at Malmstrom AFB at 10:15 a.m. It took him a few hours to mentally recover from his DC trip.

He'd spent the night in Space Systems, the expansive CIA installation embedded in a cluster of defense contractor buildings. His quarters in that facility resembled a luxurious condo, with a large open space filled with comfortable furniture, a fully stocked kitchen, and an enormous bathroom.

The CIA director had come to his room around 9:00 p.m. that evening, and brought a bottle of whisky. The two men had talked and drunk until midnight, discussing the details and timelines of the reconfiguration of the silos and the implementation of their new, auxiliary functionalities, as well as the missile upgrades.

Maurice had the impression that the ambitious timeline was about more than just readiness. It was as if Radcliffe and the president were anticipating something specific – that they were acting on a certain threat, or coordinating a larger operation of which the upgraded missile launch systems were just one facet that had to be well-timed.

After a full day's work back at Malmstrom, Maurice submitted a stack of acquisition orders totaling over four million dollars and returned to his office just in time to meet with Eduardo, who was waiting at his door at 6:30 p.m.

"Hello, Pacquiao," Maurice said as he approached and unlocked the door. "We're going to be a while. Coffee's ready."

Maurice pointed his crew leader to the coffeemaker and then went to his desk and got a notebook out of the top drawer. He then filled his own mug and sat in the upholstered chair across the coffee table from Eduardo.

"A new feature is being added to the upgrades," Maurice explained. "All the silos you're modifying will now house new, upgraded missiles." He wasn't going to reveal that they were hypersonics.

Eduardo's face distorted with concern.

"Don't worry," Maurice said as he held up his hand and forced a grin. "They've been designed to directly replace the current Minuteman III missiles. Only a few mechanical and electrical adapters will be needed, and those will be here in the morning."

"It will add time to the job," Eduardo said.

"I know – it's okay," Maurice said. "Everyone up the chain knows that as well. They're sending some engineers to help with the first install. They should be here in the morning."

"We haven't yet closed the first silo, so at least we won't be delayed with another teardown."

"You're ahead of schedule," Maurice said in a tone of approval.

Eduardo nodded. "We'll have to remove the Minuteman III that's currently in there before we can make the new alterations," he explained. "It means that this silo will be offline. In fact, they'll all be offline as we progress."

"It's okay," Maurice said. "The 91st Missile Wing will cycle on extra sites to make up the difference." The CIA Director had informed

Maurice the night before that Minot Air Force Base, the home of the 91st, would take up the slack.

They discussed the details for over an hour, making lists of new tools and supplies that would be needed as they went along. Eduardo left just after 8:00 p.m.

For the next hour, Maurice devised a security plan to accommodate the forthcoming missile extractions and transport. Afterwards, he donned his jacket and headed for the door. He'd get home around 9:30 p.m., have a light dinner – he hadn't eaten since lunchtime – and head to bed.

Things were moving at an unimaginable pace, and he hoped his mind would wind down enough to allow him to sleep.

ANDERS ENTERED Gilligan's Isle and approached a man who was wearing a black tuxedo and checking reservations at a computer. The place was crowded, and the clattering of silverware on plates and the multitude of chatting voices made it noisy. Anders submitted his alias credentials and the host led him to a table where Alina was already seated. Her hair was dark brown this time, and she wore glasses with red frames. Her attractiveness was not hidden by the disguise.

She stood, grabbed both of Anders' hands, and kissed him on the cheek.

"You're right on time," she said, smiling. It was the "all-clear" phrase.

"You always seem surprised," he responded with the corresponding status line as they both took their seats. They were near the back of the dining room, far from the wall of windows that faced the street, and not far from the kitchen. "Probably not the best table in the place."

She huffed and smiled. "It's perfect for *us*," she said and then looked closely at his face. "I hardly recognized you."

"Good," he said. "You dyed your hair."

She nodded. "And I'm not wearing perfume," she said and winked at him.

He caught a hint of forgiveness in her voice. He'd noticed she'd nixed the perfume for their previous exchange as well. "Me either."

She laughed as she opened the menu. "I think I'll go for a steak," she said. "Your treat, I understand."

"Next one's on you," he said. "I'll go for the filet mignon, and I've read that this place has good soups."

"And desserts," she added.

A wine specialist came to them and they ordered a hundred-dollar bottle of merlot – Alina's choice.

"Were you followed after our last meeting?" he asked. He wanted to know whether the man who had supposedly followed Alina to the club that night – the same one Anders had encountered at the bar while meeting with the Chinese courier – had been following him, or her.

"A *woman* followed me out of the bar that night," Alina replied. "The man left when you did."

"So, a *team* might have been surveilling us," he concluded. That was not a good sign. "I saw that same man at my exchange last night, here, in New York."

"Really?" she said as her eyes widened. She seemed to think for a few seconds and then sighed. "It makes me worry about what we've gotten ourselves into."

The wine arrived and, after giving Alina a taste, the server gave them each a heavy pour. Even though Anders was no wine connoisseur, he could tell that the wine was good. It was something about its heavy texture.

Anders got Alina up to speed on current events, including the questioning of the president's niece. He then shared what he'd learned from Barney about the jostling of Chinese and Russian nukes, and their respective personnel.

"Are you aware that things are happening at *your* missile installations as well?" she asked.

He was going to try to feign that he knew about them, but it took him off guard. "Only rumors," he said. "What have you learned?"

"Like everything else, this is only a rumor," she explained. "But I've heard from other ops at my firm that the US is reconfiguring a group of silos and control stations to launch hypersonic missiles."

He grinned.

"What?" she asked.

"It's just that, again, the rumors are exactly the same for all three players," he explained. "They're all accusing each other of interfering with their respective launch sites, and now each country is supposedly reconfiguring their nuclear assets and upgrading to hypersonics."

"You don't think it's serious?"

"I think it's all gravely serious," he replied. "But I don't know how much of it is true."

"Suppose we assume the rumors *are* true," Alina said as she looked over the menu. "What would we do differently?"

Anders was about to speak when a man came to take their orders. Alina ordered a rib-eye steak as Anders fumbled through the menu and found the filet he wanted. They both also ordered the soup – crab bisque.

"I don't know what we could do differently," he said when the server left. "I suppose one option would be to resign."

Alina's expression went blank for an instant, and then her face turned pale.

"I don't think that's an option for me," she said. "I'm in this too deep."

Anders understood, and quickly became concerned for her. He was aware of the cutthroat actions her home government enacted against spies. He then wondered how deep *he* was into the mess. After all, even the president's niece had been hauled in for questioning.

"I suppose another option would be to find a way to read the devices we've been passing around so we'd at least know what we're mixed up in," he said. "But that's a tricky thing, and it could get us into trouble."

"Probably killed," she said. "But there are some other rumors – about your CIA and the president."

"Yes?"

"He was in the CIA, correct?"

Anders nodded. "That's a fact, not a rumor."

"The *rumor* is that he was in some secret society of CIA people," she added.

Anders knew exactly where she was going, and was shocked that she knew about it. She was probably referring to the same "secret society" to which his father had belonged. He kept his composure.

"Subgroups are formed within the CIA to compartmentalize information," Anders said. "But I've not heard anything about secret societies."

"I've heard that these CIA subgroups are effectively autonomous," she explained. "And they sometimes have agendas outside those of the mainstream government – and even in *opposition* to an administration's policies."

"I see – you're talking about the so-called deep state," he said. "That's been around for a long time, and it does just what you're saying."

She shook her head. "This is different."

Anders knew that. He was trying to divert the conversation.

"The 'deep state' to which you are referring," she continued, "is composed of intermediate and high-level employees that cause problems in various ways. What I'm talking about is different: this is a complete, cohesive entity that has specific goals, and is well organized."

"And what kinds of goals are you talking about?" he asked.

She shrugged. "One-world order, socialist transition, end of days – "

"End of days – what's that?"

"It's just conspiracy theory stuff."

"Explain."

"It's simple," she said. "There are people who want to wipe humanity off the Earth."

"What? Like extreme environmentalists?" he asked. "Remove humans to save the planet?"

She laughed. "Maybe. But that's not what I mean," she said. "There are cult-like groups that just want it all to end. Some of them are wealthy crazies who want to instigate a war – a humanity-ending war. There's a story about a billionaire who donated most of his fortune to the building of the particle accelerator at CERN."

"The Large Hadron Collider," Anders said. "Why?"

"Not for science," she explained. "Rather, he was hoping that the energetic collisions would create a black hole and destroy the planet."

Anders laughed. "And why would these people want to end humanity?"

She shrugged. "Maybe it's some religious thing," she said.

That wouldn't surprise him.

"On another topic, do you not find it strange that the leaders of the three countries involved in this all came up through their respective intelligence services?" Alina asked.

"Yes, I did find that peculiar," he said. "I'm not entirely sure, but the only other US presidents involved in the CIA were appointed, and that doesn't count: those people are considered outsiders to career CIA people."

Just as their food arrived, another couple sat at a table too close for him and Alina to carry on their conversation in private. Instead, they ate and chatted about English Premier League football – Alina was a big fan of Arsenal – and then about vacation spots in Greece. At the end of the meal they ordered dessert – they shared something called a "chocolate mountain," – and then exchanged devices.

Before the check came, Anders passed her a mobile phone given to him by DMS and said, "We need to go into dynamic mode next time."

She nodded – indicating that she knew exactly what that meant.

Anders arranged for a ride through his phone app, and then paid the dinner bill – $275 with the tip. He realized that high-end dating in New York would render him homeless very quickly.

He stepped outside into the chilly night and caught up with Alina at the curb. Just as a SuperLift car pulled around the corner a block away, he spotted a man he recognized exiting the restaurant. A few seconds later, a blonde woman – early to mid 40s – appeared and caught up with him.

Anders grabbed Alina around the waist, brought her in close to him, and turned her to face him. He leaned in close as if he were going to kiss her, but pressed his cheek against hers and whispered, "We have visitors."

"Who?" she asked, but didn't turn to look.

"The guy you saw at the Orion," he replied. "Same one I saw last night. But I've never seen the woman who's with him."

As the SuperLift car pulled up – a Jeep Cherokee – Anders opened the door and let Alina get in first. She slid over, and then he got in and closed the door. As their car pulled away, he saw the man hailing a taxi, but he didn't seem to be in a rush. He and Alina were in the clear.

Alina looked out the back window and said, "That's the woman who followed me out of the Orion."

"And the man?"

"I can't see his face," she replied, and then the car turned a corner and their stalkers were out of view.

During the 10-minute ride to another Manhattan restaurant where they'd drop off Alina, they speculated about who their trackers might be. Anders' money was on the CIA. Alina's was on the Russians.

When the car stopped, Alina suddenly kissed him on the lips, looked at him, and said, "Your beard is itchy." She got out and closed the door.

As his car drove away, Anders' mind spun for a few seconds in response to the kiss.

When he recovered, his thoughts went back to what happened at the restaurant. He knew that, if their pursuers were persistent, they'd eventually catch up with them.

AFTER THEIR UNPRODUCTIVE DINNER, which Tim had been calling a "steak-out," at Gilligan's Isle the night before, Candace had located the address of Adel Pinkton, the widow of a former CIA officer, Carl Pinkton, who had died in a covert mission in Norway in 1992. The woman, now in her 80s, lived in rural Maryland, and Candace and Tim were already 50 miles west of New York City at 7:00 a.m., in an FBI-issued SUV. Candace was driving.

"Why did you choose this one first?" Tim asked. "She's not the closest – there's one in DC. We're heading pretty far out of our way. We could've flown back to DC first."

Tim was still bellyaching that she'd changed their plans last minute and decided to drive, rather than fly, back to DC. He'd also complained about the indirect route.

"Wilfred Carrigan put *two* checkmarks next to Carl Pinkton's name for some reason, and I want to see Mrs. Pinkton as soon as possible," she replied. It reminded her that five people were already dead, including Wilfred and his wife.

"You're thinking Mrs. Pinkton was involved in the SWA?" Tim asked.

"Maybe, yes, or at least she might know something about it," she replied. "It's a nice day, enjoy the ride."

"I suppose we wasted a couple of days on this trip already. Why not a couple more?" Tim said without veiling the sarcasm, referring to how they'd dropped everything they were doing in DC and scrambled to New York after getting a tip from counterintelligence.

Candace was starting to suspect that they were being purposely misled in order to obstruct their investigation. The recent tips had been a complete waste of time. Although, she thought she had recognized a woman in the back of the restaurant. She'd taken a picture of her and sent it to FBI Headquarters for facial recognition, but she had little hope that it would turn up anything. She was with a man Candace hadn't seen before. Tim also managed to get a pic of the man's face before they'd left the restaurant.

After the wild goose chase from the night before, Candace was anxious to get to Frederick, Maryland to interview Adel Pinkton. They'd arrive just before lunchtime.

RATHER THAN FLYING, Anders rented a car for the trip back to DC. He'd gotten out of New York City before 7:00 a.m., and by eight o'clock was traveling south on Interstate 95, approaching the outskirts of Philadelphia.

His mind wandered as the road rolled beneath him, and his thoughts bounced between his discussion with Alina at dinner the night before, and the call with his mother that afternoon.

It was reassuring that Alina had drawn some of the same conclusions that he had about the connections between current events on the world stage and the rumors they were hearing. It was verification that his imagination wasn't overplaying his observations, and he wasn't just being paranoid. He also wasn't being paranoid about the man who had now shown his face at his last three rendezvous locations. It meant that information was getting out, and it was more likely connected directly to him, rather than to the Russian or Chinese couriers. Was there a leak at DMS? Or a mole in the White House? Supposedly, only the president knew about the operation in the White House. On the other hand, multiple people at DMS were involved. It meant a leak coming from DMS was more likely.

Anders supposed it was possible that someone was spying on the president, but he had no idea how that could be unless Crownbrook talked in his sleep. Of course, the CIA or NSA might have tapped his computer, and possibly even the secure phone that DMS had provided him. But even if they intercepted the phone messages, they'd have trouble getting through the encryption. It could also be something as simple as hidden cameras installed in every conceivable place within the White House so that they could see Crownbrook's computer and phone screens – therefore getting the outgoing messages as he typed, before they were encrypted.

Anders stopped for a bathroom break at a gas station, and picked up a hamburger and fries at a drive-through a little after 11:00 a.m. He got to DC just after noon. He parked the rental car a half mile from DMS and walked the rest of the way, meandering a bit to follow the usual evasion protocols. Having not flown back – a decision he'd made on the way to the safe house after dinner with Alina the night before and seeing his stalker for the third time – he was less likely to have been followed. Airports were risky places in his line of work.

He entered the DMS complex at 1:00 p.m. and went directly to his office. Alina's mention of secret groups within the CIA ignited his urgency to access the files on his father's thumb-drive.

He retrieved the device from a locked drawer in his desk and plugged it into his desktop computer. A dialog box appeared that prompted him to "upload the passcode." That the access code had to be *uploaded* made it clear that it was nothing simple, like a short string of characters.

Anders called his mother, who explained that she'd just finished lunch and was about to head out to the flower bed beneath the gutter he'd replaced when he'd visited.

He told her about the passcode prompt.

"Can you snap a picture of the screen and send it to my email?" she asked.

He did as she instructed as she went to her computer. A few seconds later, her computer chimed in the background, announcing that she'd received an email.

"Got it," she said. "Let's see here."

After just a few seconds, she said, "I know what this is, but it's not exactly good news."

"Oh?"

"Your father used the encryption software that I suggested at the time – it's probably about five or six years old, obsolete nowadays," she explained. "It's the one you mentioned during our previous call."

"Encryptocon."

"Yes," she said. "An old version. It requires an image key – an actual digital photo."

There would be no guessing the passcode. "Any idea of what kind of image?"

"None, honey," she replied. "It could be anything and, what's worse, it has to be in exactly the right format, dimensions, and file type. It has to be the *exact* image with which the drive was encrypted."

"Did Dad have a CIA laptop at home?" he asked. "Or, do you think some of the other storage drives in the safe might have the image?"

"I seriously doubt he'd keep the passcode files with the encrypted drives," she said. "Your father was paranoid about security. And his CIA computer is back in their hands."

"Do you know what kinds of photos he'd used in the past?" he asked.

"I only know of one," she replied. "But I know what that was used to encrypt, and he wouldn't reuse it – but I suppose you can try it so that you can eliminate it."

"What was it?"

"He used an image from the internet of the big radio space telescope in Puerto Rico."

"Oh, so he didn't actually take the photos himself," Anders said.

He wasn't surprised that his dad would choose something that had to do with space.

"He could use whatever images he wanted," she said. "But he'd never use a photo of something personal – certainly nothing specific to his personal life – to encrypt CIA files. He'd never make that kind of connection between his professional and personal lives. Anyway, I'll find that telescope image and send it to you."

"I'll start trying some of the photos he sent me," he said. His father had sent him a multitude of pics in emails over the years.

"He must've sent me hundreds of pictures – in texts and emails – all while we were living in the same house," she said and laughed. "You can try them – yours and mine."

"What if I enter the wrong one?"

"There are no destructive anti-tampering options in that software," she replied. "It will, however, lock you out for some time after an incorrect attempt. You didn't find any physical self-destruct mechanisms?"

"We didn't," Anders replied. "And my firm has people who are experts in these things."

They talked for another 10 minutes about the Genesee Lake Spring Festival, and he promised to try to visit for that final weekend in May if things weren't too hectic for him. Unfortunately, he had a feeling they would be.

After ending the call, Anders went to his personal email account and searched for all his dad's messages that had pictures attached. There were over 200 such emails that spanned over five years. He'd try them one by one, and he figured that the best strategy would be to start with the most recent images and go backward in time.

The last one his father had sent – just a few days before he'd passed – was of a vintage car for sale in Genesee Lake. It was a red, 1967 Mustang convertible that looked to be in pretty bad shape. His father had written, "Isn't this the one that belonged to your friend Mark, from high school?"

It wasn't Mark's car – his was a '68, not to mention that he'd rammed his into the back of a garbage truck during his first year of college. It was a total loss, and Mark had suffered a broken leg and arm in the crash.

Anders went back to the data drive screen and clicked the "upload" button next to the passcode prompt. The software took him to his computer's file directory to select a passcode image. He clicked on the picture of the red car and hit the "submit" button.

The program responded with "Incorrect Passcode File," and a message box appeared with the words "Lockout in Progress" displayed inside it, along with a timer that started counting down from 20 minutes.

A *twenty-minute* delay? Anders was expecting no more than five. At this rate, it would take him 70 hours to get through the 200 images – a full-time job for two weeks.

He decided to go through the images more carefully and change the order. He didn't know what criteria he was going to use to rank them, but he'd just take a look at each one and try to get a gut feeling for how significant it was.

His phone chimed: it was a text message from Harrison requesting that he go up to his office. They had much to discuss.

IT WAS JUST after 2:00 p.m. when Candace pushed the button and the doorbell chimed inside the house. An instant later, dogs barked behind the door and a woman yelled from far off, telling them to calm down.

"Sounds like there are at least three of them in there," Tim said.

"Nice place for dogs," Candace said as she looked around the vast front yard. It was an old, two-story farmhouse on a large piece of land surrounded by fields and woods. Three tall, massive oaks shaded the front yard, and flowers in beds around the large porch added vibrant contrast to the view. The gravel driveway wrapped around the back where there were at least two other buildings, one of which was a classic red barn with a high-peaked, green-shingled roof. The other was a stone grain silo that was taller than the barn. It was a peculiar structure, with a conical roof over what looked to be a high deck that encircled the perimeter. It seemed like the old structure had been remodeled into a livable space – like a lighthouse. She could only imagine the view of the picturesque countryside from its deck.

Scuffling sounds came from behind the door as if someone was pulling the dogs away from it and their nails were slipping on wooden floors. The heavy, inner door opened and a thin woman faced them through the screen door. She looked to be in good shape for an 83-year-old woman as she fought off the dogs struggling to get a look at the visitors. Her gray hair was long and tied in a tight ponytail, and a pair of reading glasses dangled by straps from her neck.

"What can I do for you?" she asked.

"Are you Adel Pinkton?" Candace asked.

"I am," she confirmed. "And you are?"

Candace responded as she and Tim showed the woman their FBI credentials. "Can we talk?" she asked.

"Pertaining to what, exactly?" Adel asked.

"Your husband, Carl," Candace replied, although she planned to learn whatever she could about Adel as well.

The woman opened the door and invited them in. "Don't worry about the dogs," she said. "They're all bark."

As they entered, three large dogs investigated them closely, mostly sniffing and watching them. Two were golden retrievers – almost always friendly beasts – but the one to watch was a large, male German shepherd that looked more like a wolf than a domestic breed.

Adel seemed to notice Tim's reluctance to pass by the shepherd. "Don't worry about him," she said. "Titus was raised by a golden retriever mama. He's a cupcake."

Tim reached out his hand and Titus sniffed it, glanced up at

Tim's face, and wagged his tail before trotting away into the living room where he immediately began roughhousing with the other two hounds.

As Adel led them into the kitchen, the aroma of freshly brewed coffee filled the air. "Have a seat at the table," she said. "I'll have to brew a little more coffee."

Tim took a seat at one end of the rectangular table and Candace on the adjacent side to his right, facing a large patio door with a view of the vast backyard.

"We used to have horses," Adel said as she sat in the chair on Candace's right. Burbling and hissing sounds emanated from the coffeemaker on the counter. "But that was a long time ago, before Carl passed away under strange circumstances."

"Strange circumstances?" Tim asked.

Adel nodded. "They tried to tell me that he died during a mission," she explained. "But he contacted me after that operation was over – he was alive and well. The bad news arrived two days later – he'd been shot. But that was over 30 years ago now. Another lifetime."

"Sorry, we had no idea," Candance said.

"What do you want to know about him?" Adel asked. "Is this about that SWA thing again?"

"Again?" Candace asked. She wasn't surprised that the FBI had been there before, considering that the same had happened with the recently deceased Carrigans.

"I was interviewed about this 14 years ago," Adel replied. "Here, at this very table."

"You were aware of Carl's involvement?" Tim asked.

"Sure," Adel replied. "As he was aware of mine."

Candace *knew* the double checkmark next to Carl's name meant something.

"Are you still a member?" Candace asked.

"Of course not," Adel said. "And I'm no longer in the CIA."

Candace tried to play it as though she'd already known that Adel had been in the CIA. "Were you planted in the group by the CIA?"

"No," Adel replied. "Carl and I were *recruited* by the SWA."

Candace was starting to realize that her FBI files were shit. How had the previous investigators missed that about Carl Pinkton when they'd questioned him? And why hadn't they mentioned that Adel had been in the CIA?

"Why did they recruit you and Carl?" Tim asked.

"I don't know what it's like now," Adel replied, "but there was a large faction of CIA personnel in the SWA at that time – it's where the group got its start with the help of outside players."

"Yes, we knew about that," Candace confirmed. "It was instigated by a wealthy influencer – someone alive today who's still manipulating politics toward a one-world order. What can you tell us about their goals?"

Adel looked at her, and then Tim. "Aren't you aware of their intentions?"

"We want to hear it from you – your take – before we discuss what we know," Candace replied. "We're hoping to learn something new."

Adel seemed to understand, but now seemed edgy. "They want a single administration to govern the entire world, and they want to reduce the global population to something like 500 million."

"Do you know how they plan to go about doing this?" Tim asked.

"Their strategies are being implemented right now, as we speak," Adel replied. "In the US, wealthy influencers are still doing much of that work."

"You mean by funding like-minded politicians," Tim said.

"Yes, that's essential, but it's not enough," Adel explained. "They're also funding the elections of judges, district attorneys, union leaders, and even school board presidents. And they're bribing or blackmailing those people to do various things."

"School board presidents?" Candace repeated.

Adel nodded. "They need to get at the minds of future generations," she explained. "But there are more sinister things they believe in – like population control at all costs."

"*At all costs* – what does that mean?" Tim asked.

"It means beyond contraceptives and social pressuring," she replied. "War, disaster, pandemic – whatever it takes. It doesn't matter to them what the state of the world is afterward – even if it means a nuclear winter. The planet, and some humans, will survive, and the only power in existence will belong to those who planned the whole thing. Then, when the world government takes over, they'll control the population from the very start of the recovery – ideally keeping it under 500 million – and then living happily ever after."

"So you think they'd actually try to release a horrible pathogen, or start a nuclear war, to accomplish this?" Tim asked.

"*Think*? No," she replied. "I *know* they'd do it. I was a member, remember? Carl and I discontinued our involvement when they started talking about these crazy things. My feeling is that they're responsible for releasing the RAT-32C virus."

"You think it was an attempt to reduce the population?" Tim asked.

"Maybe," she replied. "But it was more likely a test run to study its effects, both in terms of the spreading of the virus itself and its social consequences – how people might react to government control."

"What happened when you got out of the SWA?" Candace asked, wanting to divert the conversation away from conspiracy theories. "Did they threaten you?"

"Some verbal warnings, yes, which were designed to make sure we kept our mouths shut," Adel explained. "Not so much about keeping the existence of the group secret, or even its objectives, but about keeping the identities of its members concealed, especially the leaders of the group."

"And that's why we're here," Candace said. "Will you divulge names now? Were there any prominent people in the SWA –

maybe some from the CIA, or any other government entity at the time?"

Adel stared at Candace for a few awkward seconds. "It seems you've not done your homework, young lady," she said. "With a massive investment by a private source, the SWA started as a group of CIA people – many at the very top of the food chain. Once the power of this group exceeded a certain threshold, it rapidly expanded beyond the CIA – mostly by recruiting influential people from the private sector, as well as from the intelligence and security services of foreign nations."

"How many members did the SWA have when you were still active?" Tim asked.

"Over 1,000," Adel replied. "And they were all influential people. They were given tasks to carry out, within their own spheres of influence."

That was nearly double the number of members Candace figured they had. "What tasks were given to the CIA people?" she asked.

"Most of us, like Carl and myself, were supposed to influence elections by digging up dirt on candidates, or fabricating it," Adel replied. "But others, with different skills, were tasked with taking out people who were in the way."

"Assassinations?" Tim asked with a shocked expression.

Adel stood as she spoke. "Yes, sometimes, but otherwise mostly *nonlethal* things, like setting people up – drug busts and the like." She returned with three mugs and an insulated carafe of coffee. She filled the mugs, and asked, "Cream and sugar?"

Candace and Tim both declined, and each grabbed a mug as Adel retook her seat.

"Do you know of any influential people who are *current* SWA members?" Tim asked.

"You mean, like the president?" she asked. "And the current CIA director – Radcliffe, is it?"

"Are they?" Candace blurted.

"They *were*," Adel replied. "I can't verify that they are *current* members, but they are, at the least, *former* members who are now at the highest level of government. It's just as the SWA had planned it."

"Do you know of any way we can *prove* that the president is an active member?" Candace asked. She flushed, realizing that she might come off as too eager for a supposedly unbiased FBI investigator.

Adel shook her head. "I've been out of it way too long," she said. "You'd have to find an active member."

Tim took out a clean copy – no checkmarks – of the list that Candace had given the late Wilfred Carrigan to look over and handed it to Adel. "Do you recognize any of the names on this list?" he asked.

Adel put it on the table and looked it over. "Sure," she said.

Candace handed her a pen. "Could you put checkmarks next to the ones you are certain were members," she said. "Also, if you know any other names, please write them down as well."

Adel looked at her. "The only reason I'm doing this is because I'm old, and my husband is dead. This could get me killed."

Candace nodded. She knew well that was true – four people they'd interviewed about it were dead, and a fifth one on their list had been assassinated after that. They had taken extra precautions this time – even their immediate supervisor was out of the loop on this visit.

Adel returned the list with checks next to eight names and two added ones: Crownbrook and Radcliffe.

"You're absolutely sure about the president and CIA director?" Tim asked.

"I met them both when I was an active member," she replied. "That was in 1990 or 91."

"Anything else you know that can help us expose this group?" Candace asked.

"Are you after individual members, or the entire organization?" Adel asked. "If it's the latter, you might be biting off more than you can chew."

"What do you mean?" Candace asked.

"They'll kill you," Adel replied. "And they won't care if you're FBI, the president, or an angel sent by God himself."

"We'll take care of ourselves," Candace retorted. "But is there anything else you can tell us?"

"I have no more names," Adel said. "But you should know that there are other clandestine groups that exist which have similar ambitions and, although their ultimate objectives don't necessarily coincide with those of the SWA, they may be cooperating on some things."

"What groups?" Tim asked.

"There are two that I know of," Adel explained. "One is called TS-49. It's an international group of highly influential people – politics and old wealth – which wants to rid the Earth of humanity altogether. They essentially want to return the planet to nature."

"I'd say that's about as extreme as it gets," Tim quipped and chuckled.

"It's not a laughing matter," Adel scolded. "They'd settle for a nuclear holocaust, but they really want to inflict a targeted, biological end to humanity. They have constructed research facilities around the world, and fund the schooling of graduate students to work in government labs. After all this RAT-32C stuff that happened a few years ago, you're undoubtedly aware of gain-of-function research."

Candace knew it basically involved altering known pathogens to make them deadlier, or more contagious. It had been suspected that the RAT-32C virus had been the product of such research, and she knew the FBI was still investigating that possibility.

"And the other group?" Candace asked.

"It's called the Custodial Group, or the CG," Adel replied. "I'm not sure of its ultimate goal, but I know that our president was – or is – a member."

"Wait, I thought you said he was in the SWA," Tim said.

"He was – or *is* – members of both," Adel retorted. "His first connection with the SWA came through a meeting between the CG and SWA leadership. My husband was at that meeting. So Crownbrook was actually a member of the Custodial Group *before* joining the SWA. I'm not sure about Radcliffe."

Tim scribbled in a notebook as Adel explained the common goals of the two groups, which included nuclear war as a means to their ends. Although the SWA would have settled for nearly any method of severe population reduction, the CG's only objective was a massive nuclear conflict, and it had to be carried out with missiles. The reason for this was unknown.

"Do you know of any other CG or TS-49 members?" Candace asked, realizing now that the scope of their investigation had to widen.

"I know of only two for certain – and they're both already on your list," Adel said. "Crownbrook is one."

"And the other?" Tim asked.

"Henry Bennett," Adel replied. "He was with the president during that joint, CG-SWA meeting."

Candace knew that Henry Bennett was deceased. His wife, Griselda, however, was not.

CHAPTER 9

It was a crisp, sunny, Monday morning, and Maurice relaxed as the tension seemed to release its grip on his body. He sipped coffee and watched out his office window as an empty missile transport vehicle pulled into a hangar a quarter mile away. It would be used to transport one of the missiles that was being replaced to a secure location in Colorado where it would be dismantled.

The modifications to Silo I-1 were complete and a new mobile launch vehicle, or MOLV, was ready to be tested. It had taken nearly 10 days – three days longer than planned – for the first silo upgrade, which was expected since they'd made some last-minute changes designed to accommodate the new hypersonic missiles. That first new missile was scheduled for delivery in the next week, so the silo wasn't ready for operation, but the control system could be tested while empty.

Eduardo's people would now start renovating their second site, Silo I-2, and they'd train the first launch control crew over the following weekend. Since Maurice had selected the mobile launch crew from current launch operators at active missile silos, the training was expected to go quickly. Specially trained drivers and dedicated mechanics would be assigned to the trucks to ensure that they were well-maintained and could get to the silos even under horrible weather conditions.

Even though each silo had a specific truck designated to it, any of the mobile launch stations could operate any of the silos – the crews just needed the access and arming codes for the missiles. The latter were, of course, controlled by the president. The original plan called for five more trucks than silos to account for downtime for vehicle maintenance and upgrades. The president had promised a few additional trucks, and replacement electronics, so there'd be ample redundancy built into the system.

Eduardo's crew was now on its way to Silo I-2, five miles southeast of I-1. The rest would go more quickly since a part of the crew would head to Silo I-3 midweek to prepare it for its upgrade the following week. Also, once another launch crew was trained and tested, it would train subsequent crews, leaving Eduardo's group free to focus on the mechanical upgrades. At that point, the operation could just grind away, progress could be more easily monitored, and he'd get a better idea of the projected completion date.

Even though everything was on track, Maurice still had deep anxiety, the source of which he couldn't pinpoint. At least a part of it came from the realization that the new system seemed to give the president the power to act unilaterally: the operators would get their orders through a different command structure – from the president, to the CIA, to the missile wing commanders rather than through the usual Department of Defense channels. This was explained away by Crownbrook and Radcliffe when Maurice met with them in DC: they wanted to build redundancy into the command structure. Maurice saw it more as a workaround – a way to *circumvent* the checks built into the system.

Maurice's thoughts shifted to the most recent drone incursions of just two nights before. Two sites had been simultaneously infiltrated: H-3 and J-6. They'd been shut down, and all power – including the battery backup systems – had been taken offline. In one respect, the incidents greatly disturbed him. However, they did affirm the need for the new system he was now developing.

Maurice just hoped that the mobile system would never have to be used.

It was a sunny, Monday morning, and Anders enjoyed the long, meandering walk that was the last leg of his trip to DMS. By 7:45 a.m., he was in his office examining his usual news sites. It seemed every geopolitical story that came up was related to his project, or to the rumors associated with it. The top stories focused on minor naval skirmishes between the US and both China and Russia in the South Pacific and North Atlantic, respectively.

The frustration and anxiety that the news reports incited in him made his stomach queasy. He sensed they were connected to his operation with the president but his suspicions were based entirely on the rumors passed on from his courier counterparts. The information was completely unsubstantiated – including the stories about the supposed deployment of hypersonic missiles at US missile silos. He was not privy to anything happening at America's missile sites, and could therefore verify nothing. Next, other than the bare facts, anything reported by news organizations always seemed to be speculation. They were either guessing or claiming "unknown sources" for their information.

Even if Anders blindly assumed that all the rumors were true, they didn't point to a singular conclusion. In fact, they could point to anything from imminent nuclear war to just business as usual. He wasn't going to draw any conclusions at this point – at least nothing that would warrant action on his part.

During the week since he'd returned from New York, he'd had no exchanges for his project with the White House. He'd spent the time trying to break into the data device from his father's safe. Having to wait 20 minutes between attempts made it go excruciatingly slowly, and the most tries he'd made in one day, between his other work, was 38. He was starting to worry that none of the images in his possession would be the one, but it would take him over a week to test the rest of them.

His thoughts wandered to the phone conversation he'd had with Delilah late the night before. His suspicions had been on the mark: she was dating a surgeon, but she wanted to "stay friends." Anders felt unusually comfortable, even relieved, with her disclosure. It was too hard for him to have a relationship with a "normal" person, considering the abnormal life he was leading. It made him think of Alina's kiss in the car in New York.

His phone vibrated, disrupting his line of thought. It was a text from Harrison asking him to come to his office.

There were three minutes left on the wait time since his latest failed attempt at getting into the thumb-drive, so he got the next image ready as he waited. It was a pic of an island in the middle of a lake in Vermont.

When the lockout time was up, he submitted the photo. It failed. The 20-minute timer reset and started counting down. He left his office and went to the elevator. As it ascended, he realized that the photos he'd viewed over the past days, and the emails to which they were attached, brought forth old memories. They conjured emotions, some of which were sad, but others brought on a warm nostalgia, and a smile to his face. He had over a hundred left to test, after which he'd get more from his mother.

When he entered the office, Harrison led him to the chairs and couch on the left side of the room. Harrison sat on the couch and Anders took one of the chairs across the coffee table from him. On the table was a carafe of coffee and two mugs.

"Some bad news," Harrison said. "Our Chinese courier has been taken in. It's verified this time."

"By the MSS?" Anders tried to ask calmly as he poured coffee. The Chinese side of their project had been trouble from the very beginning. It was unnerving.

Harrison shook his head. "Worse," he said. "The CIA."

Anders felt his chest tighten. "How could they know about *him* but not us?"

"My sources at the CIA tell me that they got a tip from the MSS," Harrison explained. "It's a very confusing ordeal when China turns in their own spies."

"It's because he wasn't an MSS spy," Anders said. "The MSS *must* know that the Chinese president is going around them."

"Just like ours is going around our agencies," Harrison added. "And the CIA and FBI are catching wind of it."

"Yeah, and Crownbrook's underground channel goes through *us*," Anders said, regretting his worried tone the instant he uttered the words.

"I understand your concern," Harrison said. "The CIA doesn't have the power to take in its country's citizens like some foreign intelligence services do."

"But our FBI will – if the CIA tips *them* off."

"Good thing the CIA and FBI don't play well together."

"Do you think the CIA knows something, but just isn't moving on it because of that?"

"Perhaps. The stalkers you've seen during your exchanges might be CIA – but we haven't identified them yet," Harrison said. "Your Chinese contact was picked up 24 hours after you made the exchange at the hotel bar. But since the same guy appeared at your meetings with the Russian, information must be leaking from our side."

"From the White House?"

"Maybe," Harrison said. "I doubt they've identified you, however. They would've taken you in or referred you to the FBI. I do know that they've been investigating something else that could be connected to our situation: the Single-World Alliance."

"What's that?"

"It's another secret society," Harrison replied and went on to explain its objectives, which included installing a global government, severely reducing the world's population, and establishing complete control over every aspect of society.

"How would they reduce the population?"

Harrison shrugged. "Any way possible – sterilization, disease, and even nuclear war."

"But how does the Single-World Alliance involve us?" Anders asked.

"Crownbrook. He was connected to the SWA at one time, and the FBI has been investigating it. They might be looking into the Custodial Group as well," Harrison explained. "My contacts reported that some of the sources the FBI interviewed were killed afterwards – professional hits. Four were on the West Coast – the two double murders I told you about – and a fifth was recently assassinated in Hawaii. They were all suspected SWA members."

"Sounds like a cleanup operation," Anders commented.

"Which means there could be more to come," Harrison said.

"Could these hits involve the president?" Anders asked, regretting it immediately.

Harrison smiled. "I doubt it," he said. "At least he's probably not giving orders to kill anyone."

"I didn't mean –"

"I know," Harrison cut him off, holding up his hand. "But it's a fair question since we don't really know anything at this point. The CIA was investigating the SWA internally when Crownbrook was still a CIA op. It could be that he was involved in that capacity."

"You mean he might have been *infiltrating* the group by order of the CIA?"

Harrison shrugged. "Possibly," he said. "But that's just speculation. That would've been a long time ago."

"But he was also a member of the Custodial Group," Anders said. "How does that fit in?"

Harrison shook his head. "Not sure," he said. "But I'm certain he was a *legitimate* member of the CG, considering he and your father were trying to recruit me."

"So, what's next for us?"

"A new Chinese courier will be ready in a week," Harrison replied. "In the meantime, you have two operations to carry out. One with your Russian contact."

Anders was looking forward to seeing Alina again. "And the other?"

"The president's niece."

"Really?" Anders asked, surprised. "Hasn't she been compromised?"

"As it turns out, no," Harrison replied. "The FBI only questioned her because of her frequent visits with the president during a suspicious time. Since then, she's kept up her regular visits and Crownbrook has made sure that she's either brought something in – like an antique of some kind – or left with something. She's bringing you a train car – one that needs repair."

"And there will be a data device inside," Anders concluded. It reminded him that he had a locomotive from her for which DMS still had to estimate a value. "Why not use the phone?"

"Because it's not digital this time," Harrison explained. "It's a paper document of some sort."

"That's strange," Anders said. "Why not just scan it – digitize it?"

Harrison shook his head. "All I know is that it's a small, waterproof envelope that's not to be opened for any reason – its contents cannot be duplicated."

"When is the meeting?"

"She'll be contacting you in the next few days," Harrison said. "Try to set up the meet for this coming weekend – same place."

It would be his third time at the bookstore in six weeks. He didn't like it, but at least he'd been in disguise for all those exchanges.

"Anything else?" Anders asked.

"Yes," Harrison said. "Any progress on breaking into that thumbdrive?"

"Still working on it," Anders replied.

"When you get in, please let me know if you find anything

connected to our project with the president," Harrison said. "I feel like I'm tangled in a web in the dark – all of this stuff is connected in some way but I just can't piece it together."

Anders felt the same. What was worse was that the answers to all their questions were flowing right through their hands and they just couldn't access them.

CANDACE NAVIGATED THE LIGHT, Sunday morning traffic on the highway heading west out of Savannah, Georgia. They were on their way to a little town called Genesee Lake.

"This is a long way to go without setting up an appointment," commented Tim.

"Even longer if you consider we're driving back to DC afterward," Candace said.

"What?"

"We have another stop in North Carolina," she explained. "After checking the flights, and figuring in the time it will take to pick up a rental car, driving back is quicker and cheaper."

"What if she isn't home?" he said. "Or out of town?"

"Then we'll be waiting around for a while," she replied as she exited the highway and proceeded northwest on a rural road. "Try to enjoy the scenery. Ever been to Georgia?"

"Only Atlanta," he replied as they passed beneath a long canopy of trees. "You're right though, it is beautiful around here."

"Especially compared to what it's like in DC right now – cold and damp," she said, even though she'd checked the weather earlier and learned that it was going to be sunny and mild on the upper East Coast. "Consider this a vacation."

After a 40-minute drive on a curvy road that passed through forests and fields, and around some beautiful lakes, they came to the small town of Genesee Lake, the home of the Hornets, as advertised by a tall billboard on the side of the road as they entered the central business district. The town center had two bars, a gas station, a grocery store, and a combined police-fire station.

They backtracked a half mile east on another road until they arrived at the house of Griselda Bennett and the late Henry Bennett, her husband. They turned left into the driveway at 10:15 a.m., got out of the car, and climbed the stairs to the front porch.

As Candace lifted her hand to knock on the wooden frame of the screen door, laughter came from inside the house – it sounded like a group of women. That's when she noticed three bikes leaning against the far side of the porch. Mrs. Bennett must have company.

Candace looked to Tim, shrugged, and knocked loudly on the door. The laughter continued and it seemed no one had heard the knock.

She waited until the noise died down and knocked again. This time, voices murmured from inside, and a thin, elderly woman padded to the door.

"Can I help you?" the woman asked through the screen.

"Are you Griselda Bennett?" Candace asked.

"Yes, and you are?" the woman asked.

"I'm Candace Wright and this is Tim Barilaro, special agents with the FBI," she explained as they both presented their badges and held them up to the screen. "It sounds like you have company. Should we come back later today?"

The woman's face seemed to express relief and she said, "Please. How about 11:30?"

Candace glanced at her phone for the time. "Sure," she said. "Is there a place nearby where we can get some coffee in the meantime?"

The woman instructed them to go back through town and head west until they got to the Hen House, the town's lone diner.

As they got back into the car and pulled out of the driveway, Tim asked, "What the hell was that?"

Candace knew that it wasn't usual protocol to leave once contact was made with someone they needed to interview. "She's not going anywhere," Candace argued. "Plus, I wanted this to be as friendly as possible. Maybe we can get some reliable information from her."

"When's our next meeting?" Tim asked. "The one in North Carolina."

"Whenever we get there," she replied as they pulled into the Hen House, a half-mile west of the town center. "You need to relax. Let's have coffee and bagels and gather our thoughts before we meet with Mrs. Bennett."

Tim took a deep breath, exhaled, and rolled his eyes as he pulled the door handle and got out of the car.

Candace got out and took in the sweet air infused with the smells of blossoming flowers and fried bacon. She needed to relax, too. They were in the middle of a web of information and nothing was making sense. She hoped Griselda Bennett would provide something revealing.

It was Sunday at 11:00 a.m. when Anders parked the car a few blocks down from The Page, and entered. The bookstore teamed with customers but he spotted Sara Bradbury at a table in the seating area. She was in the far-left corner, next to a display of an early-edition H. P. Lovecraft collection. He went to her and placed a cardboard box on the table that contained the train car that she'd asked him to appraise the last time they'd met.

"Hi Don," she said. "Pretty crowded today. Are you getting coffee?"

"Yes," Anders replied. "You want something?"

She declined, the usual routine, and Anders went to the back of a long line of patrons. After five minutes of waiting, and scoping the place out for possible tails, he got his coffee and went back to Sara's table.

"Sorry about that," he said. "Long line."

"Not to worry," she said and pointed to a stack of books on the floor next to her feet. "I've been paging through these."

Anders nodded to the box on the table. "According to my guy, this car would go for about $1,500 at auction," he said. "You might get a thousand in a direct sale."

"Thanks," she said as she opened the box and checked that everything was there. She pulled out a receipt of return that she then signed, dated, and slid to him. She put the box into a backpack slung over the back of her chair. "Now, on to the next thing."

She reached into a red gift bag on the floor next to her feet, opposite the side with the books, extracted a cardboard box, and set it on the table between them.

"You think you can find someone to fix this?" she asked as she opened the lid and pushed the box toward him.

Anders peered inside. He'd been given some details ahead of time so that he could at least appear to know something about trains, although the character he was playing was not claiming to be an expert.

"Looks like an LGB Santa Fe locomotive," he said as he lifted the largest piece of many out of the box. The wheels were detached and other components were scattered on the foam bottom. "An old one – with some assembly required."

She laughed. "My client said the wheels stopped turning and that he disassembled it but couldn't fix the problem," she explained. "You think you can do something with it?"

Anders sorted through the components at the bottom of the box. "Looks like all the parts are here," he said. "All I can do is take it to my guy. No promises."

"That's okay," she said. "Just let me know the verdict. When might you know?"

"My restorer is pretty busy," he said. "But I can probably get you a prognosis in a week or two, and maybe an estimate of repair costs." He thought someone at DMS must be becoming a model train expert with all of this train stuff, and hoped they were having fun with it.

"Perfect," she said as she pulled out a form that had the model and serial number of the train and a line for him to sign, indicating that he'd taken possession. "Please sign."

He signed it and slid it back to her. He then closed the box and put it into his knapsack.

She put the papers into her bag and then looked at him.

"Do you know who I am?" she asked, seemingly looking for recognition in his eyes. Her demeanor changed in an instant. Serious. "Do you know who my *client* is?"

Anders was stunned by the question, but was able to play it off as confusion. "What do you mean?" he asked, trying not to address the question about her "client."

"I *know* what I'm doing," she said, keeping eye contact. "I found the envelope inside the train – I took it apart since it was already broken."

Now Sara Bradbury was completely involved, and Anders felt bad for her, but he had to keep up the charade. "There was an *envelope* inside?" he asked, hoping to God that she hadn't opened it. "What was in it?"

"A piece of paper with two fingerprints on it," she replied. "And it looks they were made in blood."

His chest tightened and his stomach soured. "What? That's really strange," he said without the need to feign a bewildered expression: he was authentically confused. *Fingerprints? In blood?* "Do you have it?"

"I put it back inside the train's hidden compartment."

Anders was partially relieved, but his nerves were now charged.

"I figured my client had an important reason to send this to you," she added.

"I don't know what a fingerprint would mean to me," he said. "Do you?"

Her expression changed to derision, and she rolled her eyes. "Do you expect me to believe that you don't know anything about this?" she whispered.

"Maybe the envelope was inside the train when your client bought it."

"Do you know who my client is?" she asked again.

"No."

"Bullshit," she whispered as she leaned closer and stared into his eyes.

"Why don't you ask your client about it?" he asked. He hoped that, if she did, it would force Crownbrook to retire his niece from the mule service. He was tempted to suggest that she take the train back with her, but that would put the information at severe risk, even though it had already been compromised by her opening the envelope.

"I will," she said. "I took pictures of everything."

Anders' eyes watered as he tried to squelch the panic building in his chest. His worry extended to Sara's safety.

"Sara, listen to me carefully," he said. "You need to delete those pictures – don't share them with anyone. You can get more answers from your client."

"You know him," she said.

Anders just stared back at her.

After a few awkward seconds, she said, "You know, I was questioned by the FBI about my relationship with my uncle."

"I heard."

"They asked me some strange questions," she explained. "They wanted to know if my uncle was having me meet with people to convey messages. I told them he wasn't, but it made me think about some of the antiques deals he's asked me to do in the past. The train kick he's been on is new."

"How long have you been doing this for him?" Anders asked.

"Just after he started his first term – about five or six years ago."

"What kinds of antiques?" he asked. "I mean, before the trains."

"All kinds of things," she replied. "Watches, old radios, fancy jewelry boxes – some were gifts for my aunt."

They were about the right size, Anders thought. They were easy to carry and could conceal things, like thumb-drives. "Did any of them come from outside the country?" he asked.

"Many," she said. "Russia, China, the UK, India. A few from South America."

"Did you ever get the impression that there were messages in any of those other pieces?"

"No, not until the FBI questioned me about it," she replied. "Now I'm thinking there were messages in all of them."

"Sara," Anders said as he reached over the table and grabbed both of her hands. "Please, listen to me carefully."

She looked back at him with wide, green eyes that were starting to become glassy.

"Don't be startled – try to look relaxed," he said, trying to make sure that she stayed calm and didn't draw attention to them. "You need to play dumb for a while and, no matter what, never let on that you suspected that you were carrying any information. Take this up with your uncle – but you will have to be careful with that."

"What do you mean?"

"You must assume that someone is listening at all times – even in his, uh, place of work," he explained. "And nothing electronic – no phone, text, email. I suggest you get him into a private room – away from his place of employment – and bring a pad of paper and converse through writing while conducting a benign verbal conversation. Be sure to destroy the paper afterwards."

"You mean his *office* is bugged?"

"They've bugged, tapped, or are monitoring everything – or at least you have to *assume* that's the case."

"My God, why?" she asked in a hoarse whisper.

"We don't know," Anders said. "But we're trying to help him."

"And *who* are you?"

"We're a private entity."

She looked at him for a few seconds, apparently dissatisfied with his response. "What do we do now?" she asked.

"I'll have to report this to my superiors, who will notify your client through secure communications," Anders explained. "I doubt you'll be asked to do this again. I was concerned about it from the beginning, but I think your uncle was becoming desperate and felt he couldn't trust any other communication methods. You weren't supposed to be in any danger since you're only dealing with him and my firm, but you now need to remove yourself from this situation."

Her face reddened, and her expression turned from fear to anger. "He's going to hear about this," she hissed.

"Let my firm talk to him first, *please*," he said. "We'll make sure he knows you're not happy. There are bigger things going on here, and you shouldn't attract any attention. Those who have already questioned you, and others, are watching."

Her rage seemed to revert back to fear. "What's this about?"

Anders shook his head. "I just don't know. Really," he said in an apologetic tone. "My job is just to deliver messages – I can't read them. And the fingerprints? I have no idea how that fits into anything. It's just odd."

"You can look at them," she said and nodded to the box with the train car.

He shook his head. "Can I see the pictures you took?" he asked.

Sara took out her phone and showed him a series of images that detailed the stages of disassembly of the locomotive, eventually showing an internal compartment with a small envelope inside, folded once. The next image showed the extracted, unfolded envelope, which was square, and about two inches on a side. The final picture was of the open envelope and a white piece of paper with two, partially overlapping fingerprints on it, one of which was fatter, like a thumbprint, and the other thinner and oblong, both different shades of reddish brown, like dried blood.

"What do I do now?" she asked. There was desperation in her voice.

"Nothing," Anders replied. "I'll make sure your uncle knows what's happened and that you're not going to say a word about it to anyone. *Right?*" He stared into her eyes.

She nodded.

"You have to expect that every device you own – phones and computers – are compromised, and that your home and even your car are bugged. Your car might even be tracked," he explained. "And you need to delete these pictures immediately. Would you do that for me?"

Sara nodded and Anders watched as she deleted the images. Regarding the car, he knew that DMS checked it for transmitting devices the night before – in her own driveway – anticipating that the FBI might try to keep tabs on her. The car was clear.

"I'm going to leave now," he said. "You say you put the envelope back in the train?"

She nodded.

"You continue shopping for books, and try to relax for half an hour," he instructed as he stood and slung his backpack over his shoulder, the train car inside. "Then go home and carry on as if everything is normal. I'll inform your client about what has happened."

She nodded, and then took in a deep breath and let it out slowly. "I'll try."

"It was nice meeting you, Sara," Anders said. "Goodbye."

"Goodbye, Don," she said.

Anders headed for the exit.

CANDACE KNOCKED on the wooden frame of the screen door.

The sound of a cabinet closing and footsteps came from deep in the house and, a few seconds later, Griselda Bennett opened the door and invited them inside. The woman was about five-foot-seven, thin, and her black and gray hair was pulled into a ponytail. She smiled. Her eyes looked intelligent and kind.

"Follow me," Griselda said as she led them through a foyer and into the kitchen. Her walk was agile for a widow in her mid-70s. "I made tea, but I can brew some coffee if you prefer."

"Tea's good with me," Tim said as they each took a seat around the kitchen table. He pointed out the large window facing the backyard. "Looks like you have a big garden."

"There's a little of everything in there. I do a lot of canning," she said as she poured tea from a ceramic pot into three cups. "But you're here to talk about Henry."

"That's right, Mrs. Bennett," Candace said.

"You can call me Gigi," the woman said. "What would you like to know?"

"Henry was a CIA operative and, later, an analyst, correct?" Candace asked.

Gigi nodded.

"It's our understanding that he was also a member of a group called the Single-World Alliance, or the SWA," Tim said. "Were you aware of that?"

"No, I was not," Gigi replied, and then shrugged. "But I'm not surprised. You see, Henry infiltrated a number of groups while he was with the company."

"But this group had its origins within the CIA, and then expanded outward," Candace said. "He would've been investigating some of his own colleagues."

"That also doesn't surprise me," Gigi explained. "Although Henry only ever spoke in generalities about his work, he was often disappointed about things he discovered during his investigations."

"Did he ever work with Thomas Crownbrook?" Candace asked.

"He did," Gigi replied. "They were on a few missions together."

"Do you know anything about those missions?" Tim asked.

Gigi smiled. "Of course not," she said. "Henry never spoke of the details of his work. It was something that bothered him – that he couldn't share things that happened to him – but he always said that it was to protect the family."

"You have kids, Gigi?" Candace asked.

"I have a son."

"Where is he?" Tim asked.

"He lives in Virginia," Gigi replied.

"What does he do there?" Candace asked.

"He's a computer scientist."

"Does he work for the government?" Candace asked.

Gigi shook her head and took a sip of tea. "His father wanted him to follow in his footsteps and go into the CIA, but my son chose his own path," she explained. "After some initial disappointment, Henry finally accepted that."

"What is your profession, Gigi?" Tim asked.

"I'm retired four years now," Gigi replied. "But I was a translator. I worked mainly from home, but would take temporary positions at US embassies when Henry was stationed abroad."

"What languages?" Tim asked.

"Russian," she replied. "I know some Mandarin, but not well enough to translate."

"What kinds of things would you translate?" Candace asked.

"Almost anything," Gigi replied. "But mostly business paperwork, manuscripts for publishers, and court transcripts."

"You don't do it anymore?" Tim asked.

"Only a few *pro bono* jobs for the local library and newspaper," she said. "But I'm thinking of taking on a couple of projects for extra cash. I'm on a fixed income now."

Candace thought the woman seemed sincere and was unusually calm for someone being interviewed by FBI agents. Such collected behavior comes either from good training, or from complete openness without fear of revealing anything compromising. Candace figured it was from the latter, considering that the woman really didn't carry any risk, even if her husband had been a full-fledged SWA member.

Candace pulled a sheet of paper out of her pocket, unfolded it, and handed it and a pen to Gigi. It was the printed list of names they'd been giving all their interviewees. "Could you take a look at these and put a check next to anyone you recognize?"

Gigi stood, got some reading glasses from the kitchen counter, and retook her seat. She clicked the pen periodically as she read, and marked a few names. She looked it over again and slid the paper and pen back to Candace.

Everyone Gigi identified had been dead for over a decade.

"Did you ever meet any of these people in person?" Candace asked.

"All of them – that's how I know them," she replied. "Henry rarely spoke about people in his professional life. But I met these people at official events – mostly at embassies in Eastern Europe when I traveled with Henry. I'm surprised I can recall any of their names. This all happened so long ago – in the 80s and 90s, maybe some in the early 2000s."

Just as Candace was about to wrap up their conversation, a knock came from the front door.

Gigi excused herself and went to see who it was.

"This was a wasted trip," Tim said, under his breath.

"Maybe," Candace agreed. "But Mrs. Bennett seems much too calm for someone who is talking to the FBI about her husband whom she recently lost."

"It's been three years," Tim argued. "Besides, it's not like we're questioning her involvement in her husband's affairs. It seems like she was effectively screened from his work."

"It *seems* so, yes," she said.

Tim raised an eyebrow, indicating that he wanted her to explain what she meant, but Gigi walked into the kitchen with a large cardboard box before that could happen.

"Got a delivery?" Tim asked.

Gigi set the box on the kitchen counter and returned to the table. "My son ordered some things for the house the last time he was here, and I've been getting deliveries about every day for the past week. I think this is the last of it – colored caulk for the windows."

"Your son, what's his name?" Candace asked.

"Anders – goes by Andy with friends," she replied.

"Does he visit often?" Candace asked.

"A few times a year," Gigi replied. "And he spends a lot of time doing house maintenance when he's here. I think he enjoys getting out from behind his computer and moving for a while."

"When was the last time he visited?" Candace asked.

"He was here about two weeks ago," she replied.

"Do you think Henry would have talked to your son about any of his work?" Candace asked. "Especially considering he'd hoped Anders would follow in his footsteps."

Gigi stared at her and, just for an instant, a look of panic flashed on her face. "I doubt it," she replied. "Henry didn't want to put us in danger."

"We'd like to chat with Anders anyway," Candace said. "Could we have his contact information?"

Gigi stood from the table and went to a phone mounted on the wall in the kitchen and looked at the electronic display. "I don't memorize phone numbers anymore," she said as she wrote on a pad of sticky-notes and pulled one off. She then handed it to Candace. "That's the number for his mobile phone."

Candace stood, and Tim followed.

"Thanks for meeting with us, Gigi," Candace said and held out her hand.

"You're welcome," Gigi replied and shook it, and then Tim's. "I hope you find what you're looking for."

Gigi led them out of the house and watched as they walked down the porch steps.

As they got into the car, Candace realized that she was now confused as to what exactly they were trying to find. There was something a bit *off* about all of it. Five people were dead as a result of their inquiries, and she had no idea why. What were the assassins trying to keep secret? She was sure Gigi would be safe since only she and Tim knew about the meeting.

Next would be a stop in North Carolina, and then a chat with Anders Bennett, in DC.

"She knows?" Harrison asked, startled by Anders' revelation about the president's niece.

Anders nodded in response from the other side of the desk in Harrison's office.

"This could be disastrous," Harrison said. "I'll notify Crownbrook immediately."

"One thing we got from this, however, is more insight into the messages," Anders said.

"Two fingerprints – possibly in blood," Harrison said. He'd examined the note before handing it off to DMS specialists. "The problem is that Sara Bradbury took pics."

"I watched her delete them, but they could have already been uploaded somewhere else," Anders said. "Apart from the potential disaster this could become, what do you make of the prints?"

"They're probably an authentication of some kind," Harrison speculated. "Suppose the other leaders wanted to verify that they were actually communicating with each other – that they weren't being spoofed by the other nations' intelligence services. The president's fingerprint in his own blood would be about the best he could do."

"Who's to say they're Crownbrook's?" Anders argued. "Besides, there are *two* fingerprints on that paper, and they look very different."

Harrison shook his head. "Yeah, I can't come up with a reason for that."

"What do we do now?"

"Two things," Harrison said. "First, we take our own high-resolution images of the fingerprints on that note. I'll have them run through the FBI's database. Next, we scrape off tiny samples of the blood. We can do a DNA analysis, and then do a database search to match whatever we get."

"Won't we be violating our agreement?"

"The message has already been compromised," Harrison explained. "We need to know how damaging this breach is. Whatever we find will remain completely confidential."

Anders looked back at him with an expression of doubt.

"I know," Harrison said, shaking his head. "It's not how we usually operate. But the envelope has been opened, and it's in our possession. No one will believe that we haven't looked inside."

"I understand," Anders said. "We're almost forced to look into it at this point."

"It's time to find out what we're dealing with – what this whole thing is about."

"Do we still pass the message along?" Anders asked.

"I'll get instructions from Crownbrook," Harrison replied. "The envelope might have anti-tampering features, so we might have to replace it – completely repackage the contents." He knew that some documents and security envelopes had special markings or electronic threads woven into them so that tampering and even photocopying could be detected. It was old technology, but effective.

"When is the next exchange with our foreign couriers?" Anders asked.

"End of the week – Friday night," Harrison replied. "But that might change after I inform Crownbrook of what has happened. In the meantime, what have you learned about the thumb-drive you got from your father?"

"Nothing yet. I'm still trying password images," Anders said. "As you know, I have to wait 20 minutes after every failed attempt. It will be a few more days before I get through everything I have."

Even though he knew that the CG files might have nothing to do with any of his ongoing projects, Harrison wanted to know more about the group that had invited him into its fold so many years ago. Although, there was a part of him that didn't want to know – he didn't want to regret rejecting their offer. He just hadn't been given enough information to make a decision at the time. He hadn't been able to take the leap.

"Let me know what you find, and I'll keep you informed of my correspondence with the president about your next operation," Harrison said and dismissed Anders, who then left and closed the door.

Harrison picked up his desk phone and placed a call to the head of the DMS biotech lab in the basement. "Put the analysis of the fingerprints as top priority – we need these results as soon as possible," he said and then ended the call.

He went to the window and looked down on the street. It was a sunny afternoon and people were milling about. There was a flower shop across the street that had set out dozens of potted plants which were now basking in the sun. It was supposed to reach 70 degrees for the first time of the year. It was already a few weeks into spring. The past few months seemed like a blur, and he wondered where the time had gone. It was worrisome: a person could get so absorbed by something that they'd suddenly find themselves with their lives behind them. To some degree, that had already happened to him – only he'd awakened in his 40s, rather than his 60s. It had been a midlife crisis that emerged at just the right time.

Now, again, he was getting in deep, but he had no choice but to see it through. It was as if a storm were approaching in the dark, and he didn't know from which direction it was coming.

JUST AS ANDERS entered his office, he got a call from his mom on his cell phone. She'd been questioned by FBI agents – they'd appeared on her doorstep without warning. He felt numb.

But it was even worse: they were going to contact *him* next. She'd only given them his phone number, but they'd soon find his home address and everything else about him that was on public record.

Although she sounded perfectly calm, he sensed that she'd been shaken by the event. He assured her that everything was okay, and told her that he'd call her back in the evening.

But everything wasn't okay.

Anders and DMS couldn't afford *any* attention from the FBI.

He went to the elevator and headed back to Harrison's office. His boss needed to know everything, and they'd need to prepare for a new FBI intrusion.

As he ascended, Anders felt a sudden surge of claustrophobia, as if the walls were closing in on him. In some sense, he knew they were. But he understood that this was precisely the time to keep his composure.

MAURICE STARTED the five-minute walk from his office building to the construction crew's hangar. He enjoyed the pleasant, Friday afternoon, which was warm for mid-April in Montana at 65 degrees. The cloudless, cobalt-blue sky made him squint.

It had taken Eduardo and his crew only seven days to complete the upgrades to the second silo, and six for the third. Tomorrow they'd start their fourth. They were on schedule, despite the extra work needed to accommodate the hypersonic missiles. The idea of sending a couple of engineers to the next site on the list before the previous one was completed was what was keeping the process on pace. Those who went out ahead could identify issues and solve them before the rest of the crew arrived. This involved ordering parts or tools whose absence would otherwise have stalled the work.

Eduardo and his crew had worked overtime this week. In the evenings, they'd trained the first launch crew to conduct a launch from the vehicles. That same crew would have to be trained again when the monstrous HG-P01s arrived. That's when the drivers would learn how to operate the eight-wheeled beasts. The big trucks were arriving next week.

Maurice entered the hangar and found Eduardo drinking a beer with the rest of his group.

The crewmembers came to an awkward attention.

Maurice waved it off. "Relax, people. You all deserve a few beers," he said, and then looked to Eduardo and pointed to the exit.

Eduardo set down his beer, and Maurice led the way out of the hangar and into the sun and cool breeze.

"What's up?" Eduardo asked as they walked along the seldomly used taxiway.

"Have you or any of your crew seen anything strange while out at the silos this week?" Maurice asked.

"You mean drones?" Eduardo asked.

"Yes, but also anything else," Maurice said. "Any unknown observers on foot, or any land vehicles?"

Eduardo shook his head. "We've seen very few people near the sites," he explained. "Only the occasional operator who might take a look at us when we're outside, but nothing more. Why do you ask?"

"There have been reports from the North Dakota missile fields of vehicles in the woods in the restricted space near some of the silos."

"What kind of vehicles?"

Maurice shook his head. "Don't know. No one has directly seen them."

"Tire tracks?"

"No tracks – these weren't land vehicles," Maurice replied. "Only fallen branches and the tops of some trees were broken, as if something had squashed them from above. Security personnel heard the cracking from a distance, but that was all. They went out to investigate, but found nothing."

"At what times did these incidents happen?"

"Some occurred just before dusk," Maurice replied. "That's why I thought that your people might have spotted something before heading back to base."

"How many times has this happened?"

"Eleven times over the past three days – Wednesday through today," Maurice replied.

Eduardo shook his head. "So, they're able to avoid the new surveillance equipment installed at the sites."

"Exactly," Maurice confirmed. "And can also evade the flyover patrols, which are randomly timed. The chances that an aerial vehicle of any kind could get that close to 11 sites in a three-day period without being spotted are small."

"And, as you said, some happened before dark," Eduardo added. "You'd think even a civilian might have spotted something under those conditions."

"From now on, you should immediately report anything peculiar that you encounter, no matter how minor it may seem," Maurice said. "If you get to me quickly, maybe I can get some aircraft into the area and we can catch these bastards."

"Will do," Eduardo said.

"How did the training go?" Maurice asked, shifting the conversation. He was referring to the first launch control crew being instructed by Eduardo's people.

"Smoothly, especially with the simulator we built," Eduardo replied, referring to a training version of one of the trucks that had all the electronics which, together with a computer program, simulated a full launch sequence. "Coming in, they all already understood the control systems in the silos. We designed the mobile systems so that everything was labeled in accordance with the permanent sites. The only new operations they have to learn are how to establish communications between the trucks and the new modules we installed at the sites, and then how to lock out the underground crews and take control of the launch systems. This first launch team will be ready for deployment by Sunday."

Maurice was impressed. It would be another milestone achieved: a mobile launch crew and three silos ready for operation. However, only silo I-1 had a hypersonic missile in its launch bay. The second silo would get its new missile in the coming week.

"Very good," Maurice said. "That first crew will be on standby, but their first job will be to train the next launch team that's arriving on Monday. You and your crew will have to oversee the training for the first two rounds of instruction."

"It's all written into a detailed course," Eduardo said. "They shouldn't have any trouble, but we'll be there to make sure things go smoothly."

Maurice dismissed his crew leader and mulled over the events of the day as he strolled back to his office. The thing that bothered him – something that he knew would keep him up at night – was that recent barrage of incidents in the North Dakota missile fields. What disturbed him most about these latest encounters was that he doubted that drones – how he understood them – would be able to crush trees. And he questioned whether they could be so quiet that guards on foot just 150 yards away could hear the snapping branches but not the sounds of their props or turbines. Even if the motors or jet engines were perfectly silent, the rushing air they produced would make noise in the trees.

The mystery was becoming increasingly perplexing as it evolved, and Maurice was now convinced that the new mobile launch network they were constructing was more than justified. It was a crucial step against an existential threat.

ANDERS MEANDERED through the DC area for 45 minutes in a trio of SuperLift rides until, after a final walk of a few blocks, he reached a combination bar and pool hall called *Bâton Noir*.

He entered the bar side of the establishment and was hit with a wall of odor that seemed to be the confluence of cigarette smoke residue and stale beer that had been soaked up by the old wood floors after decades of spills. The place was busy, and *Blondie* music played under the loud background of voices. Across the bar was a wide opening through which he spied the pool hall side, with at least six tables in view. Those who were playing looked to be serious about their games. He wondered what kind of betting was happening.

Anders was there to meet a *new* Chinese contact – now the third. His last rendezvous with the Chinese side had been with "Barney," the avid alcohol consumer. But Barney had since disappeared, and it wasn't clear who got him. Although Harrison had originally heard that it was the CIA, evidence was now leaning toward Chinese intelligence getting him – inside US borders. There was even the disturbing possibility that the CIA had turned him over to the MSS.

Anders was now looking for a woman going by "Jenny" who, based on the look of the clientele of the establishment, should stick out, as he must have, despite his disguise. He was wearing the right clothes – leather jacket, jeans, tee shirt, boots – and had a dark goatee, but there wasn't much he could do about his slight build. It seemed that every man in the place was naturally large, or at least had a beer belly to increase his presence in terms of overall volume and mass. The women, who made up a third of the customers, looked somewhat rough in both demeanor and dress. It reminded him of a biker bar, although he hadn't noticed any motorcycles outside, despite the mild weather.

The place was near full capacity. The line of about 30 bar stools was completely occupied, and all but two of the dozen tables on the floor were taken.

Anders went to the bar and ordered a beer from a woman whose skin was at least 50 percent covered in tattoos. She looked intimidating but was quite friendly.

He then went to one of the empty tables, near the back, and sat in a chair with a good view of the room. He was looking for a woman carrying a black, leather purse with a green dragon on it. That it was a dragon seemed too cliché for him, considering that she was working for the Chinese president, but he didn't control the details of their meetings.

He rolled up his sleeve to expose a black watch, with a blank, gold face, no numbers. That was *his* visual identifier.

This was supposed to be his last static meeting with any of the couriers. As a part of the exchange, Anders was going to receive a phone number to use to contact this new Chinese operative for future exchanges, and they'd execute dynamic meetings from this point forward. He was nervous about the current rendezvous, however, due to the recent disappearance of Barney.

According to his numberless watch, it was just past 11:00 p.m. The meeting was set to take place within the next 15 minutes.

The doors to the restrooms were on the wall to his left, and they were busy. He looked for the dragon emblem on the bags the women carried as they passed by, and scanned the entire room for the same. He'd spotted a few Asian men, but no women.

At about 11:10 p.m., a woman approached him with a cigarette in her mouth.

"You got a light?" she asked. She was Caucasian, with dirty-blonde hair tied in a ponytail, and wore too much makeup. She wore a black, leather jacket with torn jeans, and had a barbed wire tattoo on her neck. She had a purse, but he couldn't see the side of it. It didn't matter – she wasn't the one.

As it turned out, he *did* have a light. He even had cigarettes, as a part of his disguise.

"Sure," he said as he pulled out a silver lighter, lit it, and offered her the flame.

"Thanks," she said as she took in a deep drag and exhaled. "So, you a pool shark, or are you here for the ambiance?"

Anders looked at her for a second, confused. It was the code phrase.

"I'm not good enough to play for money," he replied with the "all safe" response.

"I'm Jenny," she said as she sat in the chair across from him and looked him in the eyes. She set her purse on the table so that the side with the green dragon faced him. "Not what you expected?"

"Not at all," he replied and glanced at her neck. "That tattoo real?"

"No," she said. "Looks good though, right?"

Anders smiled and nodded.

"It peels right off if I have to change my look on the run," she whispered.

He made a note to work tattoos into his own disguise repertoire. However, he was more interested in how a non-Asian woman had gotten into a Chinese security firm. But then he recalled that the company the Chinese leader was using was in Hong Kong.

"You're British," he said.

"Oh fuck," she said as she exhaled smoke. "I guess I need to work on my American accent." There wasn't a hint of a British accent in her speech.

Anders took a drink of his beer. "I guess you're aware of what happened to your predecessors," he said.

She shrugged. "The first one was an MSS mole," she replied. "Not sure what happened to the last one."

"He went missing within 24 hours of our last exchange."

"My client has changed firms twice now," she said. "So, if that guy was another mole, the risk was eliminated by changing to my firm."

"We thought the CIA picked up the previous guy, but now we think the MSS might have gotten him," he explained. "You've already met with the third member of our international club?"

"Tomorrow," she replied.

"Another paper exchange?" he asked, referring to the envelope he was about to deliver. Crownbrook had instructed Harrison to put the paper message in a new, waterproof envelope and proceed with the delivery.

"Nope, just the usual device," she replied as she shook her head. "Any paper exchange is unusual, but I find the whole thing odd – I mean the leaders of the three most powerful nations in the world having to communicate through secret channels."

"Have you heard anything about what's in these messages?"

"Only rumors," she replied. "Something about rules, or plans, for nuclear war between the three countries. Some think it's a plan to reduce the world's population."

"Really? Why would they want to do that?" Anders was well aware of that theory.

"There are people who think that the population of the planet should be reduced by a factor of 100, or more," she explained. "Technology has gotten to the point that we just don't need so many people. Machines can do everything that requires a large scale. Take farming, for instance. Hundreds of acres can be planted, cultivated, fertilized, and harvested by one person with a collection of machines."

"And, if there were a hundred times fewer people, there'd be no need to farm as much land," he added. Although, he knew people would still be needed for doing everything from mining the raw materials for making the parts to constructing the machines themselves. And then who would produce the industrial equipment that manufactured the replacement parts for the machines? And who would maintain everything? There was a lot of latent work involved.

"Precisely," Jenny said. "But nuclear war would destroy the planet – or at least make huge parts of it uninhabitable. Maybe that would be okay – survivable – if there were fewer people."

"Who would lead this new world?" Anders asked.

"The plan is for a one-world government," she said as she snuffed out the stub of her cigarette in a thick, glass ashtray. "But I have no idea who'd actually lead it."

She took a pack of cigarettes out of her purse and set it next to the ashtray, within his reach. Beneath it was a thumb-drive.

Anders grabbed the items and, as he tapped the pack on his palm to extract a cigarette, he replaced the drive with the tiny envelope, and set them both on the table. He then put the cigarette between his lips and spoke as he pulled out his lighter, lit it, and took a drag. He'd been a smoker for about a week in high school but was grateful that it hadn't taken hold. "Do you know what's in that envelope?" he asked as he glanced at the pack.

She grabbed the cigarettes, slipped one out, put it in her mouth, and put the pack and envelope into her purse.

Anders slid his lighter across the table to her.

"No idea," she said as she lit her cigarette and then slid the lighter back to him. "Electronic exchanges are so much more secure. This one probably carries more than just words, hence the paper exchange."

Anders knew that it did: it had fingerprints made in blood. But he didn't know what it meant. He wasn't going to divulge anything to her.

She pulled a business card out of her purse and handed it to him. On the front was the name "Jennifer Tillman" and "Elon-Tek Industries," along with contact information. Her title was "Logistics Consultant." On the backside was a handwritten phone number.

"We're going dynamic next time," Jenny said. "Better safe than sorry."

"It works best in highly trafficked areas," he said. "So we'll probably be meeting in a denser, urban setting next time."

"How long before you complete the delivery to your client?" she asked.

"Next few days," he replied. "And you?"

"I head to Hong Kong after my exchange tomorrow," she said. "And then to Zhongnanhai by the next evening."

"You're going to be on a plane for a long time."

"You're lucky that all the exchanges take place in the US," she said. "But it's best that they do. Freedom of movement is paramount in our business."

Anders agreed.

She put out her cigarette and Anders did the same.

"I need to use the restroom," she said as she stood. "You want to get us a couple of beers?"

It was the indication that their meeting was over.

"Sure," he replied as she gathered her bag and walked away.

Anders went to the bar, pulled out his phone, and arranged a SuperLift ride. He then exited the building and took a right, toward a large, chain gas station on the next corner.

Next stop, DMS, Inc. He'd get the thumb-drive scanned and then spend the night in his office. Ever since his mom had informed him of her FBI encounter, he hadn't been sleeping well in his apartment.

HARRISON LEANED back on his office couch and bit into a bagel as Anders entered and took a chair on the other side of the coffee table. It was 6:45 a.m., which was early for them both, except he knew that Anders had spent the night at DMS.

"You look tired," Harrison said and nodded toward a carafe of coffee and a white mug on the table.

"After last night's exchange, I stayed up late testing passcode files to access my dad's thumb-drive," Anders said as he poured himself some coffee. "No luck on that – I've been through nearly 200 images now. By the way, she's not Asian."

"The courier?"

"She's a Brit, and speaks with a flawless American accent."

"Interesting," Harrison said. "Does she speak Chinese?"

"I didn't check," Anders replied.

"It might've been helpful to know," Harrison said. "It would be less likely that she was an imposter if she spoke Chinese."

"You think there's a chance of that happening – an interception by another party?"

"Anything's possible in this operation," Harrison replied. "We're supposed to deliver this latest device to the director of the CIA – the leader of the very agency the president is trying to bypass by routing communications through us. Very strange."

"The CIA director is routing communications around his own agency?" Anders asked.

"Seems so," Harrison said. "But we now know for certain that there's a backchannel connection between the CIA chief and the president."

"What about the FBI? Are there backchannels between the bureau and Crownbrook as well?"

"I doubt it," Harrison replied. "The FBI is politically biased and leaks like a sieve. I have first-hand knowledge that Crownbrook doesn't even trust the FBI director – whom he'd endorsed. Radcliffe doesn't trust the FBI, either. Radcliffe doesn't even trust his own organization. There have been politically motivated leaks from the CIA in the recent past, and he's currently dealing with those responsible."

"It always amazes me how dysfunctional our government agencies are – that the CIA and FBI don't trust each other," Anders said. "That, together with the president not trusting anyone, makes it seem like we're governed by a paranoid, communist regime."

"Our nation is more fragile – in the political sense – than most people realize," Harrison explained. "Since we elect our leaders and representatives, and they, collectively, could change laws, and even the Constitution, we're always just one election away from destroying this country. And one bad administration could cause irreversible damage."

"Was Crownbrook's reelection a step in the right, or wrong, direction?" Anders asked.

"Only time will tell," Harrison said. "Now, onto business. You'll deliver the device to Radcliffe tomorrow night."

"Directly to the CIA chief?" Anders asked, his eyes wide in surprise.

Harrison nodded. "You'll meet at a fancy restaurant in Alexandria – the *Wildflower*."

"That's an expensive place," Anders said.

"I know," Harrison said as he grinned. "I took my wife there last year for her birthday. The entrees alone are around a hundred bucks. And you don't get very much, so eat something beforehand."

"How will this go down?"

"You have a reservation for 8:45 p.m. tomorrow," Harrison explained. "You'll be taking a DMS op with you who will pose as your girlfriend – both of you in disguise, of course. At 9:30 p.m., you'll go to the restroom and Radcliffe should meet you there. If it's not safe for the exchange, the backup time is 9:55 p.m. – you'll go to the restroom and make another attempt."

Anders seemed to mull it over. "You think the FBI – or the CIA – is following Radcliffe?"

Harrison nodded. "Probably," he said. "Kind of odd that the CIA will have security in the vicinity to protect Radcliffe, and a separate set of CIA ops might be watching him for other reasons."

"This is becoming quite convoluted," Anders said.

"And increasingly dangerous," Harrison added as his phone vibrated. There was a message from DMS bio-research personnel notifying him that a report had just been emailed to him. It was about the fingerprints. He wanted to wrap up the meeting to see what it was about. "You have anything else?"

"Any news about Sara Bradbury?" Anders asked.

"Crownbrook knows about her discovery," Harrison replied. "And he's convinced her to be quiet for the moment."

Anders stood. "Is the CIA director also a member of the Custodial Group – is that why the president trusts him?"

"Maybe, but I can't confirm that."

"And what about the Single-World Alliance – could Radcliffe also be a member of that?"

"It's possible he and Crownbrook are both members."

"Shouldn't we be concerned about such a radical entity existing within our government?" Anders asked. "Shouldn't our leaders be vetted before they can even be eligible for office?"

Harrison laughed. "Who's going to vet them?" he asked. "The CIA? The FBI? Who do you trust?"

Anders just stared back at him, seemingly thinking about the question for a few seconds, and then an expression of realization and disappointment came to his face. "I get your point," he said. "But what do we do if we discover these types of destructive intentions within our current operation?"

Harrison had been asking himself that same question and could only come up with an answer that caused him great anxiety. "Let's cross that bridge when we come to it," he said. "In the meantime, work on getting into your father's data drive, and prepare for your rendezvous with the CIA director tomorrow."

Anders left the office and closed the door.

Harrison went to his desk, opened the email from the DMS biological group, and downloaded the DNA report. The first fingerprint was confirmed to be that of President Crownbrook, and in his own blood. DMS had connections in many federal agencies, and also at the Walter Reed National Military Medical Center, where one of his contacts had acquired a blood sample of the president. The DNA matched.

It wasn't so surprising that the fingerprint was the president's, although it being in his blood was peculiar, to say the least. The report on the second fingerprint, however, caused Harrison's mind to spin. Harrison was now convinced that he and DMS were in too deep.

CHAPTER 10

Maurice enjoyed the sunny morning as he sipped coffee and gazed out his office window. He could hardly believe that it was already the end of May. The weather had warmed and the trees were greening and full of life. It had been nearly eight weeks since the first missile silo had been converted, and he was satisfied with the progress. They were ahead of schedule: nine silos were in full operation – including the replacements of their conventional ICBMs with the hypersonic variety – and the tenth and eleventh were in progress. They were expecting all 25 to be converted by early August.

The nighttime intrusions at the missile sites had increased during the past weeks. There were no advances in detecting the drones, and no one had seen one directly, not even when the incursions had occurred before dusk. More – *different* – control-system malfunctions had been reported during the most recent incidents, but the new incursions had turned up some useful information.

As a part of the security upgrades, new diagnostic systems had been integrated into the launch-station machinery. They were similar in function to the black boxes in airplanes, which logged all system parameters so that problems could be diagnosed after an event.

One of the missile sites in which a black box had been installed had been rendered nonfunctional during a drone intrusion. Its device recorded all the steps the drone had taken to accomplish the shutdown. The most important detail gleaned from these data was that the new *mobile* systems – the MOLVs – would still be able to launch from a site that had been deactivated by the drones; the trucks could revive them if they suffered this particular shutdown procedure, as well as all the others they'd encountered so far.

It was a great relief: had the MOLVs been deemed useless by the black-box diagnosis, the entire land-based ICBM program of the United States could have been dead in the water. It was clear that, presently, the trucks would work. However, it seemed that the drones themselves were evolving, or at least their methods were changing, so he still worried that the MOLVs would eventually be rendered ineffective.

Maurice had become more comfortable with the progress of the project, its objective, and his role in it. In another three months, the country would be safer than it had ever been.

Two weeks ago, the morning after Anders' exchange with the CIA director in the lavatory of the high-class DC restaurant, a pair of FBI agents, a man and a woman, had shown up at the door of his apartment. Anders had nearly crawled out of his skin when he'd seen their faces: it was the man who'd been appearing at his rendezvous locations – and he recognized the woman from outside the restaurant in New York. His training had kicked in, and he'd maintained his composure.

He'd invited them in – they hadn't recognized him – and they had an hour-long discussion, mostly about his father, but also about his mother and himself. He knew everything his mom had told them, so he'd been well prepared and was sure to be consistent with her story.

As for information about himself, DMS had masterfully set him up with a cover story that was akin to those used for a change in identity. According to the façade, Anders was a computer specialist, subcontracted by a few different companies over the past two years. DMS had even been doing his taxes to make sure that everything added up. It was perfect, as long as he kept the details straight, which he had.

There was another potential problem that DMS had also averted. His apartment wasn't rented under the name "Anders Bennett." The FBI people hadn't asked about it but, if they had, DMS had set up a good cover – with supporting documents – that Anders rented the apartment through an unofficial sublease from his "tenant persona," which had also been constructed by DMS. Subleasing was against the rules of the management of the apartment complex, but it would've worked.

Near the end of their visit, Candace Wright had handed him a list of about a hundred names and asked if any looked familiar to him.

Anders examined the list, but recognized none of the names except for those of Crownbrook, Radcliffe, and Henry Bennett. His first thought was to try to memorize a few – clearly, they were related to his father's business, and possibly to the CG or SWA. However, he knew that DMS had security cameras around his apartment – which he'd normally activate by means of a light switch when leaving the house, or if something else warranted it. He'd turned them on for their meeting, so he'd just held the list in front of his face at an angle so that one of the cameras, located to the right and behind him, could get a good shot of it. So he'd gotten *all* the names.

The FBI agents' questions about his background, and current job, had been superficial, and he was satisfied that the meeting posed no threat to him or DMS. However, they were clearly searching for things related to the president's actions, which *did* involve DMS, so he suspected he'd be seeing more of those agents in the future. In the end, he'd gotten more information from the FBI than they'd gotten from him. Afterwards, DMS investigated the names on the list while he was in New York, carrying out the president's information operation. They'd learned some about the members, but little about the organizations.

Now, Anders was driving his rental car south, from New York toward DC, on a mild, overcast morning. He'd been informed that, for reasons neither he nor Harrison knew, their operation would come to a halt for a while. Anders welcomed it – he was exhausted.

During this two-week stint in New York City, he'd made over 30 exchanges with his Russian and Chinese counterparts without incident. They'd been operating in the city in order to employ the more secure, dynamic method of exchange. They'd get on their phones, and one operative would guide the other while they both moved about the city. Each operation consisted of over an hour of subways, taxis, walks, and SuperLift rides before a short encounter in a coffee shop, bookstore, deli, or shopping center. Unfortunately, it left little time for him to converse with his contacts, and he'd only learned snippets of information during the meetings. The good thing was that the actual meeting destinations were known to no one – not even, presumably, the operative giving the instructions – before the meeting. It was the most secure meeting possible for this type of rendezvous.

The general theme he'd learned from the other couriers was that they, and their respective private organizations, sensed that things were rapidly accelerating. They'd concluded that, whatever the leaders of the three most powerful nations on the planet were planning, it was going to happen soon – within weeks, by their estimates.

This notion was further amplified by the fact that things were going to go "quiet" for a while. Anders knew that it was common for communications to go silent just before a large operation was to be carried out. A prime example of this was the diminished chatter between al-Qaeda members before September 11.

Despite the short contact time, he and Alina seemed to make a connection. At one point she suggested that they meet for coffee somewhere in the city: they could go in disguise and just spend an hour together. An instant later, however, she canceled the idea for being too reckless. Anders agreed, but he would've been tempted to take the risk. It was a lonely business, and sometimes a person needed more than books to keep them company.

Anders arrived at DMS at 11:00 a.m. and went directly to Harrison's office.

Harrison was waiting on the couch. "Have a seat," he said and nodded to one of the chairs opposite the coffee table from him. "We have some things to discuss."

Anders sat.

"You need to stay in for a while – here, at DMS," Harrison said.

"Something up?"

"Since your visit with agents Wright and Barilaro in your apartment a few weeks ago, the counterespionage group within the FBI has initiated an investigation," Harrison explained.

"You mean of DMS itself?"

Harrison nodded. "My sources tell me that the FBI suspects DMS is colluding with the president and meeting with foreign couriers – delivering the president's messages."

Anders' mind spun. "I'm the only one making the exchanges – they must have identified me somehow," he said as he became queasy. "Did I make a mistake?"

Harrison shook his head. "If they suspected you, they would've taken you in by now," he said. "And, if they'd ever tracked you here after a mission, they would've already shut us down – or raided us with a warrant. It wasn't you."

"Then what?"

"It might be connected to my time in the CIA," Harrison explained. "My moles tell me that the FBI, together with rogue CIA employees, has been investigating various CIA internal groups, especially the one of which the president was – *is* – a member. My name might have come up somehow, even though I never accepted membership."

"So this has to do with the Custodial Group?" Anders asked, baffled.

"Seems so," Harrison said. "But we're lucky that our operation with the president has slowed for the time being. If needed, I'll get you out of here for a couple of weeks, but let's wait on that for now."

"I'll take this time to try to get into my dad's files," Anders said. "Maybe we'll learn something about the Custodial Group." Anders had received over 200 new images from his mother to test as password files, but he'd been unable to try them while he was in New York. He'd left the thumb-drive at DMS while he was there.

Harrison nodded. "It might help us to at least see what we're dealing with," he said. "It could also reveal the president's intentions. All we have to go on now are rumors."

"Yeah, serious ones," Anders said. "The other couriers have expressed all the same concerns we have. Maybe it's time to dig up more info."

"I agree," Harrison said. "I'm also giving you unrestricted access to our daily intelligence reports – try to connect them to our project."

This was as serious as it got. Anders had never been privy to the company's intelligence reports – at least not with unfettered access.

"I'll get going on it right away," Anders said as he stood.

Anders headed back to his office. He had enough clothes for about a week's stay, but DMS also had a laundering service, so that could be extended indefinitely. He wondered how long it would be before he'd start to get cabin fever.

IT WAS rare that Candace was invited to lunch with her supervisor – whom she despised – and she was even more perplexed when she entered the trendy, Alexandria restaurant and saw the Deputy Director of the FBI at the same table with him.

As Candace approached, both of her superiors stood.

"Thanks for coming, Candace," said Jack Neumann, her direct supervisor. His dyed-black hair was slicked back. It always seemed to her like he was trying to look like a mafia hitman from the movies, although he more resembled a character that would play a snitch. His dark suit was tailored to make his shoulders look wider than they were, and his black shoes gleamed but were too long and narrow for his body. He topped off the look with a large, gold watch.

Candace had had no choice but to accept his invitation. She certainly didn't enjoy the man's company. And now it was going to be awkward as hell. Something was up. Was she being fired?

"Have you ever met our Deputy Director, Shelly Stevens?" Jack asked.

"I don't believe I have," Candace said, as the unusually tall woman stood and held out her long, bony hand. With her high heels, she was well over six feet tall. She was dressed in a shiny, gray pantsuit that somehow made her look even taller. Her hair was as gray as her suit, and was so short that it made her head look too small for her body. Her mouth, however, looked too big for her face.

Candace tried to temper her disdain for bureaucrats and smiled as she shook the woman's hand. "Pleasure to meet you, Deputy Director Stevens," she said.

"Please, Candace, call me Shelly," she said and retook her seat. "Let's eat."

Shelly ordered a salad with tofu, and Jack ordered a different vegetarian dish, although Candace knew well that he wasn't a vegetarian. Candace had pasta with shrimp, and iced tea.

About the time they were finishing their meals over benign chitchat, the real reason for the lunch invitation emerged.

"I understand you've been investigating potential leaks from the White House," Shelly Stevens said. "Can you elaborate?"

Candace had no choice, even though she preferred not to do so in a public place. "I wouldn't classify the alleged information flow as a *leak*," she said. "Rather, it's a *channel* that circumvents normal protocols. And we've not revealed much along those lines."

"What *have* you revealed?" Shelly asked.

"Definitively? Nothing," Candace replied. "But there's evidence that the president has been a member of a group within the CIA called the Single-World Alliance, or the SWA. The communications might have something to do with that."

"*Has been* a member?" Jack Neumann asked.

"We have no solid evidence that he's still an *active* member," Candace said.

"No evidence at all?" Shelly asked.

"No, and only circumstantial evidence that he ever *was* a member," Candace explained, although she wished they had more. She despised Crownbrook's administration, and she'd get great satisfaction if she could bring it down. "There's a possibility that he was *infiltrating* the organization. The CIA had been investigating sub-groups of this kind within its ranks during his tenure as a case officer."

"You mean sub-organizations like the SWA, and the *Custodial Group*?" Shelly Stevens asked.

"The CG has come up in our investigation, but we aren't sure about its objectives," Candace explained. She did know, however, that the CG and SWA might be cooperating somehow, and that Crownbrook could have been a member of *both* organizations.

"Well, I suggest you dive into that," Shelly said. "Our current president might have been a member of both groups – might *be* a member of both – and it could be quite a revelation for the citizens of this country."

She detected disdain in the woman's voice and was starting to get the picture. Candace, too, would like to get rid of Crownbrook. However, she did believe that, if something politically or criminally damaging to the president were to be exposed, there should be overwhelming evidence before it was revealed. She also thought that the allegations should be extreme – not something like acquiring suspicious campaign funds, or some sex scandal from an earlier time in his life. What the SWA stood for certainly qualified: reducing the world's population through war and various other types of extermination was about as serious as it got, not to mention taking over the entire planet afterwards. The world had already experienced someone who'd tried to do that. It was a good thing that Hitler hadn't obtained the atomic bomb or advanced biological weapons. Those horrible things did, of course, exist now, making world domination a real possibility.

Candace knew of only one overlapping objective between the Single-World Alliance and the Custodial Group: they both wanted to start a nuclear war.

"I'll dig up whatever I can on the CG," Candace said. "We've not had much luck locating former SWA members. As you know, five people have been murdered."

Shelly nodded and looked to Jack.

"We're working on that," Jack said. "It's particularly unsettling since the leak could have come from within the bureau. We know that the assassinations in Santa Barbara – the Mackenbergs – were linked to a Russian operative. We have no leads on the others."

Candace had been trying to cope with her obvious connection to those deaths. She'd taken extra care since then to make sure that only she and Tim knew who they were interviewing. For the last two interviews, she'd circumvented her FBI superiors altogether. It hit her that she was now doing the same thing they were accusing the president of doing and, just for an instant, understood why he might be doing it. It seemed that no one could be trusted.

What was the origin of this degradation of security? Candace wondered. She had some ideas. First, the vetting process for people who worked in sensitive positions – those who also held significant implicit power – had become weak. In fact, in some cases, it was so superficial that people with known, extreme biases were allowed to occupy those positions. This happened because politicians had been able to circumvent the screening protocols to get their people in place. Second, those implanted people felt emboldened to use their trusted positions to bring in their own, like-minded people. Finally, none of those people had any fear of acting in a politically biased way because there were rarely any consequences for doing so. That would only occur if you were on the "wrong" side of the political spectrum.

Candace felt she was currently on the "right" side of the political divide, but was starting to acknowledge that things had gone too far. If the president had to use backchannels to communicate with foreign leaders rather than use his, otherwise trusted, secure agencies to do the job, then the country was in trouble.

"Candace?" Shelly asked, breaking her away from her thoughts.

"Sorry," Candace said. "I was just thinking about the people who were murdered. It means this is more dangerous than it seemed at first. There are some ruthless players in this game."

"Indeed," Shelly Stevens said. "However, you need to keep going. Find out what you can about the Custodial Group, and how it's connected to both the SWA and the president."

It was becoming clear that the deputy director had an agenda. Candace supposed it was the same as hers, but she was now starting to see the danger in her own actions.

ANDERS SPENT the morning in his office trying password images and reading intelligence reports. One question on his mind was why the info exchanges had stopped. Harrison had told him that they might pick up again in a few weeks, but why would they be halted at all?

Anders figured there were at least two possible, diametrical, reasons for the pause. The first was that the three parties had come to some sort of consensus on something – or had made final plans, which they would now proceed to carry out. The second possibility was that they'd come to an impasse, and further dialogue was not expected to be productive.

The most recent news of the past weeks seemed to imply which of those two possibilities was more likely: tensions were building. The standoff between the US and Chinese fleets in the South Pacific was intensifying – warning shots had been fired on both sides. Next, Russia and the US were squabbling about new weapons – missile systems – provided to Poland by the United States, as well as the recent acceptance of Sweden and Finland into NATO. Russia threatened world war – even nuclear – which fit in perfectly with the rumors passed along from the other couriers.

There was still one other mystery that neither Anders nor Harrison had been able to explain: What was the purpose of the fingerprints? One was that of the president – in his own blood – but the other was still a mystery. The fingerprint itself was unusual in both shape and pattern and, according to the DMS biometric analysis team, was made in a biological substance that wasn't human blood. Were the fingerprints needed to prove that the US had someone specific in custody? DMS sources had not been able to match the second print to any in the government databases to which they had access – which was everything the CIA and FBI had. And Anders wondered if they'd have any luck extracting DNA from the unknown print since it hadn't been made in blood, although it could have been made in some other DNA-carrying substance.

Having unrestricted access to DMS's intelligence reports was revealing. First off, he hadn't realized the extent to which DMS had infiltrated the CIA, FBI, Department of Defense, and even the IRS. It worried him: who else had their tentacles embedded in these agencies?

In perusing the 75-plus pages of the current daily report, he'd come across something startling. The FBI was investigating a secret connection between CIA Director Radcliffe and the Secretary-General of the United Nations, Keiron Swensen, from Sweden. They were also looking into over a dozen of Swensen's directly appointed officers for a variety of things, first and foremost, however, was their connection to the recent pandemic. The RAT-32C virus had devastated the world for over two years, and Swensen and his cohorts were implicated in a number of ways, from its origins to the subsequent policies that involved everything from social isolation to vaccine mandates to how information was disseminated and suppressed.

Anders turned his attention to his father's thumb-drive – the latest 20-minute delay just ended and he was ready for another attempt. This time he tried a passcode image of a bright yellow, acrobatic plane flying through a white hoop over blue water. The picture failed. During the 20-minute lull, he'd email his mother.

HARRISON WAS in his DMS office, staring at the scientist who sat across the desk from him. It was Dennis Jones, a DMS fingerprint and DNA expert who worked in an external lab operated by the company. The scientist had insisted on seeing him in person at DMS headquarters. The slightly built man's round glasses were smeared, and the gray-black stubble on his face matched the color of his greasy, disheveled hair.

"Let me get this straight," Harrison said. "You can't find a match to the fingerprint, and it was made in the blood of an animal? This was already in the report you sent me."

Jones shook his head. "It's more than that," he said. "The fingerprint itself has unusual features – very few pattern defects like islands, lakes, and crossovers."

"What does that mean?"

"Nothing conclusive – it's just that I haven't encountered anything like it before," the scientist replied. "And the scale of it is strange as well – the lines are more densely packed. The average separation between adjacent grooves is almost half the usual distance."

"You said you'd learned something about the order in which the prints were made."

"Oh, yes," Jones said. "By the tiny amount of overlap, we've determined that the president's fingerprint is on the bottom."

"So, the unknown one was taken after the president's."

"Yes, and just a short time after – within an hour," Jones explained.

"How do you know that?"

"Before they dried, there was some mixing, or smearing," Jones replied. "The bottom one was still tacky when the second one was made."

Harrison's mind was spinning. "And the DNA?" he asked. "Have you identified the animal?"

Jones shook his head. "I need your permission to pass the sample to a colleague – a university professor – to conduct a full study."

"Too late for that," Harrison said. "The sample is gone."

The scientist's face turned pale. "Gone?"

"Gone for good."

"Damn," Jones said, clearly disappointed.

"Can't you use the original material we gave you?"

"No," Jones replied. "We used it all in the first scan. We can pass the data we have to the professor, but I'm sure he would've wanted to do some additional tests."

"Give him the data," Harrison said. "Keep me informed."

Harrison saw the man out, poured himself some whisky, and settled onto the couch. He wondered for a moment what the daily, stimulant-depressant cycle of coffee and alcohol was doing to him, physically and mentally. It was going on dinnertime, so he'd consider his drink a happy-hour cocktail, although it was a Tuesday, and he'd normally only partake in happy-hour on Fridays.

He was as confused as ever. It was clear that the fingerprints were intended to convey some important information. Other than identifying the sender as the president, it was meant to prove that the two sources of those fingerprints were in the same place at the same time.

Harrison took a swig of his drink and winced. By processing the fingerprints, he'd already broken DMS's protocols for the handling of client info. The service DMS was supposed to be rendering to the president was strictly a blind information exchange. But Harrison was starting to believe that he should know what DMS was handling.

He came to a sudden resolution: he was going to learn whatever he could about the information going into and out of the White House. If he deemed it nonthreatening, no one would ever know that he looked at it. However, if it posed a serious threat of some kind, he might be able to do something about it.

CANDACE'S IMPROMPTU meeting with her FBI superiors went late and she didn't get back to her office until almost 7:00 p.m. It was a follow-up from her lunch engagement two days prior with Shelly Stevens and Jack Neumann. The three of them had been in Shelly's office since 4:00 p.m.

When Candace entered her office, Tim was waiting for her and, before saying anything else, asked if they could go out for coffee. It was odd, since he usually went alone on coffee runs, and there was a chain coffeeshop in the headquarters complex. She'd gotten the hint: he wanted to go off-site to talk.

When they got into the car, she asked him what was happening. He put a finger to his lips to hush her. "I just needed to get out of the office for a few minutes," he said.

Tim drove to their usual, outside coffee place, parked, and then took his mobile phone out of his jacket and put it in a compartment beneath the armrest. He nodded for her to do the same.

Candace's fingers tingled as she took out her phone and set it in the compartment. Tim's face looked more serious than she'd ever seen it. She sensed fear.

They got out of the car, entered the coffeehouse, ordered beverages, and took them to a patio. The weather was mild but the late, spring breeze was getting chilly as the sun went down.

"What's going on?" Candace asked as they sat at a small table, far from two others which were occupied by patrons. They could speak freely.

"We're under surveillance," he said.

"What?" she asked, shocked. "By whom?"

"The CIA. But it's worse than that," he continued. "We might be in danger."

"How so?"

"I have a contact in the CIA – a friend from college. We were both on the baseball team," Tim explained. "He started with the CIA at about the same time I got into the FBI. We promised to warn each other if either of us found out that the other was in danger. It was a joke at first, but not anymore."

"What did he say?"

"He's on a CIA counterintelligence team that operates domestically."

"That's not legal."

Tim rolled his eyes. "Since when does that matter?"

He had a point.

"They've taken out domestic ... uh, *players*, before," he continued.

"Players?"

"Operatives, terrorists, spies," he said.

"You think they 'took out' our witnesses?" she asked.

He nodded. "And they're not done."

"What do you mean?"

"They've been following our progress," Tim explained. "They know where we've been. And they've decided that it's not the people on the list who are the problem. It's us."

"Us?"

"We're in trouble, Candace," Tim said. "And I'm not sure how far they're going to take it. There was mention that the situation might get *wet*."

"You think they're going to *kill* us?" she said in a hoarse voice. *Wet* referred to blood – a term used by the Russians to indicate a hit. "That's absurd."

He looked back at her with wide eyes, seemingly waiting for her to come to her senses.

"It's crazy, right?" she said, hearing the pleading tone in her voice. "I just got back from a long meeting with Jack and Shelly Stevens. They want us to pursue the Custodial Group and the SWA in full force, and make a connection to the president. We'll even get resources if we ask for them – we'll get a surveillance team."

"It seems that the CIA has other plans for us," he said. "What do we do?"

"Bring it up with our director."

Tim shook his head. "Can't do that," he said. "It will give away my CIA contact. Besides, he has no hard evidence – only unrecorded vocal conversations."

"With whom?"

"The CIA director."

"My God," Candace hissed. "He's the president's appointee – they must be in on this together."

"What's our move?"

Candace's head was spinning. "We can't trust anyone," she said. "Even our own director could be involved – he was installed by Crownbrook."

"But the *deputy* director must not be with him," Tim argued. "She's the one who told you to widen our scope to include the Custodial Group and charge ahead."

She was puzzled about the possibility that President Crownbrook could be a member of both the SWA and CG. It occurred to her that he could have been a member of one, but was infiltrating the other. According to Gigi Bennett, her late, CIA-operative husband had told her that he and Crownbrook had been *investigating* the SWA. But both men could still have been legit members of the Custodial Group.

"Let's focus on the Custodial Group for now," Candace said. "I have a feeling that we'll learn more about the president by investigating the CG, and more about the Single-World Alliance will be revealed along the way."

"Meanwhile, we're being watched," Tim said. "And we're in danger."

"Then we'll need to be careful," she said.

Tim's eyes widened in what seemed to be disbelief and suppressed fear.

"We'll be okay," Candace added.

She heard the crackle of distress in her own voice and knew that Tim had picked up on it. They weren't going to quit their jobs. They had to follow through. But Candace knew that they were getting in over their heads.

ANDERS OPENED his mom's email and looked through the nearly 200 pictures his father had sent her during his last two years. His dad had copied him on some of the emails to which those images were attached, so he had to remove those so that he wouldn't duplicate attempts – each would cost him 20 minutes.

After removing the duplicates, he ranked those having the least personal relevance as top priority. Therefore, there were no pictures of the family, house, yard, or anything that could be identified as unique to their family. What was left were pictures of places his father had visited, animals, clouds, stars, and antique cars and airplanes, which his dad had loved.

Anders transferred the new images from his desktop computer to his laptop and then connected the locked thumb-drive. A message box appeared, prompting him for a password file. He navigated to the first image on the new list, a classic Maserati that had appeared in an old James Bond film, and selected it. It failed, and a 20-minute timer appeared.

As the timeout proceeded, he combed through his usual news websites and found an article in *The Guardian* about a conspiracy theory that involved the US and Chinese presidents, the United Nations, and the World Health Organization. It had to do with the RAT-32C pandemic. Its author, a British woman by the name of Clair Townsend, claimed to have proof that the virus had been artificially altered to be extremely contagious, and then *purposely* released. According to the article, the virus had been modified to be only moderately – not severely – deadly, and then intentionally released as a test run for something "more permanent."

The story went on to explain that the project had two primary objectives. The first was the most obvious: to learn how the virus would spread through the world and how various countermeasures would perform – masks, vaccines, therapeutics, and lockdowns. The results were mostly expected, and largely unremarkable. The second objective was far more sinister: they wanted to see how local and global populations could be controlled through fear, the testimonies of so-called experts and authority figures, and the careful dissemination and censoring of information together with the precise administration of propaganda.

If true, it was utterly frightening that someone would, and *could*, carry out such a thing. There was no punishment that could account for the millions who had died from the virus, despite it supposedly being only "moderately deadly." For the living, however, the conclusions drawn from the event were horrifying. The results of the "experiment" established that huge populations could be dominated through fear and isolation by controlling information. People would gladly remain isolated in their homes where every bit of information they were fed was precisely monitored and measured. Between the social pressures, force-fed information, and information suppression, people would willingly confine themselves to their homes, take medications and injections as instructed, and surrender their jobs.

And there were other things. People could be tracked, and were *willing* to be tracked. People would turn in their neighbors, coworkers, and even family members for not following the rules. It was found that private companies and local governments were willing to blindly follow orders from government leaders and so-called experts who, later on, were both found to lie, and to not really understand the science of the pandemic or the virus.

Final conclusion: through the proper control of information, people could be made to "voluntarily" destroy their civilization.

The article informed that supporting documentation would appear on a whistleblower website called *WhistleLeaks* within the next 48 hours.

Anders' heart pounded and he needed to talk to Harrison. The article also implicated Crownbrook, and it all but confirmed his alignment with the Single-World Alliance. If true, and the RAT-32C virus was just a test run, what was coming next?

It was going on 9:00 p.m. when the file courier arrived at Candace's office at FBI headquarters. The woman set a dusty, accordion-style folder filled with hundreds of pages of documents on Candace's desk and asked her to sign a form.

"What's this?" Candace asked the woman and then looked over to Tim.

He seemed as confused as she was. They hadn't made any document requests.

"These files were ordered by Deputy Director Stevens to be delivered to you," the woman replied. "Please sign."

Candace signed the register and the agent left.

She pulled a document from the stack as Tim came over from his desk.

"These are confidential files from an investigation of the Custodial Group from the early 1980s," Candace commented as she flipped through pages.

"There are unredacted names in this report," Tim gasped, looking over her shoulder.

"The question is whether Crownbrook is mentioned."

"I guess it's going to be a long night."

"Better make some coffee," she said as she pulled a half-dozen files from the envelope and put them on her desk.

She was starting to feel like she was being manipulated. She didn't know what they were supposed to find, or why. She also didn't know exactly what the implications would be if the president were confirmed to be an active member of either of the secret societies.

Were she and Tim just pawns to be sacrificed in some dark, political game? Based on the warning from Tim's CIA contact, their lives *were* in danger, and at least five people had already been murdered as a result of her investigation. Even though the president might be an integral part of this threat, Candace was no longer after him exclusively. She was now intent on getting to the bottom of it all, no matter where it took her.

ANDERS WAS in his DMS office at 9:00 p.m. when his phone chimed. It was time for the next login attempt on the thumb-drive.

He clicked on the "Upload File" prompt in the login window, and navigated to an image of a bird in a steep, vertical dive with its wings swept back like those of a sleek fighter jet. He selected the file and clicked submit.

He immediately knew something was different. A timer icon appeared and spun as if the computer was working on something.

A few seconds later, a red message flashed on the screen that read: *Warning: Classified Material. It is a crime to access the files on this drive without proper clearance. Anyone doing so will suffer the full consequences of the law.*

Anders' heart thumped hard in his chest as he clicked the "OK" button on the window, which then closed, and a directory of files appeared.

"Yessss," Anders said aloud. He thought he was going to hyperventilate but managed to calm himself.

He looked over the long file list. It always amazed him how much information the little thumb-drives could store – and it wasn't even at half capacity.

He clicked again on the image file that had gotten him in, and it appeared in a new window. The filename was *Peregrine_011.jpg*.

"It's a peregrine falcon," he said to himself, taking the hint from the filename. He'd learned in grade school that it was the fastest animal on the planet, and could dive at speeds up to 240 miles per hour.

He glanced at his watch – it was 9:06 p.m. His mom would still be awake. Anders attached the picture to an email and sent it, and then called her. She answered on the second ring, and he explained that he'd gotten access to the drive and had sent her the winning image.

She immediately went to her office computer, opened the email, and downloaded the picture.

"A peregrine falcon," Gigi said.

"Does it have any significance to you?" he asked.

"None that I can recall," she replied. "But I can find the email that included it and see what it was about."

He heard her humming as she typed and then said, "Ah, found it. The subject line reads 'Speed wins the game.'"

After that, there was silence for a few seconds and he didn't know what was happening.

"Mom?"

"Just a second, honey," she said, and then a few more seconds of silence passed. It sounded like she was pressing her palm against the phone's mouthpiece.

"Okay, let me read the email to you," she said, finally. Her voice was different, and he heard her sniffle. "He wrote: 'My love, I'll be home the day after next. It's been a long two weeks abroad. I have meetings in DC all day today and through tomorrow evening, and I have a late afternoon flight the day after. Love you, Henry.' No mention of the image."

She sounded shaken. Anders felt it too – hearing his father's words. He wanted to head off her sadness, and his own. "Why do you think he attached the pic of the bird?" he asked.

"No idea," she replied. "Maybe he meant that he'd been flying a lot – he'd been in Russia and China during those weeks. Or maybe he just wished he could get home more quickly."

"Anyway, I'm in," Anders said as he scrolled through the long directory of files. He selected one at random, nondescriptly named "PS-1988-72," and opened it. The title page read "Destructive and nondestructive evaluation of material 7723-F."

He read the title and abstract aloud. It was complicated, scientific jargon.

"What is it?" Gigi asked.

"I think they found some object and were trying to figure out what it was made of," Anders replied. "They did a whole bunch of tests on the material. It mentions the term 'X-ray fluorescence analysis,' which is a scientific measurement that identifies all the elements in a material, and how much of each is there." And there were other methods mentioned that Anders recognized but wasn't sure of their purposes, like plasma analysis, X-ray diffraction, and some kind of electron spectroscopy.

He scrolled to the second page, which was a table of contents.

"This report is over 300 pages long," he said, and then realized that there was an overwhelming volume of information on the drive – over 1,000 files – and wondered how he was going to get through it all. "I just wanted to let you know that I finally got in, and thanks for your help. I'll keep you up to date, and maybe have some questions for you later."

"If you learn anything important about your father, I want to know," she said.

He promised to share whatever he learned.

She then told him about the Spring Festival, which had occurred over the weekend.

He'd completely forgotten about it. He felt horrible, not only about missing it – he'd been extremely busy – but about not even mentioning it. She was forgiving.

They ended the call after a few more minutes of light conversation, and Anders scrolled slowly through the file. He stopped on a picture of a complex device that looked like a strange, mechanical appendage. A close-up image zeroed in on a gray piece of metal that was part of a joint or hinge. They were investigating the elemental composition of that particular piece. It seemed they were trying to reverse-engineer the entire mechanism, which looked like a component from a downed plane or satellite.

He scrolled through the next 25 pages of graphs, tables, and images, one of which was a three-dimensional map of the positions of the atoms in the material's lattice structure. In the text were long descriptions of the various measurements and analyses, including magnetization and electrical measurements, and strength tests.

He then went to the last page of the report, just before its long list of references, and read the conclusions. The material was super strong, but would deform when subjected to an electric field. It could therefore be used as an actuator – meaning that it could move a part of the appendage in the picture displayed at the beginning of the document. One particularly interesting comment, however, was that they could not reproduce the material – they'd tried every known method.

Then who made it? He wondered. *The Russians?*

He searched the document but didn't find anything about the object's origin.

He then closed the file and opened another, named "Groom Lake S-4 Document 70152." There were over 50 with that same title but with different five-digit numbers at the end.

Anders flinched when the cover page appeared. It was another top-secret document, and it had been created by "The Custodial Group." The contact person listed at the bottom of the page was H. P. Bennett. His dad's middle name was Philip.

It was definitive evidence that Henry Bennett was a member of the CG.

He searched for "Groom Lake S-4" on the Internet and found links to articles about a top-secret research site at Groom Lake, Nevada, called "S-4." It was where the CIA and defense agencies tested experimental aircraft and other weapons systems, not far from the storied Area 51.

Anders scrolled to the next page of the report, at the top of which was the title, "Propulsion System of Object 4892." Below it was a short abstract and then a table of contents. The document was 410 pages long.

It took him a minute to read the abstract, which seemed to be about a thruster of some kind that they were trying to reverse-engineer. This report was about the functionality of the device, rather than the materials of which it was constructed. Terms such as "gravity repulsion" and "inertial compensation" were used, but Anders had no idea what they meant.

His father was no scientist, but he'd been writing declassified versions of black-project reports before he'd passed. Although it was possible that he'd been writing a declassified version of this document, Anders wasn't completely convinced that he hadn't collected the files for other reasons. There was no way he would've been able to write over a thousand such reports, one for each of the files on the drive. *Why did he have so many?*

He continued to scroll through the document, which was riddled with detailed drawings of parts and devices that he didn't recognize, and long, mathematical equations he didn't understand. He went to the end and read the conclusion section, which, of course, was inconclusive. In the end, they'd learned almost nothing about how the propulsion system worked, or even the physical principles on which it was based.

The document contained nothing about the origin of the object. However, if the Russians or Chinese had developed it, and US scientists couldn't even understand it, the US might be in trouble. He knew that technological imbalances between nations could lead to bad things.

He closed the file and selected another one named "Operation Starry Night." This one, again, was a product of the Custodial Group. He scrolled to the abstract and started reading.

A minute later, Anders gasped, "Holy shit!"

The abstract explained that in December of 1977, after *Voyager I* and *II* had been launched, beginning their long voyages that eventually took them out of the solar system, a secret, *Voyager III*, probe had been launched by the CIA at Cape Canaveral.

The mission of *Voyager III* differed from those of its predecessors in that it had a specific target – some cluster of objects on the edge of the solar system, and it headed in a direction orthogonal to the paths of the other two. *Voyager III* had also been equipped much differently than the others, with a separately powered communications system. In fact, in the space where *Voyager I* and *II* had mounted scientific instruments, *Voyager III* had packed in extra power sources and different types of communications equipment, including a forward-directed, millimeter-wave beacon.

Why had they sent out the third one, and why had they kept it secret? He'd never even heard a conspiracy theory about a *third Voyager* probe. His heart pounded as his excitement grew in anticipation of what specific part of all this his father wanted him to find. There were 1,189 files. Even if they averaged 100 pages apiece, that amounted to over 100,000 pages. He needed to narrow it down, or get help.

He clicked a button that reordered the files by date, with the most recent ones at the top. The result was not a listing by creation date, but rather by the dates on which they'd been loaded to the drive, which had all occurred on the same day. That date happened to be about 10 days before his father had died.

He reordered the files alphabetically and scanned through them, but none of the names stood out to him.

He leaned back in his chair and laced his fingers around the back of his head. He wondered what he should report to Harrison, and decided to wait on telling him anything until he had a better idea of what was in the files. He'd only opened three of them and his view of the world had already changed.

A *Voyager III* probe? What was its mission? And what, exactly, was the objective of the Custodial Group?

What Anders feared, however, was what he'd learn about his father and, more urgently, what would be revealed about the president, and his intentions.

CHAPTER 11

Maurice spent the morning filling out order requests on his desk computer. It was the first week of June, and his mind was finally starting to settle. Fourteen silos had been modified, and eight were already fully active – loaded with their hypersonic missiles. With two sets of training crews for the operator teams, the silo activations would soon catch up to the mechanical upgrade pace.

Even the monstrous, eight-wheelers were fully commissioned – there were now eight of them – and they had all the conventional trucks they needed, plus an additional five, to simultaneously control the full contingent of silos. At this rate, the entire job would be completed by the end of July, well ahead of the extended deadline. He could hardly believe it.

The drone incursions were becoming more frequent, but causing only minor disruptions in some systems within the control stations. However, some of the computer specialists were reporting altered software code – including "sleeper bugs," which were supposedly designed to allow the intruders to alter targeting information during a launch sequence. Maurice imagined a nightmare scenario where a

US missile was secretly reprogrammed to hit an American city just before its launch. Software manipulation was a serious problem, and it eroded confidence in the entire missile system.

Most of the latest incursions had taken place in North Dakota, rather than in the Malmstrom fields. The odd thing was that, even for the ones that had occurred just before dusk, people on the outside could not describe the aerial vehicles in any detail. Even the noises they made were ill-described as a deep hum – no rushing air, no propeller sounds, nothing.

In one case, a pair of fighter jets happened to be in the area where a drone was supposedly operating, and they'd zoomed in within seconds of it shutting down the launch computers of a North Dakota silo. Even though the fighters were in the right place at precisely the right time, the jets' weapons systems could not lock onto the craft – in fact, they didn't detect *anything*, nor did the pilots *see* anything. It was perplexing.

Maurice wondered how the upgrades in the other two missile wings were progressing. He wasn't privy to that information, but he assumed they were converting the same number of silos. If so, the three wings together would have upwards of 75 such systems – a formidable ancillary wing of hypersonics that could not be shut down by the drones. That would be enough to ward off Russia or China if they got bold enough to consider a nuclear strike after shutting down the conventional systems.

Maurice figured that the new systems would help to even the field, considering that both Russia and China already had mobile launch capabilities – decades-old technology where they launched nukes that were mounted on trucks. Why the US hadn't developed its own portable launchers, he didn't understand. At least now the Department of Defense should recognize the advantages had by Russia and China: they could interfere with our permanent launch sites but were largely immune to the same threat since they could instead launch missiles from trucks.

Something suddenly appeared on his computer screen that

caught his eye: it was an email from the Department of Defense, the subject of which read "ALERT: OPEN IMMEDIATELY."

He opened it, and was greeted with the headline, "China Accuses US of Sinking Submarine in South Pacific, Vows Retaliation."

"That's just fucking great," Maurice muttered. He read the rest of the article and found that the headline had come from Chinese state media, which meant it was more than just a rumor, although not necessarily *true*. If confirmed, however, it would mean that over 100 people were dead, and the US Navy should expect a counterattack.

With the escalation of the confrontations between the US on one side, and China and Russia on the other two sides of the geopolitical triangle, Maurice was glad his project was almost complete. However, he knew that, if the new system were ever put into use, the world would never be the same.

DURING THE TWO weeks after getting the delivery of unredacted files from FBI Deputy Director Shelly Stevens, Candace and Tim had collected an enormous amount of circumstantial information that didn't converge on anything. On one of the walls in their office was a whiteboard peppered with the names of people, organizations, and CIA and DIA operations, with a mess of lines connecting them together. It was like a vast spider web with holes in it – and the missing components were the most important.

It was clear that the president was *involved* in the SWA, but they still had nothing to prove he'd actually *done* anything to forward its objectives. He'd been operating under an alias, and there were no records of him providing resources to the group, or initiating any actions. In fact, the possibility that he'd been infiltrating the organization had become more plausible than anything else.

The Custodial Group, however, was another story. Internal CG records indicated that they knew Crownbrook was CIA at the time, and that he'd operated under his real name. However, there was still no indication of his role within that organization, nor any record of actions he'd taken, such as providing them with CIA information or using the influence of his government position to further the group's cause. The other problem was that the Custodial Group was a *government-funded* organization, at least partially. So how could there be anything wrong with the president being a member?

It all got a little fuzzy, however, when *private* money was used to expand the CG in various ways, including politically, beyond the boundaries of its government mission. That was another unknown: what, exactly, *was* its government mission? All she and Tim could gather so far was that the CG was developing defense technologies and, possibly, reverse engineering those acquired from foreign states.

Determining the president's involvement in both groups was the primary focus of their investigation, but it was the objectives of the Custodial Group that most interested her. She couldn't find anything definitive, other than that they overlapped with those of the SWA in one major aspect: they both called for nuclear war. The SWA sought population reduction by any means. The Custodial Group, on the other hand, wanted nuclear war in a very specific way: missiles. Even nuclear bombs were ruled out of their plan. It had to be intercontinental ballistic missiles, preferably using the most advanced ICBMs available, and they had to be launched from land-based silos.

"Why does it have to be land-based ICBMs with the CG?" Tim asked. "Why not from submarines?"

"Who knows," Candace replied. "They're all nuts – both groups."

"Yes, but they're not stupid," he said. "Especially those in the Custodial Group. It's composed of scientists, engineers, mathematicians, and high-level CIA operatives. And they have a lot of funding. By the way, we need to continue tracking the private money."

"That won't be easy."

"Yeah, especially since it's funneled through shell companies, offshore accounts, and laundered in various ways," he said. "We don't have the name of even one *real* company."

He was right. "But we do for the Single-World Alliance," Candace said. "Even some actionable evidence to press charges against a few people – private citizens. But it is odd that there isn't a single name we can connect to the private funding of the Custodial Group."

"That usually points to a dark money source," he said. "Do you think it's exclusively government-funded, and we just can't trace all the money back to its origin?"

"Possibly, yes."

"What does that mean?"

"It means there's a storm brewing," she said. "And we're in the middle of it."

The hair on Candace's arms stood on end as she realized the danger they were in. Tim's CIA contact had already warned them of a potential hit, and she and Tim had originally thought it was a response to their probing of the SWA. But now she was thinking that it might instead be their investigation of the Custodial Group that had ignited the danger.

"We need to find out if those five people who were assassinated were connected to the Custodial Group," she said. If they were, Candace thought that she and Tim should consider going into hiding.

IT WAS AFTER MIDNIGHT, and Anders had spent nearly two hours scanning the long list of filenames with the hope of finding one that might have more significance than the others. He was about to take a break when one caught his eye: *Peregrine_7071*.

"Of course!" he exclaimed. It had to be why his father had used the picture of the peregrine falcon for the passcode. He opened the file and read.

THE CALL WENT to voicemail and Candace hung up and slapped her phone on the desk. Something was wrong.

It had been over an hour since Tim left the FBI building to pick up food from a local Chinese restaurant. He wasn't answering his calls and, according to Ming's Palace, he hadn't picked up their order.

She looked at the whiteboard on her office wall. Over the past couple of days, they'd filled in some of the holes in the web of interconnected names of people, operations, and events, and they were getting close to a revelation of some sort. She could feel it.

Over the past two weeks, they'd been expanding their investigation and had requested and received sensitive files on all sorts of things related to the Single-World Alliance and the Custodial Group, as well as FBI files on various individuals. A few days ago, however, they'd requested files from outside agencies, including the CIA, which originally denied their access until the FBI Deputy Director stepped in. The CIA then complied, but the documents were heavily redacted, rendering them completely useless.

That response led her to believe that they were on the right track.

Suddenly, Tim burst into the office and she nearly fell out of her chair.

"Where in the hell have you been?" she exclaimed after collecting herself. "Why aren't you answering your phone?"

"It was off," he said, out of breath. "Come with me."

"What?"

"Food is in the kitchen."

His face looked gaunt and strained, like he was trying to maintain a calm appearance but was under great duress.

Candace stood from her chair and followed him out of the office and into the hall.

Tim spoke under his breath as they walked toward the kitchen. "We're in deep shit."

"What do you mean?" she whispered back. She *knew* something was wrong.

"I just met with my CIA friend," Tim explained. "I wasn't expecting him – he got to me in the parking lot of the restaurant before I went inside to pick up the food, and we drove to a nearby park. The CIA is about to pull the trigger on us. We're getting close to something."

They stepped into the kitchen. On a table were two brown paper bags that presumably contained their cold Chinese food.

"You went back for the food?" she asked.

"I had to go back to the restaurant to get my car anyway," Tim explained.

"Did you hear what I said?"

Candace stared at him in silence for a few seconds while her mind processed the information.

"They know everything we've been doing," Tim continued in a hoarse whisper. "He even showed me a recent pic of our whiteboard – with the changes we made *today*. They've bugged our office and might have installed a camera – unless someone got into our office and took a pic of our board. The CIA hasn't made the final call, but they will within the next 24 hours."

Candace suddenly felt violated by the surveillance, but it was much more serious than that. They weren't safe, and she didn't know who they could trust. The CIA was capable of bugging just about any building on the planet – and even installing cameras. Inside FBI headquarters, however, this had to be done with the help of an insider. It meant that their home base wasn't safe, and now she couldn't even trust her FBI colleagues, save maybe Deputy Director Stevens.

"The way I see it, we have two choices," she said. "We quit this project, or we go into hiding and continue the investigation."

Tim's pale face got a shade lighter. "Hiding?"

"Well, relocate," she said. "Take the files and get out of town. I have the perfect place."

"We can't take the files out of the building," he said. "They're classified, and can't even be taken out of this office without following protocols."

"The declassified docs can," she said. "And we can take our notes. Maybe we'll take a few pictures as well. We'll take everything that's legal – and maybe some things that aren't – and tell Jack that we're going out of town to interview a source."

Candace suspected that, as their immediate supervisor, Jack Neumann was also under surveillance. It also occurred to her, however, that *he* could be the CIA's inside contact. Either way, she could still use him to shield their next move.

"I'm going to tell Jack that we're going to Ohio and Indiana to question some subjects," she explained. "We'll be gone for a week – we're going to drive rather than organize a chain of flights. That should get us out of here and, once we're gone, we can stay away until we're in the clear."

"You think we'll ever really be in the clear?" Tim asked in a skeptical tone.

She shrugged. "You have a better idea?"

He shook his head. "When do we go?"

"Tomorrow morning," she said. "We'll stay here – in the office – overnight, just to be safe. We'll clear it with Jack, and leave early in the morning."

"Where are we going?"

"You'll see," she said. "You'll like it. I promise. We'll stop at our homes on the way out of town to pick up some essentials."

Candace figured a "soft" escape was the best way to avert suspicion while still pursuing the investigation.

They heated their food in the kitchenette's microwave and ate for a few minutes in silence. What were they on the verge of discovering that provoked the CIA to such a degree that they'd order a hit on FBI agents?

THE PEREGRINE CONJECTURE

ALTHOUGH THE IMAGE of a peregrine falcon being the passcode was a good indicator that "Peregrine_7071" was one of the files his father wanted him to read, there was something else that made Anders certain that it was the most important item on the thumb-drive.

The document was over 700 pages long and had a table of contents. He went to its references section and found that it cited over 1,000 other sources, most of which were included on the drive. It was clear that this was the central work.

It wasn't organized like a report. Instead, it was a *master plan*, riddled with goals, means, tactics, steps, and phases. The title of the document was different from the name of the file: it was called *The Quiet Storm*.

After reading the table of contents, abstract, and 25-page introduction, he understood the premise and objectives of the plan. It was a blueprint for changing the world.

Anders' anxiety reached an unbearable level as he realized that a clock had been ticking in the background all this time, and the witching hour was nigh. He'd send the file to Harrison immediately and then read as much as he could overnight so that they could discuss it first thing in the morning.

MAURICE GOT the order in the afternoon, in his office. The call had come on his secure satellite phone while he'd been meeting with the base's supplies coordinator. All mobile units were to be active three weeks from the next Monday, the third week of July.

All but four of the 25 silos slated for upgrading were currently ready: hypersonic missiles were in their bays, and their respective MOLVs and crews were on duty. He'd been officially informed that the other two missile wings were doing similar upgrades, but they were a couple of weeks behind Malmstrom. He was ordered to assist the commanders of those bases, if needed.

At 4:00 p.m., he got a call on his personal cell phone. It was

Colonel Travis Schulman from the 90th Missile Wing at F. E. Warren AFB, in Wyoming. They'd been hurried to complete the four-month job in three months and a week, and were now scrambling to finish it. They'd originally been given a later completion deadline, but it got moved up.

"What do you make of this rush job at the end?" Schulman asked.

"Seems like the brass are expecting something to happen soon," Maurice replied. "Or maybe it has something to do with the spike in drone incidents over the past six weeks."

"That's what I suspected at first – the drones," Schulman said. "But there have been some new developments that you might not be aware of."

Maurice hadn't been informed of anything new lately. His only correspondence with those running the show was to discuss the schedule and to make reports on his progress. "What's up?"

"We had an incursion at our *airbase* a few nights ago," Schulman said. "It was one of the drones, and it seemed to be executing a reconnaissance mission of some kind. We have Apache helicopters, which were all scrambled immediately."

"What happened?" Maurice asked. It was a brazen move to trespass upon a base. It got him thinking about what defensive measures he'd be able to take at Malmstrom – he didn't have Apache helicopters. He made a note to request some choppers since the runways weren't technically authorized for active fighters.

"The drone disappeared after just a few minutes," Schulman continued. "It never showed up on radar. It was nighttime, so the videos from the cameras at the base were useless. The eyewitnesses all said the same thing – it just disappeared, and no one had a good visual description of the craft. The Apaches searched for it but found nothing."

"What did the drone do?" Maurice asked.

"Disabled communications systems," Schulman replied. "Our radar also went offline, which is odd since it seems the drones are invisible to radar anyway. At the same time, there was a cyber-attack – I mean specifically that someone broke into our secure servers. A lot of classified information has been compromised."

Maurice felt sick. Those computers held sensitive information about the entire ICBM network, including everything from methods of operation to personnel. "Whoever's operating these things is getting bolder," he said. "It's as if they're gearing up to do something more drastic."

"I agree. But first, these craft are not 'drones' in the way that we know them. They're much more," Schulman said. "Second, I think we'd better be on the ready. We might be pressed into action soon."

"You think we're going to be attacked?"

"I do," Schulman replied. "I just don't know in what way, exactly."

"And what about Minot – what does Frank have to say about all of this?" Maurice asked. Colonel Frank Anderson was the commander of the 91st Missile Wing at Minot.

"He has even bigger problems," Schulman said. "The drones have been nosing around the bomber squadrons. His entire bomber wing is now on high alert, and live bombs – nuclear – are at the ready. It's like we're on the brink of war here."

"Have they seen the drones?"

"Again, not really – only some unreliable sightings by people on the ground," Schulman replied. "Something messed with the avionics systems of his aircraft, and they've had cyber-attacks like we've had. A lot of information has been compromised."

They promised to keep each other updated and ended the call.

The drones were expanding their activity, and now the gigantic B-52H Stratofortress bombers at Minot were on the ready. He also knew that the B-2 stealth bombers located at Whiteman Air Force Base, in Missouri, had been on high alert for the past two months. The commander at Whiteman AFB, Colonel Janis Lange, was a close friend and had confided that information in a phone call a week ago.

Whatever was going on had now come to a state where action

seemed imminent. That nuclear weapons were involved implied an existential threat of some kind – and that was the primary unknown that submerged Maurice's mind in a pool of worry.

He flinched as his desk phone rang, and then picked it up. It was his CIA contact, Christine, who kept tabs on the operation. She asked for a status report and then reiterated that it was imperative that the new missile system – all 25 silos – was to be fully active and ready for operation by Monday, July 27th. She wanted a confirmation of that 72 hours prior, which meant that the project really had to be completed the Friday before, the 24th. The deadline seemed to move up every time they spoke.

Maurice assured her that things were on track and then ended the call. His systems would be ready for deployment by the deadline, but the other two wings would be scrambling to finish.

It seemed that the calm before the storm was about to end.

ANDERS READ NEARLY a third of the lengthy Peregrine_7071 document overnight in his DMS office, getting just an hour of sleep before waking to the call from Harrison at 7:00 a.m. He'd sent his boss the file over secure email the night before. Anders was no longer worried about the security of the information – he was sure it was going to have to go public, and soon.

The door was open when Anders arrived at Harrison's office, and he walked right in. Harrison was staring at the TV mounted to the wall to the right of the entrance.

"Have you been watching this?" Harrison asked and nodded to the television.

"No, I've been buried in reading – what's happening?"

"The Chinese sunk one of our ships last night in the Pacific – a frigate – payback for us sinking their sub."

Anders suddenly felt queasy. "Sunk? Shit," he said. "How many sailors lost?"

"This one had just under 200," Harrison replied. "No word of casualties yet. I'm sure some were able to jump ship, although they said it went down quickly."

"This is horrible," Anders said. "There's going to be a war."

"Out of our control," Harrison said as he went to a worktable next to a window opposite the entrance, near the cluster of furniture arranged along the left wall. "Let's get to our business."

Anders followed and sat across from him.

"I think you've blown the lid off this thing," Harrison said. "I was up all night reading this file."

"Me too," Anders said, as he sat in the chair opposite his boss and placed a notebook on the table next to a thick stack of papers – Harrison had a printout of the document. "It's the scariest thing I've ever read, and I'm not even halfway through it."

"I don't even know where to start," Harrison said. "The overall plan? Or the parts that are currently underway?"

"How about we start with Project NIMH?" Anders suggested. "That phase has already been executed."

"I saw a reference to it but I didn't have the file," Harrison said. "You only sent me the Peregrine file."

"I'll get you the rest of them today," Anders said. "But you need to know about this one right now."

"Give me the quick version," Harrison said. "First, I didn't understand why this project was called *NIMH*. What does the National Institute of Mental Health have to do with it?"

"The acronym is not referring to the institute," Anders explained. "Are you familiar with the series of children's books called *The Rats of NIMH*?"

"I am," Harrison said and then seemed to mull it over for a few seconds before coming to a realization. "My God, they were referring to the RAT-32C virus. That's clever, and sick."

Anders explained the details as he went through his notes. The US and China had a secret program to use gain-of-function technologies to develop a pathogen that was highly contagious but only moderately deadly. The final product was a virus called RAT-32C.

"That was supposedly just a conspiracy theory," Harrison said. "It's illegal. How did it get funded?"

"The US National Institutes of Health funded some of it through research grants. The funding proposals for those projects didn't disclose the real work they were doing," Anders replied. "The rest of the money came from the Single-World Alliance, which got funds from both the government and private sources."

"Crownbrook must have been involved in this from the very beginning," Harrison said. "Not only did the RAT-32C pandemic start in year one of his first term, but I know for a fact that he spent a lot of time in China for over a decade before that – as a CIA station chief for a part of his tour."

Anders hadn't known that.

"So, they released the virus in China," Harrison said. "Why?"

"The rest of the world would be hindered from investigating anything – from its place of origin to the research labs that developed it," Anders replied. "The Chinese government would downplay the outbreak as long as it could while keeping international travel channels open for as long as possible. It would give the virus the best chance to spread to the rest of the globe."

"But I don't understand something," Harrison said. "If the SWA wants to drastically reduce the world population, why not make the virus *deadly* as well as extremely contagious?"

Anders looked down at his notes. "One objective was to study how this particular virus would spread globally," he said. "With that knowledge, they could better plan the release of a similar virus with a much higher mortality rate at a later time. But there were other, more diabolical reasons for doing it this way."

Anders went on to explain that the SWA wanted to know how large populations would respond to "authority" under such situations. Those in authority included politicians, law enforcement, and even doctors and scientists. How would they respond to forced isolation?

"For nearly two years, people confined themselves to their homes, tried to work remotely – many lost their jobs," Harrison commented. "Kids suffered greatly as well – socially, psychologically, and academically."

"And the repercussions will be long-lived," Anders added. "But there's more. They also wanted to observe how propaganda disseminated through social and televised media, as well as the censorship of dissenting information, could be used to sway opinion and control behavior."

"I think they got their answer – it worked well," Harrison said. "We're now learning about all kinds of information that was quashed that was important – accurate evidence that was deemed misinformation at the time."

"There's more," Anders said. "The virus tests – those nose swabs collected by various medical companies to detect the virus – what do you think was the real purpose of those?"

Harrison's face went blank. Anders knew that everyone at DMS had taken multiple tests during those times.

"Those tests were marginally accurate at first but, if you recall, they came out very early," Anders said.

"Just six weeks after the first report of the virus in the US."

"According to this NIMH document, those were ready to go *before* the virus was even released in China," Anders explained. "They were meant to be inaccurate – they didn't want the testing to interfere with the natural spread of the virus."

"Then why did they have them at all?"

"To collect DNA."

"What? Why?"

"To catalog everyone they could," Anders replied. "They expected to get up to 60% of the world's population in the database."

"For what?"

"To identify and track people," Anders said. "Since they eventually plan to reduce the population from about eight billion to less than 500 million, they wanted to use the DNA to weed out those with bad genetics."

"But nuclear bombs are indiscriminate, and so are deadly viruses."

"Right," Anders said. "I think a mass killing – be it bombs or pathogens – is just to get things started, and get the global government in place. After that, they thin out what's left more selectively."

"Sounds like the Nazis," Harrison commented.

"Project NIMH also proved that people would trust authorities in the medical fields to the degree that they would take poorly tested meds and vaccines," Anders said.

"Why is that important?"

"They can be used to euthanize people on a massive scale," Anders said. "In the same lab in which the RAT-32C virus was created, they were developing another virus that would lie dormant for up to a year – kind of like the shingles virus but severely deadly. This one wouldn't be contagious at all."

"So people would get a vaccine that contained this virus, and it would pop up later and kill them," Harrison said, nodding. "I'm sure the delay would be needed so that people wouldn't know about it until it was too late."

"Right."

"But that wouldn't discriminate either."

"Ah," Anders said. "That's where the DNA collected from the RAT-32C tests comes in. They – "

"Let me guess," Harrison cut in as he held up his hand. "People would be sorted before they got the vaccine, and individually tagged to get a specific shot," he said. "Then, when the time came to get it, those administering the vaccine would check the database to see which one a given person was to get, depending on whether they were supposed to live or die."

"Exactly."

"But I'd think that word would get out. I doubt that nurses and doctors would go along with the plan."

"They wouldn't know."

"What do you mean?"

"They'd be told that the new vaccines were optimized according to certain DNA traits, and they had to be sure a person got the one with which they were compatible," Anders explained. "They might have ten different types: some would eventually kill people, and others wouldn't."

Harrison seemed to mull it over, his expression conveying disbelief. "And this is all verified – this Project NIMH was really responsible for the creation and spreading of the RAT-32C virus?"

"The first phase, yes. You'll see all the data when you read the full NIMH reference. And the deadlier strain could be released at any time," Anders added. "The SWA is ready. It has verified that the global population can be controlled through mass and social media, and will yield to fear and authority."

"So the world is now primed to be taken down," Harrison concluded.

Anders nodded and sighed.

"As much as the SWA's Project NIMH is horrifying, the Custodial Group's ambitions are surreal," Harrison remarked. "It's confusing. The two groups want very different things but are somehow cooperating."

"The Custodial Group and the SWA wrote this plan *together*," Anders replied. "They found common ground that could satisfy both groups in the intermediate steps – in fact, they *needed* each other for those steps to be implemented. However, the *final outcome* will only satisfy one of them but will supposedly come about in a natural way. I don't know the details yet."

They both needed to read the rest of the document and agreed to get back to work and meet again in the evening.

The agreement between the president and DMS was now blown apart. Harrison informed Anders that he was going to decode everything he could that came through DMS from the president and read it. Meanwhile, Anders would continue reading *The Quiet Storm* and the reference files on his father's thumb-drive. One thing was clear: if any solid connection was found between the president's communications and the NIMH project or any other SWA initiatives, then DMS would publicly disclose everything.

CANDACE OPENED the heavy oak door and led Tim inside. They were at her uncle's cabin on a lake in northwest Pennsylvania, about a seven-hour drive from DC.

She turned on the lights and could tell that Tim was immediately impressed.

"You like it?" she asked. It had been one of her favorite places ever since her first visit as a little girl. It was a property that had been in her family for nearly a century, on the western shore of Loon Lake. It had been remodeled a few years ago and, while maintaining its rustic appearance, had been equipped with modern amenities, including wireless Internet, and a backup generator that ran on natural gas capable of servicing the entire place if the electricity went out.

It had four bedrooms, two on the ground floor and two on the second-floor loft. The rest was an open floor plan with a modern kitchen and a spacious living room with two couches, an assortment of chairs, a fireplace, and a large, flat-screen television. A smaller TV was mounted on the wall in the kitchen.

"I want to retire to a place just like this," Tim said.

"That'll be a while," she said. Tim was seven years younger than her, and she had at least 15 years before she could retire.

As she unpacked files and set up a small whiteboard on a tripod, she figured they'd be safe in the short term. No one knew where they were, and shouldn't be able to find them. They paid for everything in cash during the trip, removed the sim cards from their phones, and would not access anything online that allowed them to be traced.

She knew, however, that they'd eventually have to leave – if someone was looking, they'd ultimately track them down. She only hoped that she and Tim would discover something significant before that happened.

It was 8:20 p.m. when Anders knocked on the frame of Harrison's open office door.

"We have a lot to discuss," Harrison said as he stood from behind his desk. He looked frazzled – something Anders had never witnessed before.

Anders followed him to the far side of the room where Harrison sat on the couch, and Anders in a chair across from him.

"I don't even know where to start," Harrison said. "War is about to break out – all kinds of things are happening – and I've uncovered some disturbing things from the president's communications."

"You only have those that came *out* of the White House, right?" Anders asked.

"Yes, and only those Crownbrook sent by phone," Harrison replied. "But it's enough – you'll see. First, tell me what you learned today."

"A lot about the Custodial Group – how and why some of their plans coincide with those of the Single-World Alliance," Anders explained. "It's unbelievable."

"Go on," Harrison said, edging forward in his seat.

"The Custodial Group was established by the US Government sometime around 1950 – it's not clear exactly when," Anders explained. "Its primary goal was to collect something called *Evidence of Validation*."

"Validation of *what*?"

Anders hesitated. It was something he was almost embarrassed to say aloud.

"What is it?" Harrison asked, apparently detecting his apprehension.

"It's evidence of *extraterrestrials*," Anders finally responded.

"For chrissake," Harrison spat with an expression of derision. "You're kidding me."

Anders shook his head and pulled out his notebook. He, too, was a skeptic – and was trying to maintain that skepticism, but couldn't. "They've discovered a lot of weird things," he said. "I'm not saying that any of it is from aliens, but there's a lot they can't explain."

"Like what?"

Anders opened his notebook, glanced at what he'd written, and shook his head. "Before we get too deep into that, I thought we should start with the Custodial Group's members."

"Okay."

Anders handed Harrison a printout of side-by-side lists of SWA and CG members. At the top of the CG list were President Crownbrook and Henry Bennett. Other prominent members were the current CIA Director, Clay Radcliffe and the Secretary of Defense, Tillis Edwards. An addendum to the list had been added just before Anders' father had died – listing other high-ranking US government officials – which still made it outdated by three years.

The roster also included personal details of the members, such as current positions, locations, and areas of expertise.

"Note that the president and Radcliffe, and many of the others, are members of *both* the CG and the SWA," Anders commented. "However, we still don't know if they were infiltrating these groups, or were or *are* real members."

Numerous scientists were on the CG list, many of whom worked for the US Government at military research bases scattered about the country, including the storied "Area 51." The current Chinese president, Huang Jinping, and Anatoly Kurmaev, the Russian leader, were on both lists, along with other foreign political leaders and intelligence personnel from sensitive countries, including a few Middle Eastern nations, and others from the UK, Israel, Australia, France, Denmark, Sweden, and Germany. There were also numerous current and former CEOs of major US defense contractors on the list. The total membership of the CG exceeded 600 people, and the SWA had over 1,000 members. About 250 appeared on both lists, including the current Secretary-General of the United Nations.

"The CG is an impressive group – I mean in terms of influence and power, and also scientific expertise," Harrison commented. "But what's this proof they have for the existence of aliens?"

By his tone, he could tell that Harrison wasn't convinced. Neither was Anders – at least not completely. It was just too bizarre to believe, despite the compelling evidence that he was now going to present. He handed Harrison a multipage printout of a long table called the "Evidence of Validation Catalog," which tabulated thousands of items of "proof" supporting the presence of extraterrestrials from the past.

"Have a look at the item called *The Reduction of AG-922*," Anders instructed and went to the corresponding pages in his notebook.

Anders went on to explain that he'd read the referenced technical report that went by the same name, which was one of the over 1,000 files contained on his father's thumb-drive. The document was filled with intricate drawings, complex chemical formulae, and various charts and graphs. The page-long abstract explained things in terms that he could mostly comprehend, but the rest was much more complicated and he didn't understand all the science. The term "AG-922" was the label for a mechanical part that was being "reduced," which meant that it was being disassembled to be reverse-engineered.

"The 'AG' part of the label stands for *anti-gravity*," Anders said.

Harrison huffed. "That might sound like science fiction, but the wings of an airplane could be considered "anti-gravity" devices in a certain context," he said.

"I know," Anders said, now feeling like Harrison might think he was crazy. He then remembered that he and his mom once wore tinfoil hats to make fun of his dad. "This part, AG-922, was one of thousands of pieces that were recovered from a downed craft discovered in northern Alaska in 1968."

Anders went on to explain that the object in question had apparently come from the craft's propulsion system. A picture in the printout showed a cylindrical, gray-metallic object that was about two feet long and eight inches in diameter at the middle, gradually tapering to a four-inch diameter at each end. It was damaged – cracked in the middle – which exposed innards that resembled circuitry, but nothing like he'd ever seen before.

"The outer shell was so hard that it couldn't be mechanically cut – even with a diamond saw – and they ruled out using a cutting torch or laser because they didn't want to risk damaging the components inside it," Anders explained. "They instead removed what they could through the large crack in the housing, and made a detailed drawing of its interior – whatever they could see with tiny cameras and X-rays."

"I admit, it's all mysterious," Harrison said, "but it still could be just a downed satellite – maybe some experimental craft being developed by our government, or by our adversaries."

"There's more," Anders said, and glanced at his notes as he explained. "First, the scientists never determined the object's function. However, they were able to conduct chemical analyses of various things and found something they couldn't identify: it was a substance contained inside a metal cylinder from the object's interior that was a little smaller than a soda can. Elemental analysis technologies at the time the report was written, in 1988, were quite capable of identifying the chemical makeup of any known substance. However, in this case, they were unable to identify one of the constituent elements inside the can. All they could say for certain was that it was super "heavy," meaning that it was at the end of the periodic table, where the short-lived, unstable elements reside. The unknown element in the object, however, seemed stable, and hadn't decayed away for however long the object had been buried."

"They couldn't determine the elemental composition of the material?" Harrison repeated, apparently surprised.

"Not in 1988. But they have *now*," Anders explained. "An addendum to the report described a newer measurement, carried out in 2018, which identified the unknown substance as a stable isotope of the super-heavy element, Moscovium, which has atomic number 115. Moscovium was discovered – or first synthesized – in 2010."

"Let me get this straight: they discovered the downed craft in 1968, tried to determine the composition of this particular material in 1988, but were unsuccessful. Then, in 2018, they retested the same substance with newer technology and found it to be something scientists first discovered in 2010?" Harrison asked, seemingly performing the same thought sequence through which Anders had gone earlier that day.

"Precisely," Anders replied.

"Fascinating," Harrison gasped. "If true, it's quite a mystery."

"All the referenced reports and papers are in my dad's files – it seems legit," Anders said. "Even so, that alone wouldn't be enough to convince me that the craft came from aliens. But there are literally thousands of things like this. Every item I've encountered so far on that list is unexplainable."

Anders went on to detail specific items on the list, each with a physical description, a source – usually a crash site with a location, time of discovery, and estimated age – and a paragraph describing any features or functions that made it supposedly "beyond human technology." Some of the discoveries included unknown materials that humans couldn't replicate, such as that special isotope of Moscovium, or functionalities that couldn't be explained by known physics, like superconductivity at room temperature, or antigravity, which was described as the spontaneous levitation of massive objects without airfoils or propulsion systems.

"You think they can really prove that aliens were here?" Harrison asked, now seemingly more open to the idea.

"All I'm saying is that I don't think anyone can currently prove that this stuff came from us – humans," Anders replied. "And I think they're arguing something stronger – there's more evidence."

"Stronger?"

"Yes," Anders said. "I think they're speculating that the aliens are *still here*."

Harrison seemed to turn pale.

"What is it?" Anders asked.

"It's the president's messages," Harrison replied. "And the fingerprints."

HARRISON FELT as if he were being pulled into a sinkhole. It seemed that everything Anders had told him so far was not only consistent with what he'd learned from reading the president's messages, but *clarified* it.

"I have 19 of Crownbrook's outgoing messages – every one since he started passing them to us via satellite phone – and I've read them," Harrison explained. "First, he mentioned the fingerprints he sent to the Chinese president – in the envelope that Sara Bradbury opened."

"Were you able to determine the unknown print?" Anders asked.

Harrison shook his head. "Our experts still say it might've been made in the blood of an animal but they don't know what kind," he explained. "And, not only were they unable to identify the DNA, but they found its chemical makeup unusual. They say it contains unidentified proteins."

"So what does that mean?"

Harrison shrugged. "I don't know," he said. "But they're completely baffled."

"And what about the fingerprints themselves?"

"They've determined in which order they were made, and confirmed that parts were slightly mixed, indicating that they were made at about the same time – less than an hour apart," Harrison explained. "It means that the people to whom they belong had to be at the same location at the same time. I think it was meant as proof of existence of the unknown person."

"You mean as if the US has someone in custody, and they wanted to prove it?"

"Yes, and in this case it was proof for the Chinese president," he replied. "One of Crownbrook's messages to the Russian president notified him that the Chinese leader was getting 'cold feet,' and needed additional proof."

"Proof of what, exactly?"

"If we assume this has to do with the Custodial Group, I'd say it was meant to be evidence of extraterrestrials – maybe that the US has a live one in custody," Harrison said. He couldn't believe the words came from his own mouth. "Actually, it wouldn't necessarily have to be alive, would it? They could make the print with a corpse."

Anders' expression distorted with apparent skepticism, but Harrison wasn't telling him anything more bizarre than what Anders had presented to him in the first place.

After an uncomfortably long silence, Harrison asked, "Too farfetched?"

Anders seemed to shake himself out of deep thought. "No – not with what I have to tell you next," he said. "But first, did you find anything else important in the president's outgoing messages?"

"Each is just a paragraph long – ten sentences or so – and in very basic language, almost in code," Harrison explained. "They mostly describe military movements – positioning of the fleets – and were sent before the events actually occurred."

"Crownbrook was warning China and Russia of our movements in advance?" Anders asked with a horrified look on his face.

"Seems so, yes," Harrison replied. "But it looks like they weren't setting up attacks, but rather arranging well-planned *standoffs* at very specific locations in the Pacific and Barents Sea. He even provided precise GPS locations."

"And are those the positions where the standoffs are currently set up?"

"Yes, at exactly those locations."

"Why would he do that?"

Harrison shrugged. "No idea, but there's something else," he said. "In one of the later messages, he gave a specific date for the 'skirmishes to commence,' and China was to initiate the first one in the South Pacific. Maybe you can guess what that was."

"China sinking our Frigate."

"Close," Harrison said. "It was the date we sunk their sub – which is still unconfirmed."

"It was all planned," Anders said in a tone of realization. "It was all a setup."

"That's the past," Harrison said. "We need to concentrate on what happens next."

"And what's that?"

"Crownbrook mentions another date in his final message," Harrison said. "It reads, 'Initiate *Quiet Storm* on our move in the last week of July. Watch the falcons.'"

"That's just two weeks away!" Anders exclaimed and edged to the front of his seat. "What are 'the falcons'?"

"No idea. Maybe they're planning another NIMH event," Harrison suggested. "Phase two, the more lethal virus."

Harrison noticed that Anders' face looked worse than the usual pale. It looked gray.

Anders shook his head slowly.

The skin on Harrison's arms puckered in goosebumps and a chill worked its way up the back of his neck.

"I'm pretty sure it's something worse," Anders said. "Let me explain."

Panic seeped into Anders' mind as it suddenly occurred to him that he might know what the president meant by "the falcons."

Harrison, in what seemed to be a nervous reaction, filled two tumblers each with a finger of whisky, and set one on the coffee table in front of Anders.

Anders flipped through his notebook until he found the right page. "What I'm about to tell you is just as surreal as everything else," he said. "To start, have you ever heard of a man named Gunter Eriksson?"

Harrison shook his head.

"Me either, before this," Anders said. "Gunter Eriksson was a Nazi scientist who was brought to the US after the Second World War, along with the well-known Wernher von Braun, to develop rocket technology. Collecting Nazi scientists was a part of the Allies' post-war initiative called Operation Paperclip. The two men didn't get along, so Eriksson was placed in another organization, which was eventually incorporated into the modern complex of secret research sites that includes Area 51."

"Bringing a former Nazi into our most secretive military installation sounds like a brilliant idea," Harrison commented with ample sarcasm.

"Eriksson engineered new propulsion systems for advanced supersonic spy aircraft, including the U-2 *Dragon Lady* and the SR-71 *Blackbird*," Anders continued. "Just after the commissioning of the SR-71, he was assigned to Project Blue Book, a government study on UFOs, and was then brought into the so-called Majestic 12, or MJ-12, a group which was purportedly created to *cover up* what the government knew about UFOs."

"I've heard about these UFO groups from those TV shows that investigate aliens," Harrison commented. "The government now calls them 'Unidentified Anomalous Phenomena,' or UAP. The acronym itself is confusing – it's plural, so how does one indicate a singular craft? UFO is better. Anyway, I figured the government projects mentioned in those pseudo-documentary shows are real, but the conspiracy theories associated with them are just for entertainment."

"Well, here's another 'conspiracy theory' that I'm sure you haven't heard," Anders said. "Gunter Eriksson was involved in a top-secret *Voyager III* mission."

"Wait, a *third* Voyager mission?"

Anders nodded and explained that the *Voyager III* probe had been launched by the CIA at Cape Canaveral. Its mission differed from those of its predecessors in that it had a specific target – some cluster of objects on the edge of the solar system. *Voyager III* was also equipped differently than the others, with a souped-up communications system.

"Gunter Eriksson was responsible for developing a communication system that employed optical light rather than radio waves, as well as a directional, millimeter wavelength transmitter and receiver," Anders continued. "He was then recruited by the Custodial Group, which was described in the report as more of a secret society than a government entity. In fact, the CG is multi-agency, and multi-national."

"So, the Custodial Group is involved in this kind of stuff," Harrison said. "I could have been mixed up in all of this."

"It might've been best that you weren't."

"What was *Voyager III* investigating?"

"No idea," Anders replied.

"So how does this Gunter Eriksson fit into what's happening now?"

"*That* question I can answer," Anders said. "You see, the CG already had much of the evidence you saw listed in the Evidence of Validation Catalog when Eriksson joined, and the belief at the time was that extraterrestrials were watching the planet."

"Why did they think that?" Harrison asked.

"Other than the evidence that I've already described, there were some incidents," Anders explained. "The one that convinced Gunter Eriksson, however, was a missile launch that was intended to scare

North Korea. In 1972, the US launched an ICBM – with no warhead – that was supposed to land in the sea near the rogue nation. It was intended to demonstrate that the US could hit them at any time. The US had warned the Soviet Union and China beforehand so that they wouldn't react and launch *real* missiles of their own."

"I never heard of that," Harrison said, apparently skeptical.

"It's a secret that somehow never got leaked," Anders said. "And one reason it was kept secret was that the missile never reached its target."

"What happened to it?"

"It was destroyed before it reentered the atmosphere," Anders replied. "It essentially burned up while it was in space, at the top of its trajectory."

"A malfunction?"

Anders shook his head. "No. There's footage of something engaging with it in space, although it's a poor-quality video," he explained. "They speculated that a laser had destroyed it, which was beyond the capability of any nation's technology at the time. But that was just a guess."

"So they naturally thought it was aliens," Harrison said with a tone of ridicule.

"Well, they didn't know anything for sure, but some of the scientists had some ideas," Anders explained. "One scientist in particular …"

"Gunter Eriksson," Harrison interjected.

"Yes," Anders said. "He suggested carrying out some tests."

"Such as?"

"The first was to launch a second missile, but this time to make sure that it would be filmed with high-quality video, and also monitored with various instruments," Anders explained. "They tried it, but this time the missile was destroyed earlier in the trajectory – before it even left the atmosphere. The limited film footage they obtained was still poor, and the surveillance planes had been in the wrong locations. No debris was even recovered – same as the first one. They learned nothing new. But the fact that a missile was destroyed *again* was enough to convince many people at the highest levels that something unusual was happening."

"Did they try again?" Harrison asked.

"Not with ICBMs," Anders replied. "They'd already sacrificed two missiles, and their failures – likely deemed as malfunctions by the Soviet Union at the time – came off as weakness. It was making the US look bad."

"So what did they do?"

"The US Government did nothing, but the Custodial Group studied the situation thoroughly and deemed that the evidence that aliens were on or near Earth was strong," Anders explained.

"Just based on the failed missiles?"

"Yes, and the fact that, ever since those missiles were destroyed, strange craft started showing up at our ICBM sites, and even interfering with their systems," Anders explained. "By the way, this is also happening *currently*. Strange craft have been showing up everywhere – powerplants, NASA sites, naval vessels, missile fields, and NSA and CIA communications facilities. Maybe you've seen the footage by US Naval aviators from 2004 and 2015. Our own government released the videos in 2017 – the article was published in the *New York Times*."

"I've seen them," Harrison said. "Strange craft were nosing around our carrier groups. One was called the 'tic-tac' video – recorded from a fighter jet. It showed a white, pill-shaped aircraft that looked like a flying propane tank. The videos are stunning, but I'm still not convinced the objects are of extraterrestrial origin."

"Me either," Anders said. "But to the Custodial Group, those observations, along with all the other evidence they had from the past, were convincing enough to plan something drastic. Let me explain."

CANDACE SET a bowl of popcorn on the kitchen table, grabbed a handful, and started munching. A cool, night breeze soughed through the light curtains over the kitchen sink, and the chirping of crickets was the only sound coming from outside other than the occasional, distant groan of the motor of a small fishing boat making its way to shore in the dark. She recalled with fondness the midnight fishing adventures she'd had with her uncle. He'd always bring along a thermos of hot cocoa and they'd sip it while they watched their fishing lines and gazed at the starry night sky.

She resolved to come to the cabin more often.

Tim took a sip from a beer bottle and then grabbed a handful of popcorn. "We can make multiple connections between Crownbrook and both the Single-World Alliance and this shadowy Custodial Group – by the way, I'm still not clear on the CG's overall objective. However, all of his suspicious involvement is explained away if he just says that it was his mission while in the CIA to infiltrate these organizations."

"That only works for periods when he was in the CIA," Candace argued. "We need to find a *recent* interaction between him and them."

"Once in the CIA, always in the CIA," he said.

"Please," Candace said and rolled her eyes. "That doesn't count when you're in a position where you can fire the director of the CIA who, by the way, is also a member of both organizations."

"Fair enough," Tim conceded. "All I'm saying is that the president has two years left in his second term, and whatever we dig up will be suppressed for at least that long before it sees daylight – if it ever does. And, even if it does get out earlier than that, it will be seen as misinformation fabricated by his political adversaries."

Candace nodded. "I know," she said. "And the Attorney General is in his back pocket as well, so the DOJ will drag its feet." She'd witnessed the Department of Justice quash one of her embezzlement cases against a former colleague of the president. She realized that the aftereffects of that case were part of what invoked her angry persistence in this one.

"What I've found interesting is the unusually large degree of collaboration between the two groups," Tim said.

"They have a symbiotic relationship," Candace said. Although it was speculation, she thought she understood what their bond might be. "The Custodial Group is mostly scientists, along with some intelligence people – but even those are mostly technical people. The Single-World Alliance, however, is comprised largely of politically connected people, wealthy sorts from the private sector, and intelligence operatives with a more HUMINT bend."

"Human intelligence operatives could have both technical and political skill sets," Tim argued. "But I see where you're going. In order to initiate a nuclear missile attack, they'd have to overcome both technical and political obstacles."

"I get the politics part to some degree, although it's my understanding that the president could order a launch without the approval of Congress," Candace said.

"The Secretary of Defense must approve it but cannot veto the order," Tim explained. "But I'm sure that there could be some kind of refusal from inside the military if the president just ordered a nuclear strike without provocation."

"Or maybe Congress could declare him unfit for office before the order could be carried out," she said. "That aside, I'd think the technical part was already taken care of by our military. What would be the technical obstacle? Why would technical assistance be needed?"

"I don't know," Tim said. "Maybe they intend to acquire some missiles somehow and launch them on their own. Or maybe they're planning to get some nuclear bombs and conduct their own bombing raid."

"Remember, just missiles – no bombs for the CG," she said. "And I'd think CG operatives launching missiles themselves would be crazy. First, they'd have to *obtain* the missiles, and then figure out how to *launch* them."

"I suppose they could convince the missile silo operators to launch the missiles," Tim suggested. "The president has the Gold Codes – the launch codes – and the nuclear football. He could just give the order, and the operators would launch without question."

"I think they're supposed to do that anyway," Candace said. "But maybe the SWA or CG having their own people as missile operators would guarantee no resistance."

"You think we could get the names of the operators?" Tim asked.

Candace shook her head. "I doubt it," she replied. "Besides, we've already collected the names of a large number of suspected CG and SWA members, and none of them were missile operators."

She went to the refrigerator and returned with a beer. She popped it open and took a swig. "Something is going to happen soon, I can feel it," she said. "Like a huge terrorist attack but on a global scale."

"Add in the fact that five people have already been assassinated, it would seem we are at a crucial juncture."

"And those five are only the ones we *know* about," she added.

"And *we* could be next," he said and chuckled.

Candace laughed, but it bothered her. They really *could* be next. But it only strengthened her resolve. They were on the right track.

Anders shifted in his seat, grabbed his whisky glass from the coffee table, and took a gulp. It burned all the way down. Harrison asked for the punch line and now he was going to give it to him, no matter how crazy it sounded. Anders was starting to believe that what he was about to describe was really going to occur, and soon.

"First, Gunter Eriksson made the argument that, if extraterrestrials were really present and keeping quiet, there was a reason for it," Anders explained.

"They're following the *prime directive*," Harrison blurted.

"Possibly," Anders said, knowing that the "prime directive" was a term used in the *Star Trek* TV series referring to the protocol that forbade them from interfering with underdeveloped civilizations in order to avoid influencing them in any way. "But they've already violated that policy by destroying those missiles and exposing themselves to our military."

"Then why are they here?" Harrison asked.

"According to the Custodial Group, one reason is that they want to make sure that we don't destroy ourselves," Anders replied. "And they'll eventually reveal themselves when we've reached a certain level of development."

"That sounds like the prime directive to me."

"Except that they'll intervene if we try to do something crazy."

"Like destroy the planet with a massive nuclear war," Harrison said.

"Right," Anders said. "But there are possible variations on this concept, beyond the idea that they're looking out for us – protecting us from ourselves."

"I see where you're going," Harrison said. "Maybe they're looking to protect the *planet*, and not necessarily *us*."

"Yes," Anders said. "In fact, they might view humans as destructive pests they need to eradicate before taking over the planet."

Harrison huffed. "So now we're talking about an alien invasion – *War of the Worlds* style?"

Anders ignored his derision. "That's one possibility," he said. "But it's irrelevant – whether or not anyone is watching us doesn't matter. We have to worry about our side of the equation, meaning, what are the CG and SWA planning?"

"And what is that?"

"Gunter Eriksson had the idea that, no matter why the extraterrestrials were here, they would intervene if we did something drastic that threatened the planet," Anders explained. "His idea, called the *Peregrine Conjecture*, was to launch a massive nuclear missile attack – ICBMs – which humans wouldn't be able to stop. The aliens would then be forced to step in and take out all the missiles, and would have no recourse but to reveal themselves. Unequivocally. Their presence would be proven without a doubt."

Harrison's expression went from one of contemplation to that of realization in a few seconds.

"What is it?" Anders said.

"All three leaders are on both the CG and SWA membership lists," Harrison said. "Are they purposely driving their nations into nuclear war, with the intent of testing this ... uh,"

"Peregrine conjecture?"

"Yes," Harrison said. "All of this recent geopolitical turmoil might be contrived to set up the final act – a massive nuclear attack."

Anders had come to the same conclusion, especially after learning the content of the president's outgoing messages.

"The peregrine is a falcon," Anders said. "Maybe the president was making a connection to Gunter Eriksson's Peregrine Conjecture when he said, 'watch the falcons.'"

"Possibly," Harrison said. "But I still don't understand why the two groups would cooperate to such a degree. The final objectives of the CG and SWA are so different."

"The larger plan, Quiet Storm, contains a decision tree," Anders explained. "The base of that tree is the launching of ICBMs, which, of course, is no easy feat. The CG and SWA have been cooperating for decades in order to achieve this."

"Suppose that occurs, what happens next?" Harrison asked. "How does this 'decision tree' work?"

"It's more like a flow chart. Once the missiles are launched, two things can happen," Anders explained. "One, the aliens take them out – no nukes land – and the CG has proven the existence of extraterrestrials along with their current presence on our planet."

"And what will the SWA do then?"

"That's not clear, but it's assumed they'll postpone their own objectives until they see what the aliens actually *do*," Anders replied. "The Custodial Group seems to think that the aliens will make contact with us, although some of its members think they'll invade."

"And what if there are no aliens?" Harrison asked. "The nukes will land."

"Yes, and then the Single-World Alliance gets what it wants," Anders explained. "The missiles strike their targets, the SWA initiates the teardown of society as we know it, and a one-world government gets instated. The CG will just bow out at that point."

"It would be chaos," Harrison said. "Millions would die."

"Yes, but it won't be enough," Anders said. "At some opportune time, they'll commence the second phase of the NIMH operation, shut down global communications, and organize and cull the masses."

"*Billions* need to be slaughtered if they're going to reduce the population to 500 million," Harrison said.

"How do we stop this?"

"Release all the documents," Harrison replied. "Through internet leak sites, to start."

"Will that be fast enough?" Anders asked. "According to Crownbrook's own secret messages, something big is happening in the last week of July. That's less than two weeks from now."

"We can also try the FBI," Harrison suggested. "I don't think I trust the CIA at this point, considering the director is a member of both the CG and SWA."

"You trust the FBI director?"

Harrison shook his head. "No," he replied. "But how about the agents who questioned you in your apartment? They seemed to be after the president, and were investigating both organizations."

"What if they don't understand the urgency, or just don't believe us?"

"That's why we'll release it publicly at the same time," Harrison said. "We'll give the FBI people a couple of days to act. The leak sites take time to vet the information before they release it anyway."

"I have a business card with one agent's phone number," Anders said. "Should we contact her?"

Harrison nodded and placed a call on his mobile phone. He set up an untraceable call for the next day through DMS's communications department, ended the call, and looked to Anders. "Load a thumb-drive with the files you want them to have," he instructed. "You'll make a drop sometime tomorrow, and we'll give them the pickup location. After that, it's up to them."

It was about the quickest they could move, but a dark feeling in the back of Anders' mind told him that they might already be too late.

CHAPTER 12

Candace and Tim stared at the TV in the cabin's kitchen. It was 7:15 a.m., the coffee just finished brewing, and the morning sun was shining through the patio door that overlooked the lake at the bottom of the hill. It didn't feel like a Monday.

Cable news stations were reporting that an American aircraft carrier in the Barents Sea was ablaze after being struck by either a missile or a torpedo, it wasn't clear which. It was clear, however, that Russia was responsible for the attack, which resulted in the loss of life, although the casualty count had not yet been reported. Russia accused the US of sinking one of its submarines just 12 hours prior – something that hadn't been reported in the news until now.

A ticker streamed across the bottom of the screen saying that China was accusing the US of sinking another one of its submarines, the second in two weeks. China had responded to the destruction of the first sub with an attack on a US frigate, sending it under the waves. Now it seemed China would retaliate again.

"They're saying that we struck first in all cases," Tim said. "What the hell is happening?"

Another ticker message announced that the sunken Russian sub was the *Kolpino*, sometimes referred to as the "Black Hole" due to its supposed silent propulsion system. If true, it would be an enormous loss to the Russians.

"I think we're on the verge of all-out war," Candace commented.

Her attention was then drawn to her buzzing phone, rattling on the kitchen table. She looked to Tim, who was sitting across from her.

They'd spent the last two days poring over the files they'd brought with them, many of which they'd illegally digitized and were reading on their computers.

Amongst the cottage's modern amenities were wireless internet access and satellite television. They had to be extremely careful about the former, and only used the cabin's computer for anonymous tasks, like internet searches and news updates. They couldn't use any of their own devices, and she'd taken the precaution of routing incoming calls on her FBI phone to a burner, which was now vibrating on the table.

"I don't know that number," she said as she examined its screen. She'd already ignored two calls from her immediate supervisor, but it otherwise seemed that no one was looking for her. She answered it. "Hello?"

"Is this Agent Wright?" someone asked. It was a woman's voice.

"Who's calling, please?" Candace said.

"I need to talk to FBI Agent, Candace Wright," the woman said. "I have urgent information for her."

Candace put the phone in speaker mode and set it on the table so that Tim could hear the conversation. She looked at him, and he nodded for her to speak.

"Okay, this is Agent Wright," she said. "What's the information?"

"We're making a dead drop in a park in Alexandria," the woman said. "It's a data drive with crucial information. You need to pick it up. How much time do you need?"

Candace's mind seemed to freeze for a few seconds. She looked to Tim, who shrugged and nodded for her to continue. "I'm not doing anything until I know what the information is," she said.

The response came after a few seconds of silence. "It connects the president to the Single-World Alliance and the Custodial Group," the woman said. "On the thumb-drive are top-secret files that prove this, also connecting the president to current events. The situation is urgent. You can get the files today, or you can wait until they're released to the public, two days from now. Your call."

Candace's heart pounded in her chest. She glanced at Tim, whose eyes were wide and his head nodded dramatically for her to agree to the pickup.

"We're at least seven hours away," Candace said. "We can be in DC tonight."

"Write down this number," the woman said and then recited it as Tim wrote it down. "Call when you're ready for pickup instructions."

The phone went dead.

Tim's face was now pale.

"You think it's a trap?" she asked.

He shook his head and shrugged. "Does it matter?" he asked. "We have to do it."

"It sounds like they're telling us exactly what we want to hear — giving us precisely what we're searching for," she said. "It's too convenient."

"They say the information will be out in two days anyway," Tim said. "If it were a trap, why would they tell us that?"

"Right, why give us a reason to decline their offer?" she said.

"We have to go," he reiterated.

She sighed. "I could've used a couple of weeks here," she said.

"Three days isn't enough," Tim agreed. "I didn't even get to go fishing. Not that I could've enjoyed it under these conditions."

"We'll come back when all of this is over. You can fish next time," Candace said. "Let's pack up and get out of here."

Someone knocked at his door, and Anders swiveled his chair 180 degrees away from his gigantic computer monitor and faced the entrance to his DMS office.

"Will the FBI agents pick it up?" he asked Harrison, who was standing in the doorway. Anders was referring to the thumb-drive that he was to hide in a local park.

"Tonight," Harrison replied as he entered and sat down on the couch against the wall to Anders' left. "They're out of town – seven hours away – but they're coming back for the files."

Anders felt some relief, but he still had more to do. "I've been working with our computer people," he explained. "We can make the files live to the public as early as Thursday – three days from now – if the leak sites move at their usual pace."

"Good, but wait until I give the okay to submit them," Harrison said. "I want to make sure to give our FBI contacts a chance to move on this, maybe make some arrests. We informed them of the planned public release in *two* days – so that should light a fire under their asses."

"It feels like we're acting as double agents," Anders said. "It's hard to believe that the president is involved in something so bizarre. But I can't get myself to ignore the circumstantial evidence."

"It's even worse than that," Harrison said. "We're just one of many parties in this situation, and no one trusts any of the others. Now we even mistrust our own client."

Anders' next task was to figure out which files to release to the public, and which to give to the FBI. DMS document specialists helped him search all the files for those that mentioned his father's name, of which there were about 100. He'd read through them and removed or electronically redacted all instances of "Henry Bennett" from the batch being released. He then did a search for all other sensitive names, including Harrison's, Anders', Anders' mom's, and a few other DMS employees. Harrison's showed up three times, and

Anders' mother's showed up in two, but mostly in reference to his father. Anders then had them search for his mom's maiden name, and they found two additional files. Anders' name didn't show up anywhere, as he expected.

He learned through this process that his mom was much more involved in the spy world than she'd led on. She'd participated in actual *missions* – not just translating and analyzing. She'd managed some assets in Eastern Europe and had acted as a courier on occasion. And she'd kept it all secret – more so than his dad had, although that was because his position had become administrative, and therefore much more public. He wondered now if he should have followed in his parents' footsteps and joined the CIA. He quickly concluded that things had worked out for the best: he was in a unique position to disseminate crucial information that might help avert a global disaster. He doubted he would've had the same opportunity had he been a CIA employee.

He just hoped he wasn't too late.

CANDACE WENT to the park in disguise, which amounted mostly to wearing a dark-brown wig. Tim had told her that she looked good in it and suggested she wear it more often. She figured he'd been attempting to relieve the tension.

It was a cool evening for July. She wore black yoga pants, a dark green sweatshirt and matching headband, and stylish headphones, which were feeding audio from Tim, who was in a minivan parked within sight of the drop area. She had a small handgun in a fanny pack strapped to the small of her back, and she had Tim's German shepherd on a leash. She regretted bringing Greta along, but she was a former service dog that had experienced real combat conditions, so she figured the canine could handle a little violence, if it came to that.

The reason for Greta's presence was that the thumb-drive was hidden in a dog park, in a drain next to a pole that held a roll of plastic bags used to pick up the mess after someone's dog did their business.

It was getting dark, and only a few dogs and their humans were spread out in the vast park. The sun was going down, but she could still see the orange sunset through the trees. The automatic lights along the path had already illuminated. It was just past 8:30 p.m.

"Looks clear from here," Tim said in her ear. It had been his idea to use a walkie-talkie app that linked their phones together without bouncing signals off cell towers. That way, no one could get location information from their phones. Her headphones were, in turn, connected wirelessly to her phone.

With Greta leading the way, Candace pulled the leash to the left side of the path and went to a bag dispenser – the one described in the instructions.

"That must be it," Tim said. "The drain is just a few steps off the path, to the right of the dispenser. See it?"

She couldn't answer but looked for it in the area he mentioned.

"Pull Greta near it and walk around the area for a while," he instructed.

Candace knew the plan but was grateful for Tim's direction. His voice was calming. The idea that the CIA might have a hit out on them made her twitchy. All she did was get a phone call telling her to go somewhere and pick up information that they'd been seeking for months. That call had been forwarded directly from her FBI phone. How stupid was she? Anyone could have made that call and set a trap. There could be a sniper somewhere in the park, hundreds of yards away and completely out of sight.

"See the drain?" Tim asked.

Candace refocused on her task and spotted a metal, circular grate, about eight inches in diameter, and ten feet from the metal pole that supported the roll of doggy bags. She guided Greta toward the grate and let her nose around the area.

"Grab a bag and pretend to pick up some dog crap," Tim instructed.

She went back to the dispenser, rolled out a bag and tore it off, and stuck her hand in it. She then went to the drain, squatted down, and carefully pulled on the grate. It gave way and she slid it aside, keeping it flat and low, below the grass level, so that someone observing from a distance couldn't see what she was doing. She peered inside the drain and was surprised to see that there was no pipe. It was just a shallow hole, about six inches deep. It was a *fake* drain.

There was nothing in it – just dirt.

She was about to panic when she got the idea to reach her bagged hand into the hole and rake her fingers through the dirt. She felt something hard. To her relief, she'd unearthed a flat, plastic box, about the size of a cigarette lighter. She grabbed it, extracted it from the hole, and pulled her hand out of the bag, turning it inside out in the process. From a distance, it would have looked as if she'd picked up some dog excrement and bagged it.

"Looks like you got it," Tim said. "Replace the drain cover and casually head back."

Candace slid the grate over the hole and guided Greta back toward the park entrance.

Five minutes later, she, Greta, and Tim were in a rental van, heading toward a hotel in Gaithersburg, Maryland, where they'd analyze what they'd collected.

The operation was a success but she had a bad feeling in her gut. The person who had contacted her about the info said that the information was "urgent." It meant that time was running short on something.

ANDERS SIPPED his first coffee of the day in front of his computer at DMS. It was 6:00 a.m., and he'd just gotten word that the FBI agents had picked up the data drive the night before. It made him nervous, but he knew he was doing the right thing. The entire cache would go public in three days.

A different anxiety sourced from the feeling that he'd gotten the information too late. His dad might not have anticipated the rate at which the situation would develop. Geopolitical maneuvering usually occurred at a glacial pace, with ample forewarning to those whose job it was to observe such things. However, that was not the case this time, although it could have been that those observers had acted to conceal, rather than expose, the incremental events that had led to the volatile state in which the world now found itself. Ships had been sunk. People had died. If war wasn't already here, it was just around the corner.

A buzzing from his desk drawer startled him from his thoughts. He opened it and found a vibrating mobile phone. It was the one he'd set up for meeting with Alina Petrova, his Russian courier contact. He answered it.

"I'm in your area. Can we meet?" It was Alina's voice. "Soon."

She sounded stressed.

"I'll have to clear it," he responded. "I'll call you back."

"Please hurry," she said and ended the call.

He called Harrison. After a short discussion, he okayed the meeting but insisted on having DMS support in the area, which Anders welcomed.

Anders called Alina back and set up a rendezvous in a chain coffee shop less than 10 minutes from DMS. It would be a static meeting, which Harrison thought was okay based on the urgency of both Alina's call and the current global situation. The shit was about to hit the fan, in Harrison's words, so some precautions had to be overlooked for the time being.

DMS operatives dropped Anders off at a street corner where a SuperLift car picked him up and drove about three miles before dropping him off at a grocery store, next to which was a "Captain's Coffees," a popular café chain.

He arrived five minutes early, went inside, ordered a coffee, and took a seat next to a window, as far from other patrons as he could get. When Alina arrived, they'd get a table outside.

At 8:00 a.m. sharp, Alina walked into the café, glanced at him, and then joined the long, but fast-moving line of patrons who were hurrying to get their morning hits of caffeine. He surfed news websites on his phone as he waited and, a few minutes later, she approached with a cup in hand.

"Shall we go outside?" he asked.

She nodded, and then led the way out a glass door to a concrete patio, on which were a dozen circular tables with large umbrellas that shaded them from the morning sun. He followed her to one in a remote corner, far from two mothers with young children on the opposite side.

"It sounds urgent," Anders said.

"It is," Alina said. "We're about to have an all-out nuclear war. The Russian president is in on it – along with your president."

"In on it? How, exactly?" he asked. It was something he'd suspected, but hoped she had more evidence to confirm that their leaders were conspiring.

Alina reached over the table and grabbed his left hand with both of hers. He felt her place a thumb-drive in his palm, but maintained her grasp afterwards.

"What's on it?" he asked.

"We have proof that the Chinese and Russian subs weren't sunk."

"What do you mean?"

"We intercepted orders from the Chinese naval command instructing their submarine captains to head out of the area and lie dormant," she explained. "We also detected an outgoing communication from the *Kolpino* just six hours ago. It was supposedly destroyed early yesterday – 24 hours ago."

"So they're faking the attacks as an excuse to assault the US vessels?"

"It's more than that," Alina said. "The US *knows* those vessels weren't destroyed. There have been no reports of engagements through the US Naval Command – no reports that US ships fired upon foreign vessels, and no US subs have launched torpedoes."

"That came from where – US military intelligence? A leak?" he asked.

She nodded. "And there's one other piece of damning evidence on that drive that proves we're on the brink of a completely manufactured war," she said.

Anders could hardly maintain his composure.

"The one US surface ship that was sunk – the frigate – was *evacuated* before the attack," said Alina. "We have satellite camera footage of the crew actually deboarding and being taken to other ships in the fleet hours before it was taken down."

His mind seemed to fog with astonishment. "That's crazy – they just let someone sink it?"

"Yes, and they knew it was happening well in advance," she said.

"And what about the US carrier that was attacked?"

"No casualties," she said. "That's all I have on that incident right now."

"You're sure about this?"

"The intel on that drive is definitive: it's multi-sourced, and each is independent and consistent with the others."

"I don't work for the CIA – I don't have power to act on this."

"And I'm not working for Russian intelligence," she said. "But we're both on the periphery, which might make us more influential in this case since there's no chain of command in which this information could get stuck. We have no constraints."

She was right. They were in an unusually flexible position compared to a typical intelligence operative who would just pass the intel up the line.

"There's going to be a huge release of information to the public in three days," Anders revealed. "It's going to blow the lid off of this – it exposes two subversive groups which are behind it all, and reveals their members. The leaders of our two countries and the Chinese president are at the tops of those lists – members of both groups. There are also documents that prove that what has been happening – this phony war – is part of a massive scheme. But I'm not sure it will break in time. We might be too late to stop this."

"What do you mean it's going to be *released*?" she asked. "Through something like WhistleLeaks?"

"Yes, and similar sites."

"Perhaps you should also leak the info I just gave you," she suggested. "It has been scrubbed of sensitive personnel info – it will not compromise our sources."

Anders agreed, and they parted ways. He arranged a SuperLift ride and then walked a block to a street corner where it picked him up.

He was anxious to see the new information. It added intense urgency to a situation that was already at its boiling point. He was sure Harrison would also want to forward this new intelligence to their new FBI friends.

As they got closer to his first drop-off location, Anders wanted to get out of the car and run. His anxiety was hardly containable. War was imminent.

It was going on noon and Candace shuddered as a light rain pattered on the window of their ratty hotel room. Tim looked up from the stained, upholstered chair where he'd been since 5:30 a.m., reading the files on the thumb-drive she'd extracted from the faux drain in the park. They'd both read most of the night and were now functioning on two hours of sleep.

Whoever had provided the files was smart enough to include a priority list of the most important documents to read first. She was sitting at the room's tiny desk, trying to determine their next move.

"This is damning information," Tim said. "The president is screwed. He should be removed from office immediately. He's a fucking lunatic – and so are all the members of these bizarre groups."

"Just his connection to the pandemic should be enough to put him away forever," she said. "This sounds like the conspiracy theories that propagated through social media over the past few years, but the sources are all included. This is hard evidence. We can actually follow its development and interrogate the people involved. Who would ever believe that RAT-32C was a part of a *plan*?"

"This scares the shit out of me," Tim said. "If the second phase of *Project NIMH* is ever implemented, the world as we know it will be over."

"According to the master plan, *Silent Storm*, it won't start until after the nuclear strike," she said. "They need some cataclysmic event to get things rolling."

Candace's phone rang. The phone number of the contact who'd provided them with the thumb-drive appeared on the screen.

"Hey," she said as she stood and then sat on the edge of the bed. Tim got out of his chair and sat next to her as she answered the call and put it on speakerphone. "This is Agent Wright."

"I assume you have evaluated the information we provided," said a woman's voice.

"Much of it, yes," Candace replied. "We plan to act."

"Something else has come up, and we need to meet immediately," the woman said. "It's urgent."

"Okay, we'll meet with you," Candace said. She now trusted – *had* to trust – whoever it was who had given them the files. "Where?"

"We want to bring you into our facility, but under restricted conditions," the woman explained. "We cannot reveal our identity."

The woman went on to explain the procedure, which included blindfolding and car rides, and no phones or weapons. Candace balked at the idea.

"If we wanted to harm you, we could have done it in the park, and we wouldn't have given you sensitive information," the woman argued.

"Give me a minute," Candace said. She muted her phone and turned to Tim. "What do you think?"

They discussed it quickly and Candace unmuted the phone. "We agree to blindfolds and no phones, but we want our firearms."

"Agreed," the woman said without hesitation, and then informed them of the time and place for the pickup.

When the call ended, Candace started packing up her things. "We'll put a copy of the thumb-drive in my safety deposit box, and the rest of our files in the trunk of the rental car, which we'll put in a long-term parking garage, just in case things get crazy," she said. "We'll take a cab to the pickup point."

Tim nodded and started packing, and then called his fiancée and asked her to pick up Greta at noon from the veterinarian's office. He'd dropped her off after their operation in the dog park the night before. He'd said she was due for a checkup anyway.

As Candace zipped her small suitcase and slung her backpack over her shoulder, she tried to remember a time when she'd felt so much anxiety. There was a feeling of utter panic in her gut.

Despite the damning evidence they had in their possession, they were probably already too late. It seemed the world was a hair-trigger pull away from nuclear annihilation.

ANDERS WATCHED AS THE BURLEY, masked DMS operatives led the two, hooded FBI agents into the interrogation room – something that he hadn't known existed until an hour prior. The agents weren't cuffed, and even had their firearms with them. It was, of course, not a forced interrogation, but just an operation in which one party – DMS – wanted to ensure its anonymity.

The agents were led to side-by-side seats at a rectangular table that faced a silvered window. On the table were coffee mugs, a carafe of hot coffee, and a plate of cookies.

The DMS operatives left the room, and Harrison, who was sitting next to Anders behind the glass, opened the intercom and spoke.

"Thanks for coming, Agents Wright and Barilaro," Harrison said. "Please take off your hoods and have a look at the screen above the window."

Above the window was a large computer monitor that displayed a duplicate image of the screen of the laptop on the counter in front of Harrison, who sat to Anders' right in the side room. The slide showed a flowchart that looked like a complex web with three boxes at the center that contained the words "POTUS," the acronym for the President of the United States, "Russia," and "China." Also prominent in the tree were "Single-World Alliance" and "Custodial Group," and various leaders of US and foreign government agencies."

"As we see it," Harrison explained, his voice electronically altered when piped into the room, "this is how current events are related to the president and other officials in the US government, China, Russia, and the Single-World Alliance and the Custodial Group."

The two agents studied the monitor above the window as Harrison used the electronic pointer on his screen to point out key features as he explained them.

"Currently, we're mostly concerned about the Single-World Alliance," Harrison continued. "This group is responsible for NIMH, and the current geopolitical state of the world."

"We've come to the same conclusion," Candace said. "But you mentioned that you had *new* information."

"We have proof that the Chinese subs that were supposedly sunk by the US were given orders to leave the area and go dormant. They have *not* been sunk," Harrison said. "Also, communications from the missing Russian sub were intercepted yesterday, at least 18 hours after it was supposedly destroyed. The US is aware of this, of course."

"So they're faking all of this to start a war?" Candace asked.

"We think the US is *colluding* with them to start a war," Harrison explained. "We base this on the fact that the US frigate that was sunk had been evacuated hours before the attack."

"What?" Tim exclaimed. "You have proof of this?"

Harrison went through the slides and explained the intel Anders had received from Alina, including satellite photos showing the evacuation of the US ship. "Note that there are multiple sources confirming this information."

Anders could see the confusion and then worry form on the faces of the two FBI agents. He recognized their reactions as being parallel to his own when he'd seen the information for the first time. His response had now gone a bit further – he was barely fending off his growing panic.

"Why are you giving this to *us*?" Candace asked.

"Your investigation is in direct line with ours, but we're not a government agency," Harrison replied. "We do not have a direct channel to action. You do."

Candace and Tim glanced at each other.

"We've been on the run for the past week," Candace revealed. "We got a warning from a CIA source that there is a hit out on us."

Harrison looked to Anders with wide eyes. Anders was stunned as well – the CIA putting out a hit on FBI agents?

"And we're not sure who we can trust in our own agency," Tim added.

"Your deputy director, Shelly Stevens, seems to be anti-Crownbrook," Harrison said. "Perhaps you could convince her to act."

Anders wondered how Harrison had gotten that information.

"We've been AWOL for over a week," Candace said. "We're going to have a lot of questions to answer. After explaining our absence, the questions will be about the meaning of all of this. What do I say?"

"We're clear on means, but not entirely certain about the final objective," Harrison replied. "As you know from what we've already provided, the desired outcome is either the establishment of a one-world government, the discovery of aliens, or both. Revealing the means of accomplishing this should be enough to derail their plan."

"And what's your version of *means*?" Candace asked.

"The president wants a nuclear war and has manufactured a situation to start one," Harrison replied. "He is colluding with the Russian and Chinese leaders to accomplish this."

"Just tell our superiors that our president is in cahoots with China and Russia to start a war and establish a global government?" Tim summed up, seemingly apprehensive about relaying that message.

"All evidence points in that direction, yes," Harrison replied.

Anders had discussed this with Harrison multiple times, but hearing him say it to someone else had a more chilling effect, especially since he was explaining it to the FBI – an organization that should be able to act on the information.

"And you must be extremely careful," Harrison warned. "There are other high-level agency personnel who've been appointed by the president who cannot be trusted. The most prominent on that list is the CIA director – Radcliffe."

"You say all this information will be made public in two days," Tim said. "Why the delay?"

"We're not the cause of the delay – it's the leak website operators," Harrison explained. "They already have the information but won't publish it until they've read it over themselves and assessed it. On top of that, we don't know where they stand politically. Maybe they won't release it at all."

"We prefer to use multiple channels," Anders added. "And also the quickest path to action, which is through you."

"Are you willing to push all of this up the line – to your deputy director?" Harrison asked.

Both Candace and Tim nodded in agreement.

Harrison put two thumb-drives in a metal drawer beneath the window and passed them to the interrogation room. "This is all the latest intel we've acquired," he said. "Two copies, including the satellite photos of the US ship being evacuated in the South Pacific."

The two FBI agents stood from behind the table, and Candace approached the window and took the drives. At that moment, two masked, DMS operatives entered the room and asked them to don their hoods.

"Again, sorry about the hoods," Harrison said. "If we can be of assistance, you can call the number we used to contact you. Good luck."

After the agents were escorted from the room, Harrison looked at Anders. "I think that's all we can do," he said.

"Now we just sit and wait?" Anders asked, hearing the frustration in his own voice.

"We'll continue to analyze the information and act on anything we can," Harrison replied. "But I think we've handed it off to the right people."

CANDACE PULLED the rental car into the parking lot of their rundown hotel, which, as its only positive feature, had an outdoor entrance to their room. She was sure she'd spotted a drug deal going down in the parking lot the night before and, based on visitor traffic and noise, suspected some sex-for-money operation was happening in the room next to them, but those criminal activities were nothing compared to the imminent threat of nuclear war.

They ordered a pizza as they fired up their laptops and dove into the files their new, secretive acquaintances had given them. That a private company would reach out with such extreme risk to themselves for the greater good encouraged her to take some risks of her own.

They pored over the files for an hour before the pizza arrived, and then discussed what they'd read as they ate.

"It was all a well-planned deception – a ruse," Candace said. "No one was killed on those ships and subs. Have you noticed that no news reports mention how the US ship was sunk?"

"I just assumed it was a missile," Tim said. "What other method could there be? A plane – a bomb? Maybe a torpedo."

Candace shook her head. "I'd think any approaching planes would have been intercepted," she argued. "It was a carrier group, after all."

"So, what then?" Tim asked.

"If this whole thing is a trick, then I imagine they could just put a bomb on the ship," she explained. "Why make it more complicated than that and bring a plane or missile into the plan?"

"Fair enough," he said. "But, again, why do this?"

"To start a war."

"And why start a war?"

"The SWA intends to reduce the population and destabilize the world," she said. "And then establish a global government – they're completely nuts."

Tim shook his head. "The Custodial Group is even crazier. Aliens? *Really?*"

"It doesn't matter which group the president belongs to," Candace said. "Both want to launch a massive nuclear attack. And you saw the full plan: the CG just wants to launch the missiles to see if extraterrestrials will stop them. If not, the SWA takes over, and the CG is out of the picture. That's why so many of these people are members of *both* groups."

"I think we have what we need then," Tim said. "Let's turn this over to Shelly."

It was disconcerting that they could only trust the deputy director of the FBI, and not the director himself. So far, the conspiracy was at the tops of all levels: the director of the CIA, the president, and maybe the director of the FBI. She wondered if the Secretary of Defense was in on it, and quickly concluded that he must be. In fact, he was crucial, since he must've been involved with the plan to execute the faux attacks on the US carrier groups. She figured that a great number of highly placed people were involved in the operation.

"I think we should go into her office for this," Candace said. "We should be safe going into FBI headquarters in broad daylight."

"Okay," Tim said, but he didn't seem convinced.

"Let's organize this evidence to get the point across quickly," Candace said. "Shelly usually gets into the office early – 6:30 a.m. We'll be waiting for her."

It was going on midnight. Candace didn't know how she'd keep her anxiety at bay until morning.

DAYLIGHT WAS BARELY BREAKING when Candace pulled the rental car into the main parking lot of FBI headquarters and turned off the engine.

"You ready for this?" she asked Tim, who was sitting next to her, sipping a coffee that he'd insisted they stop to get before arriving. She'd gotten one, too. They'd both hardly slept the night before, thinking about what the morning might bring.

"Let's do it," he said as he opened his door and stepped out.

They went into the building and, as they got into an elevator, another agent joined them. When the door closed, the woman asked, "Where in the hell have you two been?"

"What do you mean?" Candace asked. "We've been working a case. Is someone looking for us?"

"You have no idea what's going on, do you?" the woman spat.

Just then, the elevator door opened on their floor, and she and Tim got out. The other woman remained and the doors closed.

They made their way to their office and didn't say a word until they were inside with the door closed.

"What the hell was *that* about?" Candace asked.

Tim shook his head.

At that moment, Candace's burner phone vibrated. She'd stopped call forwarding from her FBI phone, so she knew it had to be from their secretive contacts.

She looked to Tim, and then pulled out the phone. It wasn't a call, but a text, which read, "Get out of town now. DD out of picture.

Expedited release of docs on WhistleLeaks. Good luck." It was clear to her that "DD" stood for Deputy Director.

"My God," Tim hissed as he read it. "What the hell is happening?"

They both twitched when a firm knock sounded behind them. They looked to the door in unison. Tim opened it.

A senior FBI agent, Kenneth Linde, stood in the doorway.

"You two have been hard to reach," Linde said with a stern expression and wide eyes.

"We've been in the field," Tim said.

"Look, Ken, we're a little pressed for time," Candace said. "We need to talk with Deputy Director Stevens immediately."

"Then you haven't heard," Linde whispered as he stepped inside and closed the door.

"Heard what?" Candace snapped.

"Stevens is dead," he said.

The words hit Candace like a kick in the gut.

"What?" Tim gasped. "How?"

The man shrugged and shook his head. "Not sure of the circumstances, but she was found in the trunk of her car – in her own garage – her throat slit ear to ear."

"My God, that's awful," Candace said, realizing that the same might have happened to her had she and Tim not gone into hiding. "So who's the acting DD now? Jack?"

She figured her direct supervisor, Jack Neumann, was next in line.

Agent Linde shook his head and rubbed his temples before he replied, "Jack was shot and killed two nights ago in front of his home – reported as a mugging gone bad."

"A mugging?" Tim mocked. "That's bullshit. They were both murdered."

"I know, I know. We have a task force working on it right now," Linde said. "I'm now the acting deputy director, so you can report whatever you have to me."

Candace caught a worried glance from Tim but ignored it as she tried to maintain her composure.

"It's a report that Shelly wanted directly, and as soon as possible," she explained. "She wanted us to look over a list of people who might have been potential conspirators – members of subversive groups – but they all ended up clean, best we can tell. We've been out of town conducting the investigation all this time. We discovered that most of the people on the list were already dead, or there was no definitive evidence that they'd been involved in the groups."

"And which groups are we talking about?" Linde asked.

"The Single-World Alliance, and some organizations associated with it," Candace replied.

Linde studied her with an expression of skepticism. "I want the full report on my desk by tomorrow morning," he said. "As you know, we're on the brink of war here. Your duties might change in the next 48 hours."

Candace's chest relaxed, even though her heart seemed to pound at 200 beats per minute. "We'll write it up today," she said as Linde exited and closed the door.

Tim looked at her with a grave expression. "We have to get the hell out of here," he said under his breath. "We're in danger."

"In so many ways," she said. "We'll stay here until noon – and then make it look like we're just going out to lunch, and never come back."

"Where will we go?"

"I'm going to pick up my husband and head back to the cabin. You and Janine are welcome to join us," she said, extending the invitation to Tim's fiancée.

"We will," Tim said without hesitation.

"We need to do one more thing before we get out of Dodge," she said. "Set up a dozen thumb-drives, each with a full set of the documents. Before we leave, I'll write a quick report explaining everything we know. Every major newspaper is getting a thumb-drive and a letter before we leave town."

"Hell yeah," Tim said and grinned. "Let's do it."

Candace felt numb, and her mind was spinning as if she were in the midst of a bad dream. Was this really happening?

FOR THE TWO days after delivering the cache of sensitive files to the two FBI agents, Anders continued reading the files on his father's thumb-drive. Although he'd finished the 700-page master document, Peregrine_7071, there were over a thousand other files on the device, most of which Anders figured were the references cited in the main report. But there were a few that hadn't been directly cited, and one of those caught his eye. It was named *Global Controls.*

The file was both a research paper and a planning document that was first written in 1982, and then updated at the end of Crownbrook's first term. After just a few minutes of reading, Anders concluded it was copasetic with the primary objective of the Single-World Alliance. In fact, it contained all kinds of things that would likely be implemented soon after the nukes or virus, or whatever else they planned, ripped civilization to shreds.

The premise of the paper was that a one-world government could not be created, and certainly not maintained, until "global switches" were realized. It meant that there had to be a means to control various things around the entire globe with the pulling of a single "lever." There would need to be switches for communications, information, energy, transportation, money, identity, privacy, and even food.

Most of these things were not globally controllable in the analog, or pre-digital, age. In the not-so-distant past, communications had been transmitted exclusively through telephone landlines or radio, or even paper mail, and could be carried out anonymously. For instance, payphones, which were a virtually untraceable form of communication, were ubiquitous in the 1980s and earlier. Those modes of conveying information were difficult to stop, at least in a precise and controlled manner. In the present day, most people relied on cell phones and computer communications, which could be tracked or shut down in an instant.

The paper cited a joint CIA-National Security Agency study that outlined the method needed to shut down global communications, including all mobile and satellite phones, and Internet services. It would take the cooperation of only a few countries to suspend those services to over 90 percent of the world. Assuming all analog land-line capabilities were shut down, this could be accomplished within 24 hours.

Anders pondered that hypothetical situation. No one would be able to talk to anyone, other than face to face. It would be a comprehensive and immediate "digital isolation," which, when including information control, was precisely the term coined in the paper to describe the process.

Most people depended on the Internet for information, from learning how long to boil eggs to how to repair the carburetor of a lawn mower to how to solve a physics problem. All of that could be shut off in a snap of a tyrant's fingers. Most people didn't have paper books anymore – at least not general references like dictionaries and encyclopedias. And almost no one kept those thick phone books, either. Everyone would be unplugged and would have to rely on what was in their heads.

Another part of the information switch was the media – propaganda. All TV, radio, and Internet information could easily be controlled by the government. People would only be exposed to government-generated information, and not allowed to publicly share any of their own. Advances in computer-generated imagery, like the CGI used in movies to simulate all kinds of scenes and events, as well as "deep fake" technologies and artificial intelligence, which could be used to alter existing videos or to create new ones to make it look like someone was actually saying or doing something that they weren't, could be used to influence the public.

The next thing on the list was energy, which was a literal switch that could be thrown at any time, even before entering the digital age. Now consider eliminating gasoline – another energy source – and that leads to the next thing on the list: transportation. Freedom of movement could be eliminated with roadblocks and the abolition of ownership of private vehicles. Aids to navigation could be easily removed: GPS service could be taken down, as could all cell phone navigation. Most people didn't have paper maps anymore, and the plan even called for removing all road signs. Anders imagined being dropped in some vast, unknown rural area: With no phone or road signs, he could be anywhere from the US Great Plains, to Europe, to South America. People would have to resort to navigating by the stars.

Money would be easy to regulate: there was already a push to move to digital currency, which afforded numerous facets of control. First, it could be personalized – connected with a specific identity that was also effectively digitized – so that the government could restrict what their money could be used to purchase. For instance, someone could be forbidden from buying alcohol, or high-calorie foods, or anything from a specific company. And companies themselves could be driven out of business with a simple check placed in some box in a computer program run by the authorities. On top of all this, the government could keep tabs on everything an individual purchased.

Next, identity and, more importantly, *anonymity*, are what kept Anders' profession alive. But identity and privacy were constantly being eroded by policy and technology – something that had already been occurring for over a decade. The *Global Switch* plan devised by the SWA would have biometric sensing and tracking that utilized everything from fingerprints to DNA. They were planning to track the movements of every human on the planet. Anders was sickened to see that the DNA collected through the testing for the RAT-32C virus, through Project NIMH, was referenced as one set of data used to implement the cataloging of the population. Even more surprising was the use of existing data that were submitted voluntarily through commercialized DNA ancestry companies. It shocked him to learn that two of those companies – the two largest ones – had been established by a wealthy SWA member.

Finally, money was useless if one couldn't obtain food. Not only had the SWA arranged for the purchase of huge tracts of farmland in the US and globally, but they also planned to control food distribution through transportation. If there were no trucks or trains, and people weren't allowed to drive on the roads – or even own cars – food sources could be cut off at any time. The global government would have the power to prohibit private food production – and actively search for "illegal" gardens and livestock and destroy them, and punish the offenders.

The final conclusions section of the report succinctly summarized the current state of the world: 90 percent of the global population could be controlled by digital means, something that had only become feasible within the last decade as comprehensive digital dependence set in. With the added obedience to perceived authority, something that was proven by the first phase of NIMH and the effects of the RAT-32C pandemic, the entire world population could be controlled. And, once the population was reduced to optimum levels – less than 500 million globally, as determined from a control and sustainability model carried out by the SWA – its obedience could be maintained *indefinitely*. In fact, control would become even more solidified as technologies continued to advance.

Anders shuddered. All the switches were already in place. The only thing they needed now was a singular event with a devastating, global impact. A nuclear war – even a limited one – might be enough to send civilization over the edge.

"This is Colonel Spelling," Maurice said, answering the call on his desk phone.

"This is Christine," the woman said. "I need confirmation that you have 25 silos fully functional – meaning ready for action immediately."

"They are," he said. "We're just awaiting word for the official activation."

"Are the teams on duty?"

"Yes ma'am, and they're currently at the ready," Maurice replied.

"Then they are now officially activated," she said. "We're going to spring the trap on the next multiple-drone incursion."

"How do you define 'multiple?'"

"When there are incursions in at least two missile fields simultaneously."

"That's happening regularly," Maurice said.

"We know," she replied. "And it's time for that to stop. And this is how it's going to happen."

As she explained the steps, he realized that things were happening quickly.

"Upon initiating the trap," she continued, "the president will temporarily raise the readiness level to DEFCON-1, and you'll head to your bunker at that time."

Maurice's heart picked up pace. The Defense Readiness Condition level was what the Pentagon used to indicate the degree of threat upon the US from the outside, which then set the US military readiness level in response. This had an immediate impact on nuclear missile launch networks. DEFCON-1 was the highest level, which meant that the proverbial "gun was cocked." The current status was DEFCON-3, which had been raised from level four a few weeks prior, after the naval confrontations had developed. Why it hadn't ratcheted up to DEFCON-2 after ships had been destroyed on all sides, he didn't understand.

"Be on the ready; the trap could be sprung at any time within the next 48 hours. It's imperative that you are completely quiet in the meantime – no additional preparations or warnings to your people that something is about to occur. A leak of any kind will ruin the opportunity," Christine explained. "Understood?"

"Yes," he replied, and they ended the call.

He hung up the phone and took a sip of coffee. His stomach suddenly gurgled and burned, and he set down his mug and took a swig of bottled water. The US had never been at DEFCON-1, not even during the Cuban Missile Crisis. It meant that an attack on the US was imminent, and so was its response. It was an extremely precarious position. And, when the trap was sprung, the upgraded silos would go into a launch sequence. It was as close as one could get to destroying the world without actually firing the missiles.

Four drone incidents had been reported in his missile fields the previous night, including an incursion at one of the upgraded sites, and a dozen others were reported by the other missile wings. It was the most ever reported in a 24-hour period. He supposed the president, and the Department of Defense, had finally had enough.

At DEFCON-1, every active missileer and auxiliary crewmember would be on duty. They'd be scattered about in bunkers around the area – only a fraction would remain at the base since it would be a high-priority target. Level-one status was difficult to maintain, so he concluded that, if something was going to happen, it would occur soon after the level was elevated.

Maurice just hoped that the president knew what he was doing.

CHAPTER 13

Anders was at his DMS desk around midnight when Harrison called him to his office. It had been 24 hours since they'd uploaded the information to WhistleLeaks, and two days since they'd handed off the second batch of intelligence to the two FBI agents. He thought something should have happened by now, but there was nothing in the news.

When Anders entered the office, the odor of cigar smoke was strong, and a TV on the wall next to the entrance blared the news.

"Come in," Harrison said as he reduced the volume of the TV with a remote. He was on the couch, and a lit cigar was in the ashtray on the coffee table in front of him. He gestured to one of the chairs across from him. "Please, sit."

"What's wrong?" Anders asked as he took his seat. His boss looked distraught.

"The president has apparently fled to an underground facility in the Nevada desert," he said. "There's a vast underground tunnel network there that could get him almost anywhere, but he'll probably end up under a mountain somewhere in Colorado."

"He's *evacuating*?"

"That's what our sources say," Harrison replied. "I got one last message from Crownbrook indicating that he will no longer be communicating, and that our services are no longer required. Any residual information that we have about our business with him is supposed to be destroyed. My Secret Service contacts confirm that Air Force One left for Arca 51 at noon yesterday."

"Shit," Anders hissed. "You think we're on the brink of war?"

"I do," Harrison replied. "The president wouldn't run for the hills unless he thought something was up."

Anders felt the same.

"And, since I think this is a legit threat, I'm taking the precautionary measure of getting DMS people out of DC before the panic starts," Harrison said. "I want everyone out of this city before it turns to complete chaos and they can't get out."

"You mean evacuate the whole company?"

"I can't rely on the possibility of fucking *aliens* stopping the ICBMs," Harrison spat. "I just sent out the evac orders. Maybe you should go to your mother's place – your hometown is far from any major targets. My wife and I are going to Indiana – her parents' place. All other DMS personnel have just been given the shutdown order and a list of places not to be in case of the worst – God forbid."

"Is DMS dispersing for good?" Anders asked.

"We'll see," Harrison said, and then took a puff of his cigar and blew out a dense cloud of smoke. "It will be a secure, but recoverable, shutdown. All DMS records will be with me, and I'll decide whether or not to destroy them later. The funding for DMS facilities and employee salaries will continue for now, and our clients will be okay regarding fund disbursement – retirement management will continue. However, the check-ins will be suspended, and everyone will be on their own regarding personal security for a while. If this is a false alarm, all our files will be preserved and we'll restart. Otherwise, the information I'm carrying will be destroyed – there will be no direct employee records of any kind."

Anders felt sick to his stomach.

There was a knock at the door.

"Ah, perfect timing," Harrison said as he snuffed out his cigar in the ashtray and stood. He went to the door and let in the computer expert.

"This is everything," Diana said as she set what looked like a hefty briefcase on his desk, and opened it. "The backups in the basement will be erased when you give the order."

Anders went to them.

"There are six, 100-terabyte drives mounted to the chassis, and the access point is here," she said as she pointed to a console that had a keypad and various plug receptacles. "This has a battery unit and a hardwired power cord. Plug into an outlet if you're downloading a lot of data, or if you want to execute the self-destruct operation. If fully charged, the battery should do the trick in a pinch, but otherwise you'll want to be on the safe side."

She went on to explain how to go about downloading data and entering commands through the keypad. "The only command you should probably memorize is the self-destruct code."

Diana then closed up the briefcase, buckled its hefty, built-in lock, and handed him the key.

"Go ahead and erase everything else," Harrison said as he held out his hand. "Diana, thank you for everything. I hope we can get through this."

She shook his hand. "I'll be back with you if we do."

Harrison looked to Anders and then back to Diana. "You both should be going now," he said. "You have the list of places to avoid."

Anders shook Harrison's hand. "Thanks for everything," he said. "Best of luck."

A minute later, Anders was in the special elevator that took him to his office. He'd pick up a few things, hire a ride to his car, and head south.

They'd done everything they could, but he concluded that they had ultimately failed. Despite acquiring an enormous amount of damning information, they'd gotten to it too late. On top of that,

Harrison had informed him that the Deputy Director of the FBI – the person who was supposed to get the information from Candace Wright – had been murdered, along with Candace's direct supervisor. He hoped the two agents were okay – that Harrison's text-message warning hadn't arrived too late. He also hoped that they'd managed to get the info to someone else who could do something. Perhaps that was the reason the president went into hiding.

Being on the so-called "good side" was a discouraging and frustrating business. It seemed that it was only a matter of time before evil eventually won out. The struggle between good and evil was like two boxers in a fight. One boxer was much better than the other – in better shape, stronger, quicker, and more skilled – but was blindfolded and not allowed to throw a punch. It was just a matter of time before the weaker fighter got a punch through his blind defenses. It was an unwinnable fight in the long term.

It was looking to Anders like a punch had finally landed.

Maurice figured it could have happened during any of the previous four days, but this night the incursions were particularly egregious. Three had occurred simultaneously in his fields – Malmstrom – but even more happened in the other two wings at the same time. Add in the sunken naval vessels on all sides, including the recent strafing of an American cargo ship by Chinese fighter jets – and it was the opportune time to spring the trap.

Maurice had gotten word at 10:00 p.m. Mountain Time that the threat level had gone from DEFCON-3 to DEFCON-1. It got his adrenaline going, but he was calm since he knew it would only be a mock launch, all of which would be carried out by the MOLVs at the upgraded silos. The defense and intelligence agencies were closely watching various locations in China, Russia, and other countries to see who would react first, and in which way. What they planned to do once they identified the culprit, he didn't know.

A woman burst into his office – a young lieutenant who was responsible for the evacuation of the base and transportation to the hidden control station, which was a bunker located under the base of a mountain.

"Colonel," said the uniformed woman. Her green eyes were wide with panic. "We've gone to DEFCON-1."

"I know, Tracey," he said, trying to keep her calm. "I'll be ready to go in a few minutes – just waiting for word from the secretary." The Secretary of Defense had to confirm the delivery of the launch codes, and Maurice preferred to wait, especially since he knew that everything was going to stop short of launching, and that no one was currently attacking the US. He did feel bad, however, for Tracey, and anyone else who was thinking that what was happening was the real thing.

Maurice flinched when a loud, chirping noise came from his desk. He twitched again when his cell phone vibrated in his front pants pocket.

He pulled out his mobile and checked it – there was a text. It was a message he'd hoped he would never see in his lifetime. It read, "CODE GOLD ACTIVATION." It meant that presidential authentication had already occurred – the Secretary of Defense must have confirmed the order – and nuclear launch codes were being distributed to the launch sites. It was just a part of the charade.

Maurice followed the chirping noise to a device vibrating on his desk. It was a little black box with a flashing white light that had a number pad and a small screen on its top surface. A prompt on the screen read, "> Enter Command Code Delta-Omega:"

He went to a safe mounted in the wall behind his desk, opened it, and extracted a card that was called "the muffin." It was an authentication code table that corresponded to the list of Gold Codes on the card in the president's possession that was called "the biscuit." Maurice looked up the proper response for "Delta-Omega" on the muffin: it was an eight-character code "I5JZ23S7," which he immediately entered on the box's keypad.

A few seconds later, two words appeared on the screen: "Codes Delivered."

It meant that his missileers now had the launch codes and were awaiting final orders to open their small, red safes to get the two launch keys. It meant they were just one, final step from launching: the US had never been to this stage. The gun was cocked, the safety was off, and the finger was on the trigger.

Suddenly, Maurice's gut churned and he scrambled to a garbage can. He bent over it and vomited a concoction of coffee and stomach acid that burned his throat and mouth on the way up and out.

Why am I throwing up? – this is all fake, he thought.

He looked to Tracey, whose face went pale, and he suspected she might throw up as well. She left the room quickly.

His office phone rang, and he went to it as he wiped his mouth on his sleeve. The caller ID indicated that it was his direct supervisor, Brigadier General Sampson. Maurice answered.

"Colonel Spelling, you've gotten the orders?" Sampson asked.

"Yes, sir," he said. "I've transferred the codes. All systems and personnel are functioning and at the ready – initiating their duties."

"That's why I'm calling," the general said. "Have you gotten reports of a wave of drone intrusions, as the others have? Multiple shutdowns have already occurred."

"Shutdowns? No, sir," Maurice replied. "Only incursions."

"You'll be getting shutdown reports soon," Sampson said.

Just as the general finished his sentence, Maurice got a call on his mobile phone. It was from one of the missile launch stations.

"Sir, I'm getting a call right now on my cell – from a launch station," Maurice said.

"Take it, I'll wait."

Maurice answered the call. The man on the other end explained that all power to his launch station had gone down. He'd only been able to get the call out with a battery backup.

Maurice got another call on the same line, and then another on the office phone.

Next, the head of his office staff knocked on the door.

"Come in," Maurice ordered.

The woman rushed in – she looked panicked. "Colonel, I have three launch sites on the line – they say their facilities are malfunctioning," she explained. "They all report unauthorized aircraft in the area."

Maurice went back to General Sampson's line. "Sir, we're getting the drone reports now," he said. "Some facilities are off-line already."

"Figure out what's wrong and get those systems back online," Sampson ordered. "Get your mobile launch systems deployed immediately, if they aren't already."

"Yes sir," Maurice said.

"The final order to launch will come within 24 hours. No changing of launch teams at this time," Sampson said. "We have fighter jets on the way to your sites to fend off the intruders, and the Marines are sending helicopters."

"Understood, General," Maurice said and ended the call. His head seemed to fog up as if he'd just awakened from a bad dream. But he was *living* the nightmare.

It was surreal; ever since taking the leadership post at Malmstrom, Maurice had known that what was happening now had always been a real possibility ... *But it's fake* ... Now he had to follow through with his responsibilities. The launch orders were phony – just a little more than a drill – but the drone incursions were *real*. It was as if the mock launch had already triggered a reaction from whoever operated the drones, but there was still no way to tell who that was until there was a reaction in their home country. He hoped the spy satellites would identify the perpetrator quickly so that they could truncate the mock launch sequence as soon as possible. It was scaring the hell out of everyone.

There were now 13 calls awaiting his attention. He addressed each one in turn and notified them that they were in imminent launch status and on lockdown. If their stations were disabled, they were to try to remedy the problems. Maurice wondered if the approaching fighter jets and Apache helicopters would scatter the intruding aircraft. This time, however, he suspected that they'd leave the launch facilities inoperable – their interruptions during the previous months had been test runs for this moment. This was the real thing.

It seemed to Maurice that it was more than a coincidence that the new, mobile launch system was deemed fully operational just the week before. It was as if the looming war had been planned, and everyone had been waiting for the new system to be in place before starting it. It had worried him from the beginning that the portable systems could be used to override authorization protocols – the president could bypass Congress, the Department of Defense, and whoever else might get in the way. Now, however, with the night's invasion of drones, it seemed fully justified.

Maurice left the office and headed to the main hangar that served as home base for the MOLV project. The crews were gathering and he would see them off. They'd position themselves within a mile of their respective launch sites. He didn't know what he was going to tell them, but he figured the words would come to him when he needed them.

After that, he'd go to the command bunker.

It was 6:00 a.m., and Anders was heading south on the highway, just north of Raleigh, North Carolina, when he heard on the car radio that the US president, and the Chinese and Russian leaders, were all missing. He already knew that Crownbrook had gone to a bunker somewhere in the west, so he figured the other leaders had gone to their respective safe places. It didn't bode well for the world, although it wasn't as if the general public was reacting in any way. The people he'd encountered seemed oblivious to what was happening. He stopped at gas stations along the way, and business was as usual – both with the employees and patrons.

At 5:30 a.m., he'd stopped at a gas station and heard a guy who was fueling up a truck with the words "Donny's Plumbing and Pipe Fitting" on its door joking with another man. He'd said that he didn't know why he was even going to work: the world was going to end soon anyway, and the president had already flown the coop. Both men laughed and went on their ways.

Anders caught himself speeding multiple times and had to work hard to distract himself from the long drive. He'd usually been content with listening to the news during lengthy trips, but it didn't work this time. He switched the radio to a music station for a while, and then turned it off, but his anxiety skyrocketed after just a few minutes of silence. What if there was an attack and he didn't even know it was coming?

The thought put him into the hypothetical situation of a nuclear attack. He suddenly realized an emotional dichotomy. On one side was utter horror. On the other side, if the proverbial lights just went out, it wouldn't be as frightening, but that wasn't how it would work in reality. The people on the periphery of the explosions would suffer long, painful deaths. And, much later, others would endure the long-term effects – cancer. And then there would be the birth defects, the contaminated areas, the social destruction, and the ensuing conflict. People would starve, die of diseases, and all sorts of other horrible things.

Anders thought he might rather be at ground zero than suffer in the world that would be left behind. If he had a wife and kids his outlook might have been different.

He turned on the radio again and tuned in BBC News. He finally heard something promising. A competitor of WhistleLeaks, called The Drum, had finally published the files DMS had submitted to them days ago. Anders had suggested that DMS submit to multiple sources simultaneously, and The Drum was the first to analyze and then release not only the files, but an overall summary of their contents, which the newscaster read to the audience.

Something else he learned, which he didn't expect, was that the

New York Times had already published a front-page article that morning, saying that they'd gotten the information from an anonymous source in the FBI. The radio newscaster claimed that the leak websites and the newspapers – *The Guardian* had a parallel release – had gotten their stories out simultaneously, which gave credence to the authenticity of the information. Anders concluded that the decision to pass the information to Candace Wright had been a good one.

The gist was that the US president was part of a conspiracy to start a nuclear war.

Anders suddenly felt sick. It sounded like any other tabloid bullshit that people would either reject or just laugh at. He feared it would make no impact in the short term. It was something that should have come out months ago if it were to have any effect.

As he was contemplating the possible outcomes of the news releases, he heard a buzzing sound in the back seat. He realized it was coming from his backpack and reached his arm back and unzipped the front pocket. It was one of his cell phones – he'd taken four of them from DMS. He found the vibrating device and pulled it out. It was the phone he used for dynamic meetings with Alina. He answered.

"Alina," Anders said. "Where are you?"

"I'm in DC," she replied. "Can you help me?" She sounded shaken.

"What's going on?"

"The FSB is searching for me," she said. "My president is in hiding and they're rounding up everyone. I've already had two close calls. I can't go back to Russia – I won't make it through an airport. Can your organization take me in?"

"My company has shut down – disbanded," he replied as a feeling of helplessness overtook him. "Can you travel domestically – do you have a car?"

"Sure, but where can I go?" she said. "There are no safe houses anymore."

"Drive to Savannah, Georgia," Anders said. "There's a bookstore there called *The Mint*. Call me when you get close and I'll come get you."

"I'll do that, but I can't leave until tomorrow," she said. "I can't explain – I have to go now. Thank you." She hung up.

Anders didn't completely trust Alina – which was definitely not her real name. Then again, he didn't fully trust any of his contacts. Even so, he'd help her if he could. He could hardly imagine being trapped in a foreign country with war looming. She likely had no friends: the US would see her as a spy, and Russia would see her as a traitor.

During the rest of the drive, he listened to the biased bickering on the radio between various groups of political characters, some for the president, some against. Some were saying it was a ploy by Russia or China to destabilize the US at this critical time – which was the obvious argument. As he predicted, it was just muddy water in the end. There would be no immediate action against the president – which might be difficult, anyway, since he was probably under a mountain in Colorado by now.

It was now out of his hands, and Anders just wanted to get home and be with his mom. He didn't want her to live through this alone, and neither did he.

CANDACE, her husband, Anthony, and Tim and his fiancée, Janine, just finished lunch and were having coffee at the wooden table in the cabin's kitchen. Greta was on the floor by Tim's feet, and the large German shepherd was a welcomed guest. Although they were hiding out because of the assassinations of Shelley Stevens and Jack Neumann, their evacuation couldn't have been better timed. The world was on the verge of all-out war. They had enough supplies to last a month.

As they watched the news, Candace and Tim glanced at each

other as the anchor reported that the president had gone to a remote location due to reliable intelligence that an attempt on his life was planned by an adversary, probably Russia, as a first strike to initiate war. Candace wondered, however, if the president was instead making himself scarce because of the information they'd passed on to major news outlets the day before. All the information she'd originally intended to pass along to Deputy Direct Shelly Stevens, now deceased, was now available to the public – published by the *New York Times* – despite the CIA's attempts to take down the leak websites through which their mysterious friends had released it. Other major newspapers were now on the bandwagon as well. It was too late to stop it.

The next bit of important news was that the Chinese and Russian leaders had also gone into hiding. She figured that the released information was as damning to them as it was to Crownbrook.

Candace was pleased with the outcome – or at least with the way she projected it would go. Crownbrook would probably be impeached, and might even go to prison. At the very least, there was little chance that his vice president, or anyone else from his party who won the nomination, would win the White House in the next round.

The newscast switched to a co-anchor, who reported on the leaked files. She gave a short synopsis, and then said, "CIA experts tell us that the timing of this document dump is suspect, and that much of it might be Russian or Chinese misinformation. The real difficulty occurs when accurate information is mixed in with fabrications, and it will take time to sort this out. We're told, due to the present geopolitical climate, only minimal resources will be allocated to the task ..."

"What?" Candace spat.

"It means they're going to do nothing," Tim commented, clearly annoyed.

Candace's heart sank. How long were they going to have to hide out? She'd gambled that the document dump would create a tsunami of action, and that they'd be in the clear in a couple of weeks. Now it looked like it was going to be a long, drawn-out process, and she and Tim would eventually be located and either killed, or taken in and charged with something – at the very least for mishandling classified information.

She looked at Tim. His face had turned to a ghastly shade of light gray.

"We did what we thought was right," Tim said.

Candace thought so, too. But it was probably going to cost them their careers, and maybe much more.

Anders pulled into the driveway at 12:15 p.m. and turned off the car.

His mom was sitting on the porch. He'd already told her about everything on the phone during the drive.

As he got out of the car, Gigi walked over and hugged him.

"You did what you could, honey," she said. "I saw on the news that the files were released to the public – there's been a huge uproar. That's a good start."

"They're saying it's just Russian and Chinese misinformation, trying to muddy the waters."

"I know," she said. "It's politics, as usual, that's hiding the truth. Our politicians have been our downfall. But at least the info is out there now."

Anders grabbed his things out of the car and followed her to the porch. "I picked up a few cases of water and dried beans and rice in case things get hairy," he said. He'd told her what Harrison thought might be happening with the president going into hiding. He now wondered whether Crownbrook's disappearance had to do with an impending nuclear strike, or if he were just hiding from the consequences of the document release.

"We also have at least a year's worth of canned goods from the garden," she said. "And this year's harvest will start in a few weeks."

He laughed. "It's as if you planned for this," he said.

They went inside, Anders dropped off his bags at the foot of the stairs, and they went to the kitchen where the TV was on and the smell of something good was in the air.

"There's vegetable soup if you're hungry," she said.

He nodded that he was, and she ladled some out of the slow cooker on the counter into a bowl and set it on the kitchen table.

He sat and took a deep breath. A cable news station was on the TV, covering everything he'd been hearing in the car. The way they were talking about the released documents – that they were misinformation and a ploy of some kind – got Anders thinking that the president might have disappeared prematurely. It would take months or years for investigators to get through all the information and verify it. It would take even longer for charges to be brought forward and, by then, Crownbrook would be out of office. And he'd probably try to pardon himself before charges could be made.

He shivered for an instant as his thoughts drifted toward the reason that Harrison had sent all DMS personnel out of town in the first place: a possible nuclear strike. The idea hadn't sunk in at the time – Anders thought it was just a precaution, although a pretty drastic move.

It didn't matter to which of the two groups, the Single-World Alliance or the Custodial Group, Crownbrook had pledged his allegiance. Both required nuclear missiles to be launched and Anders, like Harrison, wasn't putting his money on extraterrestrials preventing them from annihilating their targets.

It was going on 9:00 p.m., and Maurice was in the command bunker, located 35 miles west of Malmstrom AFB, 150 feet beneath the base of a mountain. He and the full contingent of his central command crew, which totaled 64 people, had been there for nearly 24 hours awaiting the final call on the mock launch. It seemed to him that it should have been initiated the night before, in immediate response to the flurry of drone incursions. It was possible that the elevation of the threat level to DEFCON-1 was enough to cause their adversaries to react, and that the launch would no longer need to be initiated. He hoped that was the case, even though the elevated DEFCON status had not yet been made public.

It was 10:00 p.m. when his main communications officer, Lieutenant Jerry Tanner, informed him that they'd lost contact with the mobile launch control vehicles. Tanner and the rest of the central command crew were briefed on the MOLVs and their purpose when they arrived at the bunker. It was "need to know" for them now.

Drones? Maurice thought as his stomach sickened. *Or a malfunction?* "How many?" he asked.

"All 25, sir," Tanner replied. "And I can't connect with any of the backup vehicles, either. Everything was online just five minutes ago."

"*All 25*? Is it an equipment failure on our end?"

"No sir," Tanner replied. "It seems we've been locked out."

What the hell is happening?

"What about the conventional stations?" Maurice asked. He needed to know if they'd only been locked out of the trucks, or if all silo communications were out of commission.

"The conventional systems are still online, sir," Tanner replied. "Including the modified silos – the ones the trucks are designed to override."

"So, everything is good except for the trucks?"

"Not exactly," Tanner answered. "We're getting calls about another wave of drone incursions – and warnings of the same from the other wings."

That wasn't unexpected. He figured whoever owned the drones had been practicing for this event for months. It had occurred to him, just for an instant, that maybe they didn't belong to any nation. What if some high-tech company – maybe a defense contractor – had made a breakthrough and was now instigating a war?

A technician called out to him in a worried voice, and Maurice went to her station.

"Sir, operators from silos I-2 and I-4 are reporting lockouts and launch initiations," she said. She then put her finger to her earbud and looked to him. "And now two more with the same report. Those at I-8 and J-2. They're extremely alarmed, sir. What should I tell them?"

Those were all modified sites, so it probably wasn't drones – it was the trucks. Maybe this was it – the trap – and Maurice couldn't give away that it was a mock launch. He had to let the process play out to the very end. After the launches were aborted, he'd do his best to calm everyone down and explain what had happened. He felt bad, but it couldn't be helped.

"Order them to do whatever they can to shut it down," he said, knowing that they couldn't.

Maurice went back to the communications tech. "Have you figured out the problem with the truck comms yet, Lieutenant?" he asked.

"It's not a malfunction, sir," Tanner said, shaking his head. "I've confirmed that it's a deliberate lockout – their comm thread is completely offline."

Maurice pulled out his phone and called Col. Frank Anderson, the commander at the 91st Missile Wing, at Minot, North Dakota.

"Are you locked out of your mobile units, too?" Anderson asked without saying hello.

"Yes," Maurice replied. "What the hell's going on?"

"It's the same at the 90th," Anderson added. "We're all locked out – and no way to contact them. This wasn't part of the plan as I understood it."

"Same here," Maurice said.

"We've had over 40 silos disabled by drones so far," Anderson said. "We'd be completely out of commission by midnight if it weren't for the trucks."

"We have 37 conventional silos out of commission now, plus five of the upgraded types, which we hope are still operational – using the MOLVs – despite whatever the drones have done to them," Maurice said.

"Gotta go, Spelling," Anderson said. "Getting a call from the top brass."

Immediately after ending the call, a young female officer waved him over to a red phone. "It's SecDef," she said.

It was the Secretary of Defense.

Maurice grabbed the phone. "This is Colonel Maurice Spelling," he said.

"Spelling, this is George Hallister, SecDef," said the man in a gruff voice. "What the hell is going on out there?"

"We're having comms issues and some silo shutdowns," Maurice said. "We're sorting it – "

"No!" Hallister cut him off. "Why in the hell are you initiating launch sequences?"

"What do you mean, sir?" Maurice asked, confused by the question. "The president authorized this – we received the codes."

"I have *not* given the authorization," Hallister yelled. "Terminate all launches immediately."

Maurice's mind froze for a few awkward seconds.

"Spelling?"

"I'm sorry, sir," Maurice replied, stuttering. "You do not have the authority to terminate the president's order." He suddenly felt lightheaded.

"Dammit, Spelling! Do you want to start a war?" Hallister screamed.

"Where is the president?"

"We don't know."

"Where is the vice president then? – I assume he has taken over if the president is absent."

"Vice President Schuller is also gone."

"Gone?" Maurice felt queasy. "Has the speaker of the house assumed control?"

"No – we're in limbo here, Spelling," Hallister yelled. "I have to contact the other missile wings now. Time is running out. Just stop the launch!"

Hallister hung up, leaving Maurice to make a choice. *Didn't the Secretary of Defense know that it was just a mock launch?*

All conventional launch systems were either on standby – with no launch orders – or shut down by drones, which was expected. The 25 MOLVs, however, were not communicating – *intentionally* locked out.

Maurice now wondered if he was being tested – to see if he would follow protocol. The order to stop a launch in progress could only come from the president, or the official acting president. Secretary of Defense Hallister was neither. Maurice had to proceed.

The only glitch in the plan so far was that he didn't have direct communications with the mobile launch teams. He couldn't stop the launch no matter what he decided to do.

ANDERS SIPPED tea at the kitchen table as his mom paced between the TV and the stove. The mainstream news channels kept revealing fragments of information that were keeping them tuned in – it was going on 11:00 p.m., well past Gigi's usual bedtime.

There were reports of mysterious aircraft around military installations that, as the reporters speculated, were Chinese or Russian drones designed to interfere with operations. The drone traffic was particularly heavy in the missile fields of the Western Plains.

The next tidbit was that, not only had the president evacuated to a remote location, but the vice president was missing as well.

"Then who's running the country?" Gigi blurted.

"I'm sure the president is running it from a bunker somewhere," Anders said, although he didn't know what he really believed anymore. The president was crazy, and in trouble, and Anders wouldn't be surprised if it came out later that he was dead – taken out by the CIA, or secretly arrested by the military.

A red banner suddenly appeared at the bottom of the TV screen and the newscaster lowered her eyes to read something on the desk. "This just in," she said. "In the past 24 hours, the Defense Readiness Condition, or DEFCON status, has been elevated to level one. I repeat, we are now at DEFCON-1. This is the highest level it has ever been, and it means that we're at maximum readiness, and set for an immediate nuclear response. We have retired General Argus Temboldt here for his perspective on this development."

The camera went to an elderly, bald man in a suit.

"What does this mean, General?" the anchor asked.

"The highest we've ever been before is DEFCON-2, and that occurred at the opening of the 1991 Persian Gulf War and, of course, the Cuban Missile Crisis," he explained. "DEFCON-1 means nuclear war is imminent. The added fact that our president is in a bunker somewhere, and the VP is absent, means we're in an extremely perilous situation. Naval vessels have been sunk, and people killed, on both sides. Enemy drones are acting inside our borders – at our military bases and nuclear missile sites. We will have a response. The situation looks dire, and the next hours will be critical."

The anchor went back to old news, but alarming messages kept scrolling across the lower banner of the screen ..."President Crownbrook said to be in Colorado bunker ... Enemy drones interfering at military sites across the US ... The Defense Readiness Condition elevated to DEFCON-1 ... A flurry of activity detected at Chinese and Russian nuclear missile facilities."

"This looks really bad," Gigi said.

It looked *horrible*. He wondered now whether the disclosure of the files had prompted the president to rush his plan. Had Anders' actions triggered these events to occur prematurely? After some contemplation, he decided that, if that were true, it was a good thing. Perhaps forcing the president to execute the scheme early would induce some errors that could be exploited.

His mom gasped, and Anders looked to the scrolling banner on the TV. It read, "... Launch preparation activities detected at US ICBM sites ..."

Anders' gut seemed to twist itself into a knot. There was nothing he could do.

Captain Eduardo Pacquiao's driver pulled the enormous eight-wheeler into the hidden vehicle shelter near the base of "Red Mountain," which was the code name for Malmstrom's underground command center. As the head missile technician, he was to be at the wing commander's side during these situations, and this was the first time he'd ever been in the bunker.

Just as he entered the main control room, Maurice rushed up to him.

"We've lost contact with the mobile launch vehicles," Maurice said, clearly shaken by what was happening.

Eduardo's gut tightened. "Are they unable to operate?" he asked.

"They seem to be functioning as designed – they've been overriding the launch stations – but the comm link between us and them is down," Maurice explained.

"We're locked out," a communications officer at a nearby station added.

Eduardo became lightheaded but managed to maintain his composure. What had he done?

"I need you to get to one of the trucks – the closest one is at H-10," Maurice explained. "We need to know what's wrong. If you can figure out the problem with one truck, maybe we can get comms back for all of them."

"I'll do what I can," Eduardo said, even though he knew exactly what was wrong, and that he could do nothing about it.

"Go – and hurry!" Maurice ordered.

In less than ten minutes he was back inside the eight-wheeled beast, heading southeast toward silo H-10. He was rushing the driver, who had heard the Colonel's orders, but it would be a futile effort.

When Eduardo had gone to CIA headquarters in early May, he'd been there for more than just a polygraph test and background check. He'd been given instructions on how to integrate a lockout and redirect module on the mobile launch vehicles that would cut off communications to one party and open them to another. That modification had been deemed top-secret and he couldn't tell anyone what he'd done – not even Colonel Spelling.

At the time, the CIA engineers had explained that it would be an added redundancy in the system so that they'd have another option in case communications to the command bunker were somehow severed. He was naïve: he should've realized that it was also a way to circumvent the local command structure.

Eduardo looked at the screen in the truck's dashboard that displayed the statuses of the hypersonic silos. Some had gone from white to red, which meant systems were preparing for immediate launch. He considered the handgun mounted to the side of the passenger door. He wouldn't be able to live with himself if the worst happened.

"Sir, we have silo operators reporting the initiation of final launch countdowns," a man yelled from across the command center. "They're panicked."

Maurice rushed over to that monitoring station and examined the display screen. "Which ones?"

The tech ran off a list of 25 silos that Maurice recognized as those controlled by the trucks. It was part of the plan. All the countdowns started within 30 seconds of each other, starting at t-minus five minutes to launch. He could hardly imagine being an operator in one of those underground stations and watching this happen.

"Put the countdowns on the main screen," Maurice ordered.

Various status windows cluttered the largest monitor on the far wall. Those windows were then rearranged into a five-by-five grid, all still readable from a distance. Each panel displayed various parameters associated with a given silo, including the active countdowns, all now under four minutes.

"What's the comm status with the trucks?" Maurice asked.

"Still locked out, sir," came the reply. "Captain Pacquiao's truck is also offline, so I can't reach him for an update."

Maurice was starting to sweat. He couldn't stop the countdowns if he wanted to. The operators in the trucks would carry out the operation as if it were a drill. The operators in the silos were locked out of their controls, but could still see everything that was happening.

He had to remember that this was the level the trap had been designed to attain in order to force the perpetrators to reveal themselves. He thought that the offending nation should've reacted by now. It then occurred to him that it was possible that the drones really couldn't monitor the launch status in real-time: maybe the CIA had overestimated their capabilities. Or, what if the guilty country was just slow to react? Or what if they refrained from reacting knowing that it was a ruse? How close were his superiors willing to take it? Cancel with two seconds on the clock? He wanted to vomit.

Maurice noticed a smaller monitor that showed a mainstream news station. The banner on the bottom announced that a flurry of activity had been spotted at Chinese and Russian nuclear sites.

Thank God, he thought. *Some countries have already reacted. The countdowns could cease.*

He glanced at the main monitor: the countdowns were all below the two-minute mark.

The countdowns need to stop. Now.

Maurice's nerves were on fire. He nearly jumped out of his shoes when his phone chimed. It was Frank Anderson at the 91st Missile Wing.

"When are these countdowns supposed to stop?" Anderson asked, his raspy voice revealing severe stress.

"I don't know," Maurice replied. "But this has gone far enough."

"We have no control – no contact with the mobile stations," Anderson said. "Same is happening at the 90th."

"We're at the mercy of the president."

"We don't even know where the president is," Anderson argued. "Is Crownbrook – or his people – even in control of the mobile units?"

"I don't know," Maurice said. "All I know is that we're not in the loop anymore."

"Gotta go – SecDef is on the other line," Anderson said and hung up.

They were approaching one minute to launch, and he assumed he, too, would be getting a call from the Secretary of Defense any second.

Thirty seconds.

When is it going to stop?

No call.

People were starting to murmur, and one woman screamed frantically, "Stop it! Stop the launches!"

"Send the order to back down to all operators – terminate the launch sequences!" Maurice shouted, even though he knew they couldn't.

Ten seconds.

Maurice regretted the order the instant he gave it – he had to trust the people who had designed the trap. They needed to catch the trespassers.

Five, four, three, two ...

"Silo I-2 has commenced launch," someone yelled.

Maurice couldn't believe it. It must be a part of the ruse – a part he didn't know about.

Five, four, three, two ...

"Silo I-4 has commenced launch," a technician screamed.

"What the hell are we doing?" a man cried on the far side of the room.

... three, two, one ...

Another launch, and then another, and another.

"Do we have confirmation of these launches?" Maurice yelled.

"They are confirmed, sir," a comms officer reported. "On screen."

Maurice found the monitor. It showed a map with the locations of all of Malmstrom's silos, with flashing red dots at the locations of those that had launched. Two more had appeared since he'd looked to the screen, and he now counted 17 launches. Then 18.

"Do we have visual confirmation of these?" Maurice yelled. He hoped to dear God that there would be no visual confirmation, and this was all part of the trick. They were just people watching computer screens – no one inside the command center would know the difference between a simulation and the real thing. He again had confused regrets about giving the global stand-down order. Maybe he was being tested.

His phone rang. It was his wife.

He didn't want to answer, but he needed to hear her voice.

He answered. "Carmen?"

She said something and the phone dropped out of his hand and clattered on the floor. The words rang in his head. She'd asked him a question.

She'd asked, *Why do I see missiles going into the sky?*

It was going on midnight when Anders and Gigi finished an entire pot of green tea and half a lemon pound cake. The news was just repeating the earlier stories and interviewing various so-called political and military experts.

"I'm exhausted," Gigi said. "I think I've had enough excitement for one day. Time to sleep."

Anders felt the same, although he wasn't sure how well he was going to sleep. "Let's see where everything is in the morning," he said, although he'd probably watch the news for a while longer on his phone in his bedroom.

Gigi put the teapot on the counter and the dishes in the sink. She turned out the lights in the stove area and headed out of the kitchen.

Just as Anders pointed the remote at the TV and was about to turn it off, the screen flashed a warning at the bottom.

"Mom!" he yelled.

"What is it?" she asked as she rushed back into the kitchen and looked at the screen. A red banner at the bottom read: *The US launches ICBMs.*

At that instant, the channel was taken over by the public service system and horrible warning sounds blared from the TV's speakers. A mechanical voice informed them that a nuclear attack on the United States was imminent, and then announced instructions to get indoors and shelter in low-lying areas.

"My God," Anders said, almost under his breath.

Next, Anders' phone buzzed, and then Gigi's a few seconds later, both of which then displayed text versions of the same warning messages. Jokes flashed into his head that he'd heard in grade school about what to do in the case of a nuclear attack: sit on the floor, put your head between your legs, and kiss your ass goodbye.

"It's really happening," Gigi said.

At that moment, the outdoor warning sirens sounded – the ones that Genesee Lake used to warn its citizens of tornadoes. It was an eerie, droning sound that made his chest seem to constrict around his pounding heart.

The TV channel went back to the news. The newscaster, who remained calm but whose facial expression indicated severe tension, announced that the first strikes would occur in fewer than 30 minutes, and would hit targets on the coasts.

They both stared at the screen in silence for more than a minute.

"We're on the coast," Gigi finally said. She seemed perfectly calm. "What are we going to do?"

"What can we do?" he replied. "I don't think Savannah is a high-priority target. Besides, we're over 45 miles west of the city."

He was glad they weren't in DC or New York, or anywhere in the Northeast. "Do you have Dad's emergency kit handy?"

Gigi went to the pantry and came back with a heavy knapsack. "Your father was always ready," she said as she set it on his dad's chair at the kitchen table.

Anders opened the bag and pulled out an emergency radio, which had a hand crank generator they could use when the power went out. The kit also had medical supplies, flashlights, batteries, and, importantly, a fold-out solar panel to charge things like cell phones. It occurred to him, however, that the skies might not be clear in the coming days, depending on how long it took the predicted nuclear winter to set in.

He put the radio and flashlights on the table. "I'm sure the power will go out – power grids across the whole country will be dead."

"We have candles, and the generator," she said. "It works on propane."

The house needed liquid propane for heat, but it was summertime.

"We just filled the LP tank in the spring," she added. "It's full."

"Good, we'll set that up in the morning if we need to," he said and turned back to the TV.

The news went to a field reporter on the streets of DC. The city's outdoor sirens were sounding. The man's expressions and mannerisms indicated stress and barely-tempered panic. He looked into the camera. "I'm surely at ground zero for one of the incoming ICBMs, and there's no way I can get out of the city in time," he said. "For my wife, Carla, and my two babies, Jake and Josie, I love you. We'll all be on the other side in about 25 minutes. See you there."

Anders looked over at his mom. A tear streamed down her cheek.

She looked back at him and said in a hoarse voice, "This is just awful."

"I know," he said. He was glad he was with her.

He wished they'd gone to bed five minutes earlier, but then realized their phones would have delivered the warning anyway.

If only he'd been able to figure it out sooner – what his dad wanted him to do, the password image, and the public dissemination of the files. But his regrets were irrelevant.

Maurice shook his head violently, hoping he'd wake himself from the nightmare.

The other two wings had also executed their launches, so the US now had over 70 hypersonic missiles heading toward Russia and China. There were now about the same number incoming, collectively from those two nations, which had been spotted by US satellites upon launch.

A large monitor displayed a spaghetti mess of lines that represented the trajectories of both outgoing and incoming missiles, but something was wrong. Some of the outgoing trajectories flashed red, and their otherwise solid lines turned to dashed.

"What the hell's going on?" Maurice yelled.

"We've lost tracking on four of our missiles," a technician replied. "Just as they reached apex."

The "apex" was the highest point in their trajectory, which was just above the atmosphere.

"Did we lose a satellite?" Maurice asked.

"Negative, sir," the man replied. "Anyway, losing just one wouldn't do the trick – they'd have to take out the full network, and there are 24 in this group."

"Well, find a way to get tracking back online," Maurice ordered. Although, he knew it didn't matter in regard to the missiles getting to their targets. They would act autonomously if they lost contact with control – they'd reach their targets no matter what. The only problem was that there could be no redirect at the last minute if a command was given to abort. He currently didn't have that option anyway – his command center was locked out. His people were contacting everyone they could to try to figure out how to reestablish control.

A horrifying thought came back to him – the nightmare that the drones had altered the targeting software and reprogrammed the missiles to hit US cities. He brushed it off. Enough missiles were coming in from China and Russia to destroy every major American city anyway.

Maurice's phone vibrated and he answered it. It was Colonel Schulman from the 90th Missile Wing, in Wyoming.

"We're losing our missiles," Schulman said. "Tracking goes out at the halfway point."

"Same here," Maurice said. "I'm told that the satellites are still functioning – just no response from the birds." He suspected that they were being locked out on purpose – same as for the comms with the mobile launch vehicles.

"I suppose we'll know when they find their targets in about 12 minutes," Schulman said.

"Colonel!" a woman yelled to Maurice from across the room.

Maurice turned and looked at the monitor to which she was pointing.

"Travis, I'll get back to you," Maurice said as he hung up and stared at the screen.

He stepped closer to the monitor and studied the frayed bundles of lines of incoming and outgoing missiles of all types. Now *all* tracking was gone. "What the fuck is going on?" he yelled.

"All tracking satellites are responding to pings," the communications officer replied. "And the status reports indicate that they're all functioning normally."

"Display last known trajectories all the way to projected targets," Maurice ordered. "Incoming and outgoing."

"Yes, sir," a woman at one of the control consoles said as she tapped at her keyboard. "On screen seven, now."

The curved trajectories were composed of solid lines, indicating their detected paths, and dashed lines extended from them as projected trajectories – *predicted*, instead of tracked, based on last known data. Incoming missiles from both China and Russia were projected to hit numerous major US cities and installations, and vice versa.

"What's the total missile count?" Maurice asked.

"There are 68 birds incoming," a man reported, "and 71 outgoing."

"And between Russia and China?" Maurice asked.

"There are 52 from Russia to China, and 47 the other way," the man answered. "Also from China to Japan and South Korea – 10 missiles – and Russia and China to India – 18 in all."

He could hardly believe it: there were over 250 nuclear missiles in the air, each capable of delivering a yield between 150 and 600 kilotons, or more. The Russians had some nasty weapons, including the so-called *Czar Bomba*, an aerial bomb with a yield of more than 50 megatons, although he was unaware of any incoming bombers. But the smaller-yield missiles were going to be devastating – they were targeting the most highly populated areas.

"What's the first US target that will be hit, and when?" Maurice asked.

"Looks like DC will be first with New York about a minute later," the man explained. "DC in t minus 11 minutes."

"Is Malmstrom on the target projections?" Maurice asked.

"No sir," the officer said.

It was maddening. The clock was ticking, but they couldn't *see* anything. They were blind to the rest of the world. They'd only know that something was hit from news reports – as long as public communications stayed online.

Something suddenly occurred to him: the thought about *Czar Bomba* came back to him. He went to the satellite communications officer, a woman whose face looked like she was holding back sheer panic. "Lieutenant Jackson, get me information about incoming bombers and missiles from submarines and surface ships."

"Yes sir," Jackson replied.

Maurice watched as she tapped away at her keyboard. After half a minute, a confused expression came to her face, and then she rattled away at the keys some more. Flurries of typing followed, separated by brief moments of still hands and perplexed looks.

"What's the trouble, Jackson?" Maurice asked.

"Sir ... the information must not be updating," she replied. "I'm making all the proper comms links – they seem to be active – but there are no reported launches from submarines or surface ships. And no incoming aircraft."

"What about outgoing – our bombers and subs?" he asked.

"Negative. Neither incoming nor outgoing," she replied.

What the hell is going on? Maurice pulled out his phone and called Colonel Schulman at the 90th.

"Travis, do you have any info on submarine or surface ship missile launches, incoming or outgoing?" Maurice asked.

"I'll let you know in a minute," Schulman replied.

Maurice held the phone away from his ear as Schulman barked orders to his crew. Thirty seconds later the man was talking again.

"Nothing incoming, and nothing outgoing from our side," Schulman said.

"What about bombers – have ours taken off yet?" Maurice asked.

"No – nothing," Schulman replied, and then remained silent for a few seconds. "This is all-out nuclear war – why is the navy not involved? Why aren't our bombers in the air?"

"I don't know," Maurice said. "But we have about nine minutes before the first impact. I'll let you get back to your duties. Good luck, my friend."

The call ended and Maurice stared at the scene before him, his mind spinning. Why would they not utilize every weapon they had? He then supposed one strategy might be to preserve resources for a second wave, where mobility might be key. For an instant, he thought how nice it would be to be a submariner right now. They could stay underwater for up to six months and be perfectly safe from the holocaust on the surface. But they'd have to surface eventually. And, when they did, they'd emerge into a dead world – or a world on fire.

As he gazed out over the control room, the multitude of screens suddenly changed – each went either to pitch black or bright blue.

"Sir," a technician yelled across the room. "We've lost all satellite communications."

To some degree, Maurice had expected that to happen. Every country was probably trying to destroy each other's assets in space. "Get them back online or reroute, pronto," Maurice barked. "In the meantime, put whatever land links we can get on screen."

In the next minute, a screen lit up with feeds from other military installations, the main one from NORAD, but they were suffering the same satellite blindness that was crippling his own command bunker. NORAD did, however, have ground links to all land-based detection systems, but they were still showing clear skies – no missile tracking.

The first incoming missile was set to hit DC in seven minutes.

"Can we get a national news station on one of the large monitors, please?" Maurice ordered.

A few seconds later, one appeared. It was a woman and a camera crew with a mobile transmission station in rural Pennsylvania, 65 miles due west of New York City. The woman looked visibly shaken, but Maurice thought she was holding up well considering the circumstances.

"New York City is behind me, and we're told it will be the second target hit, just minutes after DC," she explained. "I'll stay with you as long as I can."

Me too, Maurice said under his breath.

It was supposed to have been a ruse, he thought. *Did something unexpected happen that caused this? Or had this been the plan all along?*

It didn't matter now. He still had 120 disabled missiles under his command and he needed to get those silos back online for the second round, even though he wasn't sure he'd live that long.

CHAPTER 14

Anders studied the target map on the TV: Savannah was not going to get hit in the first wave of attacks. However, Atlanta, about 250 miles to the northwest, was. That Savannah was safe made him think of Alina, who was hopefully on her way there.

Anders sipped coffee that Gigi had brewed and stored in an insulated carafe for when the power went out. It was just after midnight, and the first missile was due to strike DC in 6 minutes. He'd set the alarm on his phone to sound at that time. The TV station had a woman planted about 65 miles west of New York City, explaining the data shown on the screen, which was just a mess of projected trajectories over a map of the United States. Anders was impressed that the news network had gotten someone out there so quickly.

"We lost all live trajectory data about 15 minutes ago," the newscaster explained. "So what you're seeing on the screen are *projected* paths, based on the last known data. Our communications with defense outlets have gone quiet." The woman then went into the safety procedures that all the other networks were repeating: people in those areas were to get into their basements, or internal rooms with no windows – closets or bathrooms. And then *kiss their asses goodbye*, she forgot to add.

The countdown on his phone passed the three-minute mark.

He went to the kitchen counter, refilled his coffee mug, and grabbed a plastic container of chocolate chip cookies as he went back to the table. His stomach felt like a churning pit of acid, but the coffee and cookies were psychologically comforting to him. He started nibbling nervously, like a mouse in a hole in the wall.

"Should we be able to see the blast in Atlanta?" Gigi asked as she set candles on the table and kitchen counter.

"It's nighttime," Anders said, "and the bombs usually detonate far above their targets. So we could probably see it from here, 200 miles away – it should light up the sky. But we shouldn't be looking at it anyway, or even be outside."

"Maybe we should go into the movie room – watch the news in there," she suggested. "No windows."

Anders agreed, grabbed his coffee and cookies, and followed her into the interior room where she turned on the large, flat-screen television. She switched the channel to the same news station that was on in the kitchen, and placed three candles on the coffee table in front of the couch along with a long-nozzled butane lighter.

It was pitch black behind the newscaster as she squinted into the camera and seemed to be talking for the sake of avoiding dead time. She looked to be shivering despite the mild summer weather in the Northeast. She kept looking behind her, in the direction of New York City, which was not visible in the night.

"We're going to move behind this concrete structure to shield us from the initial blast," the woman explained as she walked into an alley. "It should occur in approximately two minutes. We have no idea what to expect from this distance, but we're taking reasonable precautions. We should probably be in a basement – you viewers should go to your basements, if you have them, or to an internal room or closet on the lowest level of your homes. We're told to warn you not to look in the direction of a potential target: the initial blast could be blinding – even from a great distance. Also, it's too late to evacuate the cities: most are in gridlock and you'll be caught in traffic during the blast. Stay home, and batten down the hatches."

"Atlanta gets hit in five minutes, according to that graphic," Gigi said. "And Los Angeles at about the same time."

"Our missiles will hit Moscow and Beijing at about the same time Russia's hits Atlanta," Anders said, referring to the same chart. Beijing has like 20 million people."

"Tokyo has 40 million, and Delhi about 30 million," she said. "They're targets too, even though they weren't even involved in this conflict. I find that strange, and saddening."

"But they *are* targets of the Single-World Alliance," he said. He'd already told her everything he knew about the SWA and CG.

Gigi shook her head in disappointment. "It's a shame that our government has allowed internal factions to develop within it," she said. "I know it would be difficult to do, but they should have investigated, and then exterminated, those who wanted to undermine the government from within, or redirect it for their own agendas."

Anders agreed. And he probably took the word "exterminate" to a more extreme level than she did. Those who would work from within to weaken the country should be rooted out at the least, and literally eliminated in the worst cases. It sounded harsh, but look at where inaction had landed the country, and the world.

"We've been receiving reports of people jumping to their deaths from high-rises in New York City and LA, and committing suicide in other ways," the newscaster said. "This has been the nightmare that was predicted from the very beginning of the nuclear era – from when I was a little girl in Kentucky. I never thought it would actually happen. Two minutes until impact on New York, and just a minute and 15 seconds until DC."

The camera stayed on the woman as she sat on the ground with her back against the red-brick building. The camera descended to her level as well, indicating that its operator was also kneeling or sitting.

The reporter pressed her finger against the earbud in her left ear and tilted her head slightly.

"I'm in direct contact with our man outside DC who's standing by to confirm detonation there, which should occur in about 20 seconds," the woman informed. "Ten seconds ... five seconds."

Anders nearly jumped out of his skin when a loud noise sounded from somewhere in the room. It took him a few seconds to realize what it was. His phone was blasting a heavy-metal song: he'd forgotten the alarm he'd set for the first detonation. He looked to Gigi who stared at him with wide eyes and her hand on her chest.

"Sorry," he said as he shut down the alarm.

The newscaster sat in silence for another 10 seconds with a blank expression on her face, glancing up at the camera and down to her phone, apparently to monitor the time. "See anything, Roger?" she asked.

After a few more seconds of listening to the feed in her ear, she said, "Nothing yet?" and then looked into the camera. "Apparently, the DC strike is behind schedule. The New York strike is anticipated in 40 seconds."

She went silent again, seemingly listening into her earpiece, for about 20 seconds. "Anything, Roger?" she asked, listened for a few more seconds, and then looked back to the camera. "Nothing yet in DC."

The screen then split into two side-by-side windows, one of which was black, except for what seemed to be a few outdoor lights in rural areas, miles away.

"What you're seeing on the split screen is the feed from a camera mounted on a tripod in a wheat field just a mile east of our location, pointing toward New York City," she explained. "We're coming up on the New York strike time ... ten seconds ... three, two, one ..."

The woman's eyes widened as she waited for something to

happen. Another ten seconds passed, then 20, then 30. She pressed her earbud again.

"Roger? Anything in DC?" she asked, and then listened and shook her head at the camera.

"Nothing in DC, and nothing seen here, outside New York City, now 45 seconds past the predicted New York strike time," she said. "Los Angeles is now over a half-minute past their zero hour as well."

Anders caught a hopeful glimpse from his mom and he shook his head. "I'm sure their trajectory estimates aren't perfect," he said, although he, too, hoped for a split second that the strikes had somehow been averted.

They sat in silence, eyes glued to the TV, while the reporter kept getting updates from her contact in DC with no verification of an explosion. Five minutes passed, then ten, as reports of more missed deadlines came in.

Anders felt queasy.

"We don't know the reason for the delays," the reporter said. "We've been told that the NORAD satellite links have been disabled, so times of impact are just estimates. However, we were originally told that the error would be plus or minus three minutes. We're now beyond that error window by over eight minutes."

Anders wasn't convinced their estimates had only three minutes of error. There was always some excuse – and he fully expected to hear, years after the holocaust, that they'd failed to figure in the change in the arctic jet stream, or something like that. He reconsidered: perhaps he wouldn't survive to hear their explanations.

"What the hell's happening?" Maurice muttered. None of the ground-based detection units sensed incoming missiles. Were they offline, too? They were now at +12 minutes – the incoming missiles were extremely late. There were no satellite feeds of any kind, and therefore no indication of detonations anywhere on the planet. If any had occurred, he was sure the cable news stations would have reported something by now.

"Still nothing from DC?" he asked one of the comms officers.

"No, sir," she replied. "And nothing from our observers outside Moscow or Beijing."

Those first arrivals – the hypersonics – were now at $t = +14$ minutes.

"Get me MOLV-1 on the line," Maurice ordered. It was the Mobile Override Launch Vehicle – Team 1 – which launched from Silo I-1. They'd reestablished contact with the trucks just after the last missiles missed their predicted delivery times. It was further evidence that they'd been purposely locked out.

"On speaker now," the comms officer said.

"This is MOLV-1, Lieutenant Jacobs," a voice boomed out.

"Colonel Spelling here," Maurice said. "Did you have visual confirmation of the launch from I-1?" It was the one that targeted Moscow.

Although Maurice believed his wife when she said she'd seen missiles being launched, he needed direct, eye-witness confirmation from his operators.

"Affirmative, sir," Jacobs replied. "We watched it go."

"Did you see other launches?" Maurice asked.

"Affirmative – we saw at least a dozen from our launch location," Jacobs replied.

"Stay in position and await instructions," Maurice said and ordered the comms channel shut down.

They were now 15 minutes beyond the first strike time – for incoming and outgoing.

"What's the status of Beijing?" he asked.

"No impact observed," was the reply.

"Have there been any detonations anywhere on the goddam planet?" Maurice shouted.

His control-room crew frantically tapped away at keyboards and talked on headsets.

After 30 seconds, Maurice yelled, "Anyone?"

A flurry of verbal negative reports came from all directions. Nothing in the US, China, Russia, India, Japan, Pakistan, or anywhere else.

They were now 19 minutes past the first projected impact, and that was well beyond any errors in calculations.

"We have detection arrays in Guam and Hawaii," Maurice said. "What are they saying – have they detected anything at all?"

"They spotted our missiles outgoing to the west, and incoming from China, all of them only on the way up, sir," a tech replied. "And ships in the North Atlantic detected the Russian launches. But no one has seen anything coming down – nothing approaching any targets, anywhere."

In an attempt to explain the situation, Maurice thought that one might envision that a country had developed a technology to shoot down missiles before they got to their targets, but he was certain that the US hadn't perfected anything capable of that, and he was pretty sure that China and Russia hadn't either. Hypersonic missiles made it even more difficult. Besides, would a country shoot down its own missiles as well? Nuclear blasts should be happening *somewhere* on the planet.

At 29 minutes past the projected first detonations, Maurice called NORAD directly and asked for an explanation of what he was seeing from the bunker.

What they told him was the most shocking thing he'd ever heard.

It was 36 minutes beyond the first projected impact time and Anders' hopes were rising. Was the whole thing just a stunt? If it was, it was a complicated one since news agencies had supposedly acquired footage of the actual launches from the missile fields out west. If it was a sham, who could ever trust the media again? Or the government?

He then thought about the reason the Custodial Group wanted to launch nukes in the first place. No one was going to convince him that the world had been saved by aliens.

The reporter was out of her crouch now, leaning her back against the building. She was yammering on, constantly updating the time, and repeating negative reports of strikes around the country, and around the world. *Nothing in the US ... nothing in China ... nothing in Japan ... nothing in Russia ...*

Not only were the incoming missiles late hitting the US, but there were no reported strikes anywhere on the planet.

"What's happening?" Gigi asked, her voice weary with fatigue.

"I don't know, Mom," Anders said. "Those missiles could have made it to their targets and returned by now. Something's wrong."

"My God, your father ... you don't think ..."

"No Mom, I'm not figuring extraterrestrials were involved," he said. "Not yet, anyway."

Anders sent a text to Harrison, "Any idea what's going on?"

"No idea. A trick? Aliens? We're hiding out in Indiana. Stay safe," Harrison replied.

Gigi shook her head and huffed. "If this is all a ruse, I think heads should roll."

"I don't think the launches were a stunt," he said. "There are numerous videos – and not just from the US. Many clips are from private citizens. The launches happened."

"Then where are the missiles?"

"I don't know," he replied. And he didn't care, as long as they never landed.

"Where in the hell did they go then, Major?" Maurice yelled into the phone at a man from NORAD who he'd had on the line for the past five minutes. "Those missiles were supposed to land nearly 50 minutes ago – there were over 70 of them. They don't just disappear!"

"I'm sorry colonel, I just don't have an answer for you," the man said. "We lost contact with all missiles when they breached the atmosphere, incoming and outgoing."

"And what happened to the comms?" Maurice asked. "Were the satellites destroyed?"

"No, sir," the man said. "Those satellites are again operational – went back online five minutes ago. The feed to your facility needs to be reestablished."

"So?" Maurice said. "What do our satellites tell us?"

"Nothing – they stopped collecting data midflight."

"There were no detonations anywhere. Are you suggesting they all just evaporated?" Maurice asked in a sarcastic tone. "Each missile has a transmitter that chirps encrypted telemetry data. Have you searched for records of those signals?"

"Of course," the man replied. "We've been looking for the missiles ever since satellite comms went down."

"What about missiles fired from subs and surface ships?" Maurice asked. "Do we have bombers in the air? Are we expecting a second wave?"

"We're on the lookout for a second wave," the man said. "But there has been no indication of one. Regarding the subs and bombers, I can't tell you anything."

"Sir!" a woman yelled from somewhere in the control center, causing Maurice to pause his conversation. "It's the president – he's going to be on TV."

He followed the woman's pointing finger to a television monitor that was tuned to a cable news station.

Maurice hung up the phone.

It surprised him. He realized that, in the back of his mind, he'd been thinking that the president was dead. Maybe now he'd get some answers.

Anders had never been more nervous in his life, and now had to pee like a racehorse. He went to the bathroom and, when he came out, he heard his mom turn on the television in the kitchen. Evidently, she'd had enough of the windowless TV room, even though it was the middle of the night.

"Anders, come quickly!" she yelled.

His heart sank as he scurried down the hall, expecting the worst – he'd just gotten himself to believe that the missiles weren't coming.

He got to the kitchen and went directly to the TV. "What is it?"

"They're saying that the president is going to speak."

When his heartbeat came back to its normal rate, Anders wondered when they were going to arrest Crownbrook: he'd now been exposed through the most damning document release in recent times.

A red banner scrolled along the bottom of the screen saying that the president and other world leaders were going to speak shortly, and that viewers should stand by since it could happen any minute.

"What on Earth is going on?" Gigi asked. "No missiles have hit anywhere in the world – I'm not complaining, but how is he going to explain that?"

Anders grabbed a box of graham crackers from the pantry and commenced his nervous eating as they waited.

Suddenly, the screen showed a rectangular table with three empty chairs on one side, facing the camera. The space was small, and the walls were gray – as if it was a room on a warship. The audio caught some indiscernible chatter – Anders couldn't even tell if it was in English – and shadows fluttered about in the bright lighting, but no one passed into view of the camera. There was a large flat-screen monitor on the wall behind the table. It was dark.

After five minutes of this dead time, the audio quieted, and a man that Anders didn't recognize came on screen, stood in front of the table, and smiled into the camera. He looked tall, early forties, with short, black hair, and his white teeth contrasted with his dark complexion. He had old-time, movie star looks, and wore a dark suit and tie. He seemed out of place in this scene.

"Hello citizens of our beautiful planet," the man said. "My name is Dimitry Nikolaou, and I'm here with you to celebrate avoiding our third world war, and perhaps the destruction of our little blue oasis in the cosmos."

The man spoke with a slight accent and, in light of his name, Anders figured he was probably Greek.

"Who in the hell is *this* clown?" Gigi blurted.

Anders chuckled. "I have no idea," he replied. "I've never seen him before – but the name seems familiar somehow." He pulled his laptop out of his backpack that was leaning against the wall behind him. He powered it on and searched for a file while he listened to the TV.

"You have been through a lot during the past few hours, and also during the weeks leading up to this final event," Nikolaou continued. "The leaders of your respective governments have as well. What you are about to hear is a description of a gambit, the magnitude of which has never been taken in our history. And it was a winner."

"Gambit? What the hell is he talking about?" Gigi said.

Anders thought he knew exactly to what the man was referring, but just listened.

Nikolaou looked away from the camera, seemed to nod to someone off-screen, and then looked back to the viewers. "We're ready to begin," he said.

Three men filed in, and each stood behind a chair at the table.

Anders gasped. Left to right were Crownbrook, the Russian president, Anatoly Kurmaev, and the Chinese leader, Huang Jinping.

Anders brought up the list of SWA members from his father's files and found the name.

"Dimitry Nikolaou is a wealthy entrepreneur from Crete," Anders informed his mother, whose eyes were locked on the TV. "He's also a member of the Single-World Alliance."

"What the hell is this?" Maurice exclaimed, his eyes, and everyone else's in the control center, were glued to the largest monitor in the room.

The leaders of the three warring superpowers were all seated at the same table.

The president of the United States cleared his throat, glanced down at some papers on the table in front of him, and then looked into the camera.

"I'm sure you are all very confused," Crownbrook started. "For those of you in the US, it's between midnight and 3:00 a.m., but what we are about to reveal is for the entire world to see. I will first give this address in English, and then my counterparts will deliver the same information in Russian and Chinese so that their respective peoples can hear it directly from them."

Crownbrook looked to the other two, who then nodded for him to continue.

"In the past hours, and even the weeks leading up to this event, you have likely experienced the most frightening time of your lives," Crownbrook said. "I'm currently on the *USS Abraham Lincoln*, in an undisclosed location somewhere in the South Pacific. As you may know from the news, this carrier group was supposedly attacked, and suffered significant casualties. To the families of the crews on these ships, your loved ones are alive and well, and we apologize for the anguish you have surely experienced. They will be contacting you in the coming hours. You'll soon understand why we've taken these extraordinary actions."

Crownbrook took a sip from a bottle of water and cleared his throat. "We're at least two hours beyond the impact times for all launched missiles – on all sides of the exchange," he continued. "I'm sure you're wondering what happened to them. There have been speculations – in the media and otherwise – that they were never launched. I can assure you that they were, and we have proof of that. Other rumors are that the missiles weren't armed with nuclear warheads and self-destructed before they descended. We can verify that they were armed, and have proof that they did not self-destruct. Every missile launched on all sides was armed and had a specific target – including highly-populated areas and military installations."

The screen behind the three men came to life and showed amateur footage of various missile launches from locations around the world.

"What we, the leaders of the three most powerful nations on Earth, have carried out, is a great gamble," Crownbrook continued. "It was a maneuver that has exposed a secret that will change our understanding of the universe, and drive us into a new age."

Maurice sat on a desk and stared at the screen. He'd seemingly, and unknowingly, played an integral part in some grand ruse. All he could do now was listen.

WHAT ANDERS WAS SEEING on the screen was simply bizarre. Three enemies at the same table, right after mutual attacks that could have wiped their respective nations off the Earth – and could have destroyed the entire planet in the process.

The president continued.

"For three-quarters of a century – since World War II – the US government and other nations have been studying evidence of odd phenomena and objects that have been appearing in our skies, and discovered in the ground and under ice," Crownbrook explained. "The most sensitive evidence of these objects has been passed through dark channels all this time, meaning through clandestine groups within government agencies, such as the CIA, and those related to national defense. Even US presidents were not privy to certain things – even if they asked direct questions about them."

Anders knew Crownbrook was referring to evidence of extraterrestrials.

"Unlike previous presidents, however, I worked my way up through the CIA ranks, starting as a young case officer," Crownbrook continued. "I was groomed, and then selected, to be a member of what might be described as a secret society within the intelligence community, which included people from the CIA and other agencies, private defense contractors, and even foreign intelligence services."

"The CG," Anders blurted.

Crownbrook looked to the Russian and Chinese leaders, apparently looking for their approval before he continued. The other two men nodded, and Crownbrook looked back to the camera.

"You see, this is the first time in history that all three major world powers have leaders who are members of this society, and who therefore understand and support its purpose," Crownbrook continued. "One of its first priorities – which was needed to fulfill its primary objective – was to create this rare opportunity, so that we three, as representatives of this organization, would one day be sitting together at this table, and in this current situation. The secret society of which we are members is called the Custodial Group."

HARRISON STARED AT THE TV. His vision blurred for a moment and he felt like he might pass out.

He and his wife, Lauren, had gone to her parents' lake cottage in central Indiana to distance themselves from high-priority targets. The lodge was small, but comfortable, and had all the essentials, including internet and TV. They also had a gasoline generator in the garage, with enough fuel to keep the fridge going for about a week.

The weather was perfect, so there'd be no need for air conditioning or heat, and there was a fireplace for the latter if needed. They were surrounded by woods on three sides, so there'd be enough firewood if it came to that, and Clear Spring Lake made the fourth side. The fishing was great in the lake, so they could get some protein in a pinch.

They seemed to have averted nuclear war, for now, but he wasn't sure that they were out of danger. He was nervously awaiting what was to happen next. He had some ideas of what was in store but kept them to himself for the time being.

They were sitting on a couch that faced a large TV mounted over the fireplace. It seemed that he'd made the right call by closing down DMS and getting out of town. He wished he'd been wrong about everything, but here they were.

The *Custodial Group*. The president had just admitted publicly to being a member, and Harrison's heart skipped a beat in anticipation of finally seeing what they had done – how their plans had come together.

"The Custodial Group has been in existence since 1950," the president continued. "Many things happened around that time, including the first use of nuclear weapons in 1945 and the start of the nuclear arms race that followed. But other, more peculiar things occurred between 1945 and 1950, some of which have been disclosed to the public, but many of which have not."

"Was this the group you were recruited to join?" Lauren asked.

Harrison had told his wife about many of the unclassified things he'd done while in the CIA, but he'd only mentioned that a "secretive group" had recruited him, and that he'd declined. Sometimes he regretted passing on the offer, and she'd seemed to sense it.

He nodded.

"The Custodial Group was covertly formed by CIA members to explore these odd things," Crownbrook continued, "and then to keep what they found secret, and to maintain their concealment until the time was right to reveal them. The time for full disclosure has now arrived."

Lauren squeezed his arm. "You're finally going to know what it was about."

Harrison already *did* know what it was about from the files Anders had gotten from his father. He was now going to learn the consequences of his failure to expose the CG – and the SWA – before they'd accomplished their objectives. A sense of doom seeped into his mind and his chest tightened.

"The reason why now is the time to do the things we've done, which I'm about to describe, is connected to strange craft which have been meddling with our secure military installations, including our nuclear arsenal, for decades," Crownbrook explained and then looked to the other two leaders. "And not only with our facilities, but also with those of our friends."

"Friends?" Lauren huffed. "Didn't they just try to kill us?"

Harrison tightened his grip on her hand.

"More recently, we've detected drones flying around our missile silos which somehow have the ability to render them nonfunctional," the president said. "Even more alarming, they seemed to have the ability to *launch* the missiles, as my Russian counterpart reported to us years ago. In the beginning, each of our three countries thought this meddling was being conducted by one of the other two, of course. But we eventually got together and figured out that it was *someone else*. If the three of us hadn't been members of the Custodial Group, we might have missed this opportunity."

"Opportunity?" Lauren blurted.

"The Custodial Group developed a black-funded wing in the 1970s that went by 'CG,' composed of top scientists and engineers based at Area 51 and other secret sites around the country," Crownbrook explained.

"Black-funded?" Lauren asked.

"Off the books – unofficial," Harrison replied. "It's a degree more secret than dark-funded."

"You see," Crownbrook continued, "since the 1940s, we've collected some strange artifacts, their ages dating from thousands of years ago to present day. The only objects of which the public is aware – and which have sparked numerous conspiracy theories – are those we acquired in 1947, in Roswell, New Mexico. But there were numerous other incidents that were better concealed which provided ample evidence, some of which was technological, and some biological."

"Holy shit," Harrison hissed. His thoughts went to the unidentifiable fingerprints on the note the president's niece had opened.

ANDERS NOTICED his mouth was hanging open and closed it before looking to his mom, whose jaw was still dropped.

"Roswell, New Mexico?" she asked. "Is he suggesting that *aliens* are involved in what happened today?"

"Dad and his aliens – he loved those conspiracy theories."

Gigi nodded to the TV. "Maybe they weren't just theories," she said.

"For a long time now – since the first nuclear test at Los Alamos in 1945 – we've known that someone has been watching us, interested particularly in our space and nuclear programs," Crownbrook continued. "And they became increasingly more brazen about their incursions as time went on, from the so-called drones interfering with our missile silos to our actual sightings of objects – crafts – nosing around our warships and toying with our fighter jets, the videos of which were leaked to the public years ago."

"I've seen those clips," Anders said. "They're all over the internet, and the US Navy even admits that they're real, and that they can't explain them."

"In order to explain to you what has happened today, and why, some history is in order," Crownbrook continued. "After World War II, the US and Russia basically split Germany's rocket scientists and brought them back to work on our respective space and missile programs. This, of course, had broad implications in both the Cold War and the Space Race."

On the screen behind the three leaders, a picture appeared of two men standing next to the launch pad of a Nazi V-2 rocket. The man on the right was tall, with wavy, brown hair, and looked like he could have been a movie star from the 1950s. The other was shorter, thin, with sparse blond hair and round, wire-rimmed glasses.

"The man on the right in this photo is Wernher von Braun, whom many of you might recognize," the president continued as he stood and pointed to the taller man on the screen. He then pointed to the shorter man. "But this man you might not recognize. His name is Gunter Eriksson, another talented scientist."

"My God," Anders said, and nearly coughed. "He worked at secret US bases on all kinds of things – rockets and airplanes and the like. He was a member of the Custodial Group."

"Wernher von Braun was the leading rocket scientist of his time, and is often given credit for the US winning the space race and getting us to the moon," Crownbrook continued as he retook his seat and looked into the camera. "The reason we are sitting here today, however, under these bizarre circumstances, is because of Gunter Eriksson."

Two more pictures of Eriksson appeared on the screen. In the first, he stood next to an SR-71 spy plane, as indicated by the caption.

"Eriksson was involved in a CIA project codenamed Archangel which developed the SR-71 *Blackbird*, which replaced the U-2 spy plane in the 1960s," Crownbrook explained. "These represent technologies that have been known to the public for decades."

Anders knew there was a lot more to Eriksson than those planes. There were numerous other secret projects in which the man had been involved. And he'd had some strange ideas, beyond science.

"But Eriksson was involved in, and directed, other projects of which you are most certainly unaware," the president said.

A color image of an older Eriksson – in his mid-60s at least –

appeared on the screen. He was in what seemed to be a well-lit airplane hangar, standing next to a complicated object about the size of a compact car. It was shaped like a fat, silvery donut with hundreds of glowing, white tubes protruding from its walls, making a weave of complex bends and turns, and merging into an aesthetic pattern at the donut's center.

"This is the drive – the engine, if you will – of a craft we dug out of the ice in Antarctica in 1974," Crownbrook explained. "It contains technologies that we do not understand to this day, a half-century later. The object will float in mid-air, as if it were being levitated by a giant magnet. But it's not magnetic. Most interestingly, however, is its age. Based on its depth in the ice, and other measurement methods, our scientists estimate that it's about 3,000 years old, give or take a couple hundred years. Due to the absence of any other viable conclusions, we understood that these objects could not have been constructed by the human race on this planet."

"He *is* talking about aliens," Gigi gasped.

It wasn't unexpected, based on what Anders had learned over the past months, but it still made him lightheaded.

"How your father was able to keep all this secret is unimaginable," she continued. "He must've known about this the entire time. And we wore *tinfoil hats* at dinner to make fun of him."

They'd mentioned it numerous times in the past weeks, but Anders still felt his stomach tighten as he remembered the scene. His dad was laughing and enjoying the ribbing. And he recalled his father telling them a few things he'd learned from the TV shows about aliens, which Anders now knew weren't mere conspiracy theories. He'd told them about strange observations in Antarctica, sightings by naval aviators, and interference at military installations. It seemed that all that information was true – and had even been leaked to the public in some way – but people just brushed it off as conspiracy or fiction.

"There has been a long history of mysterious objects probing our military facilities, starting after the successful testing of the atomic bomb, and its subsequent use," Crownbrook continued. "The most well-known event of those early times was the Roswell Incident, in 1947, as I previously mentioned, but there were numerous others of which the public has been unaware. What has not been publicly disclosed, until now, is that the frequency of these incursions has been increasing to the present day. They've become more brazen, and have been meddling with the functionality of our missile silos, bombers, and nuclear-capable naval vessels."

Anders knew where the president was heading. He was not only disclosing that aliens *were* here at one time. He was saying that *they are here, now*.

MAURICE'S VISION sparkled and he felt like he was going to faint.

"Is this some kind of joke?" a woman asked from her communications desk.

Maurice didn't know what the president was up to, but the situation was shaping up to be the most elaborate deception ever played.

"Most recently, these so-called drones have been incapacitating our missile silos, both shutting them down and, in some instances, initiating launch sequences," Crownbrook continued. "It wasn't clear, early on, if they really wanted to control the sites, or just show us that they *could*. During the past year, the frequency of these incursions reached a level where we had to do something about them. And that's where Gunter Eriksson comes into the picture, even though he's been dead for nearly 30 years."

"Colonel, you ever hear of this guy?" a young lieutenant asked him.

"No, Barnes, I haven't," Maurice replied. And he thought that was strange. As a former test pilot who'd flown everything from the newest fighter jets to spy planes, he thought he'd at least recognize the name of one of the top scientists who'd developed the SR-71.

"Gunter Eriksson was tasked with studying these strange

phenomena when the incursions first began, and he came to the conclusion of extraterrestrial involvement," Crownbrook explained. "Assuming this, he came to three possible reasons as to why these so-called extraterrestrials were doing what they were doing. First, with our use of nukes immediately after their invention, they figured we'd be apt to use them again. The aliens were therefore stepping in to prevent us from destroying ourselves and the planet. The second possibility was that the extraterrestrials were planning a takeover, the first step of which would be to disable our nuclear capabilities. Finally, his third idea was a confluence of the first two: the extraterrestrials wanted to protect the planet until they were ready to take it over at a later time."

Maurice couldn't believe what he was hearing, or that he'd fallen for the story that China or Russia had been responsible for the drone incursions. He'd been so convinced, in fact, that he'd barely questioned the construction of the mobile launch stations that circumvented launch protocols and safeguards. He'd overseen the launch of 25 nuclear missiles – intended to kill millions of people. He felt violated. He'd been tricked into doing something he otherwise would not have done.

"So the aliens were going to protect us from ourselves?" Anders yelled at the television.

"That still doesn't explain why all three countries attempted to carry out all-out nuclear attacks," commented Gigi.

"In 1972, we'd had enough of the saber-rattling by North Korea, which was being instigated by the Soviet Union, and wanted to demonstrate our capabilities to them and the rest of the world," Crownbrook continued. "We launched an ICBM on track for North Korea – reports of which were never made public. It had a non-fissionable warhead, and was meant to self-destruct near Pyongyang."

"I never heard about this, did you?" Gigi asked.

"It was in Dad's files," Anders replied.

"That missile mysteriously disappeared before it reentered the atmosphere," Crownbrook said. "We have satellite imagery that captures the event – there were strange, luminous spheres that appeared around the missile when it reached space. The ICBM then vanished before our eyes, along with the glowing objects. It was a shocking mystery, and it was kept secret, despite some leaked stills from the video, which were quickly dismissed as phonies by public media."

A video played on the screen behind the president with a caption that read, "From the Earth Resources Technology Satellite (ERTS), November 30, 1972." Anders found the video grainy and unremarkable, at least compared to others he'd seen on the alien-enthusiast TV shows.

"Back to Gunter Eriksson," Crownbrook continued. "He argued that, whether the supposed alien observers had benevolent or aggressive intentions, we should someday take advantage of their apparent inclination to protect the planet in order to expose them. He devised a hypothesis, which was based entirely on the idea that, when presented with a full-scale, global nuclear attack, the extraterrestrials would step in and stop it. If hundreds of missiles were launched, and subsequently disappeared, the aliens would be revealed, and the evidence would be incontrovertible."

"Crownbrook is out of his mind," Anders said. Anders knew all about Eriksson's crazy plan. "And so are the other two if they believe this bullshit. They scared the hell out of the entire world. People committed suicide because of this, for God's sake."

He'd said it aloud, and believed what he'd said, but he knew that the president was about to reveal a new age for the human race.

Maurice pulled a pack of cigarettes out of his jacket pocket and lit one. He knew it was against regulations, especially in the bunker, but he no longer gave a shit. They calmed his nerves. Besides, he was in charge.

Maurice learned that there was evidence early on that would have exposed the ruse, and he was angry that he and his people had missed it. According to the tracking data they had on incoming and outgoing missiles before they disappeared, each targeted city had at most *one* missile heading toward it. Washington, DC would be a primary target of both China and Russia, and would likely be struck twice, but that's not what the projected trajectories showed. It would be the same for Moscow and Beijing, but they, too, only had one missile targeting them. In fact, not a single city on the planet was double-targeted. It just wasn't possible unless the players were conspiring.

He looked back to the TV screen and took a deep drag of his cigarette. He thought Crownbrook looked smug as he delivered his speech.

"A year later, in 1973," Crownbrook continued, "we attempted another mock nuclear attack with a single, unarmed missile. This one was mysteriously destroyed before it even left the atmosphere."

Maurice knew nothing of either of the attempted fake attacks.

"Since they blew it up in the atmosphere where it would have contaminated a large area had it been carrying a real warhead, we concluded that they – the aliens – could distinguish between missiles that contained fissile materials and those that did not," Crownbrook explained. "Our so-called *watchers* then seemed to change their focus to controlling the launch sites. We concluded that they'd changed their approach: rather than intercepting the missiles after launch, they'd make sure they never got off the ground in the first place. We assumed that this was the objective of the most recent drone incursions into our missile fields. As I said earlier, they are able to take over our launch systems remotely."

Maurice had seen that happen a hundred times in the past six hours. All of his silos had been rendered inoperable.

"Due to this fact," Crownbrook explained, "we had to develop new measures in order to circumvent the complete takeover of our nuclear launch sites. We had to act while we still had time. We were being backed into a corner."

Maurice now understood the importance of his part in this grand deception. He felt the need to backtrack his outrage, however. He was starting to understand the urgency of the situation, and didn't see any other way: capitulation to whoever was trying to take over the country's – *the world's* – most devastating weapons was not an option.

ANDERS WAS EXHAUSTED but wide awake. His nerves were electrified and nearly burned out. That's when he got the text from Alina on his burner phone. It read, "Stuck in Charlotte. Police directing everyone off the highway. Might not get there until tomorrow."

Anders had already explained to his mom what was happening: Alina had been abandoned by her firm and she was on her way to Savannah, and would then come to Genesee Lake. They both decided that she wasn't a danger: she wasn't affiliated with Russian intelligence. Even if she was, Anders had nothing of use to them. The only risk was the desk in his dad's office, but Alina knew nothing of it, or even that his mom and dad had been in the CIA.

Anders texted her his mom's address.

"Alina's stuck in North Carolina," he said. "She probably won't get here until tomorrow."

"Poor young lady," Gigi said. "She's all alone in this mess."

Anders was concerned for Alina's safety even though he knew she was far more resourceful than the average person. Her training would help her get through the initial hunt by Russian intelligence.

After that, when DMS was running again, Harrison would set her up with a new identity and relocate her, if that's what she wanted.

Their attention went back to the president.

Gigi paced back and forth between the stove and TV as she listened. She was clearly nervous, and spent from stress and lack of sleep.

The president went on. "Gunter Eriksson's hypothesis was the basis for the actions that have transpired in the last few years, culminating, finally, in the events of the past hours," he explained. "His idea is called the *Peregrine Conjecture*."

"My God, your father was trying to warn us – the *peregrine falcon* image as the passcode," Gigi said. "It was already too late when you figured it out. We had no chance to stop this."

"The concept was originally called the *Eriksson Hypothesis*," the president explained. "The name was changed when hypersonic missiles were woven into the plan – they're the fastest nuclear missiles that exist, just like the peregrine falcon is the fastest animal on the planet. When in its lethal dive, the peregrine gives its prey little time to react. In the same sense, we wanted to force a quick reaction from our observers."

Anders thought that added even more risk to the ploy: what if the extraterrestrials weren't quick enough to respond?

"It was a risky gambit that went as follows," the president went on. "The most powerful countries in the world would feign a war, and initiate an all-out nuclear attack. Our observers would then be forced to intervene – stop the missiles somehow – if they wanted to preserve the planet. We, however, would set up detectors and cameras everywhere – land-based and in space – to record *everything*, and therefore collect irrefutable evidence that the aliens exist, and are currently present in our world."

"They risked our entire civilization on this bet?" Gigi spat. "For what? To prove that someone was out there – aliens? There must have been another way."

As if Crownbrook had heard her through the TV, he went on,

"One might ask what was to be gained from such an existential gamble. Through the assessments of our CIA and Department of Defense, in conjunction with the corresponding agencies of our friends – Russia, China, the UK, and others – it was determined that a global attack was imminent. That is, we concluded that those who have been watching us would attempt to take us over in the near future."

"We're in danger of an alien invasion?" Anders scoffed. "This is crazy."

"And then there's this," Crownbrook continued. "The NSA and private industries discovered other types of intrusions – informational, digital. And I'm not only talking about classified military and intelligence files. I mean personal data on every citizen of the United States, and those of every other country that keeps digital files on its people. We have to assume that they have everything that has been stored in computer records, appeared on the Internet, or been transferred electronically by any means – email, social media, cloud-type storage, cell phones, and so on."

"How does proving the existence of extraterrestrials help us in any way?" Gigi asked.

Anders had the same question. "Yeah – it seems like what they've done could accelerate an attack," he said. "Otherwise, the aliens could just ignore us and carry out their plans in the future – maybe the *far* future. How did they know that an invasion was *imminent*? And what could we do about it anyway?"

"Before I explain what happens next, let me show you what we've learned from this ordeal," the president said as a video played on the screen behind him.

It was footage from a high altitude – maybe on the edge of the atmosphere – that showed a missile rising into space.

"This is one of our missiles," Crownbrook explained. "It's near the apex of its trajectory, just barely above the atmosphere. Watch what happens."

A massive, dark object suddenly appeared – perhaps a half-mile from the camera, though it was difficult to tell with only the rocket as a reference. It had facets, like a flat gem, but otherwise had no structural features that he could see.

"Holy shit," Anders gasped.

The missile then seemed to freeze in place, list slightly, and then disappear, along with the object.

"What happened to it?" Gigi asked.

"And here's another one," Crownbrook said as another clip started, showing a similar scene, but from a different angle.

This camera was zoomed in on the alien object a little more tightly than the previous shot – more of an overhead look – and he could see it was shaped like an equilateral triangle. A missile came into view, and then seemed to evaporate into thin air, or *vacuum*, as the case may be. This time, Anders thought it got blurry just before it disappeared, simultaneously with the object.

"Every missile that entered the atmosphere disappeared in a similar fashion," Crownbrook said. "This includes each of our country's hypersonic missiles, which are faster than conventional ICBMs, and follow shallower trajectories."

"Not a single missile made it to its target," Gigi said. "Amazing."

Anders suddenly felt anxious. It frightened him: whoever, or whatever, swallowed those missiles had basically proven that the military technology of Earth was no match for them. He would've felt better had China or Russia been responsible, developing some new technology that elevated them above the others. At least then he'd know that other countries – including the US – wouldn't be too far behind. If extraterrestrials were really responsible for what had happened, there would be no catching up for humanity. The aliens were apparently advanced enough for deep space travel. They could be centuries ahead of humans.

"Look at the ticker at the bottom of the screen," Gigi said.

It stated that the sailors on the ships and submarines that had been attacked had started contacting their families.

"We've exposed something that has probably been happening

for centuries," Crownbrook continued. "The question I'm sure you all have is *what is going to happen next?*"

"Of course we do!" Anders yelled at the TV. He was feeling like the world had just poked a gigantic hornets' nest. If the so-called observers had been around for centuries and hadn't bothered us, why not leave them alone?

"Before that, there's something else that needs to be revealed to the population of the world as further evidence from our past," the president continued. "The Cuban missile crisis was averted for mysterious reasons – something of which I only became aware through my colleagues in the Custodial Group. You see, both the Russian and US weapons systems had simultaneously malfunctioned at exactly the right time, just as an attack was about to commence. Both sides, for obvious reasons, hid these facts from the rest of the world. It wasn't until our connections through the Custodial Group facilitated communication through unofficial channels that we were able to compare notes, so to speak."

Gigi took a sip of tea. "Fascinating," she said. "Although, I'm not sure I believe it."

Anders felt the same, even though he might have been involved in delivering those communications. He really wished that his dad was still alive to corroborate these stories. If he had to keep the secrets that his father had, it would have driven him insane, especially for the amount of time he'd had to sustain them.

"Now, to our extraterrestrial observers – those who have intercepted our missiles – if you are listening, we invite you to meet with us," Crownbrook said as he looked into the camera. "Not that you need it to locate us, but we are broadcasting a beacon from our position in the South Pacific."

"I'm not sure that's a good idea," Gigi said.

Crownbrook cleared his throat and again looked to the camera. "Citizens of our planet, our next step is to await their response," he said.

Anders could hardly believe what he was hearing. Were they

really trying to contact extraterrestrials? Was this some kind of joke, or the delusions of a madman?

"For those of you sheltering in place at home or elsewhere, you're safe for now," Crownbrook said. "Go back to your lives. You'll get more information when we do. I now turn this presentation over to President Kurmaev."

The Russian president began speaking in his country's language. Since Anders and his mom both spoke Russian, they realized he was giving the same speech that Crownbrook had, and seemed to be reading from a teleprompter.

"So, what do we do now?" Gigi asked.

"I suppose we just wait," Anders replied. "At this point, I think I can tell you how I've been involved in this." She already knew a lot, but he wanted her to know everything.

He started from the beginning – from that first meeting with the president in February – and explained everything he'd seen and done since. There were still some things for which he had no explanation, and on the top of that list were the mysterious fingerprints. Harrison probably knew more by now, and Anders would ask him about it.

Although Anders was somehow relieved to tell her his story, in light of what had ultimately occurred, it all seemed irrelevant. However he'd gotten to where he currently was didn't matter anymore. Humanity had entered a new era. He was wary, however, that it might still be a trick.

Anders' phone buzzed. It was Harrison.

"Can you believe this?" Harrison asked.

"Do *you* believe it?" Anders asked.

"I don't know *what* to believe," Harrison replied. "I am convinced, however, that the missiles were launched. I'm just not entirely sure what happened to them. If they were able to deceive the entire world to justify launching them, I'm sure they could be tricking us about the rest of it."

"And what about the videos of the objects – the things that made the missiles seem to evaporate from existence?"

"I don't know, Anders," Harrison admitted. "You know what they can do with videos these days. Everything could be fake – just good CGI. We'd have to analyze the original videos to see if they were artificially created."

Anders had thought the same when he'd seen the clips. The CGI, or computer-generated imagery, and also "deep fake" technology, was so good now that it would be impossible to authenticate the videos without having the original files.

"What would be the purpose of faking all this?"

"It depends on how cynical you are," Harrison replied.

"Very."

"Well then, assuming the most diabolical plan that doesn't involve space aliens, it could be a ploy to intimidate and cage the population of the planet," Harrison explained. "The people will be malleable after this – controllable. Just like during Project NIMH. This might be the global event they needed to set the next phase into action."

"To what end?"

"To establish a global government," Harrison replied. "We know that the president and other two leaders are members of *both* the Custodial Group and the Single-World Alliance. What if they just used the CG to get the missiles launched, but they devised a plan so that the missiles would all fail – maybe self-destruct? It would give the false impression that aliens had done it, and the population might be so shocked that they'd do anything they were told afterwards. The perfect setup for the SWA."

The thought had crossed Anders' mind – that their actions were consistent with the goals of both groups. Except for one thing.

"I figured the SWA would have wanted some of the missiles to land," Anders said. "Given that they want to reduce the population."

"Good point," Harrison said. "They could've played it that way – gotten both the population reduction they sought along with the alien scare."

It would have been the perfect amalgam. They would have

reduced the population – let the nukes take out the most populated cities – and then they'd argue that we needed to combine forces to fight a mysterious, alien enemy.

Before ending the call, Harrison informed him it would be a few weeks before DMS headquarters would be reactivated – depending on whatever else transpired – and employees would be called back into action at that time.

"That was Harrison," Anders said to his mom as he set his phone on the table. He then explained what they'd discussed.

"It's so confusing," Gigi said. "It's almost impossible to know what's real and what isn't. All we know for sure is that the missiles didn't land. But we can't even be certain that they were really launched – or at least, if they were, that they were *real* and were headed for actual targets."

"Yes, they could have launched a bunch of duds into space and just let them burn up in the atmosphere, or self-destruct in some way," Anders said.

Another ticker scrolled across the bottom of the screen. The Vatican – the pope – was claiming that the missiles were destroyed by God.

Anders was now more confused than ever.

It was 4:00 a.m., and Maurice had been chain-smoking since midnight. His crew continued to monitor their stations but were frequently distracted by the television. He didn't mind. He was lucky anyone was awake after almost 36 hours without sleep.

The idea arose that the ruse the three leaders had pulled off had involved the fake launches of missiles – or unarmed missiles that just harmlessly self-destructed when they reached the upper atmosphere. Although he was certain they had been launched, Maurice was now extremely suspicious of the possibility that the missiles were designed to fail, considering that the only ones that had been launched were the new, supposed hypersonics – all recent and secret replacements. In China and Russia, it might have been easier to replace their conventional missiles with duds without having to devise an elaborate scheme to trick everyone into going along with it. In the US, they'd have to go to greater lengths to make replacements if they did it by the books. Perhaps Maurice and his equivalents at the two other missile wings had been conned: they were the weak points in the system, and were exploited in this grand deception.

But there was a counter to his argument: what would have been the purpose of the *drones* in this alleged charade? That aspect of the plan would have been too elaborate to carry out without mishaps. He was convinced they were real, and therefore maybe everything else was as well.

But his confidence in what he understood about any of it was wavering. Could the drones also have been contrived? Could it be that someone had been able to install software in the control stations to make it look like someone on the outside was meddling with them? After all, there were no clear images of the drones, and no convincing direct sightings. Even the satellite images shown to him by the CIA director and the president when he'd met with them in DC could have been fabrications. How far did the scam actually go?

Maurice bounced back and forth between which events were undoubtedly real and which could've been faked. He was certain that his missiles had been launched, and was also convinced that Russia and China had launched theirs – every independent detection source to which he had access reported the same thing.

The simplest explanation of their disappearance was that they self-destructed. But suppose they didn't. In that case, what destroyed them? He didn't believe the president's story about aliens, and he'd never be convinced that the videos showing the missiles disappearing in space were authentic. One couldn't trust any digital media – anything could be faked.

He was certain that no country was capable of taking out all the ICBMs. And why would they take out their own? The possibilities therefore reduced to those described in the ticker-tape messages the news channel was scrolling at the bottom of the TV screen: either extraterrestrials stopped the nuclear holocaust, or it was God himself who'd intervened. The most likely possibility, however, was that it was all a grand deception, the true purpose of which had yet to be revealed.

CHAPTER 15

Anders rolled out of his bunk after just two hours of restless sleep. It was 6:30 a.m. when he found his mom in the kitchen. She looked exhausted.

"Any word from your Russian friend?" Gigi asked.

Anders shook his head. "I'm worried," he said. "I've heard nothing from her since she was pulled off the highway in Charlotte. I sent her a message last night. No response."

"Oh dear," Gigi said and sighed.

They watched the news all morning while they drank coffee and nibbled at their bagels. Anders was a mess, both physically and mentally. His nerves felt like they'd been burned by an electrical current.

They decided to turn off the TV for lunch, and then took a hike around the lake behind their property. It was hot outside – a normal late July day in Georgia – but the light sweating and blue sky helped to clear his mind. Imagining the mountainous white clouds that were slugging their way overhead replaced with the mushroom clouds of nukes helped him to keep things in perspective. They were lucky.

The events that had already occurred were unprecedented. He did feel relieved that the threat of nuclear war was seemingly over but he knew that the whole sequence of events was a prelude to something much larger. Whether that meant the formation of some kind of global government, or the unmasking of so-called extraterrestrial "watchers," he had no idea, but something big would happen next, and it would be transformative, and irreversible.

There were now three prevailing theories regarding the events of the past 24 hours. The first was that it was an extravagant hoax, the purpose of which had yet to be revealed. Second, the missiles had been swallowed up by aliens – the theory the governments of the world were pushing. And, third, God himself saved humanity from self-destruction, the idea proposed by the pope and the leaders of some other religions. All three factions were already building their bases of believers. Even though Anders wasn't religious, if given the choice, he'd of course choose the third option to be true. Who wouldn't? The most likely possibility, however, was that it was a hoax. The true objectives of the event would reveal themselves in the next few days, and he had some ideas of what they were.

When they got to the far side of the lake, the north shore, they sat at a picnic table under a tall oak tree, just a few yards from the calm water. It was the "swimming hole" he'd frequented as a kid.

"If the alien story is true, what happens next?" Gigi asked.

"That could go any number of ways," he said. He'd read a lot of sci-fi in his lifetime, and questions of this type had crossed his mind many times. "They could just remain quiet and concealed."

"But they know that *we* know that they're there," she said.

"True, but our proof is just some videos that don't show very much – of their vessels I mean," he said. "It is clear, however, that the missiles abruptly disappeared. And there are 50 or more clips showing that happening." He kept in mind that all those videos could have been faked.

"What if we've just poked a bear, and now they – the extraterrestrials – decide to move against us?" she asked. "What if they want our planet, and have now come to the conclusion that we'll ruin it unless they act immediately?"

"I'm sure we'll ruin it eventually," Anders replied. "Even *we* admit that. But I think we're at their mercy anyway. I'm not sure what our leaders thought they'd accomplish through all of this."

"What do you mean?"

"If these so-called extraterrestrials can hang out in space – coming from some distant place, cloaking themselves in orbit around our planet, and intercepting and diffusing our most deadly weapons – then they could take us down at any time," he said.

Gigi's expression seemed to turn sad. "It's a shame," she said. "If only they waited another 50 or 60 years."

"Why?"

"You would have gotten to live your life."

"I *am* living my life, Mom," he said. "We're fortunate to be living in these times. If it really is aliens, then we have witnessed *first contact*. If they destroy us, well, I guess that's not good, but our lives will not have been boring."

"I prefer boring," she said.

"Besides, 50 years won't be enough," he said. "Then *my* kids will still have their lives ahead of them."

"Oh," she said. "I'm still waiting on grandchildren."

"I'll first need to find them a mother," he said, laughing. In his profession, that was going to be a tricky feat.

As they trekked back to the house, he contemplated his inner thoughts – those which he'd usually suppress during daylight hours, when his mind would otherwise be distracted by his work. He acknowledged that his perspective on life had changed in the past days, and more gradually during the past few months. Until now, his reality focused on a specific place and time – his local position on the surface of the planet, and on the present. But there was so much more.

Maurice had gotten two hours of restless sleep between 10:00 a.m. and noon in the bunker before getting the orders to return to normal status – meaning that everyone got to go home. The readiness level was reduced to DEFCON-3, but he thought it should at least remain at level 2 since there were supposedly alien ships around the Earth. He then realized that it didn't matter for him – all remaining missiles were deemed nonfunctional. This time the drones had done permanent damage which would take months to repair. It was the same story for the other missile wings. The rumor was that similar damage had been exacted upon the Russian and Chinese missile systems. He hoped that was the case.

He was still numb after hearing the president's revelation on world television and realizing the part he'd played in the scheme. Crownbrook, and the other world leaders, had taken an enormous risk that had immediate and existential consequences – and it was all based on the whim of a former Nazi scientist. The man's hypothesis was founded on pure conjecture: it was high-risk gambling with human existence as the ante.

Gunter Eriksson's idea was simple: aliens were hidden – perhaps orbiting our planet undetected – and watching us in case we were going to destroy the Earth, in which case they'd step in and prevent that from happening. Eriksson's proposition was simply to force them to do so, using a method in which their interference would be undeniable – and unequivocally revealing. The most extreme thing of which the human race was capable was all-out nuclear war.

Apparently, it had worked. But the evidence still wasn't definitive: videos could be faked.

Supposing it was really true – extraterrestrials *had* intervened – what was going to happen now? What if the "aliens" had now concluded that humanity is an imminent threat to the planet, which they'd planned to take over eventually, and now decided to exterminate us before we destroyed it? Perhaps we've provoked them into acting prematurely.

What was he saying? Was he buying into the alien story? He

knew there was a more sinister, *terrestrial*, explanation for the entire event. Although, it would be challenging to come up with a viable, alternate theory that accounted for the disappearance of over 200 nuclear missiles from the three superpowers. It was either aliens or God, or all the missiles on all sides had been *designed* to disappear. Maurice went with the simplest explanation: the missiles were duds. They self-destructed.

It was 2:00 p.m. when he ordered his people to go back to normal operations. This meant that regular staff members would resume their duties at the base. Even those who were permanently stationed at the bunker and missile silos couldn't do much more than monitor satellite feeds: they didn't have any missiles left to launch, and neither did anyone else. Although, there were still bombs on airplanes and missiles on naval vessels.

Maurice would stop at the base, and then head home to his wife. The kids were going to be arriving in the evening. There was great relief considering they'd just averted nuclear destruction. However, the air around him seemed to be electrified by his own anxiety, fueled by a sense that something even more devastating was still looming.

ANDERS AND GIGI got back to the house at 2:45 p.m. It was a hot day – now in the mid-90s – and they were having iced tea in the kitchen.

He still hadn't heard anything from Alina.

The television was off – they were both sick of seeing the same footage over and over again, and hearing a million speculative takes by reporters who didn't know anything new.

Anders had never seen his mother so flustered. Her thoughts seemed to be going everywhere, and she'd expressed her feeling of impending doom multiple times during their excursion around the lake. He was feeling it, too.

"Regardless of how this turns out, the president should go to jail," she said. "Along with everyone else involved."

Anders agreed, but then realized that *he* was involved, although mostly unknowingly. A massive investigation would eventually reveal DMS and its employees, although it would take a good amount of time – many years, he figured.

Right on cue, Anders' phone vibrated and Harrison's name appeared on the screen. He answered.

"Are you seeing this?" Harrison asked.

"What?"

"You're not watching? Turn on your TV!"

Anders motioned to his mom to turn on the television.

"Call me back later," Harrison said and ended the call.

Gigi found one of the cable news stations, which showed a female reporter talking at such a quick pace that Anders could barely understand her. The woman kept looking back over her shoulder as she spoke, as if she were expecting something to happen. She was in DC – the Washington Monument and Capitol Building were in the background.

"What's going on?" Gigi asked as she leaned closer to the screen.

"President Crownbrook is due to speak within the hour," the reporter continued, "along with the Russian and Chinese leaders, and the Secretary-General of the United Nations. Just 14 hours ago, the three leaders were on an aircraft carrier somewhere in the South Pacific, and we've been informed that they arrived in the United States 20 minutes ago."

"Why are they coming here?" Gigi asked.

Anders shrugged and shook his head.

"Something's happening," Gigi gasped as the feed went to a different reporter, now on the South Lawn of the White House. There was a stage and podium set up in the grass, with a gaggle of reporters milling about nearby.

"We can see and hear Marine One now, approaching from the southeast," the man said as he shielded his eyes from the sun and then turned to look in the direction of the incoming, iconic helicopter. "It will be just a few minutes before the president will address the nation."

The aircraft made a swift landing, and the engine whistled as it slowed. The rotors halted after a few minutes and the stairs lowered. It took another minute before President Crownbrook appeared at the door and waved to the crowd. As he proceeded down the stairs, Huang Jinping, the Chinese president, looked out the door and descended, followed by the Russian leader, Anatoly Kurmaev. A fourth man, whom Anders didn't recognize, was the last to exit and the men gathered and faced each other on the lawn, about 20 feet from the stairs of Marine One.

The three leaders wore suits. The fourth was thinner, shorter, and younger than the others, and Anders couldn't tell what country he represented – neither by his physical characteristics nor his uniform, which was white with some strange, black markings on the shoulders and chest. The Secretary-General of the United Nations, Keiron Swensen, then joined them, apparently escorted from the White House and across the lawn by US Secret Service agents.

After what seemed to be a short conversation amongst themselves, the five men broke formation. Crownbrook led them to the podium, where he stepped onto the stage as the others flanked to his left and right, a few feet behind him. A herd of reporters – now up to about 50 – crouched within 15 feet of the president and aimed cameras and microphones in his direction.

"Good afternoon," Crownbrook said into the microphone mounted to the podium just below chin level. "I've been known to make an entrance, but I admit that this one was over the top."

This brought about light, nervous laughter from the reporters.

"As a group, we decided to address the world from here – Washington, DC – and in English, so that the message will be most globally disseminated," the president continued. "It will be translated in real-time in all languages, and to all nations."

Crownbrook looked to the only man in the group that Anders didn't recognize, and waved him forward.

"What an odd-looking individual," Gigi commented.

With Crownbrook as a reference, Anders figured the man was about six feet tall – a few inches shorter than the president – and about 170 pounds. His large, dark eyes were wideset on his olive-colored face. His hair was pitch black, and his ears were average size but stuck out at funny angles.

The man stepped up to the microphone, looked out over the crowd of reporters, and said, "It is not important that I tell you my name, or from where I came."

"My God, what's wrong with his voice?" Gigi gasped.

When he spoke, it sounded like two people were speaking at the same time, as if a higher-pitched and lower-pitched tone blended into a single voice that came out as a dissonant chord, like simultaneously hitting the middle-C and the adjacent C-sharp keys on a piano. It was odd, and unpleasant.

Beneath the strange tone, Anders thought the man's accent resembled Portuguese, but not quite. His opening line already made the hair bristle on the back of Anders' neck.

"Our scientists have been observing your civilization for more than 5,000 years. In the past century, we were tasked with making sure that you did not destroy yourselves, and this planet, as your technology advanced," the man said. "Your destructive capabilities increased rapidly during and since your Second World War, especially with the dawn of fission and thermonuclear weapons. There have also been other disastrous things that you have nearly stumbled upon in your scientific research about which you are unaware. As a result, we had to increase our presence and initiate more proactive measures to ensure the safety of this planet."

Anders didn't like the tone of the man's voice, or where he sensed his monolog was leading.

"Are we looking at an extraterrestrial?" Gigi asked.

"I don't know," he replied. He knew they were at least trying to make him appear as one.

"Your leadership has organized a clever but high-risk ploy to expose our presence," the man continued. "This has forced us to make a difficult decision."

The expressions of the three leaders and the UN Secretary-General remained unchanged, and Crownbrook even seemed to nod in agreement.

"Earth will now be annexed by my civilization, and all nations will be reconfigured to fall under a single structure," the *alien* explained. "Your population is too large, and will be reduced in the coming days. Those of you who remain will be given certain duties to sustain yourselves and your environment. Your militaries will be eliminated – you will no longer have a need for them since we will protect you from the outside – and we will enforce nonviolent behavior within the citizenry."

"My God!" Anders blurted.

"I think the aliens are taking over," Gigi said, staring at the screen with her mouth open.

"No," Anders said. "They're establishing a *single-world government*."

His mind spun, inducing a mental vertigo. Was the Custodial Group responsible for this, or was it the Single-World Alliance? He was now convinced that it was *both*. He was now certain that it was all a fantastic production – tricking people to fall in line because the so-called *extraterrestrials* were now running things.

"We have identification and biometric data on approximately 85 percent of Earth's inhabitants," the *alien* continued. "Expect instructions through your social media accounts. Those who refuse to comply will be the first to be removed from the population. Opportunities will be provided to those who want to *volunteer* to be removed."

"What does he mean by 'removed from the population?'" Gigi asked.

"I think it means *exterminated*, Mom," he said. "They're going to kill us."

"All personal electronic communication capabilities will be terminated shortly," the *alien* continued. "Your phones, electronic mail, and social accounts will no longer have their normal communications functionalities. You will, however, be responsible for all messages and orders directed to you through these media by your new authorities. Your current governments will be fully dissolved within the next 24 hours, at which time new local leaders will be appointed. Obey all instructions or there will be severe consequences. Those involved in socially destructive behavior will be removed from the population immediately. Local military groups are now being deployed to high population areas to maintain order."

Reporters started shouting at the strange-looking man. When he held up his hand as a gesture to indicate that he wouldn't be taking questions, there were gasps. Anders had to look more closely at the screen to see what caused their reaction.

"Look at his hand!" Gigi exclaimed.

It was deformed – it didn't look human. There were three, equal-length fingers, and a thumb that was about a third longer than them. On the heel of its "hand" was a protruding point that looked to have a flat nail on it.

The man then turned to the other four men near the podium, said something, and then walked toward Marine One. The Russian and Chinese leaders followed him as Crownbrook stepped up to the microphone. The UN Secretary-General remained to the left and behind him, and he seemed to be suppressing a grin as the president spoke.

"There will be profound changes to all of your lives, and they'll be implemented immediately," Crownbrook said. "You should make sure to follow instructions without hesitation: it could strongly affect your life, and the lives of your families."

Ignoring the barrage of questions from reporters, some of whom tried to follow them to the helicopter but were stopped by the Secret

Service, President Crownbrook and the UN Secretary-General hurried to Marine One and climbed the steps. Both men went inside without looking back, the door closed, and the engine started its high-pitched whine.

"What the hell does this mean?" Anders asked. "Was that a threat?"

The television suddenly went silent and the screen turned bright blue: the signal was lost.

Anders picked up the remote and went through the channels – they were all offline.

"That's odd," Gigi said.

Anders didn't like the timing. A few seconds later, the screen went black and a message appeared on the screen. It read, "Check electronic mail and social media for individual instructions."

"Individual instructions?" Gigi said. "Are we supposed to *do* something?"

Anders went through the other channels and they all displayed the same thing. He then picked up his cell phone and placed a call to Harrison. A second later, a busy signal droned in his ear. It was a rare thing to hear in the digital age. He tried again, same result.

He then tried to call his mom's phone. Busy signal.

"Mom, try to call someone on your phone," he said. "Not me – a friend, anyone."

Gigi picked up her phone, dialed, and looked at him. "Busy."

She tried another, same look. "What's going on – have they shut us down already?" she asked.

It was then that Anders' phone buzzed, and then Gigi's chimed a second later. He got an email from "US-GA-1574@GlobeStation.str, which read, "Test communication for Anders Henry Bennett." In the email was an image of a map, on which was a bright, red pointer to his current location, along with some other relevant data including his parents' names, his employer, bank, Social Security Number, date and place of birth, and a description of his car and license plate. The email ended with, "REMAIN AT YOUR CURRENT LOCATION

UNTIL AUTHORIZED TO MOVE. Instructions will follow within 12 hours."

"What *is* this?" Gigi asked as she looked up from her phone, clearly frightened. "They have all our information."

"They even know where we're located," he added. "Probably based on our phones."

"Why do we have to go to the high school tomorrow?" she asked.

"What do you mean?"

"That's what the message says."

"Mine didn't say that," he said. "Let me see."

Anders took her phone and read the email. She was to report to the Genesee Lake High School gymnasium at 8:00 a.m.

"Why would *I* have to go but not you?" she asked.

They went to the kitchen counter and Gigi switched on the radio. Only static crackled from the speakers as she tuned through the entire range, AM and FM.

Anders then opened his laptop – the Internet connection was intact, but he couldn't navigate to any websites. He went to his email account: he could get into it – just like he could with his phone – but he couldn't start a new email, even though the information for all his contacts was still there. After a few minutes of probing, it was clear that he could now only *receive* emails.

Gigi checked her email – a different provider – and had the same result. Anders watched as she tried to navigate to a news website: the title of the site was still there, but there were no links to stories, or even pictures – just a message that read, "FOLLOW INSTRUCTIONS DISSEMINATED THROUGH PERSONAL MEDIA," and "TUNE INTO AM 720 FOR COMMUNITY ANNOUNCEMENTS BEGINNING AT 5:00 p.m. EDT."

They went back to the kitchen, sat at the table, and speculated about what was happening.

"I'm sure this is a scheme to install a global government – by *humans*, not aliens," Anders said. "This must be the work of the

Single-World Alliance – the whole thing must be their plan, a huge deception."

"So Crownbrook's allegiance was really to the SWA, not the CG?"

"Only a high-status member of both the SWA and CG could pull this off," Anders said. "As president, he is at the highest status anyone can achieve, and therefore perfect to manipulate both organizations. I think he wanted a one-world government all along. He just used the CG to accomplish the SWA's objectives."

A knock on the front door made both of them flinch.

Gigi rushed to it and let in Mrs. Bellfield, the mother of one of Anders' grade school friends, and long-time neighbor.

"Janice, are you okay?" Gigi asked. The woman looked like she'd seen a ghost.

"I stopped at Gert's on the way here," Janice said, referring to another member of Gigi's brunch group. "She thinks they're collecting all the elderly people in the same place – the high school. The Andersons didn't get ordered to go there – they're young – but the Fieldbergs did. They're in their late 70s. Both Ken and I were ordered to go."

Janice and her husband, Ken, were both in their late 60s, and it looked like Gert might be right: it seemed that the elderly *were* being herded to the school.

"Have you spoken with your daughter?" Gigi asked.

"We were on the phone while this was happening but the call suddenly dropped after the president's speech," Janice explained. "What are they saying on the news?"

"Nothing – the TV and radio are out," Gigi said.

Janice looked like she was going to faint.

"Shit," Anders spat as he realized what was happening. "We're completely isolated now. All communications are out – phones, internet, email, radio."

Both women stared at him.

Anders knew that a global takeover might not occur as it does in many sci-fi movies – be it by aliens or humans – with a massive invasion. Information technology was enough to accomplish the feat, and human civilization had become so dependent on it that it was now extremely vulnerable. Communications within the normal population could be cut off in an instant: all phones – land and mobile, Internet access, all social media, satellite communications, and all terrestrial radio and television broadcasts. Even shortwave radio sets could be traced and shut down if the government decided.

Anders shuddered: the *global switches* had been thrown.

There was something even worse than losing communications, however. Those same media could be used to *control* and manipulate the population. Only information the new government wanted the public to know would get to it. And it could be giving everyone different information, or *instructions*. With current technologies, the resolution of the control was down to the individual: the new "overlords," human or otherwise, could contact, locate, identify, and track almost every person on the planet. And the new government could divide and conquer the world if it moved *quickly*.

And it *was* moving quickly.

They didn't have to bomb us back to the Stone Age. They only had to *isolate* us as if we were in the Stone Age. They could control information, long term – including education. In one generation, we could be set back to prehistoric times, especially if they "got rid of" the older generations.

Taken to the extreme, they could eliminate everyone except for infants, and then raise humanity as they wanted it to be. They could eliminate all evidence of our previous existence – just destroy all electronic and written documents, and even exterminate certain languages.

None of this required advanced, alien technologies. Human technologies had come far enough to accomplish the objective. All they needed was control of the military, control of all digital information, foolproof identification of individuals, and advanced surveillance and tracking abilities. This would allow a government to control every resource, from food to information to transportation.

If it were a new, terrestrially-installed, global government – *humans* – that was trying to do this, then the only solution was rebellion. If it were truly a takeover by extraterrestrials, then fighting back would likely be futile – their capabilities would just be far too advanced to overcome.

As it stood currently, Anders had not seen enough evidence to come to a definitive conclusion, and thus assumed the most likely scenario: humans were responsible for all of it. But how could he know for sure?

It then occurred to him that it no longer mattered if he had definitive proof that the Single-World Alliance was responsible for everything that was happening. Even if he had video confessions of everyone involved, no one would ever see them. And, even if the videos were made available to the public, who would believe they were authentic? They could be deep fakes or CGI. Such technology was a two-fold threat. First, it could be used to trick people into believing that something was real. Second, it cultivated a severe mistrust of everything recorded – video or audio. In other words, it eroded the authentic as much as it poisoned with the counterfeit.

It reminded him of a class he took in college where they studied a relationship between science and a philosophy called materialism. Since all of our senses – sight, hearing, everything – had to be conveyed to our brains through some interaction between a stimulus and matter, they were all *secondary* observations. For instance, we only sense the effect of light through the response it instigates on the cells in our eyes, and sound through cells that react to the vibrations of our eardrums. Furthermore, those physiological responses must be conveyed through electrical impulses over nerves, which are matter, and processed by the brain, also matter. The point is that we do not even perceive the simplest stimuli in our physical world directly. Every perception is secondary, at best.

Since the brain is where all the processing and real perception occurs, why not skip the physical aspects – the actual physical stimuli – and just feed the brain information directly? In other words, make the brain *think* something is happening in the real world when it is really only happening inside a person's head. It reminded Anders of a movie from the late 1990s called *The Matrix*, where people were completely isolated and fed information directly into their brains.

By isolating the individual, and strictly controlling everything they saw and heard, the new global government could control the entire population.

The world was lost.

CHAPTER 16

The Final Chapter

Anders sipped coffee as he gazed out the window of his bedroom. The morning sun shone on the scarred earth that had been his mother's vegetable garden. He'd harvested everything and tilled under the plants that remained. Food was now provided by the new government, and all other sources were considered contraband.

Gigi had gone to the high school the morning after the first email message had been delivered, as ordered. She'd never returned. That was five weeks ago.

Within days of his mom's disappearance, a rumor had emerged that the "aliens" were euthanizing everyone over the age of 50. If true, it meant that his mother was probably dead already, along with many other people he knew, including Harrison. Although, if anyone could elude them, it was him. But Anders suspected that his mom, a former CIA operative herself, was also no slouch. It gave him hope for both of them.

Alina never arrived. Anders feared the worst. Although the

phones had been deactivated soon after the president's shattering announcement on the South Lawn, she must have called just in time to still be able to leave a voicemail message. She'd been heading south on her way to Savannah, and reported two disturbing things. First, the military was everywhere and there were dead bodies in the ditches along the highways – in groups, clearly executed *en masse*. Second, she'd gotten a message on her cell phone informing her that the "aliens" knew who she was – had her real name – and where she was located. It was remarkable, and disturbing, considering that she'd been using a *burner* phone. Evidently, artificial intelligence had somehow linked her to it, and then to her true identity and location. And AI had probably linked her to *him*, as well.

It distressed him to realize that their special skill sets as covert couriers had been rendered useless in a matter of hours. It was clear that the SWA had all the tools in place before making its move. Anders knew that links would eventually be made between him and his clandestine activities, and everything DMS was doing would be revealed. Of course, Crownbrook knew it all anyway and, therefore, so did the one-world government.

The morning his mom had disappeared, Anders had intended to go to the high school to find her and then, later, to search for Alina in Savannah. However, he'd soon discovered that he had no chance of getting to either place. The military had been patrolling the main highways, and roadblocks manned by soldiers had popped up on every road leading out of Genesee Lake. Anders had never felt so angry, frustrated, and helpless in all his life.

In all the time since then, Anders had not seen a single alien. *There were no fucking aliens.* He was sure of it. He'd not seen even one alien-looking craft, nor anything else that could've been construed to be of extraterrestrial origin. All government functions and maneuvers that he'd witnessed had been carried out by *humans*.

Unfortunately, the so-called extraterrestrial being, the man with the grating voice and deformed hands who had appeared on the South Lawn of the White House on that last day of the "previous age," had been enough to trick many people. Anders figured it had been an elaborate costume – easy work for a professional. They could've made the guy look like an authentic Klingon if they'd wanted to. But it was just a minor deception compared to everything else.

Crownbrook was still the supposed "president" of the United States, despite being over the age of 50. The rules never applied to those in the ruling class, of course. The Chinese and Russian leaders were also still in place, as was the Secretary-General of the United Nations, who was the acting "World Leader" until someone else was appointed by the aliens. Anyway, that was the story.

Crownbrook had been trying to convince the remaining US citizens that their missing older family members were getting advanced medical care at some gigantic facility in the middle of the country. There were even pictures on State News of the massive medical complex that was purportedly located somewhere in Kansas. Anders figured that the images were fakes: modern, computer-generated graphics were fantastic, and easily capable of producing convincing, three-dimensional imagery and video. The story was that our newfound, extraterrestrial keepers were so advanced that they could rejuvenate the elderly by renewing their organs, including their brains, starting at the DNA level. The public was told that the process would take up to a year, so no one should expect their loved ones to return before then.

Anders didn't buy a word of it. He would've prevented his mother from going to the high school that morning but she'd left at 4:00 a.m. without warning. They'd told her that, if she didn't go, there'd be extreme consequences for her family. According to the note she'd left, she'd taken that threat as saying they'd *kill* her family if she didn't comply. He was all she'd had for family. And now he had no one.

In order to shore up the extraterrestrial narrative, State News reported often on alien events, including realistic videos of alien ships doing things, like annihilating violent groups of rebel humans or destroying iconic structures from the "old age," like the Eiffel Tower, the Vatican, the Statue of Liberty, Mecca, the pyramids in Egypt and South America, the Taj Mahal, and anything else connected to national pride, history, or religion. Anders was certain nothing had been done by alien ships – there *were* no alien ships – but he figured that those monumental structures had really been destroyed. It was in the one-world government's long-term interest to do so, and was even stated as such in the SWA's manifesto.

Anders' only source of information that wasn't from the new global government came from listening to his dad's shortwave radio set. He'd only turn on the receiver, however. Any broadcasts were quickly extinguished – rogue broadcasters were hunted down and eliminated – which was why the messages had to be brief. They were also always broadcast from populous cities because otherwise the perpetrators could be easily located. Early on, some people had gotten the idea to hide in the mountains and broadcast from there. But they'd been easy to find in the open space, and then soldiers – humans – had been sent out to kill or capture everyone at the transmission sites.

From the cities, however, one could broadcast from atop a large building, and then scurry back inside and mix in with hundreds of other people. Unfortunately, with cameras and facial recognition technologies, those people started to get caught as well. The rebels had then adapted by setting up delayed, recorded broadcasts, each of which required the sacrifice of a valuable shortwave transmission set.

From the bits of information he'd gleaned from the shortwave blurbs, Anders knew that, other than their age, people had also been eradicated based on their education, profession, capabilities, physical health, and genetics. They were culling the human population. Those who were not needed, or posed a threat or burden to the new order, were destroyed.

The abduction of children was causing hysteria – even more than the panic caused by the disappearance of people over 50 years old.

All infants under the age of two had been taken from their families. Even though the official government story was that the babies had been admitted to a large medical facility to get a "proper, healthy start to life," the rumor was that they'd been taken to some alien mothership. More fantastic lies, Anders thought. A more likely explanation – and also a rumor – was that they were at a remote location being groomed to be the replacement generation. The running theory was that, after maturing into adults, this group of "new humans" would take over everything, and then everyone else would finally be exterminated. The entire "old world" would then have been purged. That youngest generation would be oblivious to the previous civilization, and there'd be nothing left for them to discover about it – all evidence of its existence would have been destroyed by then, except for the knowledge and technologies that would be carried over, the origins of which Anders imagined would be a great mystery to them. They'd be taught a single language – something not currently global, perhaps Icelandic – in order to ensure complete severance from the previous age.

To accomplish this total purge, a massive effort was being made, through forced labor, to annihilate information on a global scale. Books, films, digital media, electronic devices, and even vinyl records, were being destroyed. Only scientific and technological information was being preserved, but the names of the authors, institutions, and references to any human sources were being removed from all scientific papers and books. And there was to be no historical knowledge preserved about anything, save geological information. There would be no references to people, places, or events of the previous civilization, anywhere. Even cemeteries were being destroyed. The new global government intended to completely erase the previous world.

Anders had been assigned a job dismantling computers at the Genesee Lake Fire Department. He figured he'd been appointed to this duty because the government knew he had a computer science degree. People would bring in their computers, and Anders and a few others would replace the hard drives and destroy the old ones. The new drives and operating systems allowed citizens to correspond with the government, no one else, and only select information could be stored – no personal books, documents, music, videos, or photos. The new drives were manufactured by a well-known *human* company – the founder of which Anders knew to be a member of the SWA.

Anders still had his DMS laptop, on which were the files from his dad's thumb-drive. That computer was not connected to him in any way and, at least so far, he'd not been ordered to turn it in. He'd been spending much time reading those files in the hope of finding something that revealed an exploitable flaw in the SWA's scheme.

The SWA's master plan, *Quiet Storm*, had now been fully initiated. It frustrated him that he might be the only person not connected to the government who could see it so clearly – unless Harrison or the FBI agents were still alive. It had been spelled out in perfect clarity in the WhistleLeaks release but that entire website, along with the rest of the World Wide Web, had been shut down the day after the missiles disappeared.

The new government had already executed the first crucial step of the plan: isolating the individual – physically and informationally. Except for those under state control, all communications, including phones, radio, TV, and internet, had been completely eliminated – except for the rogue shortwave radio sets, that is. The only allowed travel was government organized. Private cars, and even bikes, were illegal, and all road signs had been removed. All gas stations were shut down and the batteries of electric cars were confiscated. Of course, there was no longer a public GPS service, and anyone caught with a paper map was arrested for "unauthorized navigation."

Food was under complete government control. Trucks delivered food daily, and individuals had to formally identify themselves to get their programmed allotment, most of which was in the form of dehydrated goods, powders, bars, and pills. Identification no longer required an ID card. Instead, it was done with DNA: a simple breath sample or skin rub was sufficient, and there was no known way to trick the system. All other food was considered contraband, and private gardens were illegal. In this way, food could be used as a control mechanism: disobedient people and their families could be deprived of food.

The entire money system had been shut down the day after the mock nuclear war. It had been one of the easier digital levers to pull: most banking was done online. No Internet, no banking. The contents of all safety deposit boxes had been confiscated by the government. In fact, all property – land, houses, apartments, cars, and anything else of value – now belonged to the state. People could be evicted from their homes on a moment's notice.

The government had ordered all precious metals to be turned in to authorities. Anders' parents had some gold stored in the safe that he wasn't going to hand over, even though it had no use in this dystopian world. He also had two handguns in his possession – one in the safe and one behind the cabinet in the second-floor bathroom. Firearms had been the very first things to be confiscated. The population had been fully defanged.

Again, there *were no aliens*, and there was no extraterrestrial technology involved in anything that was occurring. It was all carried out with human-conceived machineries, the most effective of which were digital in nature. However, on a regular basis, they still resorted to low-tech solutions: bullets.

There were rumors that no children had been conceived since the transition. It had only been five weeks, so Anders didn't know how accurate that story could be. He suspected, however, that if it were true, the sterilization had been administered through the government-distributed food. It was either that or the so-called vaccines everyone had been forced to take. When he'd been called to the high school a week after his mom had disappeared he'd worried it was another extermination event, but his neighbor had informed him that they were just administering vaccines.

Anders knew that the government would come looking for him if he didn't show, so he decided to go with the intention of finding a way to avoid the injection somehow. He'd been extremely fortunate that his former high school classmate and registered nurse, Rebecca Stiles, had been administering the shots. When she was about to stick it in his arm, he looked her in the eyes and whispered, "I don't want it." It had been risky for him to say that, and risky for Rebecca to fake it. But she'd squeezed the skin on his shoulder so that the needle passed between the folds without penetrating anything. The contents of the syringe then wetted his shirt – something he'd preserved in a sealed plastic bag in case he needed the evidence one day. Afterwards, Rebecca winked at him and revealed that it wasn't her first mock injection.

Anders knew that the "vaccines" might be a veiled, delayed execution apparatus: they could contain a dormant virus that would activate in a year or two and kill off a large fraction of the population. It was something that had been described in the SWA's plans.

He then wondered about the second phase of the NIMH operation. When were they going to release the more deadly virus? He wondered if they even needed to do that. Why create a global pandemic when they could just kill people at will? They'd already massacred a huge fraction of the population, even though he didn't know the numbers. The first NIMH operation, however, had accomplished precisely what it had been designed to do: it demonstrated public compliance.

Anders hadn't yet eaten any of the government food. His mom had accumulated a huge supply of canned goods, and he had two gigantic bags of dried beans and a few sacks of rice – enough to last him a few months. He'd had no appetite since his mom had disappeared, and was losing weight on his already light frame. Food wasn't a priority for him right now; he figured he'd have to make some drastic decisions well before the food ran out.

It had crossed his mind that sterilization would have been an effective but less violent method of reducing the population. After just a short time searching through his dad's files, he found that it *was* a part of the SWA's plan. Sterilization alone, however, was too slow, so massive kills had to be carried out at the very beginning, which they had been.

Another initiative implemented by the Single-World Alliance was a massive campaign of extravagant propaganda, continuously disseminated through all media. From shortwave radio broadcasts, Anders had learned that people in New York were seeing alien ships on the news doing things in Los Angeles, and other places in the world, but never anything in New York. People in LA, however, were seeing things happening around the world, including in NYC, but not in LA. And someone in Kansas reported that there was no massive geriatric medical facility at the declared location. It was all a sham, and it could not be checked or cross-referenced because of the communication isolation. But the public was starting to catch wind of the deception thanks to the shortwave radio broadcasts from a few brave people. Anders hoped those rebels would find a way to keep going.

A question had been on Anders' mind ever since the scare of nuclear war had passed and the missiles had mysteriously evaporated into nothingness: why manufacture such an extreme production? Nuclear war? Aliens?

The answer came from a reference in the *Quiet Storm* file. The corresponding document was titled *The Critical Phase Transition*, and it described what needed to be done to kick things off once all the "levers" were in place, and society was in a teetering, vulnerable state. Anders recognized that this unstable condition had been manufactured by world leaders through the slow buildup of events designed to be perceived by the global population as an inevitable progression toward world war. At the instant the public was at the panic point – when war was imminent – the plan called for something that would put the entire population into shock, making it pliable and unreactive to the harsh changes that needed to be carried out. At that point, all the so-called levers could be pulled, initiating an irreversible, critical phase transition into the next age. For that final push, Anders couldn't think of a more shocking confluence of events than the combination of nuclear war and an alien revelation.

There was something else in this document that horrified him and made him realize that he'd always feel shame and regret for not moving more quickly to investigate his dad's files and discover Crownbrook's true motives. The disturbing insight regarded the predicted *suddenness* of the so-called phase transition. Although the document described a buildup of events that would be gradual at first and then accelerate as time proceeded, it explained that the actual "phase transition" would be rapid, and fully executed over a 24 to 48-hour period. And that's precisely what had happened. The span of time from the initial escalation to DEFCON-1 to the statement from the "alien" on the South Lawn of the White House had been less than 24 hours. All the levers had been pulled within a few hours after that, and the transition was complete. The world had been irreversibly changed in an instant.

Even though the transition had been fully executed, Anders figured much effort would have to be exerted to maintain the new state of things. One might think it would be difficult, if not impossible, to continuously police every individual citizen. But, alas, the tools for that were already in place.

The latest population control technology that was being implemented in every home was something people were referring to as a "weasel." It was officially called a Home Surveillance Device, or HSD – the government wasn't even trying to disguise it. It was a robot, similar in appearance to the disk-shaped, robotic vacuum cleaners that were common to many households.

Like those vacuum robots, the weasels were mobile, and roamed the first floor of a person's house or apartment. They were equipped with microphones and cameras, and connected to the Internet. They were personalized, ever-present observers, and they could *talk*. They were artificially intelligent and could carry on a conversation as if the weasel were just another human living in the house. Anders recalled the controversy of AI years before, and the dire warnings from experts in high-tech industry. Their warnings had gone unheeded.

To make things worse, each weasel had its own tiny, quiet, airborne drone, equipped with a camera, light, and microphone, which could fly anywhere in the house. The drones, which people referred to as "mosquitoes" due to the high-pitched humming of their propellers, were about the size of a sparrow and would beep to force you to open doors, even if you were in the bathroom or shower. They could even go outside the house, and venture around the yard.

The weasels and their mosquitoes enforced curfews, relayed orders, and listened to and watched everything in the house. And they asked questions. *What are you doing in the bathroom, Anders? Can you show me what's in your bag? What were you doing in the backyard this afternoon?*

He'd had one particularly disturbing encounter with a weasel that he'd never forget. It had asked him why he'd been late getting home from work one night. He had explained that the government transportation – a bus – was behind schedule. The weasel had then said, "Your voice sounds stressed. Are you lying to me, Anders?" Thankfully, he hadn't been. The weasel had gone on to check the bus schedule, and confirmed the delay. Anders didn't want to think about what might have happened had his story not checked out.

The weasels and their mosquito sidekicks ensured compliance and isolation. People could not congregate, even in pairs, unless they lived together, or it was required for government-sanctioned events or forced labor. People who disobeyed the rules, or destroyed their weasels or mosquitoes, were arrested, and never seen again.

Anders kept his DMS laptop in the bathroom, where he did all his reading. If the drone made him open the door, he'd stash it behind a cabinet, where he also stored some of his dad's science fiction novels. His father's other books had already been turned in to the fire station, where they were shredded and burned. It reminded him of Ray Bradbury's *Fahrenheit 451*. And the Nazis. Anders found it both sad and maddening that the warnings of past thinkers, and history, had not been heeded.

Another obvious question that had arisen was *who* was actually watching the enormous stream of video and audio data collected by the weasels and their drones? People speculated that there was no way that *everyone* could be monitored continuously and simultaneously. But that was false. It was all monitored by artificial intelligence. AI could watch everyone, all the time, and correctly interpret what they were doing. In addition, since it was observing everyone simultaneously, it could make connections between people and their actions in real-time. AI could root out conspiracies and plans before they ever got off the ground. If a scheme were discovered, a contingent of humans would be sent by the human leaders from the human government to react – to collect those involved.

At night, Anders would listen to State News on the radio. Global orders were communicated mostly through President Crownbrook, but sometimes through the leaders of China, Russia, or the United Nations. They always claimed that they were relaying information, and commands, from the aliens. Many people believed them. The rest had no choice but to obey.

The more Anders reflected upon what had led to the imprisonment and death currently being inflicted upon the world, the more disappointed he became with himself. Why hadn't he correctly interpreted the anxiety that had been building in his mind over the past few years? Why hadn't he recognized the urgency to do something sooner?

For over a decade – ever since he'd started his job at DMS – he'd felt as if a wall had been closing in around him that was driven by the erosion of privacy, the intrusion of government, and the emergence of the digital age. These things both isolated people and controlled the information to which they had access. He'd observed an intentional polarization of society along numerous divides, driven by something he'd been unable to identify – that is, until now. It was the government. But it wasn't because of the government's inexhaustible resources and immense power. It was because of its weaknesses and vulnerabilities. It had been designed with the fatal flaw that, with some clever conniving, it could be commandeered by a handful of influential, persistent people with sinister intentions. And the American government was particularly susceptible to the incremental adjustments needed to execute such a plot.

Anders knew that others had sensed long ago that something ominous was afoot – his mother had – but the feelings should have been stronger for someone in his line of business. His intuition should have given him an earlier warning – it should have forced him to act sooner. He'd been in a unique position to recognize what was happening. After all, he was connected to the very underworld that had committed this crime against civilization and human existence.

A beeping sound came from outside his bedroom door. He stood and opened it.

It was the mosquito. It was time to go to work.

He swallowed the last of his coffee, set down the cup, and grabbed his knapsack.

Anders would comply for the time being – bide his time until he learned as much as he could about what was happening. What he would do after that, he had no idea. If it really was an alien civilization that was taking over, then there'd be little he could do to fight it. However, if it was a massive conspiracy carried out by the Single-World Alliance – *humans* – then he'd have a chance.

Maybe.

Deception is the road to annihilation.

THE END

ACKNOWLEDGMENTS

The author owes a deep debt of gratitude to Jessica Fiorillo, whose knowledge, insight, editing talents, and encouragement have made this a better book. Thanks are due to Nayeli Zúñiga-Hansen for her careful reading of the manuscript and helpful feedback.

Also by Shane Stadler

About the Author

Shane Stadler is an experimental physicist and university professor. He spent his early career at the US Naval Research Laboratory researching artificially structured magnetic materials, and his current research is funded by the US Department of Energy. He has written five novels, including the four-book, sci-fi *Exoskeleton* series, and is the coauthor of a well-known college physics textbook. He has published over 250 scientific papers on topics that range from magnetic cooling to spintronics to superconductivity.

You can contact Shane at www.ShaneStadler.com

Printed in Great Britain
by Amazon